Praise for *Veiled Promises*

"This is neo old-school romance done well . . . this book was a treat to read. It was like drinking fine brandy after having had nothing but weak tea. MacNish has a strong and distinctive style."—Ellen Micheletti of AllAboutRomance.com

"*Veiled Promises* is an excellent book, but as a debut it is phenomenal. Congratulations, Ms. MacNish."—Wendy Livingston of TheRomanceReader.com

"MacNish's debut romance, a lushly written, richly detailed Georgian historical, pushes the boundaries of the genre with a story of love, revenge, jealousy, and secrets that can be quite dark, but is also refreshingly different with its complex, realistically flawed characters and compelling plot."—John Charles of *Booklist*

Praise for *Veiled Desires*

"There's nothing veiled about the emotional power and dark sensuality of MacNish's sequel to *Veiled Promises*. With strong characters playing out a plot that delves into the deepest parts of the human soul, this is a tale to keep you riveted."—Kathe Robin of the *Romantic Times* book club

"Following her debut, *Veiled Promises* (2005), which told the story of the romance between Rogan's parents, MacNish now gives readers another delectably intense and edgy tale of passions and peril, revenge and romance."—John Charles of *Booklist*

Also by Tracy MacNish

Veiled Desires

Veiled Promises

Published by Kensington Publishing Corporation

VEILED PASSIONS

TRACY MACNISH

ZEBRA BOOKS
Kensington Publishing Corp.
www.kensingtonbooks.com

ZEBRA BOOKS are published by

Kensington Publishing Corp.
850 Third Avenue
New York, NY 10022

All Kensington titles, imprints, and distributed lines are available at special quantity discounts for bulk purchases for sales promotion, premiums, fund-raising, educational, or institutional use.

Special book excerpts or customized printings can also be created to fit specific needs. For details, write or phone the office of the Kensington Special Sales Manager: Attn. Special Sales Department. Kensington Publishing Corp., 850 Third Avenue, New York, NY 10022. Phone: 1-800-221-2647.

Zebra and the Z logo Reg. U.S. Pat. & TM Off.

ISBN-13: 978-1-4201-0169-0
ISBN-10: 1-4201-0169-2

First printing: October 2008

10 9 8 7 6 5 4 3 2 1

Printer in the United States of America

For Katrina Campbell,
and an enduring friendship so strong it became family.

May you always remember
the sweetest moments,
the warmest touches,
and the very best of times.

There are the sisters family gives you,
and there are the ones you find yourself.
I've been doubly blessed.
Thank you for being my best friend.

ACKNOWLEDGMENTS

To Kathleen E. Woodiwiss, 1939–2007, for inspiring my love of romance and setting a standard to which I will always aspire.

As always, heartfelt thanks to my mentor, Brent Monahan, who continues to teach and motivate; Mary Sue Seymour, my agent, who manages to turn this business into something gracious; my editor, Audrey LaFehr, for continued enthusiasm and the opportunity to tell Kieran's story—thank you; Peter Schulman, who listens to me talk about my books with unending patience and unflagging support; and Tracy Tappan, whose warmth and generosity make Rome seem much, much closer. As ever, thanks to Aislinn, for being the very best combination of sister and friend. I love you, Sass.

Again, best for last, my little family circle, Randy and Ethan. Without both of you, I have nothing.

Venice, 1777

There are those who grow cold over the course of time, a slow, subtle erosion that takes place over many years until they are no longer the person they once knew.

But not so for Kieran Mullen. She could pinpoint the precise event that had changed her, and she guarded the secret of that night the way a wolf guards its kill.

However, released by the costumes and festivals of Carnivale, she found a tiny reprieve from her self-imposed prison.

Kieran accepted a man's proffered hand and let him sweep her back onto the floor and into his arms.

She did not know who he was; he wore a white, beaked plague mask, a cloak, and a tricorn. His identity was concealed, as was her own. He could be a butcher or a king; Kieran did not know, and she did not care.

The dance ended, and as Kieran went looking for her sister-in-law, Emeline, a man in a leopard mask with a spotted cape bowed before her, and outstretched his hand. With abandon, Kieran accepted his invitation and whirled back onto the floor. He smelled of wine and sweat, tanned fur and raw silk, and Kieran laughed behind her mask as he twirled her once, twice, three times.

A chorus of castratos sang, their high voices soaring over the orchestral music, combining with the sounds of hundreds of conversations, laughter, and clinking glasses. Costumed people danced and drank, sweeping across the marble floor, butterflies dancing with ghouls, mermaids taking the arms of men in tricorns and animal masks. The heavy air reeked of a party, redolent of melting wax and candle smoke, perfumed bodies and spilled wine, simmering food and cured meats.

The dance ended, and Kieran declined another. Her head was hot beneath the wig and her face sweated behind her mask. She needed to step into one of the rooms that had been set aside for the women, so they might remove their masks.

She found Emeline, seated by an open window.

"Are you unwell, Emeline?" she inquired as she drew near.

Emeline's gold mask turned to face Kieran, and her eyes, visible in the jeweled openings, looked glassy.

"I was quite fine, until suddenly I began to feel fatigued and dizzy. I think I am overheated."

"Come with me, and we'll get you out of the mask and wig. You need a drink of water."

Emeline nodded and made to stand, but sat back down abruptly. "I fear I will faint." She reached for Kieran's hand and gripped it. "I have been feeling this way intermittently since we left England. I told myself all was well, just seasickness. I dared not hope, but now cannot dare ignore it. I am certain there is another child, and I fear what will become of me, being so far from home, and facing the voyage. And Rogan, he will be afraid of another miscarriage, and this will spoil his business venture." She shrugged and sighed, and her voice quavered. "I cannot bear to see him disappointed again. I hate failing him."

Emeline never revealed any fear when she became pregnant, and so it made Kieran nervous to hear her admit to it. Still, Kieran showed no sign of her own feelings, keeping her voice brisk and matter of fact.

"Nonsense. You do not fail him by trying to give him a child. You make my brother happier than I've ever seen him, child or no. And dismiss your worries regarding Rogan's business proposals. Such things are meaningless compared to his love for you. Do not worry, Emeline. All will be well."

Kieran motioned to the door, where Nilo was posted, and signaled for him to come to her aid. Her guardian and friend, Nilo was a former slave who now was paid by her brother, Rogan, to see to Kieran's protection.

Kieran could not send Nilo to get Rogan; Nilo's position as servant did not allow him access to the private rooms.

Kieran instructed him to wait, and then turned her attention to Emeline. "Just take deep breaths, and I'll be back in a few minutes."

Kieran rushed through the crowded ballrooms of the palace, her heels clicking on the marble floors as she searched for Rogan.

Since the death of their uncle, Rogan had assumed his role as the Duke of Eton with remarkable ease, taking the family fortune and making it grow with his knowledge of trade, seafaring, and shipbuilding. Whispers around England were that he was richer than the king, and while Kieran didn't know if that were true, it certainly seemed that everything Rogan touched turned to gold.

She smelled cigar smoke and heard masculine voices peppered with laughter. Kieran approached the room with a sense of caution, well aware that she was unescorted and as a female, unwelcome in such a setting. The men would just have to overlook her breach in etiquette. Emeline's health came first, as Kieran was certain her brother would agree.

Emeline had longed for a child ever since she'd married Rogan, and several failed pregnancies had not dampened her determination and her hope. Still, Kieran recognized the danger in staying in Venice too long; all of Emeline's pregnancies had miscarried in mid-trimester, and if she had been feeling it since the voyage, she was already well along. A ship's voyage possessed inherent dangers for a healthy person. Kieran hated to think what it would mean for Emeline.

She opened the door a crack and peered in, hoping that she could catch her brother's eye and not interrupt more than necessary. The room was a library, towering with bookcases. Curved niches showcased sculptures, and the giant windows were hung with red velvet. In the Venetian style, every table was carved and gilt with gold, and on the far side of the room a fire burned behind an ornate, golden screen. The men had doffed their costumes, and their unmasked faces were bright and animated as they talked politics and business over their brandy and cigars.

Kieran sighed in resignation as she spied Rogan seated by the fire, all the way across the crowd of men. She leaned in to signal him, but Rogan was deep in conversation.

Cold horror settled in Kieran's belly as she saw who Rogan spoke with. He was the man of her nightmares, the man who in one horrible night, had changed Kieran Mullen forever.

Samuel Ellsworth, the Duke of Westminster, leaned forward and conversed intently with Rogan. He was handsome for his age, dignified in carriage and refined in appearance. He wore his black and silver hair pulled into a bagwig, and his gray eyes were sharp.

Kieran knew a different man, however. She knew a man who had violated everything she knew about herself, and left her naked and broken on a dirty floor.

She watched as he talked with her brother, and the cold feeling in her gut turned to sickness.

Kieran had hidden her true feelings for three years, and would not reveal them now. With bearing as regal as a queen's, Kieran swept into the room and, ignoring the shocked look on some of the men's faces, walked over to where her brother conversed.

"Forgive me Rogan, but I must have a word, please. 'Tis an emergency."

Rogan turned to his sister, concerned. "What's wrong?"

Kieran leaned in to her brother and whispered in his ear, "Emeline feels ill."

Rogan stood, offered his excuses, and made to leave, but was stopped momentarily by Samuel, who spared Kieran an odd look before he spoke to Rogan. "Sorry to hear your wife is ailing, but do we have a deal, then?"

Rogan started walking toward the door. "We'll hammer out the details another day."

"Right. Excellent. I'll call on you tomorrow, then."

Rogan didn't reply but kept going. Kieran walked by his side. She waited until they were out in the corridor.

"What's this deal with that man? Is he not the Duke of Westminster?" she asked, struggling to keep her tone neutral.

"Aye. Just business." Rogan glanced over to her, his pace never lessening. "Did Emeline get sick?"

"No, she's only dizzy and very tired." Kieran tried to sound offhand as she added, "You've never done business with Ellsworth before, have you? 'Tis seems odd that you'd suddenly be doing so in Venice, so far from home."

"The opportunity has never arisen," Rogan replied. "Is Emeline still in the ballroom?"

"Yes, by the windows near the terrace. So, what opportunity is this?"

He frowned and shot her a look that spoke of the exasperation of one who has bigger concerns. Still, he answered her. "Shipbuilding. Venice is looking to strengthen her presence at sea because the Barbary pirates raid the moment they're out on open waters.

"There's an open bidding for shipbuilding companies like mine—this is the reason we came to Venice, aye? Right now, 'tis likely the bid will go to a much larger French operation. Ellsworth wants it as much as I do. Perhaps more. He suggests a merge of our companies, making us bigger than the French. 'Tis a good proposal."

"Do you know him well enough to undertake such a venture?" Kieran asked, and winced behind her mask as she heard the sharpness of her tone. She softened it, hoping that Rogan would not become suspicious. "What I mean is, I have never heard you speak of the man, so 'tis a surprise to me that you would trust him."

In her mind's eye, Kieran saw Samuel as he'd been that night, naked from the waist down, laughing at her.

"Trust is for marriage, Kieran. Contracts are for business."

They neared the ballroom, and Rogan looked at his sister with a piercing stare. "Why the interest?"

"Curiosity." Kieran shrugged and spoke the truth, something she so rarely did. "Were I a man, I would most certainly be involved in such pursuits."

Rogan smiled at her briefly and reached for her hand. He squeezed it lightly. "You'd have been a worthy adversary, *sidhe gaoithe*. But since you are not able to put your mind to business, why don't you do something else? Be a part of life, Kieran. I miss the sister I once knew."

Kieran withdrew her hand. "You speak nonsense, Rogan. I am very much alive." She gestured across the room. "There is Emeline; let's go see to her needs."

She saw the look in her brother's eyes before he turned away: disappointment in her, frustration with her.

As usual, it stuck a barb in her heart, but she dared not tell her brother why she'd changed, and what had caused it.

The future played out in front of her, and she knew that if Rogan did business with Samuel, it would put him in her life in a way she could not escape. Samuel would dine with them, attend their gatherings, perhaps even come to the country for their annual hunting festival.

If Rogan did as he planned, Samuel Ellsworth would be inescapable to Kieran.

That was something that she could not allow.

She'd stuffed away her shame and her self-hate, and in doing so, she'd become cold and distant from the people who loved her. It was impossible to be otherwise when she spent every day living a lie.

And now, Samuel Ellsworth thought he could conduct business with her brother as if nothing had happened? She'd kept it all secret, and now he had the audacity to think that she would tolerate his presence?

Kieran would die first.

As Rogan and Kieran made their way through the ball-room, they saw that Nilo had removed his hat and was fanning Emeline, who still leaned against the window.

Rogan knelt at his wife's side and spoke softly with her. He stood then, and turned to Kieran. "I'll carry her out. Let's go."

Kieran hesitated only for a moment. Inwardly cringing at how it would hurt them and how callous she would seem, she said, "Would you mind overmuch if I stayed on here for a time, and enjoyed a bit more of the *festa*?"

Rogan's expression became incredulous. "Emeline is ailing, and you want to dance?"

"I was merely thinking that Emeline needs to lie abed, and there's naught I can do for her. 'Tis not indifference, Rogan, but simply practicality."

"Yes, stay," Emeline said softly, settling the matter. "I have seldom seen you have such fun. 'Tis a good diversion for you, and I would be pained to have caused you to miss it."

"Thank you, Emeline," Kieran said softly, and she moved to embrace her. "I do so hope all is well with the child," she whispered in her ear.

Emeline squeezed Kieran tight. "Pray 'tis so."

"Of course," Kieran lied again. She'd ceased praying years ago, after a night spent praying to be spared a horrific choice, and months after, praying for an absolution that never came. "Sleep well."

Rogan consulted his timepiece. "Two hours, Kieran, and see to it that Nilo knows where you are at all times."

"Thank you, Rogan."

Rogan lifted his wife and cradled her in his arms. He left the ballroom by way of the terrace. Kieran took Emeline's evacuated seat and waited until she was certain that Rogan would have had time to get into a gondola and head back to their rented palazzo.

When she decided enough time had passed, she rose and turned to Nilo. "I need to go above stairs."

Her tactful phrase told Nilo all he needed to know: his mistress needed to use the facilities. The great, hulking African escorted her through the crowded ballroom and to the bottom of the steps that curved to the upper level.

Kieran ascended them, her heart pounding, her belly churning. Never mind what she felt, her determination was set. She would personally see to it that whatever the cost, Samuel Ellsworth would not enter into business with her brother.

Aboard his elegant *burchiello*, Matteo de Gama hunched over a high stakes bank of faro. They played with real money, no checks or chips. Sequins and ducats were piled around each punter, the biggest stack in front of Matteo. The banker tried to cover his dismay behind a disaffected mien. He could not, however, hide the bead of sweat that formed on his upper lip. The man was all in, and had just bet the turn. Matteo didn't mind the case keeper; he counted cards the way he seduced women: After years of practice, it had simply become second nature. Though Matteo's expression never changed, he coppered the bet and waited for the banker to make the turn.

The swaying of the *burchiello* picked up as the rowers turned onto the Grand Canal, heading in the direction of a man who had summoned Matteo to ask a favor. Because Matteo had a game slotted for that evening, the other players joined him on his *burchiello* to play en route.

The turn revealed the final three cards in Matteo's favor, and the banker let out a small moan as he slid the last of his sequins across the board and added to the glittering pile in front of Matteo.

"Time to take a break, gentlemen?" Matteo asked. He rose and crossed the marble floor to his well-stocked liquor and wine cabinet. At his orders, small, bite-sized finger foods had been set out, dried dates and cheeses, anchovies and olives. "Come, eat. We will play again after I see what Vincenzo is in need of."

The banker, Leonardo, accepted a large glass of wine and took a piece of cheese. While the other men talked and laughed about the game as they counted their remaining monies and loaded up the dealing box, Leonardo drank and ate as if it were his final meal.

"My wife will slay me," Leo said with finality. "First she will cut off my penis and feed it to the pigeons in the square. And then she will cut out my heart and leave me to lay dying in our bed."

"Playing with your wages again?" Matteo inquired.

"Worse. Playing on credit." Leo took a huge gulp of wine, glanced over his shoulder, and leaned in with a confidential whisper. "I am in debt to several men, a few of whom are unsavory."

Matteo shook his head in sympathy. Gambling, for Matteo, was a way of life. It was how he paid his rents, padded his coffers, and afforded life's luxuries. For others, however, it could become something much darker, a compulsion, and it had led to many a man's death when creditors came calling. Sadly, it seemed Leonardo had succumbed to that sickness.

"More wine?" Matteo offered.

"All I need is a few chips and a chair, and I'm certain I can recoup my losses." Leo held out his glass as Matteo poured, and as he watched the dark red liquid fill the goblet, he chewed his bottom lip pensively. "You know, for a price, I would let a little information slip your way."

A desperate man's final plea. Pitiful. "What price, and how am I assured this information pertains to me?"

Leo glanced back to the table at the bank of faro. "I assure you, if I were you, I would want to know."

The piles of coins by Matteo's seat glittered, and Leo looked on longingly. The thing about desperate men was they were often willing to go to extreme lengths to save their necks. Matteo studied Leonardo for a moment: wide, earnest eyes, sweaty brow, trembling hands. He was afraid of his wife, definitely, and was frantic to get back into the game, but was not likely lying about having information. Matteo was curious enough to wonder exactly how little Leo would take in exchange for his tidbit. "Two sequins."

"You insult me. Twenty."

"Ten, and nothing more."

"Twelve, and I will divulge names."

"Done."

Leo sent a searching look around them, making certain none of the other men listened. It was painful for Matteo to watch him; every thought, emotion, need, and desire stood out in plain relief on his thin face. It really wasn't a wonder as to why he'd been reduced to selling information.

"Gia, the daughter of Paulo DelAmicio, has gone to her father and revealed that a certain man seduced her and left her with no virtue and no promise of marriage."

Cold dread formed in Matteo's gut. Paulo DelAmicio was a dangerous man. But his lusty daughter had been irresistable.

"Whomever that man was," Leo said, his tone indicating he knew precisely who wooed the beautiful young girl, "might want to consider leaving Venice before he is divested of his head. I hear there's been a high price lain upon it."

"Interesting information, indeed, though useless. Shame on me for falling for your ruse." Matteo bowed slightly, his demeanor unaffected despite the apprehension that gripped him. He turned to the other men. "As always, our time was enjoyable, but I must cut it short. As you know, I have an appointment." He swept his winnings into a leather pouch, counted out twelve sequins and pressed the payment into Leo's waiting palm.

Matteo excused himself and left the grand room of his *burchiello* to seek out his boatmen. Within minutes the vessel was brought to the side of the canal, the gamblers were asked to leave, and a man was discretely dispatched to send word to the man who was expecting Matteo.

Signore de Gama, it seemed, had pressing matters that required immediate attention.

Kieran slipped down the servants' stairwell and wended her way through the palace until she reached the library. From the sounds and smell of it, men were still enjoying their brandy and cigars.

She opened the door and peeked inside again. She saw Samuel at a table, playing cards. He had a brandy snifter by his side, stacks of chips in front of him, and cards in his hand. He laughed and made a bet.

Kieran thought of the dagger she wore strapped to her thigh, and was suddenly set with the urge to thrust it between his ribs. Such longings were not unusual, but they were rarely so potent. She could feel his hot blood on her skin, and it sent a shameful, exciting surge to her loins.

Nilo waited for her, thinking she was seeing to her physical needs. Knowing her time was short, Kieran did not linger in the doorway. She opened the door and entered, swept across the room as she had before, as if she were above the rules of decorum.

As Kieran neared Samuel, she steeled herself. Using every ounce of her nerve, she approached him. She could smell his scent, expensive musk and spices. It turned her stomach.

Kieran leaned down and spoke to him through her mask. "Your Grace, my brother has sent me with a message for you."

Samuel's gray eyes glittered with interest as he cocked his head up to look at her, his recognition apparent on his unmasked face. "Is that so? Well, give it to me."

"Come with me, Your Grace. 'Tis a private matter."

Kieran turned and walked briskly from the room. Behind her, she heard him rise and make his excuses before following. She led the way through the palace until she found a quiet corridor. Nervousness had her in a tight grip, and she forced herself to focus. She needed to make certain that Samuel dropped his business offer, and stayed away from her.

Kieran had her dagger beneath her skirts; she was not the defenseless, naïve girl Samuel had taken advantage of, assaulted, and abused.

Samuel had donned his costume in keeping with

Venice's laws, and approached her wearing a plain white mask, its mouth curved in an eerie grin.

He drew close, his manner far too casual and confident for Kieran's comfort.

"What is the message?" he asked without preamble.

"The message is mine. Stay away from my family, and abandon this business venture with my brother. I will not tolerate your presence in my life." Kieran heard her voice tremble, but she kept her chin raised, so he would not read her posture and know her fear.

Samuel considered her words before responding. "And if I do not?"

"I will do whatever I must to ruin my brother's opinion of you. As you might recall, that shouldn't present too much trouble for me."

Her voice was gaining strength, and the chilly tone of it resembled the frigid girl she'd become, the one that caused suitors to name her ice princess when she spurned them.

"This is due to our previous encounter, is it not?" Samuel sighed as if he were deeply troubled. "Please, accept my apologies for my behavior that night. I was quite drunk, and decidedly out of line."

Behind her mask, Kieran wore the expression of one stunned. "You dare to stand before me and offer an apology? Firstly, there is no forgiveness for what you did, and second, if there were, 'tis three years late."

"Well, I cannot undo what I've done. All I can do is say that I'm sorry for my part in it."

"You are disgusting," Kieran hissed. "My brother would kill you if he knew 'your part.'"

"Kieran, please, I beg you," he began, using the sort of tone one reserves for squalling babies and agitated horses. "Try to remain calm. For three years I have seen you, at the theater, at balls, and for dinners of mutual acquaintance, and you seem to look right through me, almost as if you did not remember. Why the sudden concern over a business venture that will not involve you?"

Kieran did not speak, for no words could escape the knot in her throat. How could he be so casual about something so horrid?

"I was drunk," he continued, shrugging his shoulders as if that excused his actions. "What I recalled when I woke, however, had me expecting a visit from your brother or the magistrate the next day, the next week, the next month. I rushed to secure alibis and witnesses. I crafted denials, and I sweated the consequences." He cocked his head to the side, as if infinitely puzzled. "Nothing happened. You obviously never told Rogan. So I assumed you were not too upset by the matter."

Kieran found she was too angry to be afraid of him. His grinning mask seemed to mock her and his voice was an echo of her worst nightmare.

"Not upset?" Her voice came louder than her intention, and it echoed from the high ceiling.

"Shhh." Samuel cast a glance down the corridor and back to the room where his associates gathered. "Someone will hear you."

"You disgusting, horrid, vile man," she raged.

Samuel grabbed her by the upper arm and hauled her around the corner, and through a set of French doors to the outside. She screeched and struggled and he clamped a hand over her mask. "Hush, you fool. I will not have you causing a scene."

He dragged her further from the house until they were down by the bank of the canal, where no one was likely to hear them.

"We'll settle this now," he said harshly. "Five thousand pounds for you to do as you've been doing: holding silent. Now think rationally. This shipbuilding deal is lucrative for me, but also for Rogan. Make no mistake, he wants this—he knows it will make him richer than Midas.

I should hope you have enough affection for your brother to not stand in the way of that."

"Let go of me. How dare you lay your hands on me!" She wanted to reach for her dagger, but he held her so tightly she could not break free.

"Five thousand pounds for your silence," he repeated, his tone insistent and angry. "You've kept it secret all this time. Why change that now, when it will hurt your brother?"

"I don't want you in my life," she bit out. "It makes me sick to look at you."

"I will stay away, I give you my word. I shall take pains to avoid your company."

"No. I don't want you near my family. You'll drop this deal or I will tell Rogan."

"He won't believe you," Samuel said with assurance. "You go and toss out your tawdry slander, and see what comes of it. I'll make it my mission to paint you as a hysterical spinster whose interest I've spurned. Think on it. After all this time, who will believe you? Your brother? I think not. 'Tis been three years. A virtuous woman would have immediately called for her honor to be avenged. How will you explain your years of silence?"

"I could tell the truth," Kieran said, and she heard the doubt in her own voice. His grip on her arms was not too hard, but it imprisoned her just the same. The sound and smell and touch of him had her once again feeling the victim. It transported her back to that night, and it was every bit as frightening as the first time.

Samuel laughed lightly. "The truth is rather ambiguous, is it not? I say, 'twould be most interesting to see what would happen. My alibi places me well away from London that night, and you will make claims three years late. You'll certainly seem mad. Perhaps your brother will think you've gone daft, or more likely, he'll think you in need of a husband so you can produce a child or two and relive your hysteria. 'Tis a proven fact, you know, that women of a certain age begin to lose their grip on reality if they remain a spinster."

When Kieran didn't respond, Samuel squeezed harder, and gave her a little shake. "What will it be? Five thousand pounds and your silence, or your insane allegations matched to my alibis?"

The pressure on her arms snapped her to reality. A primal shriek of rage tore from her throat and pure bloodlust sang in her veins. She fought him with all she had. He crushed her to the bulk of his chest and tried to restrain her. But she was wild, out of control. She wanted to rake the skin from his body, to pull the hair from his head, to make him bleed and to make him scream in pain. She kicked, slapped, scratched, pinched, and punched like a wild woman, no longer wanting her dagger, but to flay him alive with her bare hands.

Matteo de Gama loved Venice passionately, but he despised Carnivale for its noise, crowds, foreign visitors, and the mess it left behind. He sought solace where he could, in the drunken English lords who couldn't refuse a bet, and in the tender beauties who lost their inhibitions while hiding behind their masks.

This night, however, he had to contemplate leaving his fair city, if only for a time. How long until Signore Del-Amicio realized that Gia had been no more a virgin in Matteo's bed than he himself had been? Matteo thought of Gia and her sultry eyes as she begged him to marry her, and how they'd narrowed in rage when she'd threatened her father's wrath if he refused.

Well, it seemed she'd meant it, enough to play the mistook virgin to her powerful, protective papa.

Matteo ran a hand through his hair and considered his options. He would need to visit his *casino* before leaving

Venice, to gather clothing, monies, and to make certain his landlady had all her rents paid for the next year. He would be back in Venice in a few months; Gia was far too lusty a young woman to go long without a lover. She would find another man, and her father's anger would be redirected.

As he sailed, he heard a female voice calling out to him from a bridge. A delay, but one he would gladly make time for.

He had his *burchiello* pulled beneath it where Mariuccia, the daughter of the butcher, leaned down to him, the high curves of her breasts the only exposed flesh available for his viewing.

"You never come to see me anymore," she pouted.

Because her mother and father were good people, he thought, and their daughter was their treasure. But he did not say that. "I am a busy man."

"Busy, busy man. And while you are so busy, I am an abandoned flower, wilting on the vine."

"Your father would shoot me if I were the one to pluck you, my delightful angel. He wants you properly wed, and a son-in-law to pass his trade to."

"Matteo, you are wicked to worry about my papa when I tell you I am so forlorn." She shifted her posture and changed tactics. "I read your satire, and I hope you would bring me aboard your *burchiello* so we might discuss it. Unless you think I am too young. . . ."

"Youth is such a charming flaw," Matteo replied softly. His *burchiello* drifted beneath his feet, the stars shone overhead, and before him a maid dipped down low so he could view her soft breasts. He would not seduce her, no matter how tempting, but as a man who enjoyed life's pleasures, he did not suffer her flirtation.

A scream rent the air, destroying the peace and sending shivers down Matteo's spine. He looked around and saw nothing out of the ordinary. He lifted his gaze back up to Mariuccia. "Did you hear that?"

She shrugged, obviously restless to be on his *burchiello* or on her way. "Do I charm you, Matteo?"

Matteo smiled softly, dismissing the sounds he'd heard. Probably a domestic dispute of some sort, or a lover's quarrel.

"Many things charm me, Mariuccia. Do you hope to be amongst them?"

The scream came again, this time full of such rage that Matteo felt his blood grow cold. It was a rare thing to hear something so primal, and curiosity, as it so often did, decided the matter for Matteo.

Without another word to Mariuccia, he called out to his boatmen and applied himself alongside them to the task of moving the *burchiello*. The vessel was low-slung, heavy in the center, and made to move with the wind, so it was with great effort that they pushed the oars into the water and heaved the craft into motion. Another sound reached them, this one the grunt of a man being injured, as if by a jab or kick, and the noises were growing closer.

Soon enough he saw them, a struggling woman in the grip of a man. Matteo could make out the sounds of her distress, muffled by the grip of his hand over her mask.

Matteo wasn't the sort of man who got involved in others' problems, but neither was he a man who would calmly sail by as a woman was assaulted.

He pulled two pistols from his belt and leveled them both on the man. His voice rang out, "Let the woman go."

They both stopped, long enough to look around. The man kept a grip on the woman, as if trying to fend her off. The woman began to fight in earnest once more.

Matteo cocked both pistols. "Let her go," he said again. And then, realizing how many visitors littered the city, said it again in French, and once more in English. "Let her go, or I will kill you."

As the man struggled with the woman he called out, "Go away. This is a private matter."

"Three seconds, and your brains feed the fish."

The man, seeming resigned, let her go.

Just as he released her, the woman swung around, and losing her balance, toppled over the side of the bank and fell into the water with a splash.

The two men looked at the water in horror, and then at each other.

"I can't swim," the Englishman said from behind his mask.

And then, Matteo de Gama, who thought he'd seen the very bottom of human indecency, watched as the man turned and hurried away, leaving them both behind.

The water filled Kieran's mask, saturated her many layers of clothes, and sucked her to the bottom. She kicked and thrashed, but could not force her way to the top.

The dark water dragged her down, cold and unfeeling; the only sound, bubbles rising from her mask. It would not take long, she knew, for death to come. Only minutes, and then it would be over.

In her mind's eye, Kieran saw her mother's face, stained with tears.

And then another image appeared, this one of the years that stretched in front of Kieran, loveless, lonely, and tainted with memory.

In all the time that had passed, nothing had taken away the shame and pain of that night. Why should she fight the one thing that would most assuredly wipe it all away?

Kieran stopped struggling and let the water take her into its silent darkness.

~2~

Matteo could not give chase and leave the girl to drown. He tossed his pistols to the deck and yanked off his cloak before diving into the canal. The water was murky and dark, and he held his breath until his lungs burned for air, his outstretched arms feeling around for her. He felt the touch of fabric, grabbed a fistful, yanked, and began swimming upward, desperate for air.

When he broke the surface, Matteo grasped her around the middle and swam back, careful to keep her masked face above water. Once alongside his *burchiello*, he handed her up to his boatmen and then climbed aboard to collapse on the deck.

Matteo's manservant rushed over. "What is happening?"

"Help me bring her inside."

Together the men made to lift the woman to her feet, but she whirled and yanked herself from their grasp.

"Do not touch me," she hissed.

Matteo waved his manservant away. Maintaining a distance from the frightened woman, he gestured to the doors of the large cabin. He spoke in English, as she had. "There are blankets and dry cloaks inside."

She glanced around wildly, her mask and wig still in place, though her hat was gone. Her cloak and gown must be heavy, Matteo thought, sodden as they were with water. Something in her posture, however, spoke of desperation, and Matteo felt a prickling on his skin that had nothing to do with the cold water.

"I will not hurt you," he assured her.

Her face snapped around, her eyes glittering behind the frozen mask of icy silver and vivid blue.

He moved to the door of the living quarters and opened it, revealing a well-lit room with walls of mirrors and creamy woods, marble floors, and velvet furniture. A huge gaming table dominated the room, and atop it a case held chips and decks of cards.

He glanced in and viewed the sumptuous room as if through her eyes, wondering why she perceived him as a threat when he'd just saved her life. "I cannot help you unless you come in, dry off, and tell me where you need to go."

She took two steps back and looked at the water, as if thinking of pitching herself back into the canal to escape him.

Matteo's patience snapped. He hadn't gone to the trouble of saving the girl only to have her take her life by jumping off the deck of his vessel. He gestured for his boatmen to grab her and haul her into the cabin.

He retrieved his pistols and shoved them back into his waistband, following his men and the squirming, screaming girl. The boatmen did as they were instructed and then left, closing the door behind them.

Matteo locked the door lest the girl get more ideas about escaping. How absurd that she seemed so fearful, as if he were her abductor.

He removed his wet jacket and tossed it to the floor, then reached for her wig and mask. She slapped his hands away and hesitated as if unsure of what to do. Finally, the discomfort must have decided for her and she ripped them away herself.

She stared at him defiantly, the silver wig dripping from her left hand, the mask dangling from the right.

Wet auburn tresses hung in thick locks around an oval face, finely boned and exquisitely formed, her skin so fair as to be likened to ivory. But it was her eyes that captivated him, dark and stormy blue, fringed by thick, spiky lashes. Water beaded on her skin like wobbling, silvery tears beneath those eyes, and her mouth was pink and full and beguiling.

As if of its own volition, his hand moved to brush away hair that clung to her damp cheek.

She pushed his hand away again, straightened her posture even further, an admirable task for one wearing several stones worth of soaked clothes.

"Your cloak," he murmured. "Take it off, and I will get you a blanket."

His fingers brushed one of the silken frogs as if he longed to undress her himself.

Kieran felt dizzy, sick, enraged. How dare he touch her?

No more, she thought. Never again. She'd had enough of being manhandled and abused to last a lifetime, and was not about to be raped aboard this Venetian's boat.

Kieran met his eyes and, with all the practice of dissembling for three years, offered a tremulous smile to put him at ease. He smiled in return, and she let out a little sigh of exasperation. "'Tis been a most trying evening."

"Of course. I understand completely," he said, but his eyes did not move from her lips and his fingers brushed the line of her jaw.

"I have a stone in my slipper. It pains me. One moment, signore, whilst I remove it."

She bent at the waist as if to take it out, and slid her hand up under her skirts to her dagger. The catch released without a sound and she was upright in an instant.

She thrust the weapon out at him, catching the edge of his shirtsleeve, just missing his arm. She lashed out again, this time aiming for his middle.

"Stand away from me." Her voice quavered and broke. She sharpened it like a blade. "Get back."

He took two steps back, his eyes locked on hers. He considered her for a moment, glanced at the slice in his shirt, and then yanked a pistol from his waist. He calmly leveled it at her. "Forgive me, but I will be damned if I will let you stab me aboard my own *burchiello*."

"Touch me again and you will die," she said, and she meant it.

He paused, his head slightly to the side. It irritated her that there was no fear in his eyes, as if she brandished a parasol and not a dagger.

"Back away," she commanded him.

Damn him, he grinned, still unafraid. "It seems we have reached a stalemate," he said. "Why do we not both set aside our weapons and don dry clothing. If you do not mind civility, we could enjoy a glass of port while I return you to your . . . keeper."

He strolled casually to the little bar in the corner and, with one hand still holding his pistol, poured two glasses of port, his eyes all the while trained on her reflection in the mirror.

Kieran considered her options. True, it seemed he meant her no harm, but neither had her cousin Simon seemed evil the night he'd convinced her to betray her word to her brother and accompany him. Kieran no longer trusted her instincts.

Her gaze kept returning to his pistol. It was crafted of light wood and black iron, possessed a long barrel, a short grip, and an ornately curved hammer. He held it with careless grace, his forefinger resting on the trigger, his thumb lightly riding the hammer.

She took a step closer to him, and he raised the gun and the port, one in each hand. "Your choice. What will it be?"

Kieran looked down at her hand. Saw the silver wink of the metal and the grip of her hand on the pommel, so hard her knuckles shone whitely. For three lonely years she had suffered in silence, and now, Samuel would do business with Rogan. She had been powerless to cow him.

And what could she do to stop it from happening? Debase herself and reveal her greatest shame to Rogan, the only person's opinion in England she cared about. Risk his disbelief, or worse, his disappointment in her.

No. She couldn't do that. And so she'd have to suffer Samuel's presence in her life, feign normalcy, and let it eat away at her like a cancer.

A lame apology and five thousand pounds, as if he could buy back the memories that haunted her days, disturbed her nights, and poisoned her soul.

She looked again at the man who held wine and a gun, as if he offered life in one hand and death in the other.

And suddenly, that pistol was liberation. Freedom. The cost of the gunshot a momentary payment for the engulfing black that would take all her pain away forever. For once, Kieran would test her fate.

She dove at him, knife outstretched and brandished like a sword.

He tossed the glass of port in her face, the wine blinding her as the glass crashed to the floor, the crystal exploding in a shatter against the marble tiles. He feinted left and grabbed her by the cloak as she lunged at him, used the fabric to yank her down to the ground. His hand caught her wrist as they went down. He landed on top of her, her breath whooshing from her lungs as he used his body to subdue her. With a deft motion he pried the dagger from her hand and flung it across the room.

Beneath his weight she thrashed like a wounded, captured beast, desperate for release. And then, beyond all her control, she whimpered, "Please don't. I cannot bear it. Please just shoot me."

He went still, his hands pinning hers to the floor as he stared down at her. His dark brown eyes were soft, velvety. His face, for all the hard angles of it, possessed a strikingly soft mouth, and it curved down at the corners with rage or frustration she knew not, maybe both. He was close, so close she could see the dark bristles of his incipient beard beneath his skin, and could smell his breath, pleasantly scented with wine. His long, dark hair hung into her face, brushing cold and wet against her skin.

Finally, he seemed to make a decision. He released his hold and moved from her. Studying her, his body coiled as if he were poised to grab her again if she made a strike at him, he smiled debonairly and inclined his head in a mock bow.

"I am Matteo de Gama, a stranger to you, and so you have no cause to esteem me. Yet, I pulled you from the canal when another man would have left you to drown, and make no mistake," he met her eyes again, his sincere and soul-deep, "if I wanted to ravish you, the deed would be done by now."

Kieran pulled herself to a seated position beside him, her breath rapid, her heart pounding. She used the hem of her cloak to wipe the port from her face before she twisted her hands in the fabric, at a loss of what to do or say.

She looked at the floor where broken glass lay in a puddle of wine on the creamy marble. He'd known what she meant to do; she'd seen the flash of recognition in his eyes. It shamed her that she'd allowed him to know something so deep and dark about her. He was speaking, she realized, asking her who she was.

She introduced herself as a shiver took her, and she tried not to let it show, holding her body as rigid as possible, clamping her jaw tight lest it chatter. He did notice, however, and he got to his feet and fetched a thick blanket. When he returned he held it beyond her grasp.

"You must remove the sodden cloak if you hope to get any warmer."

It felt like capitulation to remove it, and yet, it was foolishness to continue to wear the soaked garment. She was freezing, her corset a strangling, wet vise around her middle, her gown clinging to her like a sticky film. The cloak draped over her with its saturated weight, the only thing she could modestly remove. Finally, Kieran undid the frogs and pushed the cloak from her shoulders, letting it sag to the floor.

The blanket was warm and soft, an instantly soothing comfort as he wrapped it around her with a gentleness she did not expect, given that she'd tried to stab him in order to force him to commit a murder. She brought her eyes up to his and found him staring down at her with that same expression as before, an odd mix of curious, cautious compassion.

It was a stare that prompted her to repay his manners with her own. "I am in Venice with my brother, Rogan Mullen, the English Duke of Eton, and his wife, Emeline. We are staying at the Palazzo Morosini del Giardino."

Kieran swallowed heavily against the lump of embarrassment in her throat for attacking him with no provocation. She also knew Nilo would be sick with worry, and wondered what Rogan would think when she turned up, soaking wet and without her escort. She had many lies to tell if she wanted to keep her secret safe, and the thought did not sit well with her.

"Does your offer to take me home still stand?" she asked shyly.

"Of course." Matteo went to the door, unlocked and opened it, called for his boatmen, and informed them of their next destination.

The *burchiello* lurched into gentle motion as Matteo returned to Kieran's side. He offered her his hand, and she accepted the help in getting to her feet, as the weight of her garments would have made that task impossible without his aid.

A pair of armchairs sat on either side of a table, and Matteo gestured for Kieran to take a seat in one of them. "Do not worry about the wetness. Be comfortable. I hope we can be civil?"

Kieran nodded her assent. "Yes, of course, and I apologize. I was quite overcome by all that had just happened. 'Tis clear to me you meant only to help me."

"Think nothing of it." He avoided the worst of the spillage and shattered glass at the bar, poured another glass of port, and brought it to Kieran. "It will warm you."

She sipped and the sweet flavor burst on her tongue, the scents of currants and berries filling her sinuses. Once again she was aware of the way he studied her, and found the intensity of his stare unsettling.

"Who was that man?" he asked.

Kieran hesitated, trying to decide what she would reveal, not only to this man, but to her brother. "I don't know."

Matteo took the chair across from Kieran and openly studied her. "If that is so, how odd that he would call it a 'private matter.' That speaks of something more than strangers, no?"

"I don't know why he said that, and I don't know who he was. I am just relieved you came along when you did."

Matteo leaned back in his armchair, his soft mouth quirked up on one side. "You lie. How fascinating."

Kieran feigned confusion. "Why would I lie?"

Matteo grinned, but he didn't take the bait. "The man took you against your will, no?"

"Of course."

"And when caught, he left you to drown. Why would you lie to protect him?"

"Precisely," Kieran agreed stiffly. "Wouldn't I want the man punished?"

"Ah, good," Matteo said, as if cheering her on. He raised his glass in a toast. "Continue to answer each question with a question. It is an excellent ploy when employing falsehood."

"You don't know me well enough to make such distinctions of my motivations or my character, signore."

"Knowing when a man bluffs is how I afford the luxuries life can offer. You are good, and obviously well-practiced, but you are not the best I've seen."

He held his port by the rim, the glass dangling from his thumb and two of his long fingers as he gestured to her face with the tip of his index finger. "The color rides high on your cheeks, and your lips flatten with defiance even as your chin slightly raises. You may want to watch the chin and mouth. Practice in the mirror if you must. There is nothing you can do about the blush but try to remain calm, and most will likely mistake it for the discomfort of speaking of upsetting matters."

"You overstep your bounds."

"Indeed I do. It is my life's passion, in fact."

"You are a libertine, then."

"All Venetians pursue pleasure, art, romantic intrigues. Wine, food, beauty. The things that make a life rich. I will not apologize for taking joy in my life. Indeed, if you do not pursue the same, why come to Venice?"

"I told you, I came with my brother and his wife."

"To see Carnivale, no?"

"Combining business with a holiday. He seeks a bid for shipbuilding."

"But you said he is a duke? An aristocrat?"

"He is many things, signore. A sea-trader and a former pugilist, as well, and in England he owns multiple properties and a fleet of ships. My brother is successful in everything he endeavors." Kieran knew she sounded boastful, but she was proud of her brother. They were the children of a common sea-merchant, and though their mother had been a lady, Kieran and Rogan had not been raised to such wealth and privilege.

But when the laws of primogeniture put Rogan in succession for the dukedom, he threw himself into the position with all the grace and diligence it demanded. He'd found love with a common woman, defied convention and propriety when he deemed it honorable, and had earned the grudging respect of his peers.

Matteo sipped his port and considered her over the rim with a scrutiny that made Kieran want to squirm, but she did not give in to that urge. She leveled a glare on him, cold, withering, and unrelenting, that had repelled many a potential suitor. But Matteo did not seem to notice.

"He may well be all those things and more, *cuore solitario*. But your brother does not know you very well, does he?"

"He used to," she replied softly, more to herself than to him, "a long time ago."

Silence fell over them as the *burchiello* moved in time with the gentle current of the canal. The room was warm with candles and lamps, the light reflecting off the mirrored walls and dark windows as if they were caught in a floating cocoon.

"So what will you tell him," Matteo asked, finally breaking the silence, "when he asks what happened to you tonight? That some unknown man attacked you for no particular reason?"

Kieran tilted her head at an imperious angle. "Such things happen."

"Were you walking along the strand alone?"

"No," she replied indignantly. "I was attending a *festa*."

"Were you unescorted?"

"Of course not." She thought again of Nilo, and wondered if there was a search going on for her. She pulled the blanket tighter around her shoulders, looking for warmth in its soft folds.

Matteo continued on. "You expect your brother will believe that your escort was thwarted and you were grabbed and taken against your will by some unknown assailant?"

His eyes swept over her, taking in all her details, and Kieran felt her color deepen. "You were costumed, escorted, and in a crowd of people who were likewise garbed. No one could see the beauty of your face or the superb form of your body. So, why would he take this risk, why choose *you*, and not one of our Venetian women, many of whom stroll about unfettered by a doyenne?"

Kieran flushed deeper. This man picked apart her lies with ease, and it unnerved her even as it made her angry. She asserted herself, hiding her doubt. "My brother will believe me."

"He might. As you say, these things do happen. But if you want his unquestioning belief, you would do well to craft your story better."

The *burchiello* came to a rocking stop as they pulled alongside the bank of the canal and the boatmen called out, announcing their arrival.

Matteo didn't move, but kept his eyes on Kieran. "I suspect that you know precisely who grabbed you, and why he did so. I do not know why you would lie to protect him, but I am certain you will continue your ruse." His voice dropped and gentled. "I also suspect you would very much like to think life a better option than death."

"You do not know anything about me. Nothing at all," Kieran whispered fiercely, and she jumped to her feet. How dare he speak so casually of her darkest longing? "Good night, signore."

She whirled on her heel and hurried to the door. A moan of dismay escaped her lips as she found it still locked. Before she could turn to demand he open it, Matteo was behind her, so close she could feel the heat of him. His jaw was above her ear, and he spoke quietly as he handed her the discarded pieces of her costume, along with her dagger.

"Perhaps you should stay a while on my *burchiello*, and allow me to school you in the Italian art of vendetta. It is a tradition in my country, and we believe that when one wrongs another, they deserve to be repaid in full. There is a singular delight in serving justice from one's own hand." Matteo moved even closer to her, lowered his voice until it was an urgent whisper. "Only then can one find peace in their soul."

Kieran turned and looked up at him, her lips parted and trembling. She could not move, but was rooted by his words and the images they created in her mind.

"Ah, you have the most beautiful eyes," he murmured. "Like the canal at twilight."

He looked as if he would kiss her, and that was enough to break Kieran's reverie. She grabbed her things and held them to her chest. "Good night, Signore de Gama. Thank you for your aid, the blankets, and the port."

"I will tell my men to watch you as you approach the palace, and for them to take care they are not seen. I would not want their presence to spoil whatever false-hoods you might invent."

Matteo unlocked and opened the door, then stood back so she could depart. A smile played about his lips as he bowed. "And thank you, for a most interesting evening. It has been a long time since a woman threatened to kill me, and longer still since I met such a captivating liar. I also cannot forget that never before have I had the happy privilege of saving a life, let alone, the life of someone so beautiful. So, thank you for the many pleasures."

Matteo gave brisk orders in Italian to his men.

Kieran hesitated for a moment, but turned and walked away, her wet things clutched to her chest as the boatmen flanked her in escort. She stopped and turned around, saw Matteo standing in the open doorway, limned with candlelight, his face cast in shifting shadows.

He seemed to read her mind. "I have a small *casino* on the isle of San Giorgio Minore. I shall not be there long, as I will be traveling, but send for me if you wish. If I am available, it would please me very much to see you again."

"A casino?"

"House," Matteo corrected after thinking of the English word. "You can send for me at my house."

"I shall not."

"I understand, *cuore solitario*. Someday, when you are ready to let go of some of your hauteur, perhaps you can take back some of your pride. Until then, I wish you the best with your deceit."

Kieran found herself without words. The man knew no boundaries at all. She turned back around and stalked away, her head held high.

"And remember," Matteo called out to her departing form, laughter rich in his voice, "mind your lips and chin."

* * *

Kieran left the boatmen on the fringes of the property. She thanked them, but none of them spoke English. They smiled, nodded, and pressed kisses to Kieran's hand before sauntering away, their light-colored jackets disappearing into the darkness.

She hesitated before the two ornate, double doors, her hand on the iron handle. Taking a few deep breaths to sustain her, she steeled herself against the guilt for the lies she would tell Rogan. Kieran had kept her silence this long; she would not allow the events of this night to rob her of her privacy.

She'd be damned if she'd spend the rest of her life suffering Rogan's efforts to conceal his shame when he looked at her. She knew well what kind of honor her brother possessed. She would not allow him to find out that his sister had none.

With her mind made up, Kieran opened the door and went inside.

The household was in an uproar, and Rogan was in the process of gathering a search party. Everything stopped as Kieran entered.

"What the hell happened to you?" Rogan demanded. He strode across the room and grabbed Kieran, pulled her into a fast, fierce hug, and then held her by the shoulders for inspection. "Are you hurt?"

"No. I'm fine." Kieran struggled for normalcy as she spoke the lies she'd formed. She told as much of the truth as possible, so that if there had been any witnesses, her tale would hold up. "I had heard a noise and sought to see the source, and when I emerged into the corridor, a masked man grabbed me and dragged me outside. I fought him, and fell into the canal as a result. Thankfully, a kind man in a *burchiello* saw me fall and he rescued me as my assailant ran off. Overall, I'm fine, Rogan, other than a bit shaken. Please do not worry."

As Kieran finished speaking, Nilo dropped to his knees before her, his head bowed.

Kieran lay her hand gently on his head, her fingers resting on the warm curve of his shorn scalp. "Faithful Nilo. How you must have worried."

Rogan stood before her, his eyes hard, his face unreadable. "Nilo has asked me to dismiss him."

"That's ridiculous." Kieran turned her attention back to Nilo. "Rise, and face me. There is no room for shame. You are not at fault."

Nilo stood tall, and met her eyes. "It is my duty to protect you."

"Yes, and you have stood at my back for three years. By your own vow, you swore that not a hair on my head would be harmed under your watch, and so it has been. You had no control over the events that happened this night; you cannot protect me when you are not present."

His lips flattened but he remained upright, at attention, as she had commanded him. "Were you hurt in any way?"

"No. I swear it."

He frowned and sucked in his bottom lip. The expression tore at her heart, calling to mind the one time he'd told Kieran of his life in Africa, when another tribe killed his wife and children, and how sick he'd been on the slave ships, in body and soul. He'd been unable to save his family, and unable to save himself.

The thought that he would think he'd failed her had Kieran speaking from the heart.

"Please don't leave me, Nilo." Kieran's voice broke over the words, and she swallowed hard against the lump that formed in her throat at the thought of losing him. "Please," she whispered, and the tears that shone in her eyes were honest and real.

"I will not," he said after a time. His face softened. "I am sorry. I will not fail you again."

"Go, and think no more about this night. You are my protector, and more, my friend. I rely on you, Nilo. That will never change."

Nilo hesitated. He'd been there the night Kieran was in the "house of lords," posted as a guard by her cousin Simon and ordered to kill Rogan when he arrived. Through a crack in a shutter, however, Nilo had witnessed much of what had happened inside.

That night may have poisoned Kieran's soul and wounded her heart, but it had also deeply affected Nilo. He'd been Simon's slave then, and if he'd acted on his impulse, he would have hung the next day. Standing outside in the dark, he'd been helpless to intervene while two women were assaulted.

The day Rogan hired him as Kieran's guard, Nilo had made a solemn vow to Kieran that he would lay down his life before he'd stand by helplessly again.

And in their mutual, unspoken understanding of why Kieran held silent, their friendship was galvanized.

Nilo reached out and brushed a finger against her wet hair, his touch so light she scarcely felt it. With sadness in his eyes, he turned and left the room.

Rogan stood with his hands jammed in his pockets as he studied his sister beneath a scowl.

Kieran held to her resolve and adopted a flippant tone. "Why do you look so fierce, Rogan? I did not kidnap myself, nor set out to worry the household."

"Perhaps you take this lightly, but I don't. You could have been raped or murdered."

"But I wasn't. Why don't we put the matter to rest. I am freezing cold and exhausted. I need a bath and bed."

Rogan continued on, ignoring her. "Raped or murdered, and 'twould have been my fault for leaving you." He raked a hand through his hair and blew out a breath. "What a fool."

Kieran could not bear to have Rogan taking the

blame. "'Tis not your fault, any more than Nilo's. I should have not left the room alone."

He met her eyes, and in his she saw the need to do something, and the helplessness he felt that there was nothing he could do.

"Do you have any idea who grabbed you?" Rogan asked. "Did you see his face?"

Because she loved him, she answered his questions. But also because she loved him, she lied. "Of course not. He was costumed. If I knew, would I not demand you go find him, and see to the matter?"

She moved to stand by the fire, shivering in her wet clothes. And she ignored the stab of guilt as she over-exaggerated how cold she felt so her brother would relent in his questioning. The fewer questions asked, the fewer falsehoods she would tell.

"Was anything familiar about him?"

"No, Rogan." Kieran let her teeth chatter, providing ample proof that she was indeed quite cold.

"I don't like this. I don't like it at all." Rogan began to pace the room. He removed his jacket as he walked and handed it to Kieran. "Something feels odd."

She slid the garment over her shoulders. It hung to her knees and was warm from Rogan's body, but she kept up the shivering. "I can only surmise he had been watching me and had found out my relationship to you. He said something about me bringing a fine ransom."

Rogan grunted. "Perhaps." But he didn't look satisfied. "He spoke English, then?"

"Yes, with an accent. Italian, I think. 'Tis difficult to say. He did not speak much."

Rogan made a noise in his throat, still pacing.

"I hope I don't take ill," Kieran murmured through her chattering teeth.

He paused and glanced at her, and for a moment

Kieran thought he knew. She held her breath, releasing it as he spoke.

"Aye, you're cold. Not just from the wet, aye? You speak about your ordeal as if it happened to someone else. You're not afraid, not worried, and you don't even seem to want to find out who did it, and see him brought to justice.

"And it scares me for you. I actually worry nights, wondering if you'll ever come back to that girl you once were. I despair for it, and aye, I miss that girl. You've grown far too cold for your youth, Kieran, and I can only pray that one day you will find something to warm you."

He paused, those green eyes watching her with a cold, hard stare that made Kieran feel like a child. "For tonight, however, go to your rooms and call for a bath. We'll talk more on this in the morning."

She turned to leave, ready to put it all behind her, but her brother's voice stopped her. "The man who pulled you from the canal and returned you safely—do you know where I can find him? He needs to be properly thanked and rewarded."

Kieran hesitated before answering. In her mind she considered the possible outcome of Rogan speaking with Matteo de Gama. "No. I'm sorry. I fear I was too overwrought to think clearly, and did not even ask his name. I have no idea where to find the man, other than aboard one of the many *burchiellos* I've seen on the canals. I was in such haste to get back home, and was just grateful for his help."

Rogan waved his hand. "'Tis understandable. You'd just been assaulted and nearly drowned. Put the matter aside for now, go and take your bath, get warm, and to bed with you. Perhaps if you relax a bit, you'll recall more details."

"As you say," Kieran said softly, her guilt a weight in the pit of her belly. The feeling didn't relent even as she spoke the complete and absolute truth. "I'm sorry I can't tell you more, Rogan."

He waved his hand in her direction, dismissing her.

Kieran left her brother's presence to seek out comfort. Her rooms beckoned with the promise of a hot bath, a fire, and peaceful solitude.

Her mind, however, was anything but quiet. It spun with snippets of conversation. Most of all, with one particular sentence, spoken into her ear like a tantalizing secret. *There is a singular delight in serving justice from one's own hand.*

Kieran stopped in the hallway and looked down at her hands. Smooth, white, and slender, with long tapered fingers. She'd felt helpless to the memory of that night for so long.

The words Samuel had spoken screamed in her mind. *A virtuous woman would have called for her honor to be avenged.*

She pictured Samuel's face and imagined his suffering as she had, knowing that her honor was avenged, and that she saw to it herself.

That familiar, shameful spurt of excitement warmed her once more.

A servant walked down the corridor, his eyes downcast, step brisk, arms full of folded linens. He was a member of the palace staff, a native Venetian.

"Signore, do you speak English?" Kieran asked him.

The servant stopped and smiled. He shifted his burden so he could show her his forefinger and thumb, held apart to indicate he knew a small amount. "I am of your service," he replied in heavily accented English.

"A translation, please. What is *cuore solitario*?"

"Ah, *sì*." He fumbled through a few words in Italian until he formulated a reply. He stammered out two English words, leaving Kieran certain she never wanted to see Matteo de Gama ever again. "Lonely heart."

❧ 3 ❧

Matteo de Gama sailed his *burchiello* home to his small *casino*. The noise of the street performers jarred his nerves as his vessel navigated the waters of the canal and the *rio* that led to his home. He disembarked with his boatmen, and together they proceeded with caution. There was more than one man angry with Matteo: vengeful brothers, jealous husbands, furious fathers.

Outside his entrance, a group of adolescent boys gathered in a cluster, and Matteo grinned to himself as he wondered what mischief they were plotting. He flipped them a sequin as he passed them, and they scrambled to catch it.

He laughed at them, enjoying their youthful exuberance. Boys, like tightly compressed springs, needed to be let go with a firm, slow release. Let them go too quickly and they would bounce around, wild and uncontrolled.

Matteo had once been one of those boys himself, running the streets after dark, stealing, pick-pocketing, and cheating at cards. He knew a few things about being let go too early and with no care.

One of them wrested the coin from another and held it up to the moonlight to assess its value. Shouts of thanks followed Matteo, who waved them off.

The boldest of their bunch stepped aside, the coin in his fist. He called up to Matteo, who was already three-quarters up his walkway, with his boatmen behind him. "Not a good night to sleep in your own bed, signore."

The boys took off at a run like a pack of wolves startled by a gunshot. In the dim light he saw the door to his *casino* was ajar, and instantly Matteo was on the move, his men on his heels. It was probably DelAmicio's men, and if so, Matteo and his men would be outnumbered and outgunned.

Shouts came from inside his rooms, echoing in the entrance alcove. Matteo dashed down his walkway, ran as fast as he could, hearing the footsteps hit a few seconds behind him. They were in pursuit, but Matteo and his men had a good lead.

They rounded a corner to slip down an alley. It had plenty of doorways that led to other alleys and gardens like a maze, and had served them well in similar situations.

There were other men posted there, and Matteo was tackled and grabbed as he entered, along with his boatmen. Stilettos hit the ground with metallic twangs and a few shots from pistols rent the air in warning. Two men held Matteo's arms, one had an ankle. Scrabbling around on the gritty, dirty ground Matteo nearly broke free, but he stopped fighting and froze in place as a cold, iron muzzle pressed against his head.

"Your time is up," said the man who held the pistol, his voice muffled behind a mask that bore the face of grinning ghoul.

Kieran sat by Emeline's bedside, the two of them working on sewing projects, Kieran on a tapestry and Emeline on a baby's nightgown in a soft blue cotton. The light of afternoon spilled in through the open windows, as did the air, fragrant and fresh.

Fully recovered from the previous night's ordeal, Kieran was gowned in pink silk and ivory lace. Her hair spilled down her back in shiny, dark auburn waves, held back from her face by carved, gold combs.

The door opened and Rogan stepped in. He smiled at his wife and then addressed his sister. "A word, Kieran?"

"Of course," she replied, setting her sewing to the side. Emeline caught her gaze and lifted an eyebrow in question. Kieran shrugged a reply, and followed her brother out of the rooms with an insouciance she did not feel. Her belly flipped over and again and her palms began to sweat. She knew her brother well enough to not like the expression on his face.

Rogan led the way to Kieran's rooms, far enough away from his and Emeline's that they would not be overheard by his wife, an ominous sign. Kieran's mouth grew very dry when Rogan shut and locked her door. When he turned and faced her, his eyes gleamed like hard, glittering emeralds beneath the black slash of his brows.

"Why did you lie to me?"

A dangerous question, for Kieran had lied to her brother so many times she knew not in which falsehood she'd been caught. She remembered Matteo's words, and kept her chin steady, lips soft. "I don't know what you mean."

Rogan took two steps closer to her. Kieran planted her feet beneath her, determined not to show her fear.

"Who was the man who pulled you from the canal?"

"I do not know. I told you last night, I neglected to ask his name."

"You are lying. Why?"

"That would be such a silly thing to lie about, Rogan. Don't be absurd."

Rogan grabbed her by the arm and hauled her to his chest, his fist a hard band around her arm that burned and hurt.

"I have never been so close to smacking you, Kieran."

Real anger gathered in Kieran's chest like a thundercloud. Yes, she'd lied. That did not give him the right to threaten her. "Go ahead. Hit me. See if you feel better for it."

Rogan reached into his coat pocket with his free hand, not relaxing his grip on her arm in the slightest. He withdrew a piece of tattered, stained parchment. "This was delivered less than thirty minutes ago. Why don't you explain how a man called Matteo de Gama not only knows your name, but he also knows mine and where we are staying? And when you finish with that explanation, you can tell me why he apologizes for contacting you lest your brother find out."

Kieran tried to snatch the paper but Rogan was too quick. He held it high above her head. The action was so brotherly in manner that Kieran kicked him in the shins, hard.

"How dare you read something addressed to me."

"Aye, I dared. I suspected you of lying last night, but couldn't find a reason for your mendacity. I still cannot, but at least now I know my instincts are correct."

Rogan dragged Kieran over to the chair by her fireplace and pushed her down. He threw the letter onto her lap, and loomed over her as she unfolded the parchment. Tiny grains of sand fell onto her lap as a musty odor rose from the paper, and she noticed the handwriting, loopy and artistic amidst various blotches and smudges.

Signora Kieran,

I write to you from the Leads, trapped in a prison cell across a bridge from the Doge's palace.

I ask you for your help. There are false charges brought against me, the most nonsensical of allegations, in fact, that of freemasonry and treason. I ask, who loves Venice more than I? If there is such a man, make him known to me.

Sadly, there is a powerful man who would see me spend the rest of my days in this cell, and while I do not deny that I once loved his wife better than he, I do not care to accommodate him in this way to satisfy his vendetta.

Please go to the Doge's palace and inquire when I will be brought before the Court of the Esecutori contro la Bestemmia. Pity that it is, I am not privy to that information. Once the date and time is known to you, I implore you come and speak on my behalf to the Council of Ten. The events that transpired between us last night will provide some defense of me, as the man claims I committed one of my transgressions just this evening past.

I do so apologize if this letter jeopardizes anything you may have told your brother, but I am in the direst of straits and you are my shining ray of hope. Surely the Council of Ten will listen to you during this Inquisition, and if possible, your brother Rogan, a duke. Indeed, to have aristocrats vouch for me and my whereabouts will not hurt my case, even if they are English. I mean no offense in this.

Most sincerely,
Matteo de Gama

Kieran brought her face back up to her brother's after she reached the end of the letter. Honor demanded she do as Matteo asked. He'd pulled her from the canal when she was nothing but a stranger to him. However, she had to deal with Rogan first.

She stood and calmly laid the letter on the gold, marble-topped table by the chair. "I will go to the Doge's palace, now, if you care to accompany me."

A muscle flexed in Rogan's jaw. "You'll first explain why you lied to me."

But Kieran knew better than to back down.

"No. I won't. I lied for motivations that are mine alone, and they shall remain my private reasons. 'Tis not your concern."

"You are my ward. 'Tis nothing *but* my concern, aye?"

"Wrong. I am your sister, not your wife or your servant or your child. If I wanted a man to give me orders and demand my honesty, I would marry one of the many who have offered for my hand."

Rogan narrowed his eyes, obviously toying with the idea of turning his sister over his knee. His hands fisted and then released, again and again until Kieran thought he might actually strike her.

But she met his gaze with false calm.

"You are far too full of yourself," Rogan bit out. "You live, dress, and dine on my accounts."

"That is only because you refuse to accept recompense from Da and Mum." Kieran kept her voice level. She would not be made to feel indebted simply because she existed. "Is it my fault that I have no means to support myself, barring selling myself into marriage? Would you rather that, over the cost I bring you?"

"You speak nonsense in an effort to disguise the true matter."

"I do believe we are at the crux of the matter, Rogan. Think on it: If you did not support me as I live, dress, and dine, would you dare to speak to me as you are?"

Rogan let out a long breath. He stared at her for a few minutes until he finally shook his head, a gesture of disgust and resignation combined. "You were raised better than to be a liar, Kieran. I cannot fathom what has made you stoop so low.

"But you have always been our mother's daughter, as stubborn and headstrong as any man. I know that nothing will make you tell me the truth, even were I to try to beat it from you, and honestly, I have no desire to test the boundaries of that belief.

"You live with me because I love you, Emeline loves you, and we want you with us. The issue isn't financial, and I'm sorry I made it so.

"I will accompany you to the palace of the Doge. I do want to thank the man who saved you; he deserves that, and any help we can lend him. I care not if he committed the crimes that are laid against him. My loyalty is not to Venice, but to you, my blood."

Rogan turned and walked away from Kieran. He paused in the doorway and turned. "Just one thing. Did Matteo de Gama treat you inappropriately?"

Kieran thought about the night before, the look in Matteo's eyes, as if he understood her darkest longings. She remembered his eyes, so dark and full of amusement, but somehow still sad. And his mouth, soft and expressive, quirked up in humor, turned down in rage.

"No, Rogan. He truly did not."

His gaze met hers, full of meaning that did not need to be spoken. Not when one had been raised the way they had, with honor and conviction as requirements. "I take you at your word."

The statement could not have been better aimed to injure Kieran any more than it did. She fought the sting of tears as Rogan left her rooms. Nothing hurt more than his disappointment.

For a moment she considered running after him and telling him everything. Every sordid, disgusting detail so he would understand why she had lied. So he could comprehend the gravity of how, in the act of knowing, he could never again look at her the same way again.

Kieran pushed the thoughts away. Better for him to know her as a liar than to know her for worse. Much, much worse.

Liars did not inherit God's kingdom; the admonition from the Bible rang in her ears.

It was a small consolation to Kieran to consider, however, that by those same standards, neither would most anyone else.

And yes, she admitted to herself, Samuel Ellsworth had struck a chord. Perhaps after all this time, Rogan would not believe her. Had he not discovered what a liar she could be?

* * *

In deference to the law that forbade persons from being without costume during Carnivale, Kieran donned the half-mask that matched her gown, a pink and gold creation with cat eyes and pricked ears. It had a head-dress of pink feathers that made a hat unnecessary. She picked up her parasol and her reticule and followed her brother out of the palace.

They boarded a gondola, and Kieran sat on the small, hard bench and opened her parasol to shade her from the blazing sun. She angled it so the taut, pink fabric shielded her also from Rogan's silent regard.

The ride to the Doge's palace took less than a quarter of an hour, but Kieran felt like the entire afternoon passed before she could disembark.

They left the Grand Canal behind them as they entered by way of the Piazzetta dei Leoncini, passing the columns of Venice's two patrons, Marco and Todaro. Kieran marveled at the statues that stood atop the tall pillars: the lion of Saint Mark and the statue of Saint Teodoro of Amasea, or "Santodaro" to the Venetians.

The Piazza San Marco dominated Venice, the seat of the republic and the center of Venetians' lives. Kieran stopped, absorbing the enormity, the beauty, the scents and sounds. The ground floor of the Procuraties were dominated by several cafes exuding the tantalizing scents of pastries and coffee, along with a fair share of laughter and shouts.

Kieran had noticed that the Venetians laughed as much as they spoke, a trait as vastly different from the English as any of the more obvious.

It was the many differences of Venice that enraptured Kieran, nothing like England or Barbados, the island on which she and Rogan had been raised.

The architecture flaunted boldness and audacity without a trace of restraint. Everywhere the eye looked one could see detail upon detail, each surface and area decorated and adorned. Yet, the city wore it with a casual elegance that felt as natural as the elements of which it was comprised: water and wood, marble and metal.

Oh, and the water, she mused, sparkling in a deep green-blue when the sun hit it just so, something beyond color for its luminescence. No horses' hooves ringing on cobblestones, no clatter of wagon wheels, no cries of people hawking their wares. There was such peace in the water lapping against the black hulls of gondolas, the sounds of conversations held in cafes, and the cries of seagulls and cooing pigeons.

A woman in full Carnivale costume ran from a café, pulling Kieran's attention to her. She laughed and darted around a pillar, giggles turning to shrieks of pleasure as a man followed to peek around the column, the meter and tone of his voice obviously making it known he was in the midst of playful pursuit. He grabbed her hand and pulled her toward him, kissing up her arm until he reached her elbow.

The woman allowed him to pull her closer, and soon they were dancing to a song only they could hear.

"Looks like fun, aye?" Rogan asked.

Kieran sent her brother a cool look of disdain. They walked to the Doge's palace, pigeons flying out of their path.

All Venetians pursue pleasure . . . the things that make a life rich. That is what Matteo de Gama said, Kieran remembered.

They stepped inside the shady interior of the palace and as Rogan spoke with the attendants and guards, Kieran allowed herself to mentally answer Rogan's question.

Yes. It had looked like fun.

Good timing often comes down to chance; Matteo had already been brought in for his Inquisition in the

Grand Council chamber. Outside the huge doors, Rogan and Kieran removed their masks, left them on a table, and entered.

An enormous dais held a long, thick table of dark, elegant wood. Centered behind it was a high-backed throne, flanked by five large, carved chairs on either side. The Council of Ten had been assembled, and as Rogan and Kieran had found out, because one of the charges was of treason, the Doge, the Prince of Venice himself, sat for the Inquisition with his Council.

Matteo stood, flanked by two guards as the proceeding took place. To his side there was a man giving impassioned testimony to the Doge and the Council.

The man, his anger thinly disguised by his reddened face and clenched hands, spoke in rapid Italian, his tone accusatory. A red-lipped woman with shiny, curly hair sat at his side, her eyes downcast, her cheeks flushed. Papers littered a table in front of him, and when he reached the crescendo of his diatribe, he slammed his fist down on the documents.

When the man finished his speech, Matteo had a turn to address his defense, and he did so in measured tones. One of the men asked a question, and Matteo answered, and another asked a question, gesturing to the rear of the chamber.

Matteo turned and saw Kieran.

Their eyes met and held, and in his grim expression Kieran saw relief and gratitude. Matteo said something to the guard beside him, and a long conversation was conducted before the guard slipped away and the Inquisition continued.

"What do we do?" Kieran asked Rogan in a whisper. "What are they saying?"

"Just wait." Rogan had her take a seat. "They know who we are and why we're here."

Kieran watched the proceedings continue. Matteo

stood with his face sober. She leaned over to her brother once again. "Are Venice's laws similar to ours?"

Rogan nodded gravely. "Aye. The penalty for treason is death."

Kieran sat back and retreated back into silence, considering that if Venice executed treasonous persons in the manner in which England did, she did not want to know about it.

Still, as she studied Matteo from the back, it pained her to imagine his body dangling from a rope, those amber-lit eyes bulging as he gasped for air.

After what seemed an eternity, a guard came and gestured for Rogan and Kieran to follow him, and led the way to the front of the massive courtroom.

Kieran behaved as she would before her king, and swept into a deep, deferential curtsy. Beside her, Rogan bowed low.

A man approached and identified himself as a translator summoned by the Council, and with his aid, they addressed the Doge and the Council of Ten.

The Doge turned his attention to Kieran first.

"You claim you were with this man, Matteo de Gama, last night?"

"I was, your Serenity," Kieran answered, and she curtseyed once more. "He saved my life when I fell into the canal, and he returned me safely to my brother."

"Impossible," the patrician man screamed, pounding again on the papers. "She lies!"

"Do not call my sister's integrity into question," Rogan interjected, his voice firm and resounding in the great hall, echoing off the high ceilings.

"And you are her brother, no? You confirm this is the truth?"

"Indeed, your Serenity."

The Doge leaned over and listened to the whispered words of a counselor at his side, nodding as he took in the information and the advice. He cast his attention once more to Matteo, and his flinty, dark eyes narrowed in contemplation.

"This is not the first time you have been brought before the Council of Ten, Matteo de Gama. However, it is the first time I have heard anything that defames your loyalty to Venice."

Matteo did not hesitate to defend himself. "I have written many satires that have inflamed those who read them, it is true. I have engaged in private gambling despite the ban on it, and relieved many a man of his coin, that is also true. But what Count Carlo Gambera claims, that I turned my loyalties elsewhere and endangered Venice with correspondence and maps of our city in an effort to weaken our defenses, is not true. No man loves Venice as I."

"Nor her women." The Doge's eyes rested briefly, but knowingly, on the count who made the claims of treason and freemasonry against Matteo, and his wife who sat at his side.

The Doge leaned back in his chair and regarded the group before him. His dilemma proved sensitive. The count who made the claims had gone to great length to prove them. He was a man of influence and power. To say the count fabricated the documents would mean he would be guilty of a high crime.

The Doge chose to address Rogan with the aid of the translator. "You are a duke in England, no?"

Rogan bowed deeply. "I am, your Serenity."

"You are also one the shipbuilders who petitioned for the Republic's naval bid."

"Yes, your Serenity."

"And you say your sister was returned to you by this man, Matteo de Gama?"

"She was, and I'm very grateful for his help. If not for Matteo de Gama, she would have drowned."

"He sent you a letter from inside the Leads."

"Only his request that we come speak on his behalf, your Serenity. I will happily show the letter to you, if you would care to read it."

The Doge's gaze traveled to Kieran, the count, Matteo, and finally back to Rogan. "Would you say that Matteo de Gama is an honorable man?"

"He returned my sister to me, unharmed. 'Tis an action that speaks to me as one of honor, yes, your Serenity."

The Doge fell silent again. His counselor leaned over and whispered something else. The Doge replied in the same fashion, and the discussion continued until finally the Doge smiled and nodded. He sat up straight and laid his hands flat on the table, fingers spread. He was prepared to give his answer.

He addressed the man who brought the charges, and by way of the hushed voice of the interpreter, Rogan and Kieran were able to follow the proceedings.

"Count Carlo Gambera, the claims you make are of the most serious in nature. I do not take your word, or your proof, with lightness. Yet, we have conflicting information presented here today, in the form of an English noble. I can not disbelieve His Grace, for I am not the reader of hearts and minds, but only an examiner of evidence. I do not believe we have enough evidence to convict Signore de Gama, for we have papers that could have been given to you by a man with a vendetta. Papers alone cannot compel me to order a man's death, most especially when he has an alibi that debunks one of your documents.

"Yet, Matteo de Gama, you have troubled our city with your inflammatory writings. Simply that you have been brought before the Council of Ten for other infractions proves that while you may be a man who loves our city, you are not a man who treasures harmony. Venice values harmony. I value harmony.

"I hereby decree that you, Matteo de Gama, will be

exiled from the Republic of Venice for a period of five years. Go out into the world, and see if when you return you will be prepared to enjoy the harmony that my Republic has to offer."

A knowing gleam came into the Doge's eyes as he glanced from the count to the gambler, and the woman who had obviously come between them. "I will send you with my guards, to see to it that you find safe passage out of Venice. Farewell, Signore."

The Doge stood and left the room, followed by the Council. The count gathered his papers, tapped them in order, and towing his wife by her upper arm, approached Matteo. He leaned in and hissed a stream of Italian before he walked away, dragging her behind him. She looked back, and with a smile, blew Matteo a kiss goodbye.

Matteo stood stunned in the center of the immense chamber. Surrounded by frescos and statues and all things beautiful and Venetian, he realized the full impact of the Doge's orders.

Exile.

Five years! He'd planned to leave Venice for a short while and let the matter with Gia fall to rest, but never had he intended on being gone for five years. Five months, perhaps, but years?

No more sailing his *burchiello* on the canal at twilight. All the pleasures of Venice would be denied to him, from *Festa del Mosto*, the annual pressing of the grapes that Matteo loved to attend, to even the noise and upheaval of Carnivale, which he now knew he would miss. The food, the wine, the scent in the air, it was everything Matteo knew, and the only thing he wanted to know. He was stripped of his city, his home, his life.

Exile.

The word cut like a blade, sharp, cold, and merciless.

Suddenly his satires became insipid and contrived. His intrigues with women turned empty and hollow. His gambling and swindling left a bitter taste in his mouth. Without Venice, what would he be, where would he go? He would now be like the travelers he had scorned, plunged into a new culture where he knew nothing of their customs.

Rogan approached Matteo. He outstretched his hand in a gesture as ancient as the castles of England: It said, I am friend, not foe.

"I am sorry for your troubles," Rogan said simply.

Indeed, Matteo thought, grasping his hand in a firm grip. What more can a man say to another when he has witnessed his ultimate disgrace?

"I must thank you. I know it is a small recompense for the life of my sister, but I am leaving Venice and returning to England. If you choose, you may come with us. It would be my pleasure to allow you usage of one of my London homes, for as long as you wish to remain. 'Tis the least I can do for what you have done for my family."

Kieran heard his words and her heart dropped to her feet. No, she thought wildly: No! She could not have Matteo so close to her. Matteo de Gama saw too much, and knew too much for her comfort. How long before Rogan and Matteo became friendly enough for Matteo to tell her brother what she said that night, and worse, what she'd done.

Memories flashed in sequence. Standing aboard the *burchiello*, ready to launch herself back into the dark, killing canal; lunging at Matteo with her dagger, trying to provoke him into shooting her; the final disgrace, his lying on top of her and her words, telling him volumes. Her final plea. *Please just shoot me.*

Kieran stepped forward. "Rogan, perhaps we are presumptuous in our offer. Signore de Gama speaks French as well as English, and may find Parisian life more to his liking. I have heard that in Paris the climate is far less constraining than life in London. As a Venetian, Signore de Gama may feel quite—*inhibited*—in England."

Rogan faced Kieran, listening, and behind his back Kieran saw Matteo smile at her words. He caught her eye and with the smallest of motions he pointed to his lips and then his chin.

She averted her eyes and turned her attention fully on her brother, all the more determined that Matteo de Gama not accompany them home to England. This man must not be housed nearby. He must not be afforded entrance to their homes. He just simply needed to not be anywhere that Kieran was.

Rogan turned back to Matteo. "Whatever you decide, Signore de Gama, I am at your service. Passage to France is certainly something I can provide you."

On the heels of Matteo's greatest disgrace came a new opportunity, handed to him by the intriguing girl's own brother. He looked at Kieran, her pink dress setting that fine, fair skin to glowing. The wet, ropy hair of the night before gleamed a deep, shining auburn that begged for his fingers. And those eyes, mysterious for all their stormy blue beauty, silently pleading for him to decline Rogan Mullen's offer.

It was just as obvious to Matteo that Rogan loved his sister, as it was that he did not know her at all. How desolate it must be for her, he thought to himself, knowing that the greatest loneliness was felt when surrounded by others with whom there is no understanding. Matteo knew that truth with hard-earned knowledge, and looking at her before him, so young and lovely with her raw, ancient eyes beseeching with him to stay at a distance, his decision was made.

Matteo bowed low. "Your Grace, you honor me with your munificence. I understand your gratitude toward my helping your sister. I maintain that I did not do a great thing, but simply the right thing. However, as my circumstance has been unjustly affected, it is with deep humility and appreciation that I accept your generous offer."

Kieran stood helpless. Matteo de Gama was coming to England, and there was nothing she could do to prevent it.

He grinned at her, a recklessly inappropriate smile for a man who had just been humiliated and exiled.

She turned up her nose and sniffed, and that only widened his grin. He swept low into a bow, then straightened and turned to go. Two of the Doge's guards followed.

She watched as Matteo was stopped by a woman who'd been seated by the rear of the room, just beside the doors. Like most all young women Kieran had seen in Venice, the woman was beautiful: long, shining dark hair framing an exotic face that betrayed her Spanish ancestry. Slashing dark brows moved expressively over vibrant black eyes, and plump red lips pouted as if she held back tears. She grabbed his arm first, to get his attention, her husky voice a stream of rapid Italian. Her hands gestured wildly from her heart to her hair to the Doge's abandoned seat. She began to weep.

"*Non ci credo*," she cried. Tears fell unheeded down her cheek. "*Non lasciarmi, amore!*"

"*Mi dispiace*," he replied, his tone soothing. "*Mi mancherai.*"

Kieran studied him with interest as he comforted the woman. Matteo de Gama's appeal to women made perfect sense, she thought, as he held her hand, stroked her arm, and listened to her weep and wail. He paid attention to her the way he had to Kieran on the *burchiello*, as if she were the only woman in the room, the only woman in the world.

Matteo withdrew a linen handkerchief from the pocket of his leather coat, and tenderly wiped the woman's tears. She clung to his arm, her head tilted up to his ministrations, and she seemed to be begging him to take her with him.

He shook his head to the negative and said, "*Tesoro mio, non ti dimenticher moi.*"

These words brought fresh wails. Matteo simply lifted her hand, kissed the back of it, and walked away from her.

She called after him.

He kept going.

She fell to her knees and cried out another plea. "*Torna da me!*"

Kieran looked on at Matteo's retreating form. He strolled away as if taking a walk on a summer day, indifferent to both the weeping woman and the armed guards.

The dark-haired beauty screamed his name, her voice resounding in the great hall. She remained heedless of the people who watched her undignified display, and buried her face in her hands, dissolving into sobs.

Matteo de Gama's footsteps echoed off the marble walls and high ceilings.

He did not look back.

～ 4 ～

The Republic of Venice wore its history with an elegance borne of hundreds of years without real strife. The buildings aged gracefully amidst the peaceful lagoons and canals that comprised its unique charm; unscarred by the cannons and fire of battle. Lack of hardship, however, breeds complacency.

The Doge saw the need for strength, as the Barbary pirate attacks at sea had shown him just how defenseless the peaceful Republic had become. A law was passed; no ships left Venice unless in a convoy. Requests were put out to other countries, offering the opportunity to build Venice new ships well-suited for attack and defense.

Rogan Mullen abandoned the bid, much to Samuel Ellsworth's great disappointment. But with every one of Emeline's former pregnancies miscarrying in the second trimester, it was of utmost importance to get back to England as quickly as possible.

However, with Rogan leaving, Samuel lost the bid. It went to the French, and so Ellsworth and the other Englishmen joined the convoy of three ships leaving Venice, all bound for London.

Daybreak approached, the first few rays of light shining up from behind the sea. The crew was ready to go, and shots fired three in a row, signaling their intent to the other two ships.

Shots fired in reply, and the great triple-masted, full-rigged frigate shuddered with readiness.

Kieran was up on deck for the send-off, keeping out of the fray as the crew rushed through the final stages of departure.

The ropes were untied from the hawsers, and the ship began to move with the tide. The sails slapped and snapped with the brisk breeze and finally took the full weight of the wind, billowing tight. The keel sliced through the water, which foamed and purled around the prow as they picked up speed. The other two ships did the same, and soon they were out to sea, the Republic of Venice behind them.

Kieran watched until the sun was up, and Venice was nothing more than a dark shadow on the horizon. Her belly growled, ready for breakfast, and she was about to seek it until she saw Matteo de Gama standing alone at the rail.

She studied him discreetly. His dark, shoulder-length hair was unbound and blowing in the wind around his face. He wore garments that were similar to everything else she'd seen him wear; it seemed he favored black leather sewn with quilted, colored linings that were visible when he moved. He wore a red shirt, open at the collar, and the color set a striking contrast to his hair and skin.

He looked every inch the gambler he was, except for one thing: his expression. As he stood there, unaware that she watched him, he was unguarded, and without his usual debonair, sardonic expression, he looked young and rather lost, watching as his home disappeared.

Kieran looked at him with a woman's eye and admitted it to herself: He was handsome. Very much so, with his lean cheeks and soul-deep, amber flecked eyes. His mouth was expressive, sensual, and when he looked in a woman's eyes and smiled, he was dangerously compelling.

But now, looking like a little boy who was being carted away from the only home he'd ever known, he was ever more so, because he reached to the heart that Kieran protected so fiercely, and touched it.

He turned and saw her, and strangely, he did not guard his expression. His country faded on the horizon behind him, now barely visible, and he spread his hands as he looked at her, as if to say that they were empty and he was completely alone.

And Kieran, despite herself, had the urge to go and wrap her arms around him, and lend comfort.

The feeling unsettled her, and in her confusion, she did what she always did these three years past. She pushed aside her feelings, reached for the comfort of coldness, and turned and walked away.

* * *

Kieran sought out her stateroom and remained there the rest of the day, reading and sewing. Four lit lanterns swung from their iron hooks, casting light and shadows in equal measure. In the corner of her tiny room burned a fat-bellied coal stove, and atop it she heated water for tea. The hour was late; she should have been abed hours ago. Yet, she was still gowned, too chilled to dispense with her woolen clothes.

Dinner had been served in her room, as had her lunch. Kieran had made excuses, pleading a queasy belly so she could avoid dining with Matteo de Gama. She did not feel up to his scrutiny, nor the disappointment in her brother's eyes. He had not yet forgiven her for the lies and her unwillingness to explain the reason for her dishonesty.

Kieran sighed heavily. The seconds crawled by.

She'd long since dismissed her maid for the evening, and Nilo slept in the cabin directly across the low, narrow passage that led to the upper deck. Three locks barred Kieran's room, along with an iron bar that she slid into place at night.

She rubbed her hands together and held them over the stove. It seemed nothing could warm her when she was at sea; the dampness permeated the woolen clothes she wore and seeped to her bones.

She prepared her tea with expert motions though her mind was distracted. The golden honey slid into the hot water and melted, but Kieran did not bother to admire its amber color or earthy, sweet scent.

Her mind was elsewhere.

She could feel the hard press of him behind her when they had been aboard his *burchiello*. The feel of his breath on her ear, and his words: thrilling, obscene, and tempting.

"*There is a singular delight in serving justice from one's own hand.*"

Kieran lifted her cup and held the tea she'd brewed for its warmth. A shiver took her. She sipped her hot tea.

It did not warm her.

You've grown too cold for your youth. Rogan's words, apropos of the chill permeating her bones, echoed in her mind.

She cast a glance to her berth, and imagined the night she would spend in shivering, fitful sleep, tortured by her dreams, captive to the night.

The ship shuddered as it crested a huge swell, and tea sloshed over the rim and scalded her fingers as she struggled to keep her feet beneath her.

Find something that warms your heart. Again, Rogan, always commanding her with hard words and harsh prompts.

And in that moment, she was finished fighting.

Kieran set down the cup and grabbed her cloak. With the flare of fur-lined wool, she settled it over her shoulders and fastened it beneath her chin. She reached back and pulled up the deep hood, hiding her face in the dark cowl. She turned down the lanterns and reached for the locks of her door, hesitating for only a moment to ease the shivering tremble that seized her body.

She eased the locks open one by one, and noiselessly slid the iron bar away from the door. Then, heart racing, Kieran opened the door. The musty odors of damp wood and tallow smoke permeated the dark passage, and a few lonely, swaying lanterns sent crazy, shifting shadows roaming over the floorboards. The crack beneath Nilo's room was dark; he slept. Stepping out into the corridor, she closed her door behind her.

The ship pitched and rolled beneath her feet. Kieran braced both hands on either side of the narrow passage and walked aft. Reaching a short stack of stairs, she climbed up to another deck and saw a yellow sliver of light beneath the door of the cabin she'd heard being readied for a passenger.

Braced against the frame of the door, Kieran hesitated. What would he think? Would he laugh at her, or worse, think her of a lascivious bent as she sought him out alone in the night? She chased her worries with reason.

No, she told herself. Matteo would breakfast with Emeline and Rogan in the morning. Surely he would not attempt anything untoward. He would know better than anyone else that he'd be at the mercy of Rogan, Nilo, and an entire crew of sailors if Kieran sounded a single cry.

Buoyed by those thoughts, Kieran raised her fist and rapped on the door, two quick, hard knocks before she lost her resolve.

A few long moments dragged by, and as she was turning to leave she heard the metallic rasp of the doorknob being turned.

Matteo leaned his shoulder against the doorway when he saw her, his body limned with the light of many lanterns burning behind him. Though his face was shadowed, Kieran saw the question in his eyes. It was quickly followed by the half-smile that took his lips as he peered into the darkness of her hood and knew who knocked on his door. "*Cuore solitario*, what brings you?"

"I am here to discuss your previous offer," she said crisply. If she did not feel brave, she could at least feign it.

His smile broadened. "Ah, yes. I should not be surprised. Come in." He gestured to the tiny cabin as if it were the grand room aboard his elegant *burchiello*.

The cramped space was stuffed with steamer trunks that had been stacked and secured with thick ropes. Every surface bore piles of papers weighted with brass disks to prevent them from falling as the ship lurched and moved beneath them. A quill was bleeding on a piece of scrap paper, the open ink pot beside it smudged with use. Books were piled everywhere, the leather volumes cracked and worn. In a corner a cello had been lain in its open case, its rich mahogany gleaming in the golden lantern light.

And it was warm in the room, so warm that Kieran felt her fingers begin to thaw.

"I am sorry to intrude," Kieran said shyly, feeling suddenly out of place. She pushed the hood of her cloak down so it hung at her back. "You are obviously quite occupied."

"Writing." He waved his hand absently at the papers. "It is nothing. The story goes nowhere."

"You are a man of letters, then?"

"*Si.* Yes. *Uomo di lettere,*" he murmured softly. "For whatever that is worth."

Kieran glanced again at the cello. "And a musician as well?"

"Of sorts."

"And a scholar." Some of the books were in languages she did not know.

"One could say that."

"Anything else?"

Matteo shrugged. "Of course. I am many things. One cannot be interesting if one is not first interested."

"A philosopher, too."

"Are you here to know me better, *bella*? If that is so, you may want to take a seat. Such a venture will take some time."

Kieran became very aware of the way he watched her, his eyes lingering on her lips, eyes, and neck. His casual posture belied the look in his eyes. He was observant, and Kieran found herself the object of his study.

Time to get to the point, she thought, before he thinks her purpose to be something more than business.

"I have money," she said bluntly. "I have sold various pieces of needlework, and I have a tidy sum tucked away."

"This is good news for you."

"I am offering it to you, signore, in exchange for your tutelage. Do you recall your offer . . ." Her voice faltered and she cleared her throat. "To help me?"

"I offered you revenge, eh?" Matteo's eyes swept over her in a way that made Kieran want to run out the door. "Vendetta."

"Yes," she breathed. "Will you? I will give you all of my money."

"This is what you want? You want to pay back the one who hurt you?"

"I think I do." She faltered, but only for a moment. "I do not know. It seems wrong, the idea of revenge. 'Tis an ugly thing to contemplate, and yet, I am . . . conflicted."

"Come, sit." Matteo pulled out a chair and held it. "This is obviously something that requires deep discussion."

She hesitated. His hands were on the back of the chair, long, tapered fingers stained with ink. He saw where she looked and laughed softly.

"Ah, *cuore solitario*, still afraid of me? What can I say, but that I did not drag you from the water this time, nor did I send a letter asking you to come. You came to me of your own volition." Matteo lifted a hand and gestured to the door. "It is unlocked. And I shall stay well away from you."

To illustrate, he moved away from the chair he'd pulled out for her. Kieran took the seat and undid the fastenings of her cloak. The stove, well-stocked with coal, pumped enough warmth to heat three rooms, and she shrugged out of the confines of the garment.

Matteo poured them each wine in short, stout glasses. He set one in front of Kieran without asking if she wanted it. She looked at the beautiful handwriting on the parchment before her, but could not read the Italian words.

"What are you writing?" Kieran asked.

"Another satire. Venetian. Pointless in my exile, no?" The corners of his lips turned down, and he looked away.

He looked so disappointed that Kieran felt compelled to offer him hope. "Perhaps you could write something else. A novel, for instance."

"I have written many novels and the like. Plays, music. Some of it gets published or performed, most does not." He waved his hand as if to say it was all nothing.

Kieran nodded as if she understood, but in reality she did not. He watched her over the rim of his wine glass, and as before, he saw right through her.

"Let me explain," Matteo said patiently. "The art does not support me. It is I who supports my art."

"With your music?" Kieran asked, and she glanced again at the cello.

Matteo laughed long and loud. "Ah, if that were possible. No, *bella*, certainly not with music."

Matteo could not drag his gaze from her. The heat had flushed her skin until it turned pink and dewy and her lips were moist with wine. She kept bringing her eyes up to his, if only for a moment, before glancing away in nervousness. She kept looking at his books, his work, his cello.

"Have you never met an artist?" he asked.

"Not that I am aware of."

"Would you like to hear me play?"

"If you desire."

Yet, there was a spark of interest in her expression, and again, she looked to the corner where his instrument rested.

"It would be my privilege."

Matteo rose and retrieved his cello and bow. He returned to the table and pulled the chair further out into the cramped cabin. Taking his seat, he tightened the bow and rested the cello between his spread legs, the scroll up by his left ear, the neck cradled in his left hand.

Pausing, he glanced at Kieran again, assessing her. She was fascinating: those eyes, so primitive and fragile with pain, the exact color of the canal at dusk.

She kept her demeanor unaffected and cold. Perhaps that was sufficient in keeping men at bay in a world where female coyness and flirtatious fluttering was the norm. But Matteo didn't believe that cool exterior for a moment. He remembered well the woman he'd dragged from the canal, a spitting wildcat lunging toward a gun with eyes that begged for release. And then there was that confused woman on the deck that morning, torn by her own emotions. Oh, but she was a puzzle.

"This is a *violoncello*, or as you say, a cello. I will play a piece I wrote about a year ago, written for a character I had just created. The melody haunted me until I wrote it, but the character haunts me still." Matteo poised the bow over the strings, and then played for her. His eyes never left her face as his fingers and bow moved like the music itself.

And Matteo relished the moment, because she'd come back for him, exactly as he'd hoped when he dangled the idea of revenge like a worm before a bird.

Seduction was its own distinct pleasure, and Matteo reveled in it as he played for her.

Kieran felt the music more than she heard it, a deep, resonating melody that vibrated to her bones. It filled the small cabin, louder than her thoughts, and she wanted to close her eyes and let it take her.

His fingers on the strings oscillated up and down slightly over each note so that it wavered like a tenor's voice, controlled and expressive, like song. His bow was like a fencer's sword, slim and elegant, sometimes slow, often quick. There was poetry in the music, the man, and the instrument, moving her with the force of its beauty.

Sliding down the narrow neck, his fingers tight against the strings, the melody grew higher, more urgent. Kieran felt the music swell in her chest, and she was swept away on the crest of it, taken to a place she'd never been.

Small motes of rosin dust rose from beneath the bow, and in the light of the cabin the cello gleamed, its polished wood warm shades of mahogany and deep amber. Behind it, Matteo watched her as he played, his angular face shadowed with lantern light, his dark eyes hooded and heavy-lidded, as if he, too, were in thrall.

And then, he stopped playing.

Silence hung in the room.

"Why did you stop?" Kieran finally whispered, not wishing to break the spell, wanting more.

"It is the only piece I never finished. That is all there is."

Suddenly aware of herself, Kieran realized she was leaning forward. She pulled back to perfect posture and wiped her face of interest. "Well, you are the composer."

Matteo stood and carried his cello back to the corner. He then opened a trunk and removed a sheaf of papers that were bound with a leather cover and tied shut with thick, black ribbon. He held it up for her inspection. "Here is what you need, *cuore solitario*. This is what you came for."

Lonely heart, her mind translated. *Stop calling me that*, she wanted to shout. But she could not, for it was true, and he alone seemed to understand it in a way that she could never convincingly deny.

"What is it?" Kieran asked, her hands folded.

"It is a story of a woman just like you: cold on the outside, simmering with rage in her heart. She seeks her revenge."

"Does she get it?" And damn herself, she could not keep the need out of her own voice.

"She does. I think you will find the story very engrossing."

Kieran reached out to take it, and Matteo lifted it into the air. He smiled, and her heart began to race.

"There is a price, of course."

"I told you, you can have my money." Her voice wavered and she watched his smile deepen. He'd heard the fear in her tone. Damn him, as well.

"I do not want your money. I so enjoy taking it from those who do not want to part with it, but that joy dims when it is given freely." He reached out his other hand to her. "I want a kiss in exchange for the story. I do not think that a too high price; after all, it took me many months to write it. It will only take you but a moment to kiss me."

"No," Kieran said flatly, and she stood. Grabbing her cloak, she turned and moved toward the door. She cast a haughty glare over her shoulder as she placed her hand on the doorknob. "Perhaps you should have been more clear when you offered to help me. Had I known there would be a physical price, I never would have allowed myself to be tempted."

"But you are tempted, because you know this is what you need."

"What I need, signore, is to be left alone."

"Alone with your pain. For how long?" The tone of his voice changed, dropped low, and grew rough. "What you need is vengeance. To punish the one who hurt you. Punish him for what he did, and then you will have satisfaction. You can rise above how you feel when you think of him, and instead of the rage and the hurt, you will feel peace in knowing he paid for his sin, and that it was you who exacted payment."

Again, his words rooted her in place and fired her imagination. It was as if he offered food to a starving person. Kieran craved that knowledge, hungered for it. "How?"

Matteo held the manuscript up to her again. "A kiss."

"You are a bastard."

"You really have very little idea how correct you are," Matteo said, unperturbed. "What will it be?"

"Why?" Kieran asked in what came out as nearly a whimper.

"We all want things, *bella*. Every single human who haunts this earth wants, yearns, craves, desires. We are creatures of such need. At this moment, I desire to kiss you." Matteo shrugged his shoulders in a careless motion, and his lips quirked in a way that communicated ironic amusement. "I always seem to crave that which does not belong to me."

Kieran looked at the sheaf of papers and then back to his eyes, trying to ascertain his truth. The dark eyes were mesmerizing in their velvety softness: they glistened in the lantern light, lit with flecks of amber and fringed with long, thick lashes beneath slashing black brows. Matteo lifted a brow as she studied him, his full lips twitched with humor.

"Behold the ice princess as she weighs her decision."

She lifted her chin. "Do not mock me."

"I apologize, *bella*, but I fail to see the gravity of this trade. I am Venetian; to us kisses are like wine and food: pleasurable, to be enjoyed. Perhaps your reluctance is an English problem?"

The gauntlet was thrown down, the price named. And Kieran could not walk out of that door. Not when her mind whirled with images of retribution, an avenger of her own honor. Her decision, she realized, was made.

"There is no problem. I want the story, so kiss me and get it done with. The hour grows late."

Matteo tossed the sheaf of bound papers onto the chair that Kieran had recently vacated as he walked toward her.

Her heart was in her throat. No man had touched her since that night, not so much as a kiss had been pressed upon her glove. Ice princess, he'd called her, and the sobriquet stung, for it was a label lain on her by many a shunned suitor.

Lonely heart. Ice princess. And the truth was that Kieran hated those names because they were true and she did not know how to get herself back. She'd lost herself, and scarcely recognized the woman she'd become.

Matteo stood in front of her, and with cold disdain perfected from years of concealing any real feeling, Kieran looked up to him.

"Quickly," she said, as if impatient. She cast her eyes to the ceiling and pursed her lips.

Matteo laughed and placed his hands on her shoulders. To her surprise, he turned her until she faced away from him, her back to his chest. She could feel the rise and fall of his breath, and the slight exhalation against her cheek, warm and scented with wine.

"I said a kiss is to be savored, no?"

She felt him lower his head to her hair, heard him inhale deeply. His fingers gripped her shoulders; they bore the pine scent of rosin and the acrid tang of ink. The warmth of his hands sank through her gown, and though his grip was strong, it wasn't imprisoning.

"A woman is God's most beautiful creation," he said, his mouth by her ear. His breath was warm and humid, and Kieran tried to not feel the tingle that coursed through her body to her toes. "Her curves are like the *cello*." Matteo's left hand slid down her left arm, and grasping her wrist, he lifted it high above her head. "She is a delicate instrument, finely tuned, perfectly made, incredibly responsive."

Matteo's hand moved up and down over Kieran's bare wrist, his fingers lightly oscillating as they'd done on the neck of the cello.

Shivering despite the warmth of the room, she pulled her wrist away.

"I agreed to a kiss. Will you not see out the bargain?" Kieran heard her own voice, the tremble in it.

Matteo simply reached down and pulled her arm back up, his fingers resuming the motion that made her breath come short.

"This is how I kiss," he said softly, his mouth against her ear. With his right hand, he ran his fingers up the column of her neck until they reached her jaw, tracing the outline of her bone beneath her skin. He cupped her face and turned her head slightly until her neck was turned toward his lips.

And then, so lightly she could scarcely feel it, he kissed her beneath her ear. Sensations unlike any Kieran had ever felt coursed in her blood like liquid warmth. The brush of his stubble contrasted with the soft heat of his lips. His mouth moved and she leaned back against his chest, all the power gone from her legs. His fingers continued to slide up and down her wrist as his mouth moved over her neck, and suddenly there was no more breath in her lungs. She closed her eyes and gave in, just for a moment, to the music he was making in her body. A veritable symphony of sensations. A small, low murmur came from her throat, pulled by a force she did not control.

～ 5 ～

The sound snaked its way through Matteo's blood. Kieran was warm and fluid and supple in his arms. Beneath his fingers her pulse pounded under soft skin, fine in its fragility. He cradled her wrist, the bones of which were slimmer than the neck of his cello. And she was infinitely more pleasurable to play. He nuzzled her neck; tasted her sweetness. He moved his lips up and breathed in the scent of her hair once more. She smelled wonderful, an exotic garden of sandalwood and jasmine. Why did she wear such an unusual scent?

She was everything he pursued in life: beauty and intrigue and thinly veiled passions. She awoke in him the urge to possess her, to solve her mysteries, to unlock the heat that simmered beneath her icy veneer.

The ship rocked like a gondola, and somewhere Matteo could hear a man call out to another on the upper decks. For a brief moment Matteo considered what Rogan Mullen would think about how his young sister was spending the midnight hour.

And then Matteo pushed that worry away. No matter whose sister she was, she was a woman, not a girl, and in Matteo's opinion, desperately in need of a man's touch. Did she not sigh in his arms, melt beneath his kisses?

So why was he plagued with what was, for him, the rarest of emotions: guilt.

Even as he held her, he felt guilty for bargaining for

her kiss. So much so, that when she reluctantly gave what he had demanded, he could not take those lips beneath his own.

Not when she looked at him with those eyes, the beauty and the pain in them combined, each magnified by the other.

If he would seduce her, he would first have to find a way to dispense with his remorse.

He kissed the delicate skin behind her earlobe again, and once more the sound came from her throat. It was her noises that were feeding his lust, making it impossible to stop what he was doing, no matter how remorseful he felt for doing it. Those little sounds were of pure pleasure, won from an unwilling woman. Matteo was many things, but at the basest core, he was only human.

"Your melody," he said against her ear. His fingers were still cupping her face, and he ran his thumb across her lips. They parted beneath his caress, the wetness of her mouth touched him with erotic promise. He held her like the cello, an instrument that would sing under the right touch. "Oh, *bella*, I would love to play you."

Suddenly Kieran was aware of his size, his strength, his height. He *was* playing her, like a symphony, and the worst of it was she was letting him. Where was her pride, her resolve, her icy guard? How could she have allowed him to so easily manipulate, and yes, *play*, her? Kieran wrenched free of him and turned like a feral cat, back arched, breath hissing.

"You're finished. Give me the manuscript."

Surprise registered in his eyes, but Matteo did not otherwise react. He simply gestured to the papers on the chair. "Take it."

Kieran stalked across the tiny stateroom and snatched up the bound volume. She made a quick retreat from the cabin, lurching out into the passage as a swell took the ship. With the manuscript clutched to her breasts, she rushed back to her cabin and hurried inside. A few deft motions had the door closed, locked, and barred, and she dumped the bundle on her table before fetching a lantern. There would be no waiting until morning; she would read it now. She set the lantern, its wick burning high and bright, down beside the papers.

And Kieran damned herself again for the slight burning on her neck, where his stiff stubble had scraped her skin. It no doubt had left marks that branded her as the needy fool she had allowed him to know her to be. Well, she thought nastily, he can put that knowledge in his growing bag of insights into her character. It seemed that when it came to Matteo de Gama, she was forever one step behind.

With shaking fingers that were growing steadily colder in the damp, chilly confines of her solitary stateroom, she plucked open the ribbon that bound the papers and removed the leather cover.

A moan of dismay was followed quickly by a hot ball of rage. She pounded her fists on the table and snarled down at the words. The entire story was written in Italian, save for one small piece of paper on top, which said in English:

My dear, lonely heart,
    Please accept my offer of translation. I am available nightly. You know where to find me.

                            Warmly,
                            Matteo de Gama

And her thoughts mocked her like a Greek chorus: dispassionate and eternally amused at her stupidity. One step behind, indeed.

* * *

Morning spread its light across the ocean, a pink and yellow-tinged miracle that turned the sea to rippling gold. Kieran stood by the rail, bundled in her warmest clothes and fur-lined cloak. She held both her hands around a thick mug full of strong, steaming tea. The sun climbed the sky, the sea-winds snapped the sails, and the ship's hull cut through the waves as they sped toward England.

Off in the distance, the other two English ships were visible, and Kieran knew that Samuel Ellsworth was aboard one of them.

Men climbed and crawled all around *The Boxer*, high in the rigging, down in the galleys, and across every deck. And though many stopped to peer at Kieran's cold, pale-skinned beauty, none dared speak to her. If the sight of her frigid gaze and disinterested demeanor was not enough to discourage talk, the hulking African who stood at her side was. Kieran watched the sunrise in peace.

Rogan came from the lower deck and spotted his sister and Nilo. He clapped a friendly hand on Nilo's shoulder and turned to Kieran. "We missed you at dinner last night, but I'm glad to see you're feeling well enough to emerge."

Kieran smiled at her brother; he looked fit and rested and strong, his skin readily darkening with the sun, his eyes a sparkling green. Being at sea had always agreed with him. "How is Emeline?"

"She's doing well, I think. I arranged for her meal to be brought into our cabin, though. She was tired last night, and I asked her if she would nap after she ate."

"And she agreed?"

Rogan grinned. "She did. I didn't have to press the point; the child moved inside her late last night. She was too excited to sleep after that. Stayed awake, hoping to feel it again."

"'Tis soon for that, no?"

"I thought so. Perhaps she is yet farther along." Rogan shrugged casually, but his face bore the worry they both felt. "I am certain she will be fine, but I asked her to lie abed for my peace of mind."

"How long do you think we'll be at sea?"

"We could make it in a fortnight, if these winds keep up."

Kieran stood on tiptoes to brush a kiss on her brother's cheek, and then pressed another. "One for Emeline," she said softly, and turned to make her way back to her stateroom.

Rogan watched his sister walk away, followed, as always, by Nilo. The former slave dwarfed his sister by two heads and ten stone, and still, she managed to look completely alone.

He shook his head, wishing again that he knew how to penetrate her walls of cold silence and fragile dignity.

She'd never been the same since that night that their cousin, Simon, had taken her. Whatever had happened in that house had changed her from the petulant, bratty, funny, and precocious sister he'd once known into who she'd become: A thin shell of a girl, lovely to look upon, impossible to know.

He resigned himself to that fact that he might never know what had happened. Kieran would not discuss it, not with him, their parents, or his wife. She'd shut herself off, sheathed herself in ice, and grown distant.

Rogan sighed heavily and turned toward the horizon. He'd hoped Venice would bring a change of pace, a fresh perspective, and perhaps, a taste of another life so that she might reach for something beyond her daily, mundane existence.

Thinking of Venice, Rogan cast his attention to

Matteo, who stood at the rail on the forecastle deck, holding onto the lines and straining into the winds as if he and the ship were one. The Venetian wore a black leather coat and breeches, tightly fitted, elegantly made, and tall boots to his knees. He held a black hat to his side as his hair streamed free in the wind. He stood out like a pirate amidst the plain cotton breeches and thick wool sweaters of the crewmen milling around him.

"Enjoying the morning?" Rogan asked as he approached Matteo de Gama.

"Yes, yes, it is . . ." he struggled to find the appropriate word in English. "Awesome."

Matteo gestured to the sky, a vivid blue dotted with fluffy clouds, the horizon that stretched into forever, and the ocean, a frothy, white-tipped deep blue. Matteo suddenly laughed out loud, a deep, joyous sound, and pointed below where dolphins raced the ship, cleaving from the water in half-crescent arcs before shooting back into the sea. Flying fish joined the fray, jumping the wakes, their silvery bodies winking in the sunlight.

"Incredible!" Matteo shouted with glee. He leaned over the rail and then looked back to Rogan, his lean face alight with discovery. "One must never grow tired of this, eh?"

Rogan grinned. "Aye, when the sea is calm and the winds are good, there's nothing that compares." He joined Matteo at the rail, clasped his hands behind him and enjoyed the sea for a moment, casting off his worries and the work that never ended. The wind stung his face, full of salt and spray.

Matteo spread his arms and let the wind fill his coat, billowing it out behind him. He laughed again, an easy sound nearly lost in the winds. "Now I see why painters, poets, and writers never grow tired of trying to capture this!" he shouted into the winds. "It is *magnifico*!"

Rogan found himself swept up in the man's enthusiasm.

Seeing it through Matteo's fresh eyes brought back some of the old delight, and with it, the memory of his first time at sea.

Their father, Patrick, a sea merchant, had taken Kieran and Rogan out for a week, and his first morning had been just like Matteo's, full of wonder and thrilling joy. He'd had Kieran beside him at the rail, and he recalled how she'd been so taken with the feel of the ocean, the movements of the ship, and the invigorating rush of wind that she'd felt compelled to dance and spin on the deck. His adorable sister. Their father had taken to calling her *sidhe gaoithe,* the wind fairy.

There wasn't anything that Rogan wouldn't give to see his sister like that again.

"Enjoy," Rogan bade Matteo, before turning to leave him.

"One moment, Your Grace," Matteo said. He joined Rogan and they began to walk down the gangway together. "I am off to find some breakfast."

Rogan noticed that Matteo de Gama did not seem to mind the rolling pitch of the ship. He moved on the ship as if he were born to it. "You do well for a man who has never been out to sea."

"I live on the canals. Gondolas, *burchiellos,* and the like. An entire city built on water." He grinned. "Even the buildings move, no?"

"And you left it to follow my sister to England." He raised a brow. "I saw the way you looked at her in the Palace of the Doge."

To his credit, Matteo never faltered in his step. "I left Venice in exile, and I come to England at your invitation. However, I will admit that your sister made England look far more interesting than France."

"Are you interested in courting her, then?"

"Ah, do you play matchmaker? Surely the sister of an English duke would not curry the favor of a shamed

Venetian pauper. And certainly you would want much more for her than me, no?"

"I know you are not a pauper, and far from it, but such things are meaningless to me. I only wish to tell you this: If you're looking to increase your wealth, know that you don't have to court my sister to get at my coffers. I'll pay you well enough to stay away from her, aye?" Rogan paused long enough to make his point. He met the man's dark eyes and was surprised to see a flash of shame there, when he'd expected greed.

His estimation of the Italian stranger rose a bit more, but still, Rogan continued, "I had a man look into you before we set sail. I know what kind of man you are, signore. And forgive me for saying so, but 'tis my sister we speak of.

"I ask that you keep away from her. And while I'm not generally the sort of man to make threats, you need to know that if you do anything to hurt her, I'll see to it that you spend the rest of your days wishing that you'd asked me to take you to France."

Rogan paused before enunciating his warning a second time, hoping the emphasis would hit the point home. "Seduce her, upset her, or do anything that I might interpret as the slightest bit disrespectful of the lady she is, and I'll deal with you personally, aye?"

Matteo met his gaze evenly before sweeping into a slight bow. Rogan knew the man was a consummate swindler, but still, he thought he saw sincerity in Matteo de Gama's guileless face and cunning brown eyes.

"Your Grace, your sister is exquisite, and I, being a man, am not immune to her beauty. I am not a good man, it is true, and assuredly not good enough for Miss Kieran. I cheat, I lie, I manipulate. I do not steal so much, anymore, but I have in the past, and if the need arose, I would again."

Matteo shrugged carelessly, and his lips quirked up at

the corners. With his narrow, black leather garments, darkly handsome looks, and devilish demeanor, he looked worldly. Yet somehow he seemed unguarded, even vulnerable, as if he were a boy posing as a knave. Just as quickly as Rogan thought that, Matteo's expression changed and he was once again brashly confident. "Yet, you see, Your Grace, you must know this about me, too: I only steal from those who deserve it. The sort of men who come to my table with their money and their greed are courting my kind of trouble. They only get what they came for, eh?

"I seduce women, that is also true. Your man will have told you this, if he is worth his salt. Again, I ask you to consider that while I am a thief and a romancer, I am not entirely without honor." Matteo paused, as if considering his words. When he spoke he said, "Your sister, however, is a sad, lonely girl. I agree with you. She does not need my kind of trouble."

Nilo walked behind Kieran, and she heard him take a few deep, steadying breaths before they ducked down into the narrow galley leading to the staterooms. Nilo was alternately queasy and stricken with panic in the small, cramped interior spaces, reliving, no doubt, his experience on the slave ships. Kieran knew what it cost Nilo to accompany her on this journey.

Kieran reached out and patted his arm while they made their way to the staterooms. "Only a little longer."

Nilo looked back at her and managed a smile for her benefit. His face inspired such affection in Kieran, regal and handsome, like an African king. The bones beneath his black skin stood out prominently, chiseled and elegant, with high cheekbones and a flared, proud nose. And his eyes, sharply observant, shimmered like liquid obsidian. They walked in silence, then, as thought occurred to

Kieran. After a moment's hesitation, she asked him, "Are you lonely, Nilo?"

"I have you."

She loved how he did not hesitate. His loyalty touched her heart.

"But are you lonesome for companionship?" Her face burning, and grateful that he was not looking at her, she pressed, "For a woman?"

Nilo chuckled, a deep baritone melody. "Why do you worry?"

"You do not do anything but watch over me." Kieran did not say what she really felt: She wanted Nilo to tell her that he was satisfied, that he would never leave her, and that being her guardian was enough for him as a man. She knew better. Nilo had once had a wife, children, and a tribe of his own. Surely keeping guard over her was less than satisfactory to a man who'd had so much stolen from him. Unselfishly she said what was in her heart. "I want you to be happy."

Nilo paused in the narrow galley, his head nearly reaching the ceiling, his shoulders barely clearing the walls. Turning toward her so he could look down into her eyes, Nilo reached out and touched her cheek with the backs of his fingers.

"You first." He smiled gently. "Then it will be my turn."

"You'll have your turn, I swear it."

There was a look in his black eyes that she'd never seen before. Pity? Doubt? Before she could say anything, he turned and they fell back into step.

The night before flashed in Kieran's mind, her wrist caught in Matteo's hand, his fingers playing over her skin, the feel of his lips on her neck. The bargain: a kiss in exchange for his manuscript.

She'd tumbled right into his trap.

Matteo de Gama had manipulated her, played her, and ultimately, tricked her. And he had known all along

what she would do, what she would want, and exactly
how to get her to agree to his terms.

All night Kieran simmered with anger. She'd felt like
his fool. Rogue. Libertine. Swindler. She'd called him
every name she could think until, out of the blackness of
her rage, she realized what Matteo had done. And her
new resolve dawned with the morning sun.

Who better to instruct her?

When in Venice, Rogan had counseled her to find
something that warmed her heart.

In the darkness of her cabin's bunk, Kieran decided
that revenge would serve that purpose, and quite nicely.

"Will you wait a moment? I have a favor to ask of you,"
she said to Nilo as they reached the door to her stateroom. At his nod, she rushed inside.

She lifted a penned letter from her table and she returned to the door, handed it to Nilo. She'd taken pains
with it, written on the finest vellum in her best hand, and
sealed with red wax that she'd pressed with her initials.
"Please deliver this to Matteo de Gama."

High in the crow's nest on the mainmast the lookouts
sounded a warning: Two thundering rings of a bell that
hung from the mast, followed by four fast, sharp gongs
on the side. Smoke on the horizon.

The crew took their emergency posts. If the ship was
on fire or under siege, each hand knew what to do. Men
manned the cannons and primed the guns; others un-
lashed the lines that held oiled tarps over huge barrels of
seawater and readied hoses and pumps. Long before the
acrid stench of burning oil and wood was carried to *The
Boxer*, they were ready for the possibility of pirates or an untamed blaze, ready to give help or lend a hand in battle.
And below decks, the ship's doctor and his assistants readied bandages, instruments, medicines, and bunks.

Matteo tried to stay out of the fray, keeping to the rail of the upper deck. He saw Rogan at the helm, his hands spread wide over his instruments and his brow furrowed with concentration.

Unsure of what usefulness he could serve, Matteo withdrew his pistols and checked their priming. He was not a sailor, but if the ship came under attack, he could certainly do his part to defend it.

Soon Matteo could see the tall masts of the ship, tiny in the distance, plumes of black smoke billowing around the crisp white sails.

Sailors pulled lines and cranked pulleys to slow *The Boxer* as they approached. They could see that passengers were lined alongside the rails near the nested stack of dories that were lashed to the side. The crew of the vessel was scrambling about, calling to each other as they swarmed to try to put out the fire.

The Boxer sailed closer, until it finally slowed to a stop, bobbing on the waves a safe distance from the other ship. Dories were lowered bearing crewmen, and Rogan among them, to see what the trouble was.

Matteo watched as the sailors rowed over the giant swells.

Soon enough the problem was revealed and solved: A small fire had broken out and caught in a sail, which licked its way upward. The crew had been able to extinguish the blaze; however, the main mast had been damaged and they'd lost a mainsail.

Rogan stood in the dory and used sign language to communicate with the men who watched through their looking glasses: Bring *The Boxer* in closer; gather sails to give to the other crew so they could make temporary repairs; ready cabins, they'd be taking on the civilian passengers for the rest of their voyage to England. The closest port was Lisboa, and the ship would sail there for repairs.

Within hours they were boarding passengers from the other ship, and Matteo watched in amusement as the overweight aristocrats had to heft their bulk up rope ladders. The ladders swayed and bumped the hull, nearly knocking people off to fall into the waiting sea below. Matteo leaned over the rail and hoped to see a particular man get dumped; he wore enough velvet, brocade, jewels, and furs that he would no doubt sink to the bottom of the sea. Red-faced and indignant, he cursed the captain of his former ship as sailors leaned down and grasped his upper arms, finally pulling him onto the deck in a most unceremonious boarding.

The man scrambled to his feet, sneering at the crew as he smoothed his rumpled sleeves. "Mind yourselves, chaps. This coat is worth more than all of you combined."

Rogan ascended the ladder, easily brought himself aboard, and ran a hand through his wind-ravaged hair. He turned to Samuel, the Duke of Westminster, annoyance and dislike written on his face for all to see. "Ellsworth, while aboard my ship, mind your manners, aye? I'll not have you insulting my men."

Samuel drew himself up to his full height but said nothing.

Matteo watched the man, paying especial attention to the jewels that studded the collar of his coat and sparkled from his necklace and rings. There was something familiar about his speech, and Matteo tucked that tidbit away to think about later.

Ellsworth, Rogan had called him. Matteo made note of that, and of the arrogance of his posture, the way he sniffed at the crewman who mopped too closely to his feet. A curl of excitement tightened in Matteo's belly as he studied what came only second to the pleasure he took at looking at a beautiful woman. His next mark.

* * *

Hours passed. Kieran paced the tiny cabin. She wrung her hands, agitated. The needlework did not soothe her. Her books could not hold her attention. She kept returning to tap Matteo's papers neatly in alignment.

A knock sounded, and Kieran swung around. She grabbed the doorknob and held still, eyeing the three bolted locks. "Who is there?"

"Matteo de Gama. I come at your invitation, no?"

Relief had her sagging against the door.

"You certainly took your time." She heard her tone, cold and detached and full of resentment.

After a pause, she heard him ask, "I should go?"

Nothing like presenting a dignified appearance, she chided herself. Humiliation stung her cheeks. Could she do nothing right anymore? If she could only forget the memory of Matteo de Gama holding her like a cello whilst he kissed her neck, perhaps she could feign a semblance of normalcy. Kieran opened the door. "No. Of course not. I apologize."

Matteo de Gama stood, a puzzled look on his face. He offered a crooked smile. "If you are angry that it took me so long to respond to your note, I received it only moments ago, and it was not my intention to keep you waiting. Indeed, would I not run to see why a beautiful woman summoned me?"

Matteo leaned on the doorjamb. He offered her a seductive smile. "What do you want?"

Kieran ignored the thrill that ran through her and moved to allow him entrance, then spoke to Nilo. "Would you wait out here, please? I need to speak with Signore de Gama privately."

Nilo tapped his ear and grinned down at her. "I will listen for you, Miss Keerahn."

"Thank you, Nilo," Kieran said softly, grateful as ever for his presence. She closed the door, turned, and looked straight into Matteo's eyes.

He was confident in his demeanor, a swaggering smoothness in his charm. He bowed as if he were an exiled prince, and not a romancer who got caught with a married woman.

Kieran permitted a tight smile for his benefit and swept across the small room. She laid her hand on the papers for which Matteo had duped her into the exchange.

"I am ready for my translation, signore. I believe 'tis already paid for."

∾ 6 ∾

Ah, but she is fierce and lovely, Matteo thought, his gaze raking over her with delight. Never mind the conversation with Rogan.

Her shiny auburn hair caught the lantern light and turned molten, like a dark, red garnet, and the same light lit those stormy blue eyes and sparked them with icy fire. She stood her ground stiffly, shoulders back, jaw raised, back rigid.

She could have looked like a passionless shrew, he mused, if it were not for the fear in her eyes, the shadow of pain, and the absolute shimmer of need beneath it all.

Matteo walked slowly toward her and lay his hand on the manuscript, right beside hers. She did not move. She stood her ground despite the quickening of her breath.

He stood close enough to smell her: sea air, raw silk and boiled wool, and the subtle perfume of sandalwood and jasmine, a perplexingly exotic scent for a young Englishwoman.

Matteo tugged the sheaf of papers from beneath her hand. She was correct; she had paid for the story the night before, satisfied the bargain and fulfilled his terms. By all rights, he should tell her the tale he'd written so long ago.

But he wouldn't. Not yet. Not when he wanted another taste of her skin.

"You did pay for the text itself, it is true. But there has been no discussion about the cost of translation," he said softly.

Those jeweled eyes widened; her lips parted; her breath quickened even further.

"You want too much for too little," she whispered.

He saw her tensing, a slight tremor that ran beneath her skin. He felt it, too, a subtle shift in her posture. Matteo knew when to stop. He laughed softly. "I tease you. Do not worry, *cuore solitario*. You have nothing to fear from me." He took a step back, withdrew a chair, and sat. "Come, sit by me. Listen to the story. Then you will understand."

Kieran hesitated. From deep beneath the keel a swell took the ship up, then dropped it into a gully, forcing her to grip the back of the chair for support. Foam and water hit the small, round portholes with a splash, a comb fell from Kieran's hair and clattered to the floor, and the light from the lantern stretched and guttered as the oil sloshed in its well. When she'd righted her balance, she lifted her eyes to his again; this time they glittered like the dark blue ocean, ruthless and unfathomable. Tingling trepidation passed down his back like a cold hand.

"I do not think you comprehend what I am after," she said, her voice threatening for all its savage softness. "I want what you promised: a semblance of hope that someday I will find peace in my soul. Perhaps you have never longed for something so elusive. Perhaps you do not know what it is like to want what is clearly beyond your current grasp. And perhaps can not recognize what it is to remember feeling normal, and to spend each day wondering where that feeling went, and how you can re-claim it."

Glossy auburn tresses slid down over the back of the chair, and Kieran impatiently tossed them over her shoulder. A snarl twisted her lips. "What do you want? To kiss my neck? Hold me unwilling in your arms? Fine. Do it and be done. And then tell me," she said, her anger fading away. Once again she looked as she had in his *burchiello* that night: full of emotion so raw it left her desolate and desperate. "Tell me what I can do. I'll do anything."

Matteo, caught by surprise, felt the urge to help her, to do whatever he needed to do in order to make the sadness in her eyes go away. Such generosity came as a rare compulsion, completely foreign to a man whose entire life was consumed with taking what he wanted.

"Of course," he said soothing, and this time, for the first time, his motives were genuine. "Please, sit. I want to tell you why this tale is important for us both."

Kieran's legs trembled, cold sweat condensed along her spine, and she clenched her teeth together to keep them from chattering. Why did he rattle her so easily? And why did she hunger to know the story that lay be-tween the leather bindings?

As if reading her mind, Matteo de Gama began to tell her.

"Many years ago, an idea came to me for this story. I saw a woman in my mind's eye, her innocence stolen, her virtue destroyed. What would a woman do to reclaim herself when neither innocence nor virtue are something that can be restored?"

Kieran leaned forward, her hands clasped tight on her lap. He had her complete attention.

Prompted by her silence, Matteo's lips curved up on one side, and his expression grew contemplative. "I had no muse for this story. I wrote it, and aware that it was not suitable for publication, I put it aside and promptly moved on to my next work."

His grin grew broader, and somehow it seemed to Kieran that he mocked the vagaries of life itself. "How completely odd that I should meet this manuscript's muse many years later. Odder still, that I should have to fish her from the canal."

"I don't understand."

"You will," he assured her. "For you see, this is a story about a woman's retribution."

"What is revenge?" Matteo asked. "Long ago, I thought to myself that if even God sees retribution as a way to measure recompense, then why not us?

"And consider the human. So vulnerable. Able to be injured, mortally so, but oftentimes in more subtle ways. Perhaps we have been stolen from, misled, violated, or wronged. Where is the justice? What is the retribution? Even the Lord bids us to seek an eye for an eye."

He paused, studying her. Kieran wondered what he saw, wished that she could see herself through his eyes. Kieran knew her facade: gray-blue eyes framed with dark lashes, a wealth of auburn hair, a face like her mother's: finely boned, fair skinned, and pleasing to a man's eye. And she knew how she presented herself, too. Cold in demeanor, quick to anger, and short on tolerance.

Instead, what if his eyes could see down to the depths of her core, know her secret shame, ferret out her darkest truth. What if he saw how she truly felt, like a wisp of a girl, thin on courage, long on doubt.

A question rose in her mind like mist over a turbulent sea: *What is the worst that would happen if someone knew?*

She pushed the query aside. Better not to dwell on what others would think of her if they knew what she'd done that night in the "house of lords"; she'd take that secret to her grave.

Far better to dwell on exactly how to punish the man who'd turned her into what she had become, and who had the audacity to bribe and manipulate her because he wanted something from her brother.

He began to read, the story coming in fits and starts as he translated from Italian to English. It began in a small cluster of dilapidated apartments where a young girl was forced to work each day to help feed her poor family.

Kieran closed her eyes and visualized the events unfolding. She saw the girl as she carried laundry, scrubbed floors, and washed dishes. In her mind's eye she could see the long, tangled black tresses pulled beneath a kerchief, the dirty bare feet, and the oft-mended holes of her threadbare garments.

When a rich man spied her toiling and offered her a pouch of sequins in exchange for a week of work, Kieran knew the girl should turn and run the other way.

Matteo paused and glanced up from the pages. He looked around the room as if wanting something. "Do you not have wine?"

"No, forgive me," Kieran said, shamed by her bad manners. She'd not offered him so much as a drink of water. She rose and went to the door, opened it and asked Nilo to bring wine, glasses, a heel of cheese, fruit, and bread.

"I ask for wine, I get a feast," Matteo commented with a grin as she retook her seat. "If I asked for a dance, would you marry me?"

He jests, she thought, and permitted a small smile. And then, emboldened, Kieran added, "Marriage is rather like dancing: Those who do it well make it look effortless, and those who do it poorly ought not have spectators."

A long, deep laugh came as her reward. Heat flushed her cheeks. Funny how it could feel so good to make him laugh.

Kieran smiled awkwardly and shifted in her seat. "My brother and his wife make marriage look like the finest dancing. They are fluid, dreamy, and all together in time."

"Perhaps one day you will find a man whose timing matches yours."

He spoke with such carelessness that it stung Kieran for some reason, as if he was not interested in becoming a suitor of hers. Did he not know that she scorned suitors the way some women disdained outmoded fashions?

"I am not suited for marriage," she said stiffly.

Matteo's eyes grew warm and soft.

"But what of dancing, *cara*? Will you dance?" he asked, and his lips lifted at the corners in a devilish grin.

Suddenly they weren't talking about marriage or dancing. Kieran felt her face grow hot. She deliberately misunderstood him. "I used to enjoy dancing, many years ago. I have long since lost interest."

Silence fell over them, awkward and extended. The only sounds came as they always did, the groaning creak of the ship, the sibilant hiss of the stove burning in the corner, and the faraway muted shouts of crewmen at work.

"Just as your brother once knew you, a long time ago," Matteo finally said. He grew contemplative, and his mouth lost the rakish edge. "When did you cut yourself off from the people who love you, and the things you loved?"

The question was so plainly asked, and he already knew more than anyone else. He seemed to look inside her and see more than she realized she revealed.

Temptation reached out and gripped Kieran,

clutched her in an unexpected embrace. Tell him, it urged, confess it all and get it out.

She leaned toward him, straining it seemed, desperation written in every elegant line of her face, in every delicate muscle of her body.

Lord, but she was beautiful. Her lips parted and trembled like dewy pink silk. Her cheeks bloomed with color, creamy, peachy skin luminous in its translucent perfection. She had hair that begged for his hands, glossy auburn tresses that had the shades of cinnamon and garnet hidden in its depths; he wanted to bury his hands in that hair, free the coils and curls from their gold combs and spread it over her shoulders and down her narrow back. But it was not the soft youth of her skin or the shimmering tresses or even those beguiling lips that so compelled him.

It was her eyes.

Those wide, mysterious eyes, alternating in color from the cold, stormy ocean when she was troubled or angry, to the precise hue of the canal at twilight when perplexed or cautious. For the brief moment he'd made her laugh, they lit with light, turning them the soft blue of cornflowers. No matter her mood, they reflected her soul, fragile and raw and primitive, filled with secret supplication for release. For relief.

Like the shrewd swindler he'd been forced to become, Matteo could read her expression easily. She was on the precipice of unloading her terrible secret. She wanted to let it out, but had been holding it close for so long, she was afraid to let it go.

"Go on," he urged her in a whisper, afraid to break the spell. "Tell me what weighs on your heart. I swear to you, there is nothing you could tell me that I have not had done to myself, or sadly, done to another."

Matteo did not know exactly why it felt so important for Kieran to confess, but he was completely certain of one thing: He wanted to be the only one who knew what made this tender young woman turn outwardly cold and inwardly desolate.

Like the odd sensations she'd inspired in him once before, generosity and guilt, he felt a newer, stranger emotion. It started in his chest, a hot burning that he might have been able to ignore if not for the urge to wrap his arms around her, cradle her against the very place where the burning grew.

For thirty-two years Matteo had survived on pure intuition and nerve, caring for himself until the day finally came when he realized he cared only about himself.

And now, convicted of a crime he did not commit, exiled from his country, and sailing to a new land, his self-protective instincts should have never been greater. He should be in the dark belly of the ship, playing cards with the sailors, keeping his wits and skills sharp. Instead he found himself in the most peculiar of situations.

He actually felt protective of another human being.

The burning spread, growing dangerously close to his heart.

A knock sounded on the door, three quick, hard raps followed by the turning of the knob. Nilo entered, a tray balanced easily on one huge hand. "Food and wine," he said with cheer.

Kieran and Matteo were still staring at each other across the table, both locked in the moment.

Nilo glanced from his mistress to the Venetian, and back to Kieran. He studied her for a brief moment, and what he saw made his face break into a small, tender grin. He quickly recovered and set down the tray on the table between them. He patted Matteo's shoulder, turned, and left the cabin. Kieran and Matteo could hear the soft thump of Nilo in the galley, resting against the door. No one would disturb them on his watch.

Matteo broke away from her gaze and seemed to pull himself together.

Kieran felt lost, confused. Just tell him, her mind urged. Get it out and be done. And yet, her pride held her back. He'd said there was nothing he hadn't done, nothing he wouldn't understand. Kieran knew that could not be the case. Surely Matteo de Gama had never known the kind of ruthlessness that Kieran had been so shocked to find inside herself.

She sipped her wine, placed a piece of cheese on her plate, and took a few grapes. In an offhand manner, she changed the subject to neutral ground. "How did you learn to speak such excellent English?"

"One of my lovers was an Englishwoman. She taught me a great many things. English was merely one of them."

"Oh." So much for neutral territory. It seemed everything the man said and did spoke of sensuality and warmth, a blatantly displayed and altogether masculine confidence. He wore his sexuality the way he wore his narrow, black leather clothes sewn with brightly colored linings, like some sort of bold statement that declared him different, audacious, and completely at ease in being regarded as such.

She cast a quick glance to her bunk, the pristine quilts spread flat and tucked tightly, not a wrinkle or crease marring her prudish spinster's bed.

Unbidden, the memory of Matteo's lips on her neck crept into her mind. Warm breath on her skin, soft lips pressing kisses along the column of her neck, her arm raised up, his chest pressing against her back, his body radiating a heat that drew her closer.

Like a serpent, an image slithered into her mind, of another woman in Matteo's arms, her body responding like an instrument. *Lover.* The word taunted her with its meaning. A faceless, unknown Englishwoman who'd taught him her tongue and tasted his. And suddenly, Kieran's cold composure melted into an emotion she hadn't felt in years: pure, unadulterated female jealousy.

"Who was this woman?"

Matteo watched Kieran's many moods with the enjoyment of a man who appreciated women as living, breathing works of art. She changed from light to dark in an instant, turned angry on the word "lover" even as she looked to her bed with an expression of pained longing. She needed love the way Venice needed its deep blue waters and golden sunlight. Without it, she was cold, unassailable, and without the musical poetry that exists only in the hearts of those who know passion.

The story he'd written was spread out before him, the reason he'd come. Yet, this intriguing creature now seemed less interested in her own revenge than in hearing about his former lover. Amused by this unexpected turn of events, Matteo acquiesced.

"I do not usually speak about women to women, but to answer your question, she was the widow of a Venetian. She was alone in the city, far too rich and far too bored. I became something of her . . ."

"Plaything?" Kieran supplied, her voice now coolly disdainful.

"Project," Matteo corrected. "She liked to teach me many things: music, art, writing, politics, languages. She hired tutors so I could learn to converse with her about these things, and therefore, keep her entertained."

"Did you love her?" The question blurted from her

mouth, obviously taking her by surprise. Kieran's eyes grew wider and her cheeks turned pink.

He ignored the small stab of pain in his heart. The wound might be old, but it still hurt when touched.

"I thought I did. For a time, I worshipped her. She educated me, made me into the man I am today. For that, I will always be fond of her, no?"

Matteo recalled well the skinny young man he'd been, knew how he must have seemed to his lover at the time, a man-child, innocent yet curious, needy yet giving. Matteo had been running the squares and alleys of Venice since the age of eleven; it had been bliss to have someone who'd wanted to take him in, to take care of him, to play with him, to shower him with attention.

Yes, he'd loved her. Like a mother, lover, and teacher all in one. He would have killed for her, if she'd asked him to.

"And was she beautiful?"

The glint in Kieran's eyes looked curiously like jealousy. Interesting. "Ah, *cuore solitario*, does that matter to the story? And for what it is worth, I find beauty in nearly all women."

"Was she? Was she beautiful to you?"

Matteo recalled Emily's face, her form, the texture of her skin. He sighed and relented, answering Kieran's question the best he could. "She was more than thirty years older than me. She became my world, and I thought her beyond beautiful."

Matteo watched as Kieran grew flustered, her skin turned the shade of cabbage roses. She rubbed her lips together as if they felt dry. She sipped her wine and ate a piece of cheese, folded her hands on her lap, and then unfolded them so she could take another sip of her wine. Finally, she was unable to keep herself from asking, "What happened to you and her?"

Look at how she longs for a definitive answer, he

thought. She wants to hear that his lover died, or that something tragic happened to end it. How to explain that romantic entanglements are more matters of want and need than of love?

Matteo wished he could give her a better answer. Wished the story had a deeper meaning, but he'd learned the hard way just how little his relationship with his lover had meant. At least to her. "She was paying for me. Do you understand? Keeping me. I was her distraction, her undertaking. I provided her with something to do. And when I was all she could make me into?" He shrugged and spread his hands. "Well, she found something else to fill her days."

"Another man?"

Was that an indignant tone this time? he marveled. Was the girl actually taking offense in a woman turning him out to replace him with another man?

It charmed him, to fancy that. Because in truth, the rejection had broken Matteo in a way that his own mother's neglect hadn't. He'd always known his mother didn't love him, but for a short, blissful time, had believed that it was possible that someone did. That he was lovable, after all. But it hadn't been true; she hadn't loved him.

No matter how hard he'd tried, he hadn't been able to elicit that feeling in Emily's heart when his own was bursting with it. And when she refused him, when it was clear that she simply didn't love him and never had, Matteo had wanted to lie down and die.

But he didn't. He moved forward, made a life the only way he knew how: He swindled, cheated, lied, and stole to get the things he needed and wanted. And while he never could resist loving a beautiful woman with his body, he never forgot that they could, and indeed would, resist loving him with their heart.

"I do not know if she took another lover, but it is likely.

There was not much of a discussion when it ended." He heard the sadness creeping into his tone, and so he let his voice grow warm and as smooth as brandy, adding, "Other than to thank me for all of the nights, of course."

Kieran's eyes narrowed and she looked away from him, again to the bed, and then back, downcast to the table. She couldn't seem to help herself, though. Her gaze stole again to her bed for a brief glimpse. When she met his eyes again, hers were full of questions she did not allow herself to voice.

Her eyes changed from curious to contemplating, the grayish, greenish blue that reminded him of the ocean before a storm. Her high color faded a bit, leaving her skin lightly flushed, and a slight frown took her brows as she took a distracted sip of wine. Her lips were wet with the wine, and he licked his own as if he could taste the fermented grapes along with the sweet honey of the girl.

Watching her could be dangerous; spending time with her treacherous, if he were to try to avoid seducing her. Rogan's warning came back to threaten him. Matteo considered that the course of wisdom would be to leave her presence and never return to it. She embodied his greatest lure: she was a puzzle begging to be solved, a living sculpture of beauty in constant motion, and an unplayed instrument in desperate need of music to bring her to life, all in one.

She was intrigue and art and altogether bittersweet.

And to Matteo, absolutely irresistible.

The course of wisdom is such a dreary road, he mused, and sparsely populated for very good reason. He'd said she didn't need his type of trouble, but now reconsidered. Perhaps a bit of trouble could be her cure.

His manuscript sat before him, opened to the page where a woman was about to be taken advantage of, and the story that ensues as she exacts her repayment.

Before him sat a real woman who'd been abused, and

Matteo thought that while living out fantasies on the page was an engaging pastime, living them in real life might be truly gratifying.

"Why did you ask about my lover?" he asked.

She looked pained for a second, as if he'd stung her feelings. "Have you had many?"

"That is not a suitable question for a lady to ask a man," he answered with a smile. "And you have not answered me."

"She was English," Kieran said, as if that provided answer enough to explain her curiosity. She lifted a shoulder in a half-shrug and confessed, "Forgive my vulgarity, but I'm not quite a lady."

≈ 7 ≈

"Not a lady? Vulgar?" Matteo repeated. His eyes slid over her, the warm brown of them like a caress. "The men must flock around you in England."

"I do not have interest in such . . . entanglements." Soft lips on her neck, warm breath on her ear, her body moving to a music she'd never felt before. She could not even muster the inclination to push the thoughts away. Lord, she was asking about his lovers! What was becoming of her?

It was the ship, she told herself. She always felt so free on the water, and this voyage seemed to remind her of when she was a girl, twirling on the deck in the wild wind that blew across the open ocean. She'd been so contained for these years past, keeping that wind fairy in constant check.

Kieran folded her hands and tried to feign a coolness she did not, at that moment, possess.

Matteo lifted a thick, dark brow. His face was long and lean and chiseled, his mouth a soft slash of constant animation. His skin gleamed in the light of the lanterns and the last bit of light that slanted in through the small window as the sun set. He was shades of amber and chocolate: eyes flecked with gold, skin burnished with copper, hair glistening with streaks of sunlight.

His lips on her skin had caused a million little smokeless fires to burn in her veins.

If Kieran still prayed to God, this would have been a good time to ask for strength.

"Why do you ask about my lovers?" he inquired once more.

Kieran couldn't answer, for how could she admit to the curiosity that a lady should not feel?

Matteo cocked his head as if considering whether or not to speak. He frowned and glanced away. Finally he rose and went to the window, looking through the thick glass to the wavy sight of the setting sun.

The light painted him with pink and gold. From where Kieran sat she could see his profile, cast in light and shadow. He loosened his collar as if it constricted his throat. When he turned and faced her, the last of the sunlight gone and only the lanterns to light him, he held out his hand. "Come here."

Propelled by a force she could not name, Kieran stood and went to him. Standing there, her legs trembling so that her knees felt as if they would not support her, she lifted her chin and met his eyes.

He reached out, skimmed her jaw with the back of a single finger. "Know this about me, for you are a lovely girl and you deserve to know who stands in your cabin this evening. Let me tell you what I am capable of: I could make you my mission. I could turn you into the focus of my entire existence, pursue you in a seduction to which you would have no defense. I could seduce you into my life, consume you with my world, and have you willing in my bed. I could possess you. I could play you like the cello, make you feel things you never dreamed possible. I could bring you pleasure beyond your imagining, and in doing so, I would enslave you. You would lick the floor in front of me, if I asked you to. You would do anything for me. And you would be mine, for as long as the affair lasted."

His eyes changed. They grew distant, regretful. He looked as though he were turned inward, trying to figure out when he'd become this man whom he spoke of with such familiarity. "And when I lost interest in you, I would walk away."

"Just as your lover did to you, you could do it to me," Kieran said. She remembered the woman in the courtroom of the Doge's palace, on her knees, begging, screaming, and weeping. Matteo had not spared her a backward glance.

"Yes. Now you see. For reasons I do not quite understand, I like you well enough to warn you of this. So be warned."

And she did see. She did understand. He was showing her his heart: ruthless and damaged, thick with scars. He was telling her who he was, a romancer, and a knave.

She'd thought they were similar creatures. Now she knew that she'd been correct. Only Kieran knew how merciless she was capable of being; only she knew the depths of her base nature.

Kieran had never known her grandmother, Amelia, the infamous duchess hanged for murder, but she'd heard stories. Kieran knew that blood ran in her own veins, the blood of a cold shrew who was incapable of loving anyone, her own daughter, her sons. She'd been capable of loving only herself.

Kieran reached out and captured Matteo's fingers, twined them with her own. She met his eyes boldly. He was telling her that he was a user of women, and she believed him.

Matteo could use her body for his own pleasure, and not feel it with his heart.

Kieran understood that, because she could just as easily use his attraction for her to manipulate him into helping her exact her revenge. It was why she wore her best gown, pressed scented oil behind her ears, invited him to her cabin and posted Nilo at the door. Matteo was not the only one capable of using his powers of seduction to secure a reward.

She had no intention of tumbling into his bed. She did, however, have every intention of getting what she wanted.

"Signore," she whispered. "We have a story to translate, do we not?"

"I warned you. You can never claim that you did not know my true nature."

His words were warning, but the sensual set of his mouth was pure invitation.

Kieran smiled. If he wanted to kiss her and light that smokeless flame in her blood, she would not suffer to permit it. She turned and leaned her back to his chest, and with her fingers still twined in his, she lifted her arm into the air, tilted her head to the side, baring her neck.

"So I am warned, signore."

He put his face to her hair. She heard him inhale, as if he were breathing in the scent of a flower. A strange sensation bloomed in her chest. Matteo lowered his lips to her ear; she felt his breath again, warm against her skin. He hovered there, just above the slim column of her neck. Her heart began to pound.

The door to her cabin opened wide, and Rogan filled the doorway with Nilo standing behind him. Behind her, Matteo stiffened, but he remained still. Kieran watched as her brother's face darkened, his brows drew into a scowl, and both his hands balled into fists.

Strangely, Kieran felt a small kick of pride at being caught with Matteo. She did not move, but stayed in precisely the same position, like a cello cradled in a musician's sure hands.

"Good day, Rogan," she said calmly. "Do you need something?"

Rogan narrowed his eyes. "Aye, I do. I came to ask if you'd like to join Emeline and me for the evening meal." Rogan unclenched his fists, laid his hands on both sides of the doorway and seemed to beg a higher power for patience. "But I'll not bother you with that matter right now, as you're obviously quite busy, aye? I'll settle for an answer to this: For three years you've rejected every potential suitor who'd dared to come within twenty paces of you. You've spent your days and nights in what has seemed to be some sort of cold, distant place, and you've expressed no interest in men, marriage, or the like."

He seemed to give up on the patience, and his voice rose on each following word, until he was shouting, "And now you closet yourself in your cabin with this man, alone, and place Nilo, *the man I pay to protect you,* outside your door so as to preserve your *privacy*! Tell me, Kieran, what in the hell is going on inside your head?"

Kieran restrained a flinch. Her brother's anger was a fearsome thing, a wild Irish display of barely controlled violence.

Yet, she could not resist a flippant answer. "Signore de Gama was just showing me how he plays the cello."

A vein bulged in Rogan's forehead. He ground his teeth and held his thumb and forefinger a sliver apart, his voice dropped to a threatening whisper that frightened her more than any shouting could. "You are this close to me shipping you back to Barbados. This close," he enunciated. "I have long been tired of your cold silences. You have made me weary with your unwillingness to talk about your troubles. Emeline and I have tried to let you have your time, your silence, your freedom. We have done everything we could think of to bring you peace, to help you, to comfort you. You defeated us at every turn. But all of that I can stand, because you are my sister. My blood. I love you, Kieran.

"But if you think I am going to let you carry on with a man behind closed doors on my ship, you are sorely mistaken. I will pack you up and send you off, and let Mum and Da take you in hand. Perhaps they can succeed where I have failed."

Rogan turned his attention to Matteo. Kieran noticed that her brother's green eyes glittered like emeralds, hard, cold polished stones. She'd never seen quite that look in his eyes before. Fear for Matteo's safety curled in her gut.

"Perhaps you do not understand the meaning of the word 'respect.' Come with me, signore, and I will teach you," Rogan said.

Matteo gave Kieran's hand a quick squeeze of reassurance and then let go, starting to move toward Rogan. Visions of her brother pummeling Matteo into a bloody pulp pulsed in her mind. Rogan was huge, muscled, hard and tough. Matteo, however, was lithe and long, with artist's hands and a lean sinewy strength that wouldn't stand a chance against Rogan, a former pugilist. Kieran leapt into motion, blocking the path between the two men.

"Signore de Gama came at my invitation. He kissed me at my invitation, as well."

"No, no, do not worry or make my excuses. I will go with His Grace and we will work it out as men." Matteo met her eyes. "It is not your fault; I came because I wanted to."

Not your fault. The words burned like acid.

Kieran pictured those beautiful brown eyes swollen shut, bruised and bloody. She turned back to Rogan. "Don't listen to him. I sent for him by letter. When he came here, he never touched me. We talked and he read to me." She gestured to the sheaf of papers, spread open on the table. And saw the wine and the cheese and bread; it looked like a lovers' tryst. Her skin flushed, but she continued. "I wanted him to kiss me, and I asked him to do so."

"I don't care if you begged for him to take you to his bed. He is a man, full grown and self-aware. He has no claim on you, and unless 'tis marriage on his mind, he would do well to keep away." Rogan took two steps, his hands curling into fists again, anger tightening his features even further. "You'd best clear out of the way, Kieran."

"No." Kieran squared her shoulders and met her brother's anger with her own. She was not afraid of Rogan's temper, not when her own was swirling inside her. Kieran was Irish and English as well, the same blood ran in their veins, and as he threatened Matteo she felt her temper begin to boil.

"Get out," she snarled up into Rogan's face. "I am a woman, full grown as well, and not a child in need of protection. How dare you barge into my cabin and make threats. I will do as I please with my virtue, thank you very much. 'Tis mine to squander or treasure, and I ask you to keep your mind out of my skirts."

Her crudeness shocked Rogan into speechlessness. When he found his voice, he said, "'Tis as if I no longer know you at all."

His words cut deep. Rogan had been her childhood hero, her big brother who knew everything, who could do anything, and who never seemed to mind having her around. Now he looked at her as if she were a slattern, and even worse, a stranger.

And she realized that no one seemed to know her anymore. Except perhaps Matteo de Gama, who saw her as she was now, instead of whom she had once been.

Rogan cast his cold, green gaze on Matteo. "I saved you from one prison, but now, will place you in another. You'll be confined in your stateroom for the remainder of your stay aboard my ship. A guard will be posted at your door, and I'll decide what to do with you when we dock in England." His lips flattened as he glanced to Kieran once again, and he said, "Be glad my sister can make me angrier than you can, signore, because you were very nearly food for sharks."

Late in the night, Kieran woke to the sound of scratching on her door. The sea was rough, causing her to stumble from her bunk as she reached for her wrapper. She staggered through her small cabin, at once wide awake. Clutching her robe tight around her, a fistful of fabric clenched at her throat, she leaned close to the door and asked who was there.

"Nilo, Miss Keerahn."

Relief swept over her. She turned the locks and opened the door. In the dim galley stood Nilo, his nightshirt hanging to his knees.

Kieran shivered in the drafts from the cold passageway and gripped her robe even tighter.

"Is all well?" she whispered. She looked up and down the hall, and just as did she could hear it: the low, warm tenor tones of the cello. She pictured it, between Matteo's legs, cradled in his arms, played like a lover. The moody melody resonated through the wood of the ship, it seemed, vibrating down to Kieran's bones. Suddenly, she did not feel quite as chilled.

Before she could say anything further Nilo handed her paper, rolled into a cylinder and tied with a scarlet ribbon.

Kieran accepted it and brought her gaze to meet Nilo's. "'Tis from Signore de Gama, no doubt?"

"His guard is my friend," Nilo answered, and a wide grin broke over his face. The lantern light cast Nilo's face in shadows, but she could see the shine of his eyes. Perhaps it was a trick of the light, but Kieran thought he looked impish, an expression completely at odds with his size and appearance.

Once more, Nilo brought the backs of his fingers to her cheek. He stroked her skin as if he touched a glass sculpture, reverently, yet aware of its fragility. "De Gama makes you warmer. Softer. For that, he is my friend, too."

Kieran touched the ribbon with her right hand, and her left rose to cup Nilo's, holding it against her cheek. Her throat felt tight with emotions she could not express. If she let one escape, they all might come pouring out.

Kieran clutched the papers to her chest. "Oh, Nilo, you shouldn't have done this. If Rogan finds out . . ."

"Mister Rogan wants to protect his sister. This, I understand." Nilo lifted his broad shoulders in a shrug. His face bore the expression it had on the night she'd stumbled out of the house after being held captive by her cousin Simon and Samuel Ellsworth. Nilo had pulled her to her feet when her own legs could not bear her weight. He'd looked at her with sorrow then, a smile meant to comfort her, and a strong hand to lend his own strength. "I told you once about the men who came to our tribe. They raped the women, killed the children, and took the men. Took us away, put us on ships. I saw my woman die. My children, too. There was no protection; too many men against our tribe."

Nilo's hand rested on Kieran's shoulder, the weight and warmth of it a comfort. "I saw you that night,

Miss Keerahn. Too many men against you, and you alone and frightened."

Kieran stiffened but could not order him to silence.

"Since then, you cry at night. I hear you, and I pray for you."

"Pray for yourself, dear Nilo, and your lost loved ones," she whispered. How could he have borne such loss and spend his worry on her?

"You do not understand. I saw you," Nilo persisted. He seemed to struggle with his English, his accent thickening in his battle for the right words. "I stayed on the outside. I did not help. Two girls alone and I stayed outside. That Simon promised me Africa, if I stay and guard the door. But there was no Africa left for me, and I still stayed outside."

"Those men had pistols, and they were white men. English. If you'd come inside, they would have killed you without a second thought. And if you'd managed to stop them with violence, they would have seen you hang the next morning."

"You are right. Too many men, even for Nilo," he said softly. "So why does Miss Keerahn feel she could have done better?"

The cello music continued, the low tenor floating through the corridor. The assault on her senses caught Kieran in a weakened condition, newly awakened from a dream and feeling as if she'd stepped back into an old nightmare.

"Please, Nilo, this is not a good time."

"When is a good time for sadness?"

"Not now. The hour is late, and I am fatigued."

Nilo seemed to weigh his words before he spoke. The pressure on her arm increased slightly, as if to keep her attention on his words. "After the men took me from my tribe, I felt bad a long time. Nilo did not even fight them.

Did not even fight on the ships. Then I got a chance to fight! Fight in the ring, get back to Africa. So I fought.

"I lost. So I guarded the door to get back to Africa. All the time, I am thinking: Nilo wants Africa."

He shook his head, vigorously, and in the light of the lanterns, his bald head gleamed. "After I see what happens to Miss Keerahn, it makes sense to me. There are bad men everywhere, England, Africa, no different. I cannot fight for this kind of man. I must fight for myself."

Kieran stood still and let him speak, for how could she silence a stoic man who rarely strung together more than three sentences?

Nilo continued despite the effort it took to speak. "Some day it will make sense to you. Some day you will see for yourself, Miss Keerahn. There are bad men everywhere. But there are good men, too. Men like Mister Rogan." He smiled shyly and said, "And Nilo. I hope I am more good than bad in here." He thumped his chest.

"Miss Keerahn, you are more good than bad. The time has come to put that night away. It is time for you to do what Nilo did: Fight for yourself. There have been too many days of cold and silence. It is time for warmth and music for Miss Keerahn."

He gestured to the roll of papers she still held. "Mister Rogan put Matteo de Gama in his room. He wants to protect you. I understand this. I want that, too."

Nilo let go of Kieran's arm and again touched her cheek, his fingers dry and warm. "But if you won't fight for yourself, maybe it is time for Nilo to help a little bit."

He smiled to lighten the mood, held his hands into fists and pulled his arms up in the traditional boxing stance. He bounced on the balls of his feet, and then pretended to take a swipe at her. When Kieran dodged the playful air-punch and let out a little laugh at his antics, Nilo grinned wider and said, "Nilo is a good fighter. Ask Mister Rogan."

* * *

Kieran did not wait for the morning light. She turned her lantern's flame up high and lit two others, carried them over to the table so she could see what Matteo de Gama had sent to her.

So low as to be barely audible, she could hear him playing his cello. She visualized his long, artist's fingers, stained with ink, scented with rosin, deftly maneuvering the bow across the strings.

She shivered and pulled a quilt from her bunk, wrapping herself in its warm confines as she sat at her small table. She uncurled the paper only to find there was more than one. In fact, there were four pages of laboriously written words, the handwriting she recognized as Matteo's.

And on top, a letter.

Dearest Miss Mullen,

It seems I am destined to correspond with you in this manner.

I submit a few translated pages of my story. Please overlook any errors in spelling and grammar. Written English comes more difficult than spoken, I am afraid. I will, if it pleases you, send more pages tomorrow night. I do believe you paid for them, no?

I am isolated but for my cello, my writing, my books, and my painting. It is perhaps not the punishment it is intended to be. As inclined as I am to work, however, my mind drifts away from the task at hand, and leads me to another more interesting dilemma. What, I keep wondering, is that scent you wear? It haunts me in my sequestered cabin, and as I reach for my cello, know that there is a far more interesting instrument I wish I were playing.

Inexorably,
Matteo de Gama

Kieran held the paper close. In the privacy of her stateroom where no one would see her, she lifted the page to her face and inhaled.

And allowed herself the girlish fancy that she could smell the amber-sweet pine scent of rosin mingled with the bitter tang of ink, the citrus-fresh scent of bergamot, and rich, masculine leather.

The papers were tightly scrawled with the translation, his handwriting loopy and difficult to decipher. None of that mattered. The story sang to her from the page, as if her own soul were speaking to itself through Matteo de Gama's written words. She saw herself in the girl whose innocence was ripped away, who'd thought she'd lost all hope, and who saw an opportunity to punish the man who took it. Innocence and virtue cannot be reclaimed. But pride can, the girl realized, and as that realization dawned on the girl, it dawned on Kieran, as well.

When at last she set the final translated page aside, Kieran reached for her own blank paper with a hand that trembled beyond her ability to control it. She stripped a quill, dredged it in ink, and wrote:

Signore,
  'Tis with bated breath that I await the next installment of your compelling drama.

She paused, biting her lower lip. Did she dare?

A warning was whispered in her mind, to be careful not to get lost in the game. Matteo de Gama understood the rules of romancing and seduction. Kieran was nothing more than an inexperienced player.

Oh, but it felt good to try to reach for something new. Now there was revenge to be had, pride to be reclaimed, a flirtation to pursue, and more, there was meaning in her life again.

With a reckless abandon she attributed to the lateness of the hour, Kieran dipped the quill once more and added,

> *Sadly, your current status does not allow for lessons in the art of playing the cello. I hear your music, however, and it lends a certain brightness to the long days and nights at sea. Keep playing for me, signore, when you are not occupied with translation, and know that your music reaches my cabin, my ears, and dare I admit it, my heart.*
>
> *Until next we meet,*
Kieran Mullen

She read over her words, and decided against crumpling the paper and stuffing it into the coal stove. No, she would send it, and let him wonder if she told the truth or played a game.

It did not matter. Did he not already warn her that such flirtations were nothing more than a diversion for him? He told her he could walk away, and she believed him.

What Matteo de Gama did not perchance realize, is that she could do the same.

With a new sense of purpose, Kieran rose from the table and retrieved her small atomizer from the trunk that contained her toilette items.

The oils contained in the glass came from the islands, a rare, precious blend of fragrances. She sniffed it and inhaled the scent of warmth and starry skies, night-blooming flowers, and silent woods.

She sprayed the letter to Matteo with a fine mist of the perfume, rolled it up, tied it with a ribbon, and set it aside. When morning dawned she would ask Nilo to deliver it.

And then, surrounded by the scent that she loved so, she listened to the creaking of the ship and the groans of the floorboards. Beneath the keel spanned the deep blue sea; above the masts spiraled the endless night sky.

Another tap sounded at her door. With a smile, Kieran lifted the scroll and rushed to the door to give it to Nilo.

She pulled it open and froze. It was a waking nightmare, and like a person caught in one, she could not move or scream, but was frozen in time.

Samuel Ellsworth leaned casually against the doorframe. "Good evening."

Sweat beaded on her skin, ran down her back. Never mind that he was seeing her in her nightclothes; the man had seen her naked.

The thought made her stomach sick.

"How?" she breathed. It was all she could say.

"A fire on our ship, and your brother gave rescue. You did not know?"

She struggled for composure, reminding herself that he could not hurt her; she needed only to scream and Nilo would hear. Yes, she'd felt the ship slow, but had assumed nothing more than a problem with a sail. "Had I known, I would have had my man toss you overboard."

He smiled at her, his gray eyes traveling over her face as if reading her every expression. She smelled gin on his breath as he said, "Fate keeps bringing us together."

"You are mad."

"And you are whispering," he replied victoriously. Samuel glanced up and down the dark, narrow galley. "Why do you keep the secret?"

Fear and rage made for a messy clog in Kieran's throat. "I don't answer to you. Go away."

"For three years it puzzled me, and then in Venice you sought me out, and now my curiosity is renewed. Is it fate, do you think? I have begun to think that I must reconcile with you."

"Be gone. There is no fate, only chance, and it has not favored me." Kieran held her hands to her throat and tried to swallow over the lump that blocked her airway. "Go, or I shall break my silence. Go, or I shall scream for my man and at my command he will fillet you into tiny pieces."

Samuel sighed as if he found her threats annoying rather than frightening. "I came to tell you that I cannot swim. I truly did not wish for your drowning, and knew the other man would save you. There was really nothing I could have done for you, but I am glad you were not hurt."

Kieran found that the anger burning inside her was far more powerful than her fear.

"How dare you," she hissed up into his face. "You have done nothing but hurt me. Every day for three years, you've wounded me with your mere existence."

Samuel looked affronted, perplexed. "How so? I admit that I was unkind to you in Simon's house, but I did not hurt you. And though 'twas belated, I offered money as recompense, and I apologized. How can you say I have hurt you for three years, when I've done nothing but keep away from you?"

"You jest in the most untoward manner," she whispered. Glancing up and down the galley once again, Kieran saw they were still unobserved. "If there is a name vile enough for you, I do not know it. The best I can do is evil. You are evil. You changed me in a way from which I shall never recover, and if that were not horrid enough, you have the audacity to propose to do business with my family, all but daring me to come forth or else suffer your presence."

Samuel held up a hand, and when he spoke, his tone was one of eminent reason. "There is more to the story than this skewed version. I did not set out to do those things that night. I was drunk, caught up in the moment and egged on by the other men. I never would have done any of that when sober. I realize that's not a justification, but I assure I am not evil. I take no delight in the memory of that evening."

Samuel sighed and spread his hands. "I came tonight to tell you that my offer of monetary recompense still stands. 'Twould be ungentlemanly for me to retract it, and 'tis true that I do feel ashamed at how I treated you."

Kieran's mouth hung open, and she regarded him as one who was truly insane. He stood before her, draped in rich garments, his handsome face noble and dignified. "I don't want your money. I don't want anything from you but your suffering, and barring that, your distance."

"I do not believe you."

"You what?"

"You would have told your brother what I did if you truly wanted to see me punished."

Aghast, Kieran could only blurt the truth. "'Tis not my liking to reveal my deepest shame."

Once again, he looked puzzled. "What shame? You emerged from that house no different than you are now. I didn't hurt you." He frowned, deep in thought. "Did I? I was quite drunk."

"Your temerity knows no bounds," she said incredulously. "And my patience is gone. I am closing this door, and if you dare to approach me again on this voyage, I will see to it that my guard finds you alone, drags you into the bowels of this ship, and teaches you precisely what an African luguru ax is made for."

Kieran closed the door, turned the locks with shaking fingers, and backed away from the door, her knees like sand, her blood like ice.

The room was utterly quiet, but in her mind she screamed, a long, primitive shriek that went on forever.

~ 8 ~

London, England

No fanfare greeted *The Boxer* as it sailed down the Thames. The great river teemed with activity, every manner of seafaring conveyance littering the murky, black waters. Along the docks people seethed in a constant sea of activity, harlots, merchants, sailors and traders consumed with their work. Wagons rattled, horse hooves clopped, lusty seamen yelled out and bawdy women laughed as ribald exchanges were tossed to and fro.

Overhead seagulls wheeled and called, their white bodies stark against a steel-gray sky. The sun burned in a hazy, vaguely yellow smear on the horizon, and a light, misty fog seeped across the waters and rolled onto the land.

Matteo de Gama found himself frozen in place, staring in awe. He felt not like he was in another country, but in a different world.

He'd expected London to be strange, far different from Venice, and perhaps even overwhelming. What he hadn't prepared for was the complete sensory overload of smells and sensations and sights.

The people clogged the docks and Matteo strained to see them, immediately noting their pasty white skin and somber clothes, tricorn hats tilted low over the brows of the cloaked men, the women clothed in homespun wool or harlot-bright satins.

All around him hung the stench of offal, rancid fish, coal smoke, and horse dung. The soot-stained buildings sketched forbidding, stark lines against the bleak, metallic sky.

And then beside him, like a vision, an angel, appeared Kieran Mullen, as ever shadowed by her hulking African escort. She wore a cloak of indigo blue, embroidered with gold threads and trimmed with fox. The fur hood framed her face, the fine bones of her cheeks and jaw like a painting, the jeweled beauty of her eyes like the mysterious ocean, and her lips, shaped like a flower's bud, pink, soft, and dewy. She looked untouched by the filth and darkness, like a princess whose feet have never trod upon anything but rose petals.

Her eyes lit when they met his, and her lips curved into an enigmatic smile. "Good day, signore. Here is London. What do you think of her?"

"Beautiful," he answered, his eyes never leaving Kieran's face. "She is extraordinary."

A shy blush crept across her porcelain skin the way the dawn paints the sky. She turned and faced the city. "I recall my first impression was darkness and stench."

"I see nothing but the fairest beauty. In fact, it makes me long to paint her, to sculpt her, to compose sonnets and music in tribute."

She lifted a brow in an expression of cool disdain that was made charming by the blush that rose beyond her control. "Sonnets for a city?"

"Would the city listen, do you think? Or would the paltry words fall on deaf ears, a pathetic man's tribute to a rare, but uninterested, beauty."

He watched her hesitate, saw her fascinating eyes turn a deeper, stormy blue. She glanced away, but not to be coy. He could see she simply was not sure how to answer.

Finally she brought her eyes back to his, and this time they were the deep indigo of her cloak, framed by sooty lashes. "She would listen."

Somewhere on the docks a prostitute called out a lewd proposition, and it seemed to break Kieran's mood. She added, "And she knows that no matter how lovely the sonnet, the poet will leave London behind without a second thought, and move on to admire a new, different city."

"The poet is not a writer of tragedies. The city would soon forget him."

Kieran's countenance turned thoughtful. "Perhaps you are on to something, signore."

"What did you think of my book?" he asked, unable to help himself from showing his weakness, the needy writer inside him who clamors for a scrap of praise, knowing he will not believe it, anyway.

"'Twas kind of you to labor over the translation."

"My fulfillment of our bargain," he said, waving away her gratitude. *The book*, his mind repeated. *What did you think of my story?*

"'Twas quite an interesting tale, signore."

"I was afraid that it would not hold up in translation, but I do believe the thoughts came across."

"They did indeed."

Before he could speak further, he noted Rogan appearing from the lower deck, his wife at his arm.

They made a stunning couple: Rogan tall, muscled, and recklessly handsome; Emeline long and curvy, golden hair gleaming against luminous skin.

Behind them came Ellsworth, the duke that Matteo soon hoped to meet across a gaming table. The man moved with pomposity, caught up in his own importance. He gave a few curt orders to some crewmen, and then looked around. He spotted Kieran, and his demeanor changed. He turned curious, his head cocked to the side. His mouth parted with words he did not utter.

It seemed, Matteo noticed, that the Duke of Westminster was besotted with the lost and lonely ice princess.

Matteo assessed Kieran, who had turned her shoulder so she did not have to look at him. Her face had grown pale and her lips were set in a tight line. Interesting.

Ellsworth shot a final glance at Kieran before letting himself be ushered off the ship, along with others whose trunks were being carried down the gangplank.

Something niggled at Matteo, and he made a mental note to look into Ellsworth further. There was more there, and his instincts told him it could be worth a tidy sum.

As Rogan caught sight of his sister standing with Matteo, his slashing black brows drew together in a scowl. But he could hardly reprimand her for speaking to a man while escorted by Nilo and surrounded by an entire crew of sailors. With his wife's hand firmly in the crook of his elbow, he approached them.

"I hope 'twas not too trying to be kept alone in your cabin, signore, but you do not look worse for wear."

"I had plenty to occupy me." Matteo bowed and when he straightened he met Rogan's eyes with the guileless charm that had seen him through many a bad spot. "Thank you very much for passage to your beautiful city, Your Grace."

Matteo could feel Emeline's scrutiny of him. What does she look for? he wondered. He stole a glance and met her eyes, saw the question there that she did not voice. Emeline's gaze drifted to Kieran's, and the look of her changed from questioning to compassionate. With a gentle hand, Emeline reached out and smoothed Kieran's cloak. "'Tis lovely, Kieran. Is it new?"

As the women exchanged pleasantries, Matteo studied Kieran. Her manner had grown stiffer at the appearance of Emeline and Rogan. She turned guarded and distant, those stormy eyes turned as cold as the ocean in winter. He ignored what they were saying, meaningless exchanges as they wished each other good health and traded compliments.

Matteo instead watched in fascination how Emeline clung to Rogan, her body in perfect tune with his. He noted the way Rogan sheltered her without a second thought, his hands constantly on her body in some way: cupping the small of her back, brushing aside a fallen tendril of her hair, covering her hand with his own as it rested on his arm.

Marriage had never looked quite so intriguing.

Matteo pictured the baby in Emeline's womb, curled safely in her body, a physical, living manifestation of their love and their hope for the future.

A wave of unexpected longing gripped Matteo, for family, a place in this world, and for someone to love him. He turned his attention away from the married couple, dropped his lashes over eyes that likely shone with envy. He knew better than to covet what he could never attain.

"Signore de Gama, you must join us for dinner this evening," Kieran invited, her voice cutting through his thoughts.

He brought his eyes to hers and saw the glitter of something unspoken. "If it is acceptable with His and Her Grace."

"Yes, of course. Please do join us," Emeline said.

Matteo saw it, the subtle shift of Rogan's body, and the answering squeeze of Emeline's hand on his arm. They communicated like two hearts, beautiful to witness, painful to long for. No wonder Kieran stiffens when they approach; their love was palpable, and turned one's lack of it into a sharp, sudden agony.

Rogan caught Matteo's gaze. His startling green eyes

gleamed with a warning, plain and bright. "I've a house in mind for you to take up residence. You'll be comfortable there."

His meaning was abundantly clear: You'll be kept as far from my sister as possible.

"My thanks. I would be delighted to accept your generous offer, Your Grace, though I insist on paying the proper rents."

"'Tis unnecessary," Rogan replied. "I've no need for your coin, and as I said before, 'tis the least I can do for the man who saved my sister's life."

"I am not in need of charity, Your Grace," Matteo said stiffly.

Kieran stood by silently, watching him from the cowl of her hood, and Matteo realized with a shock that he actually cared what she thought of him. The thought had him stammering, "How do I say . . . it is a matter of significant pride that I pay my own way."

Something changed in Emeline's posture, and in response, Rogan shifted his weight and took a far less menacing tone. "I do appreciate your offer of payment. 'Tis something to recommend you, that you do not expect anything from me."

Emeline's sapphire eyes studied Matteo; he could virtually feel her gaze on him. She glanced to Kieran, back to Matteo, and then turned innocent eyes up to her husband. "What about the property you recently acquired, love? 'Tis in desperate need of repair, and you're far too busy to see to it. If Signore de Gama were to live on and oversee the renovations, he could do us a favor and remove the burden from your shoulders. That would be an arrangement that would profit all of us, I think. And of course, with the child coming, I was truly hoping to be able to count on you to help plan the nursery."

Matteo watched as Rogan looked down on his wife with an odd mixture of tenderness and exasperation.

She smiled up at him, a dimple skirting the corner of her lips, and a gleam in her eyes. She continued speaking, her demeanor one of utter helpfulness, seemingly oblivious to the fact that she put both Rogan and Matteo in an awkward position.

"No offense intended, but I don't think Signore de Gama has the experience needed for such an undertaking," Rogan said.

Emeline would not be dissuaded.

"Signore de Gama is an artist, Kieran tells me. 'Tis an artist's eye I want for the project; a foreman can see to the more technical issues. We would, of course, provide hired hands, let him hire the needed skilled laborers, and allow him a budget. Then Signore de Gama would not have to worry about paying his way, because he would be doing us a service," Emeline added, and managed to somehow make it seem as if all the ideas had only just occurred to her.

Rogan held his fingers to his forehead in a manner that suggested an incipient headache. He shook his head, then sighed. His lips tightened in a way that indicated he would not argue with his wife or contradict her in front of others, and most especially not when she carried his child. He sighed again, this time one of resignation. "Fine. Yes. Excellent suggestion, Emeline."

Matteo hesitated. Did they make this offer out of genuine need, or was this only a slightly different variety of charity? Pride had him stiffening. He was more than capable of taking care of himself.

Or perhaps that was the problem? he wondered. Were they offering him other work out of concern that Matteo would swoop down upon the hapless denizens of his city, bilking the rich aristocrats of their vast inheritances?

Pride had him wanting to toss aside the offer, but in another part of his heart, he wondered if he were up to the task. Matteo had been many things in his life; he'd never, however, been honestly employed.

Apparently, Kieran read his expression, because she offered him a way out, should he want it. The wind whipped the cowl of her cloak's hood, and carried her voice to him. "Signore, perhaps you will want to see this property before you make the commitment to take on such a task. If 'tis the one I am thinking of, it borders the far west end of our London holdings, an ancestral home in near ruins. Whilst on a ride not too many months ago, I came upon the house and am fairly certain I saw a family of raccoons taking up residence. 'Twould be better to burn it to the ground and rebuild, than to try to rehabilitate it, in my opinion."

"It could be grand," Emeline insisted. "I begged Rogan to buy it, and 'twill make a wonderful place for guests to stay. Since we are staying in London until after the child comes, 'tis a perfect time to see to the renovation."

Rogan shrugged, his hand on Emeline's lower back. He'd obviously grown bored with the conversation, his attention drawn to the retinue of carriages that lined the dock.

Their coaches had been brought to bear them home, the ship had been secured, and the crew was preparing to unload the cargo. Ready to disembark, he steered his wife toward the main gangplank. He tossed a final comment over his shoulder, managing to challenge and insult Matteo, all at once. "Go see it, and decide if you have the vision for the task. If you do not, I'm certain I can find someone else who will. Either way, I'll accept no rents from you. Your money is useless to me, and I'll not grow wealthier on winnings plucked from my peers, no matter how much you may decide they deserve to have it taken from them."

* * *

Rogan and Emeline's manse came into view as the long line of carriages approached, a mammoth gray stone structure that glimmered in the afternoon light like a mirage. Sunlight winked from gabled windows, spires speared the sky over turrets that sat on either end, calling to mind fairy tales with imprisoned princesses and foreign princes.

Servants rushed to open doors and unload steamer trunks. Despite the wintry cold, blooming flowers of red and white had been cut and woven with evergreen boughs and placed near the huge double doors, a welcoming burst of color and cheer. Pleasant chatter filled the frosty air, coupled with the stamping and snorting of horses and the squeaking of carriage springs as footmen jumped down, drivers dismounted, and the passengers alighted.

The doors yawned open as the trunks were carried indoors, and out wafted the homey scents of beeswax candles, smoke from blazing wood fires, and lemon wax. Maids milled out, blowing breath into their hands to warm them against the cold as they welcomed their mistresses with warm smiles. A few of the barn cats came from around the rear of the house to investigate the commotion, slithering around the carriage wheels and sniffing the luggage.

Kieran spied Matteo as he took it all in, noted the way his dark, hooded eyes widened ever so slightly, and the way his soft lips lost their usual curl of amusement. He hung back, away from the servants and the duke and duchess, as if he felt out of sorts and out of place.

Matteo turned and reached into one of the carriages that bore nothing but trunks and luggage. Gently, he lifted his cello case and righted it by his side, his arm around it in a protective gesture.

A sudden feeling took Kieran in the chest, a stab of compassion for this man who had been uprooted from everything he knew, and who now lived in a strange land, with virtual strangers. Unaware of her perusal, his expression was unguarded. In that moment, he looked younger, vulnerable, his lips soft and his eyes sad. She had the urge to go to him, to hold him and to shush in his ear that all would be well.

The impulse shook her. Kieran slid her trembling hands into her fur muff and glanced away. Her gaze caught Emeline's.

Pure female knowing glowed in Emeline's sapphire eyes, and she curved her lips in a small smile that looked at once victorious and encouraging.

"'Tis a fine day, and I could use a ride after being confined so long on the ship and in the carriage," Kieran said, forcing her tone to sound offhand. She turned to one of the stable hands. "Would you saddle a fresh mount for me, please, and one for Nilo, as well."

With a smile that could only be defined as wicked, Emeline's voice overrode all other sounds in the huge, circular driveway. "Why not take Signore de Gama on a ride with you, Kieran, and show him the property. 'Twould be most helpful to Rogan and myself as we are anxious to be settled." She turned to Rogan with a sweet smile. "My love, I need to lie down. Will you build me a fire and keep me company, please? 'Tis so good to be home."

Rogan met his wife's eyes with a look of warning in his own, but relented as Emeline leaned in and fingered the buttons on his waistcoat. He consulted his pocket watch and turned to Kieran. "Two hours is plenty of time to show the property and be back." He cast a cockeyed glance to the cello cradled at Matteo's side. "And no music lessons, aye?"

Kieran felt her face burn, despite the chill in the air. Damn Rogan and his superiority. "I do not feel up to quite that long a ride, thank you," she said haughtily. "Perhaps

Signore de Gama can go on his own. A man who navigates canals can surely find his way a few miles west."

"Do not feel the need to worry about what I will do to while away my days, I beg you all. As for now, I must decline the invitation to ride out to the property. I cannot sit a horse," Matteo said. His tone was subdued, mild, and completely at odds with the burning in his eyes.

"No?" Kieran asked, her interest suddenly piqued. "How so?"

"How so?" he repeated with a smile that looked pasted on. "I shall tell you 'how so.' I am Venetian, and horses are not welcome within city limits, the outside of which I rarely traveled. I had my beautiful *burchiello*, a light, quick gondola, and small, comfortable *casino*. No horses on water, eh? And little reason to rush to learn to ride one."

"You're something of a fish out of water here in England, no?" Kieran said.

"A man out of country," he corrected, his expression betraying his offense. "I do not expect a welcome worthy of an ambassador, but perhaps it would not trouble you to reach beyond your own knowing."

If her cheeks had been hot before, they now flamed with humiliation. "You mistook me, signore. I meant no offense."

"How can I know what I have not been taught?" Matteo asked softly. The annoyance had faded, and was replaced with an expression of which the meaning was not lost on Kieran. She understood him full well.

Heat gathered in her belly, and she was grateful for the blush that already stained her cheeks, lest Rogan and Emeline see how his words had further unsettled her. It was a quote from his book and a fresh challenge all in one.

"Then I shall teach you to ride," Kieran offered, wanting to make up for her nasty comment. Memories of her mother, Camille, sprang to mind and the story she'd often told of the day she and Kieran's father, Patrick, first met. Patrick had been new to England, as well, and as he was a sea-merchant, had never ridden a horse. He'd asked Camille to teach him, and so began their courtship.

But this was not the beginnings of a love affair.

"You would teach me?" Matteo repeated, incredulous. "I do not know about that. You are, after all, and do not trouble with the observation, a woman."

"Indeed, she most certainly is, and a lady, too," Rogan said, and he caught his sister's eye. His own gleamed green and bright with what looked like amusement. He grinned at her in a way that reminded her of when they were young. "Go along, *sidhe gaoithe*. Go show Signore de Gama who is the finest horsewoman in all of England. We'll see you at dinner."

Rogan and Emeline turned and climbed the steps into the great mansion. Matteo reluctantly allowed a servant to take his cello, watching as the big leather case was gently hauled inside.

Nilo wandered off in the direction of the stables, whistling a nameless tune, his hands jammed in his pockets, his face turned toward the sun.

Matteo turned his attention to Kieran and arched a brow. "*Sidhe gaoithe?* This is not a language I know."

"'Tis a name from my childhood. My da used to call me by it. It means 'wind fairy' in Gaelic."

A slow smile curved his lips as his gaze drifted over her, slowly perusing every detail. Kieran knew what he saw: A rigidly formal girl in a traveling gown of fine, thick champagne velvet and an indigo cloak embroidered with golden threads. Her auburn hair was twisted into a taut coil behind her nape to keep it smooth and sleek as she traveled. Everything about her spoke of unyielding control, tightly laced garments, tightly coifed hair, stiff smiles, and an even stiffer demeanor.

"'Twas a long time ago," she added unnecessarily.

"You were a different girl then, eh?"

"I suppose I was."

"And now? Who are you, now?"

"*Cuore solitario*, no?" Kieran answered, trying to sound offhand. She turned away lest he read her eyes, knowing what they would show, all too well. Especially to Matteo. Must he read her so effortlessly? He left her with no-where to hide.

Horses' hooves clip-clopped on the cobblestones as the stable hands led them up the long drive. They came into view, three gorgeous coppery beasts, shining, sleek muscular flanks, long legs elegantly prancing, flashy white blazes between big, expressive eyes.

Nilo stopped one of the hands and took a gelding by the reins. He swung up into the saddle with the easy motion of one accustomed to the task.

The other two horses were brought to Matteo and Kieran, and she dismissed the lads. She placed the reins of the gentler gelding in Matteo's hands and led her horse to the hitching post, tethered it there and re-turned to Matteo's side.

He stood there, rooted it seemed, head tilted up and eyes wide as he assessed the beast. "It is a big ani-mal, no?"

"You do not have to do this," she told him. "'Tis not a challenge for you to ride with me. I can call for a coach to be brought around and have you driven there."

"I have never been so close to such an animal," he said, not moving. He eyed the beast warily, holding the reins in his hands as if poised to drop them at any moment. "Does it bite?"

"No, not him. He's a lovely boy, and far too sweet to bite," Kieran replied. She moved closer and rubbed the horse's face with her hand, then her cheek. It was good to be home in England, and once again in the quiet company of her beloved animals. "This is Lyman. He'd rather graze in a meadow than gallop across one, and he's more likely to nudge your pockets looking for carrots than bite that hand that might feed him."

Matteo took a step toward Lyman and cautiously patted his thick neck. Lyman turned his head and looked at Matteo with mellow eyes. Matteo grew bolder and rubbed the side of his face.

"He is majestic," Matteo said reverently. "Look at the shape of his ears, the bones of his face, the proud line of his head. He is the exact shade of burnished bronze: such shine and depth to the color. And his eyes. They are wise, no?" Matteo stroked upward to the horse's ear, ran a finger over the shape of it, touched the fine, velvety smooth hairs that grew along the thin edges. The horse snorted and nodded his head, his ear twitched, flattened, pricked, and then twitched again. Matteo watched this, fascinated, and breathed, "*Magnifico.*"

Strange how Kieran would be so moved. It was not *she* he touched or admired, and yet, a compliment had never felt so personal, so meaningful. He saw the beauty in what she held most dear, and it touched her, deeply. Suddenly she felt ashamed of her earlier behavior, felt another stab of compassion for this man for whom everything was new and strange.

As if of its own volition, her hand reached out and touched Matteo's face, just as he did to Lyman. He turned and looked at her, and she stood there, rooted, cupping his cheek. "Do not worry, signore," she whispered. "You will be fine here in England. I swear it."

"You will see to it yourself?" he asked her, his lips curving upward.

"'Tis the least I can do. You saved my life."

"I did not know you from anyone else when I pulled you from the canal. How can you say I saved *your* life, when you were nothing but a stranger to me?"

"Your philosophy aside, 'tis not the canal I speak of. That night, I had scarcely any life left in me to lose," she confessed softly. "'Twas your story that I meant."

Kieran saw the realization flare in his eyes, like a lantern's wick turned up. And like a flame, Kieran felt his skin grow hotter. She wanted to pull away, to take her words back with something snide that would make him stop looking at her like that, but she could not.

Not when she had read his words, felt the poignancy of the world he'd created on the page, and understood his deeper meaning.

"We are a pair, are we not?" Matteo whispered. "Two lonely hearts." Matteo reached up and covered her hand with his own. His skin was warm, so warm it felt as if he heated her bones. "You will be fine here in England, as well. I will not leave until that is so."

~9~

Kieran dropped her hand. Beneath the thin leather of her glove, she could still feel the pressing warmth of his bare skin.

Leave. Yes, of course he would leave England. Had he not told her how easily he could walk away? He was a man who did not form attachments to people.

Strangely, however, the thought discomfited her. And why should that be, when she had been telling herself that she was exactly that same sort of person?

She knew the answer, if she wanted to be honest

with herself: Matteo de Gama was the first person who understood her.

To cover her discomfort, she began giving Matteo the basics of horseback riding. When she finished, he did as she instructed and grasped the pommel, placed his foot in the stirrup and swung up into the saddle without a hitch.

"You lie, signore. Surely you have done that before," she said. As she spoke, she could hear her mother's voice recounting the first time she'd met Patrick, teaching him to ride, speaking nearly the exact same words. And her father's answer, a foreshadowing of their life together. *I would never lie to you, my lady.*

Flustered, she turned away and moved to her own mount, hooked her knee around the horn and arranged her skirts and cloak. She expertly wheeled the horse around and took off at a slow canter. Rather than having to look into those velvet brown, amber-flecked eyes, she called out directions over her shoulder. "Using your knees, signore. Off you go. A sure hand on the reins, but not pulling at the bit."

Before she knew it, Matteo had urged his horse into a canter that matched her own, and he was riding alongside her. He moved easily in the saddle, a man accustomed to motion. He held the reins a bit firmly, but other than that, managed very well.

Kieran bit back the words of praise that sprang to her lips. This was all far too reminiscent of a love that bloomed from just this sort of experience. *Look at you, Patrick. You're riding well.*

I've had the best of teachers.

She sent him a glance certain to freeze any camaraderie he thought they might be sharing. He returned it with a grin, and damn him, a wink. That blasted man could read her better than the written word.

Kieran urged her mount to pick up the pace, leaving

Matteo behind until he did the same. Soon enough
he was alongside her once again. She looked at him and
noticed that he had adjusted his grip on the reins, now
holding them just as she did. He was also moving his
hips the way she was, his back as straight as hers, held at
the same angle. A natural mimic and a quick learner, she
observed. Well, she'd give him something to imitate.

In a single, fluid motion, she leaned forward, thumped
the horse's flanks, and slapped the reins against his neck.
The horse leapt into motion and took off at a greedy
gallop. Her hood flew back and Kieran leaned into the
rushing, cold wind. Riding on the horse as if they were
one, she felt the familiar surge of power and liberation.

It was her bliss: the thundering of hooves, the frantic,
rhythmic pace, and the wind that tore at her face, stole
her breath, and filled her with its wild freedom. She felt
the knot at the nape of her neck coming loose, and so
with one hand she reached up and pulled out the comb
so it would not fall out and get lost.

Her hair tore out of the hairpins and spilled free and
was caught in the wind, tumbling auburn tresses against
her shoulders and back. She urged the horse even faster,
caught up in the sensation that if she just went fast
enough, she could outrun herself.

She kept going, beyond the formal gardens, the
groves of fruit trees, and long rows where vegetables
would grow in the spring. She rode on until there were
no more signs of human interference, where the land
grew rough and natural, open meadows and clusters of
trees, where wild roses grew and no one pruned or
plucked them.

She had a sudden thought: what if Matteo tried to
keep up and was thrown? Bloody selfish fool, she berated
herself. What if he broke his neck?

Yanking back on the reins, she wheeled her mount
around and saw him coming up behind her. He had the

horse moving at a pretty good clip, and managed quite well, bouncing in the saddle with an easy, fluid motion. Nilo rode behind him, looking amused.

Matteo's hat had flown off, leaving his dark hair to fly in the wind, and his black leather coat hung open, revealing the quilted, red lining. His shirt was flattened against his chest, and Kieran noticed how well made his body was: long, lean, and loose of limb; sinewy muscles and narrow waist. His shoulders were not too wide, but were masculine in their breadth. He looked every inch the man she knew him to be: artist, seducer, swindler, and philosopher, a devilishly handsome man with a seductively sensual mouth.

He reined his horse beside her, grinning. He patted the neck of his mount and brought his eyes up to Kieran's. His expression softened, grew contemplative, and slid over her from the top of her head to the abundance of skirts draped over the side of her mare's flank.

She was aware of her bedraggled state, unbound hair streaming to her waist, hairpins dangling from curling tresses. Lifting a hand to her hood, she made to pull it up, but Matteo reached out a hand, holding it in the air.

"No, do not cover yourself. I beg you. You are lovely as you sit there, the color high on your cheeks, eyes bright, your hair framing your face. I have seldom seen anything more exquisite."

Kieran slowly lowered her hand, held the reins in one and the pommel in the other. She was breathless from the ride, and his words did not help her regain its regularity.

Matteo leaned back in his saddle and gazed around at the English countryside. Sunlight peeked from behind iron gray clouds and cast long, shining streams of light to the grass that rolled over the wide open meadow. Snow remained in shady patches and frosted evergreens. Naked blackthorn trees hunched in knotty tangles off in the distance, and great oaks towered beyond them, their majestic bare limbs sketched against the sky like a line drawing. Wild rose bushes abounded, their spiked, sleeping branches rising out of clumps of snow.

He turned his regard to Kieran once more. "You fit here. Just so. You are part of this land. Wildly beautiful, a study in contrasts. Look at you," he said softly, his low voice like the deep tenor of his cello. "Alabaster skin and dark, red-brown hair, eyes that change from the river to the ocean to the sky. And your lips, as pink as the roses that lie idle, waiting for spring."

He flustered her with his words, and more than that, with the way he looked at her. He continued on as if he didn't know the effect of his words. Or perhaps he did, and he fully intended just that.

"You are like this land. Dormant, fallow, frozen in a season that will end in its own due time. Seeing you here, I see you as you are meant to be, a priceless painting set in the perfect frame." He cocked his head, and those amber lights in his eyes glowed. "But your spring is coming. The rivers will run high again, the days will grow long and warm, and you, my *bella*, will flower."

He turned back to Nilo and grinned. "This is not Africa, and not Venice. But it is wondrous, no?"

Nilo returned his smile and picked up the hem of his cloak. "Not cold in Africa."

"*Si*, it is cold, and stark, too." Matteo glanced around once again and his gaze landed on Kieran. "But also smoldering with the promise of what lies beneath. I am most interested to see her in full bloom."

Matteo said all these things in the manner of a man speaking fact. There was no wooing tone, no faltering, no hesitation. He lavished her with his attention, made her feel like she was not simply beautiful, but as if she were a poem, a song, a sculpture. The breeze blew briskly against her skin, but her cheeks burned with heat. And it was not the frosty air that made her body tremble.

He might not know England's terrain, but he was pointed westward and he urged his mount into motion. "Come, my lonely one, and show me this house."

A little dazed, Kieran nudged her horse and rode.

He'd said he could seduce her; she was beginning to believe him.

Kieran made a serious vow to proceed with far more caution.

They passed the outbuildings of the former ancestral home of an impoverished baron and came upon the house.

It looked like a giant had shaken everything loose: the shutters hung at odd angles beside huge, arched windows; bare patches and dark damp holes dotted the roof where slate tiles had long since gone missing; the chimneys traced a jagged drawing against the sky where brick had fallen away. The house bore several terraces on the lower level, and they all leaked into the grass that grew around them, being slowly swallowed by nature's growth. The upper balconies listed slightly, their marble balustrades vested with moss and lichen.

"'Tis only the outside, signore. I cannot imagine the interior." Kieran let go of the reins so she could slide her gloved hands into her muff. The temperature was falling and the wind picked up as night approached; it was time to ride back. "My brother will not be offended if you decline, and Emeline will surely understand."

Matteo dismounted awkwardly and held the reins in his hands as if he did not know what to do. Kieran held out a hand and he tossed them to her, his eyes quickly moving back to the house. "No, no. The duchess is correct. It is wonderful. Look at the lines, the shape. And those windows. And all of the stone, it is no doubt from this land, eh? That stone, see how it sparkles? That is the mica in the stone, catching light. Very nice. And all of the marble, see it on the balustrades, the sills, the terrace walls? She is right; it could be grand."

"The roof leaks, half the window panes are missing, and the stone crumbles away."

"A new roof, repaired glass, repointed stone. Masonry work to make the chimneys like new. Rebuild the terraces, firm up the foundation, new columns beneath the balconies. Inside, refinished floors and replastered walls, restore the marble, tear away what may be rotted and replace it with new. Add new details, maybe a library if there is not one, some moldings, frescos, some columns perhaps. Make it grand. Better than before. It could be splendid."

He turned and looked around to the gaping, sagging stables, the stone carriage house that was nothing more than a stone shell. Beyond that a stream burbled with snowmelt, and above it swayed the long, naked branches of weeping willows and towering, stately oaks. In front of the house, in the center of the circular driveway, a long defunct marble and copper fountain stood moldering amongst a tangle of bramble bushes that had once been a manicured garden.

"Yes, wonderful," he murmured, and watching him, Kieran knew that as Matteo looked around to the house and gardens, he saw it all finished.

Kieran tried to see what he saw, the possibility of beauty, grandeur, and the restoration of a once majestic home. But all she saw was a gloomy, spooky, mildewed house that loomed large against the darkening sky.

"Yes. I will do it. It will be an amusement, I think," Matteo said, his voice brimming with enthusiasm. "We should go. *Andiamo!*" He swung up into the saddle once again.

Matteo met her gaze in the fading light, his eyes

sparkling. She could not help but feel his excitement; it was contagious. She did, however, try to speak reason. No matter his vision, the house was simply in ruins, and he was agreeing to take on the project after looking at it for only a few short minutes.

"You have not even been inside. What if 'tis even worse? What if there are things that cannot be fixed?" she asked him, hoping he would at least agree to come back again tomorrow for a more thorough inspection.

"When there is such beauty on the outside, I cannot help but think I will find something worth saving on the inside," he said to her with a grin, his tone heavy with meaning. He kicked his mount into motion, calling over his shoulder to her, "Come, lonely one. We are expected for dinner."

Kieran rode behind him, Nilo at her side. She shot him a look of exasperation and Nilo laughed out loud. "Yes, Miss Keerahn, he does good for you."

And he, too, rode off, leaving her to ride after them both.

When they arrived back at the manse, the hour had grown late. Carriages were lined up in front, a sign that they had company. Footmen and drivers huddled nearby inside a large carriage, the lantern illuminating them as they played cards and chatted amongst themselves.

Candlelight burned in the windows, a golden, wavering light that beckoned them inside. She could hear the sounds of music, and muted female laughter.

Nilo hopped down and took the reins of their horses, leading them away as Kieran and Matteo hesitated in front of the granite steps. She ran a hand down the front of her traveling gown, knowing that she was wrinkled and mussed, her wind-torn hair spilling down her back.

She would look lust-ravaged, she thought.

And now she would breeze into the house with him at her arm, and no one would realize that Nilo had been with them the entire time.

Again a feeling of pride took her, that whomever visited them might think her freshly arrived from a tussle with the handsome foreigner, just as she had felt when Rogan caught her in Matteo's arms.

It ought to feel scandalous, obscene. She should be worried for what others would think, for her reputation, for not bringing the slightest disgrace to Rogan's name.

It didn't. It felt free and careless, two things she most certainly wasn't. It felt wanton and decadent and indecent, sobriquets that no one would ever assign to her.

At least, not before tonight.

She turned to Matteo, awed by his masculine beauty. His dark hair hung in shiny waves to his shoulders, shorter than the English fashion, and unbound by English convention. His brooding dark eyes gleamed with the richness of chocolate and the amber warmth of whiskey beneath silky dark brows that moved with his every expression. His forehead was high, smooth, his cheekbones defined the hollows and shadows of his face. His lips were full, sensual, and though she was not an artist, she wished she could sketch their line.

"Kiss me," she quietly commanded him.

In the dimness, with only the distant glow of candles touching his skin, bathing half his face in shadow, she saw his surprise. He laughed, a low, warm sound. "Here? Now? Little lonely one, you are the most delightful puzzle."

She relished the audacity that gripped her, laughed as she spoke, feeling freer than she had in years. "The people inside will think you have done so, anyway. If I am to have the reputation, I do feel it should be deserved."

Matteo grinned down at her. "It is true that I have yet

to establish any notoriety here in London. I have much work to do."

"You should busy yourself to the task, signore. You do not want the locals here to get the wrong impression of you."

He took a few steps to move closer to her, and her breath caught. Again she reminded herself that she was inexperienced in this game. He caught her fingers and twined them in his own, his skin so warm she could feel it through her gloves.

"It is very kind of you to assist me in this task, *cuore solitario*. Are you certain you wish to go down the path of destruction?"

"I am not afraid of the opinions of others, signore. In fact, perhaps 'tis time for them to wonder if the Venetian artist has melted the ice princess."

"Has he?"

"Sadly, no."

"Can he?" He moved closer still, until she could feel his pleasantly hot breath on her skin.

"Are you the man who penned the story of the woman who seeks her revenge?"

"You know I am."

"Then until this day, signore, you are more the man for this task than any other."

Matteo hesitated. In the shadows he looked intense. His fingers tightened on hers. "How many men have kissed your lips?"

"Not a soul."

"Not one?"

"No."

"Why is that? Why have you set about making your life so lonely?"

"'Tis easier that way," she whispered.

His face reflected that yes, he did know that it was

much simpler to keep to oneself than to seek out human attachments.

"So why me? I am not the sort of man a woman such as you entertains."

"Perhaps that is why. You will not ask to court me. You could kiss me, and walk away." Even as she spoke her cheeks burned with her words. Never before had she been so bold.

He leaned in closer, his breath on her lips now, the humid caress of them like a promise. She could feel the heat pumping from him as from a furnace; she could smell him, the scents of leather and amber rosin, ink and essence of bergamot.

His lips were so close that only a fingertip's breadth separated them.

She did not lean forward into the incipient kiss. He would come to her.

He hovered there, for only a moment, then pulled back. In the darkness and the candlelight, he was creamy skin and broody eyes and roaming, dark shadows. "No."

"What?" She nearly succumbed to the sensations dragging at her, hot blood, cold wind, his hand tangled with hers, his breath on her skin, touching her lips. "No?"

Matteo took a step back and withdrew his hand. He glanced from the servants in a visitor's carriage who had long since abandoned their card game to watch them, to the house where they had no doubt been expected long ago.

Kieran shivered before him, and the cold breeze carried her warmth and her scent, lured him to pull her close, to wrap her in his arms and do exactly as she asked. Even in the darkness he could see her confusion, and the seeds of doubt being sown in her mind.

He ran a hand through his hair, looked away from her.

How had he gotten to this place, where nothing made sense, even the simple act of kissing a willing woman? In a new country where everything was different, surely this should be the ground on which he stood firm. This was where he knew what to do and how to proceed.

Or at least, it had been before Kieran Mullen looked into his soul and appealed to a long-buried honor he'd comfortably lived without for more years than he could recall.

He forced himself to focus on the truth of the matter.

She wanted a distraction from her pain. She did not want him, the man.

He'd not let some young girl with sad eyes and a beautiful face make him suddenly feel like he could be her hero, her savior, or God help him, something more that he dared not put to words.

He'd show her who she was toying with.

Matteo took another step back, wishing he could stop smelling her perfume. Why should that sweetly mysterious scent make him want to cry? "Do not make the mistake of thinking I am helping you with your revenge because I have nothing better to do. Worse, do not think I am helping you because you're beautiful, because as lovely as you are, you are not comely enough to engender generosity in my black, bastard's heart."

He hoped she was listening, and even more, he hoped she realized that in this moment, he had never been more honest with another human being. "I want something from you. Make no mistake: I never have done anything for anyone unless there has been something in it for me."

~ 10 ~

"What do you want?" Kieran asked in a whisper.

Standing before her, shrouded in black leather and the shades of nighttime, Matteo suddenly seemed distant and different.

And it occurred to Kieran that she did not know him at all.

Indeed, she had only encountered a player of parts. She had met the artist, the cellist, the seducer, and the swindler. She knew the sound of his instrument, the feel of his lips on her neck, the story he translated for her, but she had yet to meet the man.

The night seemed to grow colder by the second. Embarrassment gripped her. Had she just begged for his kisses and admitted that no other man had been allowed such liberty?

She wanted to slap his lean cheeks, flay him with a few well-chosen words. But damn herself, her eyes stung with his rejection and her humiliation combined. Not comely enough to warrant his generosity?

More like inept, awkward, artless. Why didn't he say what he really meant?

"Kieran?"

Light beamed across the darkness, and fell in a long, golden rectangle in the space that separated Kieran and Matteo, illuminating the chasm between them. Emeline stood in the open door. Kieran turned and looked at her sister-in-law as if in a trance. Around them the night air grew colder still, sighing through the empty boughs and whispering in the shadows.

"Kieran, we received unexpected guests. Will you be dressing for dinner and joining us?" Emeline smiled at Matteo de Gama. "And signore, I have had your trunks moved into a guest room for your convenience. Please do stay the night, and we will see to your accommodations in the morn."

Nilo came up the driveway and smiled affably at Emeline as he took up his post at the front door, waiting, as always, on Kieran.

Kieran hesitated. She brought her attention once more to Matteo, hoping that he would say something that would make her not feel like such a fool.

He did not speak. Instead, he swept into a formal bow at her feet, somehow making the gesture all at once a request for forgiveness and a mocking jibe.

She wanted to run to her rooms and hide. But she would not do that. Kieran had spent three long years preserving her pride by not allowing others to see her truest self. She'd not let this foreign romancer become her undoing.

Kieran turned and swept up the granite steps, her demeanor as coldly haughty as a queen sailing through a sea of commoners.

But she kept her eyes downcast, hiding them from anyone who might look at her and know that she had never, at any other space in time, felt more alone than she did in that instant.

Candlelight lit the long dining room, and on either end of the mahogany table, twin fires blazed. Soft moiré silk in a delicate buttery gold covered the walls, dotted now with a thousand rainbows scattered there by the crystal chandeliers that hung above the table. Tall, brass candelabras sat atop the gleaming mahogany surface, boasting long tapered candles. Creamy porcelain plates were set out, rimmed in gold and painted with the ducal crest that spanned generations of Bradburns, a legacy as tattered as it was enduring.

The room was fragrant with beeswax and wood smoke, perfume, and roasted meats. Seated at the head of the table sat Rogan, his beautiful wife at his side. Several other strangers sat at the long table, all clustered near their host as they drank wine and laughed at some silly story being recounted by one of the men.

Matteo de Gama noticed immediately that though he'd bathed and changed, he was not going to fit into this crowd. They were dressed as if for a ball, the women in silken gowns that exposed their shoulders and the high curves of their breasts, the men in waistcoats and jackets, with lacy collars and cravats tied tightly about their throats.

Jewelry dripped from the women: their ears, fingers, wrists and necks, pendants dipping into the hollows of their wobbling breasts in a way that was mesmerizingly dangerous. The men wore jewelry, too, rings on their fingers and gems encrusting their clothing. Even Rogan, who dressed rather simply, wore a single signet ring on his right hand, proclaiming him lord and master over the woman at his side, the mansion, and from what the sailors told Matteo aboard the ship, nearly half of England, as well.

Matteo stepped into the room, feeling like an intruder. He wore narrow leather breeches and high boots, his finest black leather coat and a white, billowy shirt beneath it. No cravat, no jewels, no silk, and certainly no lace.

Matteo realized he had probably never looked more

like himself than he did right then, a gambler amongst gentlemen.

It was going to be a long five years if he stayed in London.

Rogan rose to greet him. "Come in, signore, and meet our guests." One by one Rogan gestured to a duke and his duchess, an earl who was accompanied by his daughter, a dowager countess, and several ladies. Matteo bowed to them in turn, rising as Rogan finished his introductions. "Everyone, this is our guest, Signore Matteo de Gama of Venice."

"Venice!" exclaimed the one of the women. Matteo tried to recall her name. Jane, Dowager Countess of Perth. Yes, that was it. He met her attention with his own, noting her well-preserved beauty, her hair a gleaming mix of blonde and silver, her eyes bright blue. She pressed her hands to the full, upper curves of her breasts, smiling as she spoke to him. "I traveled there with the earl some years before he passed. What a city. No doubt you will be anxious to return after a few weeks of our English winter."

Her words struck like a poisoned barb to his heart. Venice, with its blue canals and golden sunlight, his comfortable *casino*, his elegant *burchiello*. They had never seemed farther away, nor had he ever longed for his home more. Five years. An eternity.

Relying heavily on his ability to keep his thoughts and emotions from his face, he smiled and swept into another bow before the dowager. "True enough, my lady, but I am finding England most intriguing. I think I shall stay abroad awhile. Perhaps visit Paris, Munich, and Madrid before I return."

"How wonderful," the countess enthused, her gaze traveling over him in a way that suggested she might be interested in just how long he stayed in England, and more to the point, where he chose to spend his nights.

Before another second has passed, she proved Matteo correct.

"Come dear boy, and sit by me. You're a handsome thing, aren't you? And your accent; 'tis most charming." She patted the seat of the chair beside her and gestured to a servant to fill the empty wine glass. As he sat, she reached over to hand him his linen napkin, her barely confined breasts brushing his arm as she did so.

Another of the ladies leaned forward to capture his attention. She ran the tip of her tiny tongue over her bottom lip as she met his eyes. Yellow ringlets bounced as she cocked her head to the side, and laughter filled each word as she spoke. "How do you find England, signore?"

A vision flashed into his mind: Kieran on horseback, her disheveled hair gleaming in the muted light, her oval face flushed, her eyes like the sea, full of storms and mysterious depth. She had been as a portrait, as wildly beautiful as the meadow framing her.

"Transfixing," Matteo said softly.

As if bidden by his thoughts, Kieran entered the room. The men rose to greet her.

She'd dressed for a war, he thought. Silken battle armor and jeweled shields. Her red silk gown displayed her curves, pressed her breasts up and nipped tight on her narrow waist, the skirt a billowing, scarlet cloud.

It contrasted starkly against her skin, like ivory dipped in blood. She wore rubies, set in gold and accented with pearls, the luster of which could not compare to the slim neck they circled.

Matteo ran his tongue over his teeth, recalled the precise taste of that neck, well displayed beneath the smooth coils of her rich, dark hair.

And without having to be near her, he knew she smelled of jasmine and warm sandalwood.

He also knew, with the intimate knowledge of having

been at the sharp end of it, that she wore a menacing black dagger beneath those voluminous folds of silk.

His eyes slid down her form, and he envisioned the weapon on her left thigh. It would be above the garter of her stocking, black leather against naked white skin.

The image was enough to have him quickly regaining his seat, for the snug leather breeches he wore offered him no room for discretion. He watched her, his blood burning, fully aroused, willing her to look at him.

Kieran could not help it, it seemed, for she brought her eyes to his. Matteo did not veil his expression, but let all the heat and passion he felt for her show in his eyes, not caring who saw.

Kieran drew her breath and held it, lips parted, eyes wide. Coming to herself, she turned her head and lifted her wine glass, sipping to cover her discomfort.

Matteo could not draw his gaze away. He'd never seen her look more remote, a princess upon a mountain's peak, lofty and unattainable. That was the facade she showed the world, however, and Matteo already knew for a sham. This was the girl who'd lunged at his pistol, wishing for death.

This was also the girl who'd sent him a letter scented with her perfume.

She was altogether compelling, a galvanizing combination of wide-eyed innocence and world-weary disdain, a dagger hidden beneath her skirts and poetry buried in her heart.

And yes, he admitted to himself, he stared at her simply because she was the most beautiful thing he'd ever seen.

The room had fallen silent. Everyone at the table watched him as he watched Kieran.

To hell with them all.

"My lady," Matteo addressed Kieran. "You are looking especially well this evening."

"My thanks," Kieran said flatly, not looking at him as she spoke. Kieran turned to the man who sat at her side. "What entertainment have I missed whilst on holiday, my lord?"

Ah, so he had stung her deeply with his refusal and his words. And now she would favor another man with her attention, turning her bare, white shoulder to him in a gesture of dismissal.

Matteo narrowed his eyes at the ineffectual dolt who apparently shared Matteo's appreciation of Kieran's beauty, for the simpleton leaned over readily enough, his eyes on her breasts rather than her eyes.

"London had never been duller, I can assure you, but things are looking much more promising," he replied.

An unimaginative reply from a drooling clod. In his native tongue, Matteo silently flayed the man with insults to his pale appearance, his lack of cranial matter, his questionable manhood.

Lord Chesney, Rogan had introduced him. This lord sat with a plump girl at his side whose resemblance of him labeled her clearly as his daughter. He appeared to have no wife, and ogled Kieran as if she was being served for the evening meal. For this alone, Matteo hated him. But he also hated him for his clipped accent that spoke of a university education, his lordly titles, and his ancestral wealth.

"Lord Chesney," Matteo said his name with gusto, thickening his accent ever so slightly. "I knew a Chesney in Venice. He was English, on an extended holiday, and was a real . . . how do you say . . . *figlio di puttana*, eh, a *cacasodo*." A son of a bitch, who thinks his feces does not stink. Matteo's smile grew genuine as he saw the man's face light with interest. "I am not certain of the English translation, but let me assure you, he was quite fun to play cards with, eh?"

Rogan made a noise that sounded a little like a snort

as he sipped his wine, and when he lowered the glass he looked down the table to Matteo. "Lord Chesney is our closest neighbor. He apparently saw our retinue of carriages in London and immediately set about spreading the word of our return. 'Tis why we are so fortunate to have their company this evening."

Rogan's expression spoke volumes to a man like Matteo, who was accustomed to reading others. It said that he cared little for Chesney, and even less for Chesney's perusal of his sister's bosom. It also said that he spoke enough Italian to know the gist of what Matteo had said.

"I was surprised to find you with guests, Your Grace. In Venice we would have given the travelers a few days to settle in at home and rest," Matteo said.

"Right chap, well, you see," blustered Chesney, his ruddy face turning a darker shade of red. "I only came with an offer of dinner in the near future, and to see how the voyage turned out. I say, what a horror this, the travails of the Duke of Westminster, and the unfortunate business of his ship catching fire whilst at sea. Made for a dreadful time. Just dreadful. What a blessing His Grace was able to make a rescue. Jolly good, that.

"We were just getting ready to leave, but His and Her Grace were so kind as to ask if we'd care to dine with them this evening, and so here we are."

Matteo glanced once more to Rogan, who said nothing but raised a brow the tiniest fraction, indicating to Matteo that the events leading to their guests' invitation had just been mightily skewed.

Two servants appeared in the doorway, both bearing huge arrangements of flowers, stunning white lilies that filled the room with their fragrance. One of the servants, a young woman, peeked around her burden. "Your Grace, a delivery. There are two cards, one for you, and one for Miss Kieran."

Rogan stood. "Thank you, Mary. Set them on the side table." He retrieved the cards, handed one to Emeline, and the other to Kieran.

"'Tis from Samuel Ellsworth, thanking us for our help in his time of need," Emeline said, and she set the card aside. A frown touched her brow, as if she were in deep thought.

Kieran held the note in her lap, unopened. With all eyes on her, she gave in and read the note. She looked at her brother, and said, "He has invited me to dine with him as his guest at a dinner with the king. I shall decline."

"He is powerful man, Ellsworth," Lord Chesney said. His florid face bore his dislike of the situation. He leaned in to Kieran to speak confidentially, but didn't bother to lower his voice. "Can't say I blame you for refusing the invite. Ellsworth is something of a libertine, if you ask me. Wouldn't want to sully your reputation being escorted about by a man such as he."

"It matters not," Kieran said, and she set the note aside. She looked disdainful, distant, and primly frigid. "I am not interested in being courted, by him or anyone."

"You'll refuse dinner with the king?" Chesney's daughter sent a pained glare in Kieran's direction, clearly contemplating the unfairness of being younger and of better birth, and yet not receiving like invitations. She folded her hands priggishly on the napkin that was spread across her plump belly and sniffed. "Such a courtship could make you a duchess in your own right. A woman your age should hardly sneer at his generous offer. And why call him a libertine, Papa, when he sends flowers and a card, just as a gentleman ought?"

Chesney patted his daughter on her shoulder. "Take my word for it. Just because a man knows how to behave as a gentleman, does not mean he comports himself as such at all times."

Kieran rose suddenly from her seat. The other men rushed to stand, and she waved them all away. "Forgive me, but I must seek some fresh air." She swept from the room without another word.

Matteo watched as Rogan sent his wife a worried look and excused himself to follow his sister.

And then Matteo suffered an eternity, waiting for Rogan to return.

"You really ought not made that comment about her age. She's obviously sensitive to that issue," Chesney said, chiding his daughter.

Matteo tried to ignore the pompous pontifications of the man and his distasteful offspring.

Inside Matteo a war waged, his base selfishness battling a burgeoning attachment to the sad, lonely girl.

Where would that lead? Matteo demanded of himself.

"Well, 'tis hardly a secret that she's put herself on the shelf," Chesney's daughter replied.

Jealous girl, Matteo thought. He turned away from them, his eyes landing on the showy flowers. He remembered Ellsworth on the ship. Another arrogant man who treated others with condescension and contempt. He could not imagine Kieran with a man like that. She deserved someone who understood her, not someone who wanted to decorate his arm with her, and keep her in his bed.

The thought had him clenching his fists.

Kieran inspired far too much affection in Matteo's greedy, self-indulgent heart. And if there was one thing that frightened Matteo de Gama, it was that sort of entanglement.

Many years ago, love had turned him into a beggar. Always begging for someone to love him, bringing his mother a flower, a sweet, a gift made of sticks and string.

She would take his offering and send him on his way, turning her attention once more to her latest lover.

"Kieran is very content with her life here," Emeline interjected. "If she chooses marriage, 'twill be because she is in love. Not all marriages need be made for the sake of titles and prestige, as my own proves."

Matteo, mired in his thoughts, scarcely heard them.

Matteo was many things. First and foremost, he was a fast learner. Begging for love turned to stealing for riches, a boy's true affection changed to a man's decadent lust, and above all, his selfishness preserved him.

So why, he wondered, did a troubled girl with a lost look in her eyes inspire such confusion?

He really should have taken Rogan up on the offer to go to France.

He really ought to have kissed her when she'd asked him to.

Rogan returned to the room, a frown creasing his brow. He smiled for his guests, but the frown remained. "Kieran is fine. She will likely not be returning to the meal, however. Perhaps the strain of travel has fatigued her."

"We should depart," the countess said, setting down her wine. "'Twas rude of us to accept the invitation to stay."

Matteo watched Rogan, saw his frustration, and understood. No one, it seemed, had penetrated Kieran's walls of ice. Except for Matteo. Why, however, should that prompt him into action?

It shouldn't, he answered himself. Yet, it did.

Against every selfish impulse urging him to stay where he was, to engage the dowager countess and convince her to finance a poor Venetian artist, Matteo rose from his seat and addressed Rogan. "Do you mind if I see to your sister, Your Grace? I think I can be of help."

Rogan hesitated until Emeline took his hand. He

nodded in the direction of the door which Kieran had exited. "Aye, please do."

Matteo didn't hesitate, but followed in her wake. Behind him he heard Rogan send a maid to fetch Nilo to chaperone. No trust would be afforded the Venetian romancer.

Through the open doors to a large parlor, he saw French doors left ajar. Cold, damp air wafted into the room, causing the curtains to sway and the fire to leap.

He found Kieran outside on the terrace. She stood facing the dark gardens, desolate and barren as they awaited spring's rebirth. The moon had shown its face, bathing Kieran in otherworldly light. It turned her skin to silver, her gown to black, and she appeared as a vision to him, a cold, untouchable beauty. She wore no cloak over those naked shoulders, and he imagined the mist that condensed on her skin, cool and moist. He saw her breath, pale clouds coming in small bursts, as if emanating from a dragon breathing ice instead of fire.

His hands immediately went to his coat, but he hesitated. He'd refused her kiss. She would refuse his coat, he knew it.

Matteo had insulted, rejected, and embarrassed her, because those lips had looked like the promise of heaven, and he was a man who walked in darker places.

He'd told her he wanted something. Well, so it seemed, he did.

In the core of his jaded heart, he realized the dangerous truth that no amount of denial seemed to obliterate: He wanted to warm her.

"This man, the Duke of Westminster, he is the man who hurt you, no?"

Kieran swung around, ready to claw at his face with her fingernails. How dare he speak that name so casually?

"Get away from me. Be gone. I cannot bear any more of your vicious games." Was that a sob in her voice? Kieran toughened her tone. "You have no right, and more important, no *cause* to continue lording your knowledge of my pain over me. Leave this home, signore, if you have an iota of compassion in your black, bastard's empty breast. Leave and never seek out my presence again."

He laughed, a smooth, easy, masculine chuckle that seemed to increase the very temperature.

It also heated Kieran's temper. She took two steps toward him and let her hand fly. It lashed out, cracking him across the face with a stinging slap.

Matteo did not flinch or otherwise react. With the same, ingratiating smile on his lean, dark face, he asked, "Do you feel better?"

Kieran swung around, gripping her injured hand to her chest. Her throat worked, her eyes burned, her hand hurt. And yet, he still mocked her. She heard him chuckle once more, and damn his eyes, move closer until she could feel his breath on her bare neck and shoulders.

She shivered.

"I have read your work, signore, and given great thought to your urgings that I seek revenge. I admit, for a time I was intrigued by the possibility, that perhaps it would make me feel different. Better." She looked down at her hands, starkly white in the moonlight. "But no more. Go away, signore. I do not wish to pursue a vendetta. I just want to be left alone. And by saying this, please know, I mean by you. I want you to leave me alone."

"You do not believe you will ever feel differently, do you? No matter what, this pain and loneliness is your burden to bear."

How could he know that, she wondered? Feeling as

she did was difficult enough, but he truly shredded her pride when she realized that with Matteo, she had no dignity left. "My thoughts are just that, signore: Mine."

"You said it yourself, my breast is empty. Heartless. I have little compassion," Matteo said.

So why was he persisting in pressing his company on her? She could not shake the humiliation of his refusal of her kiss. He confused and confounded her, and Kieran realized that she was behaving as she always did when she was frightened: She ran away, hid, shut down, and went cold.

Not this time.

"What do you want from me?"

"Your honesty," Matteo answered. "It is the one thing you give to no one else. I want it."

"Just like that, you will demand my innermost truth."

"I will. And you will give it to me."

"I will not give you anything. You waste your words and your time."

"Listen," he implored softly, and yet, it was a decree. "I have little compassion, it is true. I am not a man who feels the sorrow of others. I, myself, spent my early years mired in others' problems, and no more."

He took yet another step closer and she could feel his heat, his warm breath. She caught his scent, leather and bergamot, spices, and the faint, pleasant smell of wine on his breath as he continued speaking.

"And for this man, this Duke of Westminster, I have no compassion. I know men of his sort: selfish, indulgent, decadent. He is the man who harmed you, who hurt you, and as if oblivious of that, he sends you flowers, boldly offers to court you. For this man, *cuore solitario,* I have no compassion." Matteo dipped his head down to her ear, and whispered, "And neither should you."

Out of the corner of her eye she saw a shadow in the open door to the manse. Nilo lounged against the jamb, far enough away to lend privacy, but close enough if she were to call out.

Kieran turned and looked out over the vast, moonlit gardens and meadows. The earth slumbered beneath winter's cold spell, naked limbs reflected in frozen ponds.

Here was her England, as she'd always desired. She stood surrounded by her family's wealth and privilege, and was afforded every opportunity she could ever hope for.

On that one fateful night, Samuel, the Duke of Westminster, had taken everything away. Dashed her life to bits on his jagged soul, and shown her the deepest, darkest depths of her own ruthlessness. And then he sends flowers, as if he'd done nothing at all.

Matteo de Gama was right. Why should that man be spared while she was left mired in the wreckage that he created?

"What will you want from me, if I ask you to help me exact my revenge?" she asked softly.

"I already told you what I want. Your truth. Give it to me, and I will help you punish the Duke of Westminster."

She frowned and bit her lip. A cloud drifted in front of the moon, leaving them in nearly utter darkness. "In what way?"

"I want to know what he did to you. After that, little lonely one, I want you to tell me why you hid his actions from your family, when clearly they could, and would, have avenged your honor." Matteo leaned closer to her, and pressed his lips against the curve of her ear. His breath was warm and his words were softly spoken as he said, "And then I want you to tell me what will satisfy your sense of justice."

Kieran glanced once more across the meadows that stretched for miles, encompassing the mansion's vast property. Her foot tapped restlessly. Were she a woman of less control she would have run screaming over the frozen earth, tearing at her hair and clothes like a madwoman.

As if he knew it, Matteo took hold of her arm just above the top of her long gloves, his bare skin against hers.

"Do not fear. I will hold your secret safe," he said.

"You are a self-proclaimed liar. 'Tis insulting that you would ask for my trust."

"One liar to another," he answered with another laugh. "We ought to understand each other, no?"

Just as she'd been tempted on the ship to lay her soul bare at last and see if any relief would follow, Kieran felt the urge to confess everything.

But he was so smug, demanding, and knowing, and his confidence grated on her, because inside she felt so unsure and confused. She wanted to take him down a peg, yet even a slap in the face did not seem to accomplish that.

His words rang in her ears, and she recalled what he had said. Kieran decided that Matteo de Gama would not be the only one demanding confessions of truth.

"Whose problems were you mired in?"

The question took him off guard, just as she'd hoped.

His breathing stopped for a brief moment, and he cleared his throat as if uncomfortable. Good. If she were to be so unsettled and provoked, he ought to be, too. "Yes, tell me, signore, who managed to trouble you with their worries?"

He let go of her arm.

Kieran turned around to face him. In the moonlight he looked dangerous, his face comprised of lean, hard angles. His lips curled at the corners and he lifted a brow.

"You cannot hurt me with questions, and I am not afraid of my truths. If this is a game you want to play, I will play with you," he said.

"My mother was a beautiful whore. She only took men who could afford her to her bed, and there were many who afforded her. My father was one of her lovers, I know not which because my mother did not know. If she had, she surely would have loved to use me to fatten her coffers. Alas, she traded her sex for gifts, protection, and the very roof over our heads, and the only use she had for me was running errands for her. Her lovers were sometimes kind, sometimes cruel. A man who can hit a woman can certainly hit her child, no?"

"Forgive me," Kieran whispered, completely humiliated. "Say no more."

"No, it is nothing. You wanted to know, and here it is. I am a fatherless bastard and the son of a whore. I ran away at the age of eleven because I hated seeing my mother take men into her bed, and I truly hated being beaten by the men who despised me for looking at them as they came for my mother's sex.

"I was a ragged, bony, pathetic thief by the time my English lover took me in. And then, against everything I believed in but precisely as I was raised, I became just like my mother, trading my sex and my company for my lover's money." Matteo shrugged and in the dim light she could see the flash of his teeth as he grinned down on her, his smile full of self-mockery.

"Do not beg forgiveness for asking about my life. I am a man who knows who he is, good and bad, and who does not feel ashamed of it. I could keep it secret, but what would that change? And for that matter, what did telling you about it change?"

He reached out and ran his finger down the tiny stretch of her bare upper arm between gown and glove, and oddly, the gesture was comforting, one human to another, with nothing but honesty in its most visceral state. "See, my lonely one? The sky did not fall, the ocean did not rise and swallow us, and the ground did not shake. It is the truth of the matter, and no amount of secrecy changes anything."

"You are wrong. It changes everything," she said fiercely. And then she stopped speaking because a lump had formed where her voice once was. She could only repeat in a whisper, "Everything."

His hand kept stroking her arm in a rhythmic motion that was as soothing as the rocking swells of the sea.

"Tell me how it changes, Kieran."

It was the first time he'd used her name. Not *cara*, or *bella*, or *cuore solitario*, or his little lonely one, but Kieran. The way he said it, with his accent and inflection, made her name into something different, intimate. Something private between them. Just like this moment.

And she hoped that this wasn't the seduction he'd warned her about. It would hurt too much if this wasn't real.

"Tell me," he urged.

"Why did you refuse my kiss?" she asked. No matter that it revealed how much it wounded her, she needed to know.

"Because I wanted it far too much. I could lose myself against those lips," he answered softly. He hesitated as if he wanted to say something more, but finally just said, "Tell me. What changes?"

She glanced around, feeling trapped and afraid, and completely unable to break free. Inside her the battle raged on, and beneath it all she felt an odd stirring as she imagined Matteo de Gama losing himself at all, much less against her lips. Bringing her gaze back to his, she forced herself to answer his demand. "If I told you, or anyone, I would be seen differently.

"My pride," she whispered. "'Tis all I have left of that night: my pride, my privacy. 'Tis the one thing he cannot take from me if I keep silent."

A gust of wind kicked up, whistling through the naked tree branches and sending dead leaves skittering across the terrace. Somewhere far away, she heard an owl's muffled hooting. She pulled her arm out of his grasp.

Kieran shivered and closed her eyes. She seemed to sway on her feet, all sense of balance and surety dissipated like melted snow, leaving a cold, muddy mess in its wake. And she felt like she was mired down in it, sinking. Kieran wished for brandy, or a sleeping potion, or perhaps even death. Yes, death, where decisions are not made and mistakes are forgotten and the only reality is black, peaceful nothingness.

Suddenly, warmth enveloped her as Matteo wrapped his coat around her. She smelled the leather mixed with his scent, fresh bergamot and spice. It hung heavily to her knees, and the quilted lining, a soft, thick cotton, felt like a blanket against her bare shoulders.

And then, like magic, she wasn't cold or alone.

Kieran opened her eyes and looked at him in the moonlight, as if gazing upon a stranger for the first time. Danger exuded from his every pore, and without his coat she saw his long and lean body. The contours of his face stood out strongly, defined by the silvery light in planes and hollows, his hooded eyes dark and brooding.

Here stood a man who answered to no one, who'd known no love in his life, not even his own mother's. A self-proclaimed bastard, an admitted liar and cheat.

Here stood a man who did not fear truth, she thought. Not his own, and not hers. He might manipulate the truth to serve him, but he did not fear its reality.

If the past three years had taught her anything, it was that silence did not equal peace.

And as if she stood on the precipice of a great cliff, Kieran decided to jump.

"My cousin, Simon, told me he would take me for a carriage ride around London. 'Twas a dream come true. You see, I'd longed for England all my life. I was raised in the islands, on Barbados. 'Tis a beautiful place, and my life was happy enough, but I was not content. I was a spoilt child, never satisfied, I suppose, and I'm sorry for it. My mum and da deserved a better, more grateful daughter than the one they raised.

"My heart, my dreams, they were in England. I longed to come here, to find an English lord who would love me, and make me a lady, perhaps a countess or a baroness. I wanted to make a family here, raise them in a home that had known other generations. In short, I wanted all the things my mother left behind.

"And so when Rogan came here to seek his inheritance, I accompanied him. I fell ill on the passage, and was confined to bed for weeks. Once well, I was eager to see London, the city that had held my interest for so many years. And so I forswore my vow to wait for Rogan, and I accepted my cousin's invitation." Despite the cold, her cheeks burned, like her eyes, her throat. Her heart.

"What a petulant, spoilt girl I was," she said softly. "And what a consummate actor Simon was. I never doubted him for a moment. He was all things English: polish and pomp and aristocratic manners.

"He took me because Rogan had taken Emeline, but

I did not know that. Once I was in his carriage, I realized my folly. He immediately changed his demeanor. He tossed my maid out with a note to lure Rogan to danger, and turned to me with eyes that were frighteningly bright. I fought him, with all I had. Trying with all my might to jump from the carriage. I was certain that wherever he was bent on taking me, I did not want to go."

She closed her eyes, remembering. It seemed like yesterday, the careening of the carriage, the rattle of the wheels bouncing over uneven cobblestones and ruts. Simon's bulk blocking the door, his hands easily holding back her attack, and his initial amusement rapidly turning to rage when she bit and kicked and clawed him.

"By the time we got to the house, he was furious. He dragged me inside and threw me across the room. There were other men there, and yes, Samuel Ellsworth was one of them. Simon told him that I was in need of a little humbling." Her voice cracked like ice in water. "And so it began."

Kieran wavered, unsteady on her feet, unsure in her heart. A secret protected by pride and preserved in shame is not one easily let go. Sensing her mood, Matteo came even closer, until she could feel the heat from his body.

"He stripped me, naked." All she could manage was the barest whisper. "No one but my maid and my mum had seen my flesh since I was a babe. But there I was, exposed to those men. I tore down my hair and tried to cover myself with it, and they laughed and threatened to cut it off. I was certain they would rape me."

Kieran swallowed, hard. Matteo touched her chin with the tip of his finger and tilted her face up. She reluctantly opened her eyes and looked at him, expecting the worst: pity.

Instead, she found an odd mix of anger and tenderness. It shook and strengthened her at once.

"There were other women in the house. Prostitutes, I think, given the way they looked and dressed and smelled. But there was another girl, like me. A young girl who seemed innocent and afraid. She hid in the corner, clutching her simple gown around her. It had been slit down the front, and she held the ripped pieces together. Her face was wet with tears, but she made not a sound. I remember thinking that she was being quiet in hopes they would forget she was there.

"They did not forget her. And I was so frightened, too, just like her, but I did not want to cower or cry. I was determined that if they would rape me, it would not be easy for them. I snatched one of their cloaks and tossed it around me, and I managed to grab the fireplace poker, and I was swinging it at them like a club."

Nilo came from the shadows to stand by her side. He reached out and encircled her upper arm with his huge hand, lending strength. Kieran lifted her face to his, her breathing heavy and uneven. "Nilo, now you know my shame."

"Keep fighting, Miss Keerahn." He smiled at her in the semi-darkness. "You're doing good."

She nodded, once, and took a steadying breath. "Samuel had a pistol, and he put it to the head of the other girl, the one who wept. There was no choice. I had to do what he said, or he would have killed her. So I dropped the poker, and took off the cloak when he ordered me to do so. And then, with the whores laughing and Simon watching on, amused, Samuel offered me a choice."

Nilo's grip tightened and Matteo nodded, his face set in grim lines, already knowing.

"He told me she was a virgin, too, just like me. And he offered me a choice. Her virtue or mine," Kieran whispered. Her head dropped, her chin to her chest, and shame was a leaden weight on her heart. That night was still with her, the fear, the revulsion, the pure terror and humiliation. But she did not give voice to the emotions that had ruled her decision that night. She would not make excuses. "I chose mine."

Silence hung over the three of them for what felt like an eternity. And to Kieran, it felt like condemnation. What could anyone say? There was no nobility in sending someone else to suffer in your stead, and Kieran knew that in every painful moment of every single day.

But caught in the confessional spirit of the cold, dark night with two men serving as her confidants, Kieran continued, because telling them what she'd done felt like punishment, and that was what she deserved. "He raped her in front of me. The girl never made a sound, but just wept silent tears, while the whores and the men laughed and made obscene jests. I begged him to stop, to spare her. I offered him money. Made entreaties to his conscience. But he did not stop until the deed was done. When it was over, he unlocked the door and she ran out. Just like that."

"He would have raped her anyway," Matteo said. "It is why she was there at all, no?"

"I don't know," Kieran whispered. "The night was a blur of fear and misery. The men were with the prostitutes, and there was gin and smoke and coarse laughter. I huddled alone, wondering what would happen next, but nothing did. I feared I would lose my mind, and I was sick with myself, for allowing that poor girl to take my place.

"And then Emeline came. She traded herself to Simon for me, helped me dress, and told me to go."

The lump in Kieran's throat felt as if it were on fire. But she kept talking, needing the recrimination like she needed her next breath. "And I did. I left her there, alone with that vile man. I ran away, again. Let someone else suffer in my place."

Matteo glanced to Nilo and inclined his head in the direction of the door. Nilo acquiesced to his silent request to be alone.

Kieran was swaying on her feet, completely drained. She saw that Matteo frowned, as if in deep thought, but he was silent as he stood there. Nothing had changed. The night grew colder as the wind picked up, the hour grew late, and her shame was revealed. No relief or suffering followed her confession; either one would have assuaged her guilt in its own way.

Kieran slid out of Matteo's jacket and handed it to him. Turning her head away, she dashed away a rogue tear from the corner of her eye. Crying solved nothing, a self-indulgent luxury she rarely allowed herself.

She would not give into the tears tonight. Tonight she would reach for something more effective. Perhaps brandy. "I shall take to my bed, now. I hope you are not too disappointed in the truth you so eagerly sought. Mayhap you wished for something more sordid than a weak, fearful, selfish woman."

Damn the tears, they wanted their way with her. Kieran fought them back, but they invaded her tone. She needed to get away from Matteo before he could say anything. She only wanted the privacy of her rooms.

She had the sense he was attempting to find something to say that would bring her comfort, but was coming up short because he could not find a single thing to say. "Good night, signore."

Kieran rushed across the terrace and Matteo followed her, stopping her with a firm hand on her shoulder. He turned her then, to face him, and in the moonlight she saw that his skin bore the glistening track of a fallen tear.

Without a word, he took her hand and lifted it to his face, tracing her finger along the path his tear had taken. It soaked through her silk glove and dampened her skin.

"This is the very first tear I have cried since I was a child," he said wondrously. He looked at her fingertip with an expression of pure awe. "And I wept it for you. I shed it for your pain. No more can I claim a lack of compassion. What will become of this selfish bastard if you keep tugging at my heart?"

"I'm sorry, signore, but your empathy is wasted. I do not deserve it, as you are now well aware. I kept my secret for so long, and now that I have spoken it aloud, I can do nothing but contemplate the very breadth, width, and vastness that comprises my own weakness." Kieran felt the damp tip of her finger grow colder. "I must go. Please, let me go."

Wrenching away from him, she gathered her skirts and ran past Nilo into the manse. She heard Matteo calling her back, but on she pressed, wanting nothing more than the privacy of her rooms.

Through the echoing halls she rushed, passing by the library and music room, the ballroom and various parlors and sitting rooms. She stumbled on the edge of a wool runner, but righted herself up and kept going. Above stairs the manor was silent, the servants' duties completed during day hours. Kieran heard nothing but her own ragged breathing, the rustling of her silk skirts, and the pounding blood in her ears. At last she saw the double doors to her rooms. She burst through them and stopped dead in the center of her sitting room, breathing hard.

Her maid, Jane, slumbered in her tiny alcove. Hearing Kieran enter, she scrambled from her cot and rushed to her feet, stumbling into a curtsey before her mistress.

"Unlace me, please, and then go," Kieran said breathlessly.

Without a word Jane did as she had been told, her nimble fingers plucking open the lacings of gown and undergarments. She left Kieran in her shift and hung the gown, wiped the jewelry before putting them into their cases, and folded the stays. After bobbing into another curtsey, Jane left the rooms, closing the doors behind her.

Before she could settle her breathing, a knock sounded on her door. Thinking it Jane, Kieran called out, "I have no further needs. Good night."

She heard Emeline's voice answer her. "A word, Kieran."

And Kieran could not refuse her. "Come."

Emeline entered with the rustle of silk skirts. She looked every inch the duchess she had become, from her high-dressed hair to her opulent gown of shimmering gold, sewn with seed pearls and gold beads. She wore a pearl choker around her long, slim throat, and her fingers tugged it as she looked contemplatively at Kieran.

"I never press you, Kieran."

Dread congealed in Kieran's gut, and she wrapped her robe tighter around her frame. "To what do you refer?"

"The night in the 'house of lords.'"

Heart pounding, Kieran glanced away from her beautiful sister-in-law's probing eyes. Emeline saw more in a person than anyone she'd ever known, with the exception of Matteo de Gama. "Then why discuss it now?"

Emeline sighed softly, and from the corner of her eye, Kieran saw her rest her hand on her abdomen. "The night I came for you, there were men leaving. I turned my face from them, because I didn't want them to see me. But I caught a glimpse of the one, a man called Arthur. He is the cousin of Samuel Ellsworth, and the two are usually together whenever I see them at balls or in the company of the king."

"I scarcely know of whom you speak."

"If that is true, why does the Duke of Westminster send you flowers, if you barely know of him?"

"Perhaps he fancies himself an admirer of me."

"I am asking you directly: Was he in that house that night?"

"No," Kieran lied boldly, looking directly into Emeline's eyes as she did so.

Emeline fell silent a moment, and then nodded slightly. "As you say."

She turned to leave, but Kieran stopped her with a question. "As we are speaking of the matter, did you ever seek revenge on Simon, for the things he did to you?"

There was a silence where only the crackling of the fire could be heard. They never had spoken of Emeline's life before Rogan, and the atrocities her cruel stepfather, Simon, had inflicted on her. Kieran knew only what she'd seen and heard that night. After Simon had been killed, they'd comforted each other, and Emeline had said things that Kieran never forgot.

They'd never spoken about the matter again. Both of them had put that night to rest in their own way: Emeline by carrying on and moving forward, happy with Rogan, Kieran by growing cold, shutting down, closing off.

"When I was fourteen, I put nettles in his breeches," Emeline said softly. A faint smile curved her lips. "He beat me with a strap, but 'twas worth the price of seeing him scratch whilst soaking his nether region in a tub. Not long after, I put black cascara in his food. He was very ill, and blamed it on bad fish. I did it again, and he attributed it to spoilt milk. I did it a third time, too soon after the second, and he suspected something was amiss. He searched my room, found a wax wrapper with the apothecary's seal on it. Oh, but I was frightened. I thought he would surely beat me until I bled. But instead he beat my mother for raising such an insolent child. I dropped my revenge then, because my mother's pain was not worth the price of seeing him temporarily suffer."

"Diabolical," Kieran murmured, frozen in time, rooted in place.

"Simon learned very quickly that the way to hurt me was to hurt my mum," Emeline whispered. "He learned well the lengths I would go to protect her."

"So you never again sought reprisal?"

"Oh, no, I got mine." Emeline smiled and her hand drifted down to her belly once more. "I lived through it, I kept my heart safe, I found happiness, and I made a life that his depravity could not touch. What better revenge is there?"

Kieran did not answer. Emeline came closer to her and pressed her hand to Kieran's cheek.

"I know there is much that happened that night, and that you have never recovered."

"I hardly ever think about it."

"I don't believe you," Emeline said quietly. "And if 'tis revenge you're after to try to right a wrong that was done you, you should first think about what it will cost. You cannot practice evil to exorcise a demon. You must seek instead your grace and greatness through forgiveness."

"How could I forgive the sort of wickedness that went on in that house?" Kieran whispered.

Emeline's hand was tender and warm, a mother's touch from a woman who was instinctively maternal. "They were just men, Kieran. Not monsters. They were just men, and for that, you forgive them their weakness. And then comes the hard part: You must forgive yourself yours."

Emotions gathered and swirled like a tempest in Kieran's chest. "If you don't mind overmuch, I should like to be alone."

"Of course. Sleep well."

Emeline left, the soft thud of the door closed behind

her. Kieran locked it, and then turned and leaned against the cold wood, struggling for calm.

She took a deep breath, and then another. With trembling hands she touched her belly, holding them against the flat, narrow plane as she felt her breath enter and leave.

When her breathing settled she moved to the fire, ignoring the comfort of the chair as she sank to the floor. The flames licked the wood with hissing tongues, a mindless, hot consumption. Smoke curled upwards, caught in the draft, and Kieran watched it with envy, wishing that she, too, could rise from the fire of her memory and dissipate into the wind.

Tying the belt of her robe tight around her waist, she rummaged in the bottom of her armoire and found the prize: A bottle of brandy pilfered from the larder many months ago.

She retrieved her water glass from her bedside table, and returned to the fire. The silence in the rooms was interrupted only by the pop of the cork leaving the bottle and the gentle glug of brandy being poured. Kieran sat on the floor once again, the wool soft beneath her as she settled back against the padded chair. She sipped deeply, and felt the welcomed burn slide down her throat and settle into her belly.

She rarely drank anything but wine, but kept brandy on hand for the nights that were darker than most.

This would certainly count as one of them, she thought, and took another sip.

She shifted, staring into the fire, and set the drink beside her as she curled her legs beneath her dressing gown. The buckle of her dagger dug into the soft flesh of her inner thigh, and Kieran slid the hem of her gown up so she could remove the weapon.

The finely made buckle came open without a hitch or sound, the black, soft leather worn, but still strong.

Kieran folded the straps across the sheath and set it to her side. She picked up her drink again, sipped, and watched the firelight dance across the hilt of her dagger, making the plain, black pommel shine like onyx. Idly, she toyed with the hilt, the smoothness of it pleasing, the lethalness of it intoxicating.

Like a lover, she slowly flipped open the catch to release the blade and slipped it out. She took another sip of brandy and turned the weapon so she could admire the flashing silver blade.

And inside of her, there was an emptiness that nothing filled. A deep, dark hole of yearning for something different, something real, something new. Yes, she thought, something new. There was nothing quite like the feel of something new, a distraction, a puzzle. Or if she were a romancer like Matteo, perhaps a new flame to burn away all other thoughts. At least for a time.

A longing took her, for a new feeling to wash over her and replace her cold loneliness. And if it could replace the feeling of self-hate that plagued her more than aught else, all the better.

Her memory flashed to the rocking stateroom aboard *The Boxer*, and the feel of Matteo's lips on her neck.

Yes. That had been new, and for those moments, she'd been unable to think of anything else.

Then, on the terrace, and in the face of her greatest shame, he'd wept for her.

She'd asked for his kiss; he'd demanded her truth.

She'd confessed her sins; he'd shed a tear for them.

She lifted her finger to her tongue and tasted the salt of his tear on her skin. They tasted like her own.

She turned to look out the window, and wondered where Matteo had gone after she'd run away. Would he return to dine beside the elegant dowager, and indulge the longing looks she sent his way?

What did it matter? He wasn't beholden to any

woman, nor would he ever be. Did he not tell Kieran that on more than one occasion?

So why should the image of Matteo de Gama playing the cello for the Dowager Countess of Perth make Kieran feel so restless and angry?

Kieran sipped again, deeper still, wanting a numbing peace, even if it were temporary. Finally she began to feel the loose warmth of the alcohol wending its way through her blood. It warmed her inside, where the fire did not. Where only Matteo de Gama had managed to reach.

Kieran decided to not think about that.

She brandished the blade, transfixed by the beauty of its silver surface, with the golden light of the fire reflected within. It winked, glittered, and gleamed.

She held it up to her face and saw herself in the reflection of its fractured steel.

Tears bit at the backs of her eyes again, a burning nip that had her longing for the release that weeping brought.

Kieran denied them.

She washed them back with another swallow of brandy, and held the knife against her leg, felt the cool steel on her heated skin.

If she'd ever allowed herself the relief of prayer, this would have been a good time to indulge. Kieran would not think about that, either.

Then, without really thinking about anything at all, she turned the blade so the razor-sharp edge was against her thigh. Slowly, so slowly, as if in a trance, she dragged it across her skin and watched the red blood well from the narrow wound it left in its wake.

It felt good, like the release she longed for, so she did it again, sliding into her skin to make another long, thin wound.

It hurt, like her heart, a physical manifestation of a pain that was no longer private or secret.

It bled, like the tears she finally let fall.

She watched the blood run down her leg. It soaked into the fine white cotton of the dressing gown, like a rose blooming in snow.

Two tears slipped from her jaw and fell to her thigh, the salt burning the wounds, her tears mingled with her blood.

When the bleeding stopped, so did her tears. She stood on shaky legs and stripped. Using the clean hem of the nightgown, she dipped it in her water ewer and washed herself clean, ripped a dry strip and tied it around the cuts in a makeshift bandage.

And then, naked and alone, Kieran went to the fire and threw the bloody dressing gown into the flames. She watched it burn, the fire consuming her blood but not her pain. Her belly twisted and her head began to ache.

She looked down at the bandage around her thigh. "What have I done?" she whispered. "Worse, what have I become?"

Images came to the fore, things she'd learnt of years before, of men who would mortify their own flesh in penance of their sins.

The smell of burning cloth filled the room, and Kieran rushed, stumbling, to open the windows lest the scent bring unwanted attention to her actions.

Cold, winter air swept into the room like a chilly slap, smelling of wet earth and pine trees. It turned her flesh to goose pebbles. Shivering, Kieran found her wrapper on the floor and realized that she scarcely recalled removing it.

Her thigh throbbed and burned.

This was no sacrificial offering, and she was neither sinner nor saint before a God to whom she had long since ceased praying.

Her mother came into her mind, and Kieran hung her head in shame. Camille would never have fallen so low.

The room was silent but for the sound of the hissing fire and her own breathing. She moved closer to the fire, and its light bathed her in a halo of gold and a wave of heat stung her chilled skin.

Perhaps it was a night of self-indulgence, or perhaps it was simply time for her to allow herself the longings of a woman, Kieran did not know. But neither did she deny the longing for Matteo de Gama's arms around her, whether in seduction or in sincerity.

ꙮ 12 ꙮ

Matteo hovered in the doorway to the dining room. The candlelight glowed golden over the people who ate and laughed and chatted, and Matteo again felt like an intruder in a place he did not belong.

The dowager looked up at him from across the room, and her eyes glittered as she smiled at him, the invitation clear.

That was his true place, he mused. To take his seat beside that woman and woo his way into her bed, her life, her coffers.

So why was he hesitating? Why was he standing there, confused by his empathy for a girl who clearly did not want it, and compelled to do something selfless that served no personal need?

The dowager leaned forward and inclined her head ever so slightly to the empty seat beside her.

Matteo took a breath and steeled himself. He allowed himself a moment to remember Venice and the simple life of gambling, greed, and carnal indulgence that he'd so enjoyed.

And then, against every selfish urge he'd nurtured in his black, bastard's heart, he cleared his throat. The chatter ceased as all eyes turned toward him. Catching Rogan's attention, he said, "A moment alone, please, Your Grace."

Rogan nodded and withdrew from his guests. The two men strode through the manse, reaching a room that held a massive desk, an oaken slab that dominated the floor. Floor to ceiling bookcases lined the walls, and a fire burned in a cavernous fireplace that held court between two windows. Rogan closed the doors, took a seat in one of the leather chairs that sat before the desk, and gestured for Matteo to take the other.

Matteo declined to sit, instead stood behind the chair, his fingers gripping the supple leather. He assessed Rogan with a gambler's eye, and saw a man who did not hold himself superior to others, but who knew and valued his own worth.

"There is no time for niceties. I have a favor to ask of you," Matteo said bluntly.

Rogan raised a brow and stood. "This is to do with my sister, aye?"

"It is. Suffice it to be said that after speaking with her, I find I have urgent business in London. I come to ask for the use of a carriage and a driver who does not lack for discretion."

Both men studied the other, and Matteo saw that Rogan was weighing his words with the utmost care. The Duke of Eton was no man's fool.

"If my sister finds you worthy of her trust, so shall I," Rogan finally said. "My resources are at your disposal. I will send word to the stable hands to lend you whatever you need, whenever you need it. I ask only one thing in return."

Not surprised, Matteo relaxed. When it came to negotiating the price of things, he was on solid footing. "What is it?"

Rogan hesitated, frowning. He opened his mouth to speak several times and then seemed to decide to speak plainly. "I have tried to unearth my sister's honesty for three years. The fact that you got it in a matter of weeks is both a relief, that she has found someone in whom she can confide, and an insult, that it was neither myself nor my wife that she chose to trust.

"I love my sister. I love her enough to want to be the man who finds himself on the mission to avenge whatever hurt she has been concealing these years past. I also love her enough to not allow my pride or my wants to stand in the way of the man who she has entrusted with her secrets."

The gleam in those brilliant green eyes grew fierce and brittle, and his hands clenched into fists. "I am putting my resources at your disposal. Use my funds, my men, my carriages, and whatever else is needed to do what must be done. I will not ask for your betrayal of my sister's trust; I will stay out of your way and let you do what you feel you must. As I said, I ask only one thing."

Rogan leaned forward and enunciated his words. "Whatever was done to my sister, see it is repaid in full."

After stopping in his rooms to grab his hat, Matteo made his way to the kitchens for a few slices of bread and some roasted meat. He washed it down with tea, hoping that would sustain his fatigue. The day had been long. The end of the voyage, his first horseback experience, the abbreviated meal, and then Kieran's painful confession.

He shrugged off his weariness and left the manor, seeking the stables where Rogan had sent word for a plain carriage to be brought around. As ordered, it waited for him, a black conveyance devoid of any markings that would give a hint to the actual owner.

"You know the city well, yes?" Matteo asked the driver.

"Aye, sir," he grunted. The driver was big and stocky, thick with brawn. His face was angular, square and tough, and he wore a thick stocking cap on his head, pulled low over a curling, thick mane of light-brown hair. Matteo noted that his coat was wool and well-cut. He held the reins in wide, strong, gloveless hands.

A sailor or a hired thug, Matteo mused. Most definitely not a servant. It seemed Rogan Mullen was sending him with security. Matteo smiled at that. At thirty-two years of age, Matteo hadn't ever experienced someone looking out for his neck or watching his back. He had two pistols in his belt, a thin stiletto in each boot, a way with words and women, and a hand for cards. They'd all served him well. He'd never relied on anyone but himself for his survival, and that was a good thing, because there hadn't been anyone else who cared to do it.

Until now. And that made Matteo distinctly unsettled even as it amused him.

Matteo dipped into his purse and withdrew a gold coin. He held it out to the driver.

"His Grace pays me," the man said, eyeing the coin suspiciously.

"He pays you to drive me and protect me, no?"

"Aye." The word came long and heavily laced with mistrust.

"I pay my own way. Whatever else you are receiving for your services is your business."

The man shrugged and accepted the coin. Matteo extended his hand and shook it.

"I am Matteo de Gama."

"Sam," the driver replied in turn, his grip hard and firm.

Two footmen emerged from the carriage house. They swaggered to their posts on the rear of the carriage, both bearing long rifles slung over their backs. More guards. Matteo shook his head and sighed. The duke would obviously let him have a free hand in seeing to his sister, but it appeared the duke would see to Matteo.

"We will begin in the bordellos," Matteo instructed the driver. He opened the door to the carriage and climbed inside. Nilo waited in the interior, his huge bulk taking up nearly an entire seat. He had his African luguru ax beside him, the double blades winking silver death.

A big grin split Nilo's black face as he looked at Matteo, and in the light of the lantern his skin gleamed and his eyes shone. "You are a good man to help Miss Keerahn."

"*Grazi*," Matteo replied shortly. He removed his hat and set it on the seat beside him as he sat. "Why are you here?"

"Protection." Nilo braced himself in the seat as the carriage lurched into motion. "I am known with Miss Keerahn, so I will stay in the carriage unless you need me. London's a tough city. Mister Rogan said to make sure you stay safe."

Four guards, all armed, sent for the sole purpose of watching his back. He was a man who had never had anyone to care about his fate, much less look out for it.

Matteo sat back, crossed his arms over his chest, and said nothing, because in a rare, singular moment, words failed him.

Nilo leaned forward then, the whites of his eyes gleaming brightly in his black face. "You are looking for that girl."

Too impressed to vacillate, Matteo answered him honestly. "Yes, of course. The story Kieran tells makes no sense."

"She never told me what she told you tonight. After hearing it, I question everything."

"Indeed, and the puzzle begins and ends with that girl." Matteo shook his head in annoyance. "Kieran served no one by keeping silent. The girl could be anywhere, now. She could be dead, or have long since left London. And how to find this nameless, faceless girl?" He tossed his hand into the air. "A grain of sand in an entire sea. But I will look, no? I will try."

"Miss Keerahn was afraid to tell."

"Afraid of what?" Matteo exploded. Real anger boiled in his chest at the image of Kieran having to make that choice. Who would lay down their body to take the place of a stranger? "She did what any young, innocent maiden would have done. Imagine her fear in that moment. Imagine her agony in having to make that choice."

"I saw the girl leave that house afterward," Nilo revealed. "She came outside and there was a livery waiting for her."

Nilo gave a description of the girl, and when he described the birthmark on her face, Matteo began to relax. Nameless, yes. But not faceless. "You know where she went."

"I hear her tell the driver the address," Nilo said. His grin grew wide and self-satisfied. "I remember it."

Matteo had planned on searching bordellos, because he knew that there was no better place to purchase information, such as the proclivities of certain disreputable lords and the location of wayward girls.

But this new information buoyed his spirits. Perhaps they would locate the girl without too much trouble.

"Excellent. We will find her, and when we do, I will be one step closer to knowing the weaknesses of the Duke of Westminster." Matteo leaned into the cushions to brace himself as the carriage bumped along the cobbled, rutted roads. "Once we know his weaknesses, Nilo, we own him."

Fatigue gripped Matteo as they wended their way into the city. He asked himself once more why he was doing this, when he could be warmly abed.

The answer did not change, much as he wished it would. He wanted to help Kieran, and it did not seem to matter that there was nothing in it for him, other than the possibility of making her happier.

Matteo jeered at himself: Here he was, once more that young boy who tried to bring gifts to make someone care for him. And as much as he could laugh at his foolishness, he did not call off the search and seek out his bed. Matteo hoped to find answers that would ease the heart of a sad, lonely girl who had somehow made a selfish Venetian gambler care for her.

The address Nilo remembered was of a small rooming house. It was an ancient but tidy building with a small, hand-lettered sign beside the door. It read, *Only the God-Fearing Welcome.* They'd awoken the owner, a stiff matron with an excellent memory and a cold demeanor, somewhat softened by a few sovereigns.

The girl had turned wicked, she'd said with a righteous fervor, and had been tossed out.

The girl's name was Alva, and she was a Scottish orphan who'd used the last of her money to come to London, presumably to look for honest work as a seamstress. All had been well, until there was gossip that the girl had taken to prostituting herself to pay her rents.

The matron recounted this with disgust, and announced she'd turned her out to the streets. Then, with a dawning on her face that perhaps they were not seeking the whereabouts of the girl, but her services, the woman had slammed the door.

With that, Matteo was back to where he had planned on beginning: searching bordellos. He sighed in resignation.

There had to be hundreds of them in a city the size of London, perhaps thousands.

"We will start again tomorrow night," Matteo said to Nilo.

After their guests had left and the last of his brandy burned comfortably in his belly, Rogan climbed the stairs to the upper chambers. He knew that Emeline would be naked and warm in their bed, and he was anxious to join her. But first, he chose Kieran's wing.

Rogan swallowed heavily, and thought of his parents at home in Barbados. They'd stayed on in England until his father's business had called them back. His mother, Camille, had pressed her cheek against his for an extended time, and whispered, *take care of Kieran for me.*

Rogan recalled the precise feel of his mother's skin, the scent of her lavender perfume, and the sound of her voice, sadness and resignation combined. They'd all taken care of Kieran; not one of them had been able to help her. Kieran simply would not allow it.

He paused outside her doors, and did not place his hand on the knobs; he knew without trying them that they would be locked. Kieran guarded her privacy the way a jailer minds his cell. Only it was a prison for one, and worse, completely self-imposed.

Rogan leaned his head against the door, remembering when Emeline had been locked away in the mansion, and the odd circumstances that brought him to her door. He'd helped her gain her freedom, first her person, and later, her heart. He wished he could do that for Kieran, but she fought him at every turn.

Rogan thought of Matteo de Gama, and wondered if he were the man fit for the task of setting his sister free.

He had already gotten closer than Rogan or Emeline.

Rogan knocked, a soft rap that he hoped would not wake her if she slept.

Kieran roused at the sound of someone knocking. She rolled over and rubbed her eyes, noticing that her fire had burned out and that only a few embers glowed in the hearth. She did not feel the cold, however. The brandy still had her in its warm clutches. Despite the numbing effect of the liquor, her leg throbbed dully.

"Who is there?" she called.

"Your brother."

"Is something wrong? Is Emeline unwell?"

"She is fine. I came simply to say good night."

Kieran frowned, puzzled by her brother's mood. "Good night, Rogan. Sleep well. My love to Emeline."

Perfunctory, meaningless words, she knew. But what else could he be looking for? Something more, apparently, because he replied, "Will you not even open the door?"

"I am not presentable." She sighed, heavily, and sat up. Reaching for her tinder, she lit a candle on her bedside table and inspected the bandage on her leg, finding the bloom of fresh blood. Not presentable, indeed. "Honestly, Rogan. The hour is late, I am off-dressed, am warmly abed, and you disturb me for a peck on the cheek? Can I not give you two tomorrow?"

There came a pause, and for a moment she wondered if Rogan had given up and left, until she heard him clear his throat. When he spoke, he sounded annoyed and more than a little frustrated.

"Very well, Kieran. I had hoped you might want to tell me what you and Matteo de Gama discussed, and that perhaps you would find me just as suitable a confidant. It seems the answer is yet another no."

Kieran moved from her bed and pulled on her wrapper. She walked softly to the door, careful to not make a sound lest he hear her approach. With her fingertips against the cold wood, she thought of her family and how much she loved them. How much it would humiliate her if they knew her deepest shame.

"I am sorry, Rogan," Kieran said, and never had she meant the words more. "I wish things were different."

"Aye, me too. I won't stop coming back, *sidhe gaoithe*. You're not nearly as alone as you think you are. You're only as alone as you're deciding to be."

Her heart was breaking, could he not know that? Did he not realize that every time he came and asked for her secrets he broke it a little bit more? Kieran pictured her brother, her childhood hero, the bravest man she knew, looking at her with horror that she allowed someone else to suffer in her stead. It would never happen; he must never know. Better for him to think her a cold, heartless shrew than to know it for a fact.

"You're so stubborn, Kieran. Can you not use the strength that feeds your resolve to instead feed your soul?"

And now he would think her strong. Did his misunderstanding of her truest nature really run so deep?

"I am not stubborn," Kieran told him, and heard the sob in her throat.

"You are wrong. Think of Da. Think of Mum. Aye, think of Mum, Kieran. Her strength is in you. Her blood in your veins. Think of her, and know that you have all that she did, and perhaps even a bit more. You are just like her, you know. You're our beloved Camille, without the beatings that sapped her strength."

Kieran leaned against the door to brace the weakness in her legs. She leaned there, gulping air, trying to stem the tide of emotion that threatened to overtake her. Her thigh burned with the evidence of just how much weaker than Camille she was.

Kieran struggled to maintain some sort of composure,

but she wished that Rogan would bust the doors from their hinges and burst inside, grab her and hold her until the pain abated.

But he wouldn't. She'd guarded her privacy jealously, and Rogan respected it. Like the honorable man he was, he honored it.

As if reading her mind, he said, "Open the door, Kieran. Let me in."

No, her mind screamed. *If you let him in, you'll tell him everything in this moment of weakness.* She visualized his disappointment in her again, those green eyes going cold with shame and disapproval, and it gave her fresh resolve.

"Please, Rogan, go. Please. I beg you. I need to sleep."

A long silence filled the space between them. Kieran pressed her hands to her mouth and took three steps back from the door. *Break it down, Rogan,* her heart begged. *Come for me. I am so tired of being alone.*

But she'd succeeded in one thing: creating distance between Rogan and herself.

"Aye, I'll go," he said softly. "For tonight, anyway. Sleep well, *sidhe gaoithe*. I love you."

Kieran crumpled to the floor as she heard his fading footsteps. Alone once more, she pressed her hand against the pulsing ache in her thigh.

Unbidden, an image arose in her mind, of Samuel kneeling before her, begging for her mercy.

And it occurred to Kieran, that like it or not, Samuel Ellsworth, the Duke of Westminster, was the reason she had come face to face with the darkest nature of her soul.

Perhaps it was time he met his own.

The blood was still seeping; she would need another bandage.

Kieran rose and stood tall, and swore to herself a vow, as solemn as any made in blood and through tears: Like her mother before her, she would find the strength to take whatever risks she must.

She would find her peace, or she would die trying.

∽ 13 ∽

Morning dawned with a bright, beautiful sky. Kieran opened her drapes wide and wrapped up in a thick robe so she could take tea on the balcony. The chilly air smelled fresh and carried the fecund scent of thawing soil. She looked out over the sleeping gardens and admired how beautiful England can be in the pale winter light, when the stark, rugged landscape hides nothing.

A new day, and with it, new resolve. Soon spring would come, and Kieran dared to hope for a new season of her own life.

When her tea was drunk and her maid had placed the final touches on her hair, Kieran sought out her brother.

Kieran knocked lightly on Rogan and Emeline's doors, and when Rogan opened it and his face lit with pleasure, Kieran knew she had made the right choice.

"Good morning, Rogan. Do you have time to have a word with me?"

"Of course," he answered, and held the door so she could enter.

Their rooms were cozy and warm, the fireplaces all blazing with heat. The walls gleamed with gold silk, the dark wood floors were cushioned with a Turkish rug. The small chandeliers reflected the morning light, casting prisms over every surface, and a large round table held steaming tea and warm, fresh scones. Kieran smiled a greeting at Emeline, who reclined on a cushioned chair. She still wore her nightclothes, her golden hair unbound and shining, a book in her lap and tea at her side. She curled her legs beneath the throw to make room for Kieran.

"Come sit. Would you like tea?"

"I had mine, thank you."

Emeline's eyes never left Kieran's face. She took in every detail, and then lifted her cup to sip.

Kieran knew that Emeline would simply wait until she was ready to speak. Emeline firmly believed that people needed to do things in their own due time.

Perhaps she had the right of the matter. "'Tis Rogan I came to speak with, but I do not mind your presence at all, Emeline."

"Then please, talk to your brother. 'Tis long overdue."

Kieran nodded her agreement and seated herself in a high-backed chair, folding her hands in her lap to keep them from trembling. Rogan took the seat across from her, eyeing her with expectation. He took a cue from his wife and said nothing.

A deep breath did not sustain her, and there did not seem to be a good place to begin, so Kieran simply jumped into the conversation.

"I have kept my own counsel for some time now, as you are aware."

"Indeed."

Kieran lightly cleared her throat. Looking at her brother, with his handsome face and loving heart, she nearly lost her nerve. She gripped her hands tighter. "Yes. Well. I come here today to explain. You see, 'tis only due to my pride, and I'm sure you'll understand that, Rogan, being in possession of a fair bit of that, as well."

"Aye," he said, and she smiled because he said it like

their da, Patrick, drawn out and imbued with much deeper meaning.

"Right. Well, it feels shameful to discuss certain things with you, for I fear it will permanently color how you see me. What you think of me."

"I love you. Nothing could change that."

"I know you believe that, but the fact remains that I am not comfortable revealing myself to you in that manner." Her face grew warm and regret filled her tone. "Nor do I think I shall ever do so."

A long pause filled the space between them until Rogan said, "Aye, well, if that's how it's to be."

"There's more."

"Of course there is."

"I need to ask you a favor."

Rogan took a breath and seemed to reach for patience. "Ask."

"Well, I shall, but first I must tell you something that will very likely make you very angry with me." She bit her lip and then blurted out her confession. "I have discussed the matter with Signore de Gama."

"I take it you do not care for his opinion of you? Or is it that you esteem his regard for you as higher than mine?"

"Neither," Kieran said, and heard the wobble in her voice. "You see, soon Signore de Gama will leave England, and I shall not have to suffer his opinion. But in the meantime, he has offered me a solution to a problem that has troubled me for these years past."

"The solution?"

"I cannot tell you."

Rogan cast his gaze to his wife, and saw that she smiled tolerantly. With a small nod, she indicated that he should continue the conversation.

"What do you want from me, Kieran, that the venerated Signore de Gama cannot give you?"

"Your lack of involvement."

"Pardon?"

"I am asking you to turn a blind eye to my actions."

"A blind eye," he repeated. He tapped his fingers on the tabletop. "Tell me, what exactly does that mean?"

"I want you to allow me use of the carriages, the horses, and whatever else, and I want you to refrain from asking me where I am going or where I have been."

"You are serious."

"I have never been more so," she said flatly.

"This is ludicrous. A lady of your bearing and station requires chaperones. You are my ward, and I would be greatly remiss in my duties if I were to grant you this insanely preposterous request."

"Be that as it may, I ask it of you anyway. I come to you truthfully, with no desire to sneak behind your back. I am asking that you treat me as the grown woman I am, and that you not reduce me to deceit or subterfuge." Kieran added softly, "Please."

"Am I to presume that Signore de Gama's involvement will require you to be alone with him on occasion, such as the afternoon you decided to take an interest in the cello?"

Kieran blushed, but kept her chin up. "Yes."

"You are on very shaky ground, here, Kieran. I am not going to agree to allow you to be compromised."

"You took Emeline off alone," Kieran pointed out.

"And I married her, aye?"

"But you damaged her reputation first."

Emeline coughed and choked, took a sip of tea, and pretended to be very interested in her book.

"Are you saying you will wed Signore de Gama if you are in any way subjected to . . . being compromised, in reputation or otherwise?"

"No," Kieran said. "Which is why the favor I ask you is based on affection for me, and trust in my better judgment. I wish to take control of my life, and to that end I am willing to accept Signore de Gama's help." She held her fingers so tightly they ached. "He will eventually leave England, and I will return to my life, once again a contented spinster. I will not marry to ease the opinions of my judgmental peers. If they do not like how I live my life, I can only answer that they do not have to live it. This is my life. And for once, Rogan, for once, I would like to live it on my terms."

Beneath the table, Kieran pressed her folded hands against her bandaged cuts. She swallowed despite the thickness in her throat. "Please. Think of how little I have ever asked of you, and then think what it is to be a young woman of my station. I have so little control over my life.

"When your heart was broken, you took to the sea, and took solace in the boxing ring. You were able to do as you needed to find your way. But I am stuck like a fly in a web, caught by my circumstance and my gender. Please, Rogan, don't protect me so much that I cannot see to myself." She finished on a whisper. "Please, worry less for my reputation and my virtue, and more for my soul. I'm trying to reclaim it, to use my resolve, just as you told me. Please, let me."

Rogan frowned and rose, moving to the window to look out at the peaceful morning. Kieran waited, her head bowed. He stood there a long time, and then turned to face his sister.

"I will do as you ask," he said simply. He sighed and said, "Just please be careful, and take Nilo with you."

"I will," Kieran promised. Tears stung her eyes, in gratitude that her brother could trust her still, after the lies he knew she'd told. "Thank you, Rogan."

He nodded, and then said, "Come here. I have something to show you."

He took her hand and moved to the chair where Emeline reclined. Rogan bent at the waist and pressed a tender kiss against his wife's forehead, and then he took Kieran's hand and placed it on Emeline's belly. Beneath Emeline's soft cotton nightgown, she felt the shocking warmth of her body, and the swollen mound of her abdomen. It swelled with life, a firm, hard dome that sheltered their child. Kieran lifted wide eyes to Emeline and Rogan's, saw the pride and hope that shone in them.

"Your niece or nephew," Rogan said.

Kieran pressed a little, and felt a small thump against her palm. This is life, she marveled, in its most fragile state, kicking and fighting to live.

And she thought that if a tiny child not yet born could fight for its own life, so could she.

After Kieran left, Emeline looked at her husband with a mysterious smile curving her mouth. One hand rested on her belly, her other held her tea. "Would you care to make a wager?"

"What's that, princess?" Rogan glanced up from the ledger he was reading. Taking one look at her smile, he knew he was in for some sort of trouble. "What sort of wager?"

Emeline's smile deepened. "If Signore de Gama leaves England permanently, I will grant you whatever wish you desire. If he remains, you will do the same for me."

"Whatever wish?"

"Whatever."

Stakes to stagger the imagination, he thought. She was certain she would win.

Rogan pictured the Venetian at his dining table, out of sorts and out of place. This man was not suited to England any more than an African lion. But then again, his wife could be incredibly determined to get her way, and with such large stakes, Rogan needed to clarify the terms.

"The stipulation will be that there is no interference from either of us to sway his decision."

"Are you insinuating I would meddle?"

Her mock outrage had him fighting the grin that threatened his feigned sternness.

"I am not insinuating anything. I'm saying it plainly: Don't meddle, Emeline."

She laughed and set down her tea. "Fine, my lord. I will stay out of it."

Rogan abandoned his ledgers and went to her side. He sat beside her and snuggled her against his body. She was warm and soft and loving, his child in her belly and his heart in her hands. He would give her anything she wanted, grant her any wish, and did not need a wager to do so. But it was all in good fun, and he would not deny her that, either. "I accept your wager. Kiss on it," he said.

And they did.

Matteo leaned into the shade of an elm tree, its gnarled, knotty trunk providing some cover as he watched Kieran. She was in the paddock by the stables, exercising horses, and by the look of her face, enjoying herself immensely.

It had been weeks since he'd seen her, and watching her now filled his chest with a strange sensation.

She moved like art that had come to life, every part of her a study in elegance and earthly delight. Her garnet hair gleamed in the sunlight. She wore it unbound, and it streamed behind her like silk ribbons, bouncing over her shoulders and down her narrow back. The riding gown she wore was dun colored, and its simplicity suited her small frame, showing the tiny nip of her waist and the swell of her breasts.

Matteo could not help himself; he envisioned her

nude, from her dainty feet to her shapely thighs, the swell of her hips, the musical shape of her body. Would her nipples be pink, or would they be a darker shade of her flesh? Would her ribs trace subtle lines beneath her breasts? Did her belly stretch tight across the hourglass of her body, or did it swell slightly with a womanly roundness?

He added the visual of her dagger, black death against naked white, female flesh. Why should that image enflame him, turn his whole body tense and hard for her?

Oh, but it did. It embodied Kieran: hidden dangers and veiled passions, ready to be unleashed.

This was why he'd stayed away from her. She was like a drug that threatened to consume him with the lure of temporary euphoria. When he looked at her, he felt too much.

Matteo forced himself to walk away. He'd go see Emeline about the renovations, as he'd planned. And though he'd seek out the Scottish prostitute called Alva again that night, he'd continue staying away from Kieran Mullen.

She knew where to find him, he told himself. Yet, she had not sought him out. This was what always happened. He'd begin to feel for a woman, and soon enough, he would realize that he was the only one with the burden of emotion.

Matteo stole one more glimpse of Kieran. Her hair was tossed in the wind, her face shone with delight, and she looked free and peaceful and happy. Matteo wished that he could ride with her again, wanted to bring her gifts to lay at her feet, longed to find a way to make her look into his eyes and smile. Instead, he turned and kept going.

She knew where to find him. He'd not chase after any woman. Not even this one, *sidhe gaoithe*, the wind fairy.

* * *

Nighttime brought rain, and once again, as they'd done nearly every night since they'd learned the name of the girl, Alva, Nilo and Matteo resumed their search.

Outside a brothel, Matteo hesitated. He hated the whorehouses. It was easy to hate them, the women were pathetic and diseased, used and tired, and each and every one of them made Matteo remember all too well that he was the bastard child of a whore. The men were worse, disgusting specimens who were for the most part, married and drunk, and who did not spare a conscionable thought for the women who they used to ease their lusts.

Nilo patted Matteo on the back. "One more, then we go back."

Matteo nodded his assent, and they entered.

"Come in, Govnas, the two o' you," a harlot said. She beckoned them with a crooked finger and a wide, toothless smile. Her lips were stained crimson red, and she wore a sheer chemise and filthy stockings. She craned her neck to look up at Nilo. "Gor, you're a biggun, ain't ye? And black as the night. I'll call our Mary for ye. She likes 'em dark."

The whorehouse stank of perfume, mildew, coal smoke, and cheap alcohol. What was once a rug rotted on the curled floorboards, moldering amidst various spillages of ale and wine.

This was their fifth bordello of the night, and each one grew more dismal than the first. According to Nilo, the girl had possessed a birthmark on her face, a dark red patch shaped like a strawberry just below her left eye.

Somewhere in the house they heard a shrill giggle, followed by the slap of hand meeting flesh. Fresh giggles ensued.

"We are here looking for a particular girl. She is fairhaired, and has a strawberry shaped birthmark beneath her left eye. She goes by the name of Alva. Do you know her?"

The woman's left hand outstretched as she scratched her head in mock contemplation with her right.

Matteo reached into his purse and withdrew a coin. He pressed it into her waiting palm, and only when her dirty fingers curled around it did she answer.

"Yer both looking fer lil bitty Alva?" She shrugged her shoulders as if she couldn't fathom they didn't want a toss with her. "She's wit a customer. Ye'll 'ave ter wait yer turn."

Upstairs bed springs squeaked in rhythmic protest, accompanied by shouts and grunts until they reached the crescendo of masculine pleasure. Then there was silence for a time, until a bleary-eyed man stumbled down the steps. He tucked his shirttail into his breeches, not seeming to notice that his shoes were on the wrong feet. As he passed Matteo he belched, and the reek of sulfur and gin filled the air.

He paused at the door, stopping to speak to the toothless prostitute. "See you tomorrow, Maggie, same time. Have Anne ready for me, eh?"

"Ye got the right of it, Harry, will do. 'Ave a good day."

Maggie shuffled over to see him out the door, and closed it behind him as she turned to call up the stairs. "Alva! Ye gots more in queue, girl."

A door creaked, floorboards squeaked, and out on the street a dog howled. Matteo smiled politely at Maggie as she ran a hand down his arm, and shook his head to the negative. Maggie shrugged and pulled up the hem of her chemise. She unpinned a knotted handkerchief, untied it and placed her coin with the other quid she had in there, and then pinned it back in place.

Matteo stood there, trying to not think about his mother and her lovers. It wouldn't do to fall apart in this ramshackle whorehouse, to fall to his knees and weep.

He was not that boy anymore, he counseled himself.

So why did he feel so sick to his stomach?

The stairs groaned as Alva descended. She came into

view, and Matteo's emotions turned to pity. She was young, bone-thin, and pretty in a pale, waifish way that would soon fade if she continued prostituting herself. Fatigue had left its mark beneath her blue eyes, and her heart-shaped face bore the expression of weary resignation. She wore her hair short, cropped raggedly just beneath her jaw, and despite being greasy and lank, it was the color of sunlight. Sure enough, she had a red strawberry mark high on her cheekbone. Her eyes widened when she saw Nilo, traveling over the sheer size of him, and then she blew a little breath out.

"Two o' you," she said with resignation, her quiet voice bearing a soft, Scottish accent. "An' at this wee hour?"

Matteo reached into his purse once again and withdrew two gold coins. "For your time and efforts."

Her eyes went round, and she turned and led the way to her bedroom without another word.

They followed her up the creaking stairs, and as they gained the landing the smells grew stronger and more distinct, mildew, unwashed bodies, excrement, and dirty laundry. The other doors were closed, and a curving set of enclosed stairs led to another floor. Judging by the thumping and grunting, a few whores still entertained guests.

Alva entered a small room in the corner. In the center sagged a small bed, and against the wall a tiny mirror hung above a chest. Paint peeled from the walls and in some places bare holes revealed the building's wooden bones. Faded floral curtains hung limply from nails above the single window, and on its sill sat a geranium, its bright red flowers the only source of cheer in the bleak, charmless house.

Alva sat on the bed and let the sleeve of her chemise fall from her bony shoulder. She tilted her face up to the two men in a tired imitation of female desire. "What're ye randy for? Double the fun or one at a time?"

From another bedroom a woman's voice could be

heard, moaning in faux passion as the bed thumped against the wall. Alva's face turned pink, an odd shade for a prostitute prepared to have sex with two men.

Nilo surprised Matteo and went to kneel in front of the girl. He took one of her hands, engulfing it in both of his. "Don't you remember me?"

She frowned in confusion. "I canna remember yesterday." Sadness shadowed her eyes. "An' I dinna care to."

"It was three years ago," Nilo prompted. "In a house of men, with other prostitutes and one young girl. She has red-brown hair. She was afraid. Do you remember?"

Alva glanced away, to the lamp that burned low, nearly out of oil. "The girl in the green dress. Aye, I kent her." She brought her gaze back to Nilo's, obviously searching his features for something familiar. "You weren't there."

"I was outside. I saw you leave."

Realization dawned, and a red blush followed. She ducked her head down, and though she tried to pull her hand from Nilo's grip, he held on.

"Do not be afraid," Nilo said. "We are not here to hurt you."

"What do you want?"

"Tell me about that night," Nilo prompted. "We will give you more money."

That brought her head back up. She narrowed her eyes. "Why."

It wasn't a question. That made Matteo smile, for he knew something about being very cautious of people who offered money in exchange for information. The girl might be young, but she was definitely not stupid.

He moved to her side, and ignoring the revulsion that her filthy bed inspired, he sat beside her. "The girl in the green dress is our friend, and she has been hurting ever since that night, sick in her soul for allowing you to take her place. We've come here tonight to find out more of what happened, and as much about those men as possible. I swear your involvement will be kept secret."

Alva frowned again, pursing her lips as she mulled over what Matteo had just said. "My place? She took my place for what, then?"

Matteo didn't know why he felt the need to be delicate when speaking of sex with a whore, but her youth and maidenly blushes had him striving for discretion. "As I was told, the girl was offered a choice: Your virtue or hers. She says she chose hers, and that the man raped you. Is that not the case?"

"Ooh, no. I was there on the condition of swivin'." Her grubby fingers touched the ragged ends of her hair. "I'd sold my hair, my clothes, all my belongin's, and even my Bible and the bitty earbobs my da gave me when I finished my schoolin'. My sewin' job was through, an my boardin' lady was needin' payment."

Alva shrugged, and stared down at her other hand, still captured in Nilo's. "An old friend at the factory was makin' extra shillin's workin' at a brothel at night. She suggested I could raise a fortune for my virginity, an' at first, I was fair affronted that she'd say such things. Oh, but I had nae money, nae options, so I did, by callin' on a woman who arranges such things.

"There was a man, she'd said, who was lookin' for a woman that was no diseased, an' was willin' to pay extra for a virgin." Alva pulled her hand away and twisted it in her lap with her other. "It all seemed a bunch of barnie, but when it was done, I walked out of there wi' enough money to pay my rents and to feed me for a month."

The blush crept back to stain her pale skin once more. "I thought maybe I'd get another sewin' job, but I couldna find one. Meanwhile, my landlady found out what I done and tossed me to the streets. I had no references, no work. An' where else for me to go, but to a place like this, aye?" Anger twisted her lips. "That cow kept the rest of my rent, too."

The girl yawned then, her jaw-cracking as she did so, and she wiped her eyes with her knuckles. It made her look so youthful that Matteo felt something even deeper than pity: He felt ashamed of being a man. Who, he wondered, could come and vent their lusts on such young girl?

Nilo must have felt the same way, Matteo noticed, for his eyes shimmered in his black face and his lips were pressed together in a grim line.

Matteo offered the coins to Alva, and when she accepted them, she began to speak again, this time telling Matteo and Nilo details about the man who'd purchased her innocence, and what had gone on in that house when Kieran had arrived with Simon.

By the time she'd finished her tale, the sky had lightened and all the rest of the brothel was silent. Outside the street was coming to life with rattling carriages and crying street vendors. Matteo heard the distant crowing of a rooster, and the cooing of pigeons.

He stood and bowed to Alva before he took her hand, pressed a kiss to the back of it, and placed two more coins in her palm. She stared at the money as if it were not real, as if she could not fathom that she'd earned it with talk.

Regret twisted Matteo's heart again, but he'd learned a lot growing up with his mother. She'd only taken one lover at a time, but she did so to pay her way, just the same. So Matteo did all he could for Alva: He gave her money and tried not to judge her.

It was time to go. "You have been most helpful."

As he turned to leave, he saw that Nilo hesitated. The hulking African seemed uneasy. He took her hand and patted it as if she were a child. "You look tired."

Poor Nilo, Matteo thought. Did he think he could save her? Did he not know that London was rife with such

girls, as was Venice, as were all cities? Did he not realize
they all had a sad story of what had landed them there?

"I've no taken well to sleepin' in the daytime," Alva said
softly, offering him a wan smile. A little breeze stirred the
droopy curtains, carrying with it the scent of hot bridies.
Alva's belly growled loud enough that they both heard it,
as she looked over at her geranium to cover her embarrassment. She rose and went to add a few drops of water and
to pinch off a bloom that had only just begun to wilt. "The
girls say as ye get used to it, but it hasna been true for me,"
she said over her shoulder.

Nilo lumbered to her side and patted her again, this
time on her shoulder. He dipped into his own pocket,
withdrew a few coins, and gave them to her. "Sleep
tonight," he said.

∽ 14 ∽

Weeks passed, and Matteo did not visit the manor.
Kieran waited each day, hoping to see him, wondering
the effect of her confession. Had his curiosity been assuaged and his interest lost?

It annoyed her that he had pursued her so relentlessly
for her truth, and then once he received it, he'd ignored
her without any explanation.

But her pride had prevented her from asking if
anyone knew his whereabouts. She would not reveal her
curiosity about the Venetian artist.

Every day a new arrangement of flowers came from
Ellsworth. She was forced to receive them as if they

meant nothing more to her than the unwanted interest of a suitor, when she wanted to dump them to the floor, shatter their vases, and trample the blooms beneath her feet.

The constant control over her expressions and actions was wearing very thin.

Why was Ellsworth pursuing her? The deliveries were odd and, for a reason she could not name, frightening.

And where was Matteo de Gama?

Restless and bothered, she paced her chambers, pausing to once again read a passage of his manuscript. When it neared tea time, and he still had, once again, not come to the manor, Kieran was forced to wonder where he could be, and what he could be doing. He knew no one in London besides her family, and those who he'd been introduced to. What could be so occupying his time, that he did not even come for a meal? And where, she wondered, could he be staying?

Visions of the Dowager Countess of Perth came into her mind, and her annoyance grew apace with her curiosity. Could he be in her company, drinking her wine, playing his cello? That woman had looked at Matteo like he was a piece of roasted meat, ready to be devoured. Had Matteo seen in her his next wealthy, English lover?

She envisioned his hands, long, elegant fingers, stained with ink, scented with rosin and bergamot, expertly playing over papery, wrinkled skin.

Kieran whirled around, scattering the pages of the manuscript with the billowing of her skirts. She caught a sight of herself in her cheval mirror, saw her pink cheeks, her snapping eyes. Her hands were curled into fists and her hair had begun to fall from its moorings. Above her pale blue, silk bodice, the skin of her breasts were blotched with red spots.

She looked like a woman in a jealous rage.

And then she recalled the woman in the Doge's courtroom, pleading, crying, begging on her knees.

Matteo de Gama would not make a similar fool of Kieran Mullen.

Outside, the sun shone brightly, and the chilly air carried the promise of spring. A ride would clear her head; it always did.

When she descended the stairs at a measured pace, her hair had been tightly coiled at the nape of her neck, and she wore a riding gown of thick, brushed green velvet. Her soft, leather boots scarcely made a sound on the marble floors as she sought out a servant.

She did not need to look long, because a servant came rushing up to her. "My lady . . ." she began breathlessly.

"Please inform the groom I require two horses to be saddled, and please let Nilo know I wish to take a ride." Kieran said, her mood thoroughly distracted.

"He is not here, my lady," the servant informed her. "He left word that Nigel should accompany you if you're to go riding."

Kieran frowned lightly. Nilo never took a day off without telling her. "Very well. Please inform Nigel. And do you know the whereabouts of His and Her Grace?"

"Yes, my lady, His Grace was called away on business, and Her Grace is in the solarium. I will inform Nigel of your wishes, and more flowers were delivered. Pink roses. And . . ."

Anger brewed in her chest like a storm, even as fear turned her belly in little nauseating flips. More flowers. An idea of how to rid herself of the constant reminder dawned, and Kieran wondered why she hadn't thought of it before. "Donate all the floral arrangements, and any future deliveries from the Duke of Westminster, to the local orphanages. Perhaps the children will appreciate them."

The servant bobbed a curtsey and began to speak, but

Kieran interrupted her again. "Do you happen to know what business takes Nilo from the manor?"

"He is helping our guest, Signore de Gama, at the other property. But, my lady, about the flowers—"

Kieran kept her manner indifferent with an effort that felt no less than Herculean. "I do not want them. If the orphanage does not take them, then keep them for yourself. I do not need to be notified every time a delivery arrives. Thank you. That will be all."

The servant persisted. "My lady, there is more you need to know. The flowers were delivered by the duke himself. He waits for you in the main parlor."

Anger and fear grew in equal measure, and Kieran was fast losing her ability to feign indifference. What was this man's game, she wondered. She would have to see him alone to find out.

"Fine. Please see to the horses and Nigel. I will be along shortly," Kieran said.

The girl scuttled off, and Kieran stalked through the manse, icy demeanor forgotten.

As she'd been informed, Samuel waited in the parlor. He wore rich garments, trimmed in ermine and jewels. He held his feathered tricorn in his hand, leaving his black and silver hair to gleam in the sunlight that spilled through the tall windows. On a low table sat a huge arrangement of pink roses and sprigs of lavender, the room redolent of their sweet, heavy scent.

His face lit as she swept into the room, and it occurred to her that if she did not find him so repugnant, she might think him handsome with his dignified graying temples, arched black brows, and a friendly twinkle in his gray eyes.

He swept into a courtly bow, and she wondered if he bothered to recall that he once stripped her naked and forced her to choose between her own suffering or to inflict it on another. He acted as if none of that had happened, as if he had never left her to drown in Venice.

Her heart pounded, but she'd gotten so adept at dissembling that she gave no sign. "Why are you here?"

"I was compelled to come and see why you have not replied to any of my letters or flowers."

"You are truly mad," Kieran whispered, and she backed up two steps, hovering in the doorway. "The flowers and the cards and the invitations to dine with you make a mockery of what you and I know exists between us."

"There is history between us, and in a perverse sense, honesty. No one else knows about that night but us."

"Perverse, indeed. Perverted, more like."

"Listen, please," Samuel entreated, tossing his tricorn to the sofa. He moved closer, his palms outstretched as if to show that he bore no arms, no threats.

Kieran recalled the precise image of him thrusting into the silently weeping girl.

"I am not the man you think I am," he said.

Kieran glanced behind her, to make certain no one eavesdropped. When she saw they were still alone, she whispered, "What do you care what I think of you? Why are you not content that I simply hold silent and leave that night buried in the past? Why can't you just leave me and my family alone, and spare me further pain?"

"You said I caused your deepest shame. You called me evil." He looked abashed. "What can I do but try to rectify what I've done, and perhaps change your opinion of me? I am not evil."

"I cannot understand you," Kieran said. "You are speaking English, and yet 'tis as if you speak another language. Allow me to be very clear: I want you to leave and never darken my door again. Do not send flowers. Do not send cards. Do not contact me. If you are truly sorry, then allow me the mercy of your absence."

He studied her for a moment, as if weighing his words

with the utmost care. "Will you please listen? Perhaps if you heard me out, you would see me in a different light, and would be able to forgive me."

Kieran's breath snagged and she felt as if the floor were dropping out beneath her.

Samuel did not stop beseeching her. "You mistake everything about me. I am here to apologize for the awful things I did to you. After speaking with you on the ship, I have pondered the fear and upset I must have caused you, and it wounds my heart to contemplate what I've done. I worry that there are things I did I do not even recall, for I'd been drinking gin as water for hours and hours before you arrived. Nevertheless, whatever I did, I want to make it up to you. I want to set the matter right. I am willing to do whatever it takes to make you see that I am not an evil man, but simply a man who did evil things.

"I've worried since you said I caused your greatest shame: Did I damage your virtue? Is this why you remain unmarried to this day?

"I come here today with the most honorable of intentions: I come to propose marriage. If I took your innocence, 'tis the only honorable thing for me to do."

"Marriage," Kieran laughed, the sound of which bore the edge of hysteria. "I tell you I despise you, and you propose marriage. You *are* mad."

"I am eminently sane, and have seldom been more serious. After my wife died, I saw no need to remarry; I have an heir and a spare, and plenty of time to pursue my interests. But I did not despise marriage, and was an adequate husband, I think. You are quite lovely, and though much younger than I, I don't find you silly or full of nonsense." He shifted his weight, and attempted a smile. "You're obviously adept at handling matters on your own, and are, as I said before, very comely. Beautiful, in fact, despite your fiercer nature."

Samuel stood at ease, comfortable in the elegant parlor. Wearing fine clothes and jewels that winked and gleamed in the sunlight, he looked like every woman's dream: A rich, handsome nobleman who proposed marriage and offered prestige, titles, and security. It had been her dream, once upon a time.

Kieran recalled his slurring words and gleeful grin as he held a gun to her head and made her debase herself.

He lifted his chin and looked upon her with an expression of noble regret. "I've given this a great deal of thought, I assure you. I was quite drunk that night, but that is not who I am. I am not a vile man. I am not evil."

Visions of that night haunted her. There was no way that protestations of drunkenness and claims of not recalling the events clearly were going to make Kieran forget how cruel and depraved the man was.

Marriage. She imagined climbing into bed with him, waiting for him to do to her what he'd done to Alva. She shivered with revulsion.

From the depths of Kieran's mind came a cold, calculated thought: He is open to revenge. Kieran realized that she would never get a better opportunity to exact her reprisal. She did not know how, yet, but she knew that he'd all but laid his head on her chopping block.

He thought he'd raped her, and offered marriage. Kieran would not correct him.

Without any remorse, Kieran wrinkled her brow as if uncertain. "How can I know you tell the truth?"

"Time will prove my true nature."

"Very well," Kieran said softly. She looked to the window as if deep in thought, and allowed emotions she did not feel play out over her countenance: anxiety, fear, and lastly, doubtful interest. "You've had your time today. Come again on the morrow."

* * *

She tossed on her riding cloak as she made her way to the rear of the manse. The moment the groom handed her the reins, she swung into the saddle and kicked the mare into motion. Clumps of clotted earth and soil flew from beneath the horse's hooves. Nigel followed her, urging his own mount to keep up with Kieran's thundering pace.

Beneath her, her beast ate up the miles as she urged it relentlessly. Kieran held the reins tight in her gloved hands, and she leaned over the back of the mare's neck, barely feeling the cold wind against her hot face.

Samuel's visit had been most interesting, and she wished she were not so angry with Matteo that she could discuss it with him. It was insulting enough that Matteo had not bothered to come to the manse after her humiliating confession, but now he appropriated the only person who made Kieran feel at ease.

Take Nilo, would he? Clearly Matteo knew that Nilo was her guard, and more than that, her companion, her only friend, and a comforting presence she relied on. How dare Matteo monopolize Nilo's time without asking her permission? And how dare Nilo leave for the entire day without telling her? She would see to it that they both got an earful they would not soon forget.

As she came up the long lane, her horse wheezed and blew, snorting as Kieran reined her to a stop in front of the crumbling stables. She left her mount in Nigel's care and stalked toward the decaying manor.

And stopped dead, her anger momentarily forgotten.

The place crawled with activity. Gardeners knelt in the soil, clearing away dead plants and pruning overgrown bushes. A huge bonfire crackled and burned in a barren field, and workers towed fallen branches from the grounds and old, broken furniture out of the house, tossing them on the fire. There were familiar faces, servants from the ducal estate, toiling to scrub the mossy stone with lye soap. A few men were building scaffolding on one end of the house. The main doors to the house were propped open, revealing others bustling around inside.

It seemed Nilo was not the only person who Matteo de Gama had "borrowed."

Kieran walked around to the rear of the house, and was not surprised to see that a few of the balconies had been boosted up into place with temporary beams. And there, coming from the stone out-kitchen, came Matteo, carrying a bundle of firewood.

He wore work clothes that he obviously used when he painted; serviceable dark cotton breeches and a white linen shirt that bore splotches of pigment. His hair was unbound and hung to his shoulders, tossed with wind and work, and his hands were abraded with cuts and scratches. A light sheen of sweat filmed his skin despite the coolness, and his thick leather boots were caked with mud.

He smiled when he saw her, his sensual mouth curved in a sardonic expression that captured the irony of a man such as himself finding pride and happiness in manual labor. He set the wood at his feet and gestured to the house. "It is already progressing, no?"

In that moment, it occurred to Kieran that while she was angry with him for taking Nilo without the courtesy of asking her if she minded, she was distinctly relieved that Matteo was not occupying himself with the Dowager Countess of Perth.

"You've already begun," she said wondrously.

"Why should I wait?" Matteo shrugged. "I do not like waiting. If there is a task to be done, I do it."

"Even so, how did you manage to do this in such a short period of time?" Kieran glanced around once more. Everywhere she looked there were servants hard at work. The air smelled of smoke, turned earth, and lye soap, and rang with the sounds of construction and demolition. "There must be fifty people here."

"Sixty-two," he corrected. "The duchess was most helpful in lining up help, and as you can see, she loaned me some of her own staff to assist with the cleaning and gardening."

"Including Nilo, I hear. Where is he?"

"He is not here. I sent him on an errand." Matteo looked at her with an odd expression she could not read. "Will you wait for him?"

Kieran felt suddenly awkward. Why was this foreigner so comfortable in England, rehabilitating old homes and commanding servants, most especially her own? "Wait? With you?"

"We are not alone, but certainly well-chaperoned, yes?" His eyes sparkled with amber lights and he smiled once more, dazzling white teeth in a rakishly handsome face. "Please, stay. It would be my pleasure to have you as my guest."

And now he invited her to remain as if he were the master of this property. The man oozed nerve.

"Come, I will show you around," he invited. Without waiting for her to acquiesce, he picked up his bundle of firewood and led the way. Despite herself, Kieran followed.

Matteo stopped by a large terrace. "Here, you see where the stones are clean? Without the mildew the marble shines, no? Beautiful stone, and look at the work along the edges. See how it is scrolled and beautiful? This house is a wonder. Every detail was put so lovingly together. The scroll work here matches the scrolling on the eaves, see?"

Kieran looked where he was pointing and saw that beneath the peeling paint, the wood was indeed carved.

He did not linger, but entered the French doors and moved into a large parlor. "And here there are wood floors that need nothing more than a good cleaning and plenty of wax. Parquet, inlaid with a hexagon pattern. *Magnifico*, eh? And look at the moldings: They are all plaster, hand done, and in need of nothing more than cleaning and fresh paint; no wood moldings, all beautiful plaster. See, the interior is really not so bad; most of the rooms were shut off and unused for many years. They suffer nothing more than cobwebs, dirt, and disuse. The main rooms that were used are worn, yes, but not beyond reform."

Kieran watched Matteo's excitement grow as he entered another room. It had been a huge ballroom, two-storied with an orchestral loft, towering windows, and alcoves behind archways.

It now seemed to serve as Matteo's chambers, as his belongings had been moved to a corner of the vast room, closest to a grand marble fireplace. A large bed had been set up in the middle of the floor, complete with pillows, quilts, and a folded down comforter. A round library table and three high-backed chairs had been carried in, and already she saw that plans for a garden had been sketched. An ancient armoire had been pushed into the room, and his trunks were neatly arranged beside it.

She saw his books were piled along one wall, and his cello leaned in the corner, a low stool beside it. Sheet music was scattered on the floor, and unlit candles filled the room in tall pillars, on the table, in the dusty, dangling chandeliers, and all around the bed. He clearly had chosen to live there during the renovation.

Matteo dumped his firewood into a large, old copper pot and dusted his hands on his breeches before turning toward her.

Kieran glanced once more at the cello, and felt her face heat as she recalled his hands moving with elegant, sensual precision over the delicate skin of her inner wrist.

He noticed, damn him, because he missed nothing, and he smiled again, this time a slow curve of those soft-looking lips. "I chose this room for the acoustics," he said softly. "They are amazing. Do you want to hear?"

"No," she said abruptly, and she turned around so he could not see her face and know exactly how much she hungered for just that.

He came up behind her and put his hand on her wrist, his fingers lightly touching the veins where her pulse throbbed. Kieran tried not to notice that he smelled of clean sweat and sundrenched linen, the cool air lingering on him still, scented with turned earth and the bonfire's smoke. His breath was warm on her ear. "I should have kissed you when you asked me to. I was a fool to say no."

"I shall never ask again. 'Twas a moment of madness, of rebellion against my own spirit, and nothing more. The moment has thankfully passed."

"Your spirit," he whispered. "Yes, I have given that some thought, Kieran."

He said her name again, and it shook her as it did the first time. Did he feel the tremor that took her body when the word passed his lips?

"You have the spirit of the sun, the moods of the moon, and the will of the wind," he said against her hair, the heat of him warming her in ways she did not want to think about.

His poetic words were nothing more than tools in the arsenal of a seductive man of letters. She cautioned herself to not take them more seriously than what they were: Words. Nothing more.

"My spirit, my mood, my will. I want them all back. That is why I am here," she said softly.

"Tell me. I await your pleasure."

She trembled again. Just the touch of his hand on her wrist was enough to have her wondering what his lips would feel like, what his body would feel like pressed to hers. The thoughts were indecent. But she did not push them away.

"You'll recall our last conversation?"

"Of course. Every word."

"And so you know my true nature." Kieran could not keep her voice from shaking, like her body, like her hands.

"That was," he began, but she cut him off before he could say more.

"Call it what you will. I did not come here for absolution."

Matteo said nothing. Kieran closed her eyes and waited, listening to the sounds of servants at work, and of hammers hitting nails. Perhaps now he thought that she got what she deserved: a guilty conscience.

His silence hurt her, and made her wonder just how much she was allowing the opinions of the Venetian to matter.

His hands came down on her shoulders, a gentle pressure. He turned her to face him.

"Do you see me as a man who would judge you?" he asked softly. "I am a thief, but I've dueled men who I caught stealing from my gaming tables. I am a seducer, but I guard my freedoms and my heart. I am a swindler, but I resent those who try to cheat me. I am the last sort of man who passes judgment."

"Why have you stayed away for weeks?" she asked, hating herself for the breach of her pride. But she needed to know.

He did not answer right away, but she did not retract the question.

"You did not come see me," he pointed out.

"Were you waiting for that?"

"You came today."

"Because you took Nilo."

"I should have asked for him weeks ago, to lure you here," he said softly. "It is good to see you."

Kieran squared her shoulders beneath the pleasant weight of his hands. "Samuel Ellsworth came to see me. He offered an apology, and then, he offered marriage. It seems he has the impression that he violated me, and is seeking to set the matter right."

Matteo's brows shot up.

"I invited him to return on the morrow," Kieran added.

And Matteo smiled a slow grin that made her think of soft velvet and aged whiskey. "Well done."

A strange feeling of pride had Kieran softening.

"If you need my help with anything, the offer stands. You only need to ask."

With the relief that he would be there if she needed him came another thought. Matteo de Gama had gone to great pains to tell her what kind of man he was. It would not do for her to forget that when he told her that he never did anything unless he had a vested interest.

"What would you want in return?" she asked, lifting her chin up another notch. "What is in it for you?"

A strange look came over his face. "So we shall move now to negotiations?"

"I suppose. There is nothing free in this life."

Just as slowly, that smile faded, and the look in his eyes changed. Was that hurt she saw? It couldn't be. She only played the game by his rules.

"Nothing is free. Of that, you are correct," he said, turning away. He moved to pick up his sheet music, and he tapped it into a neat pile, set it on the stool. "A kiss, the length of which is to be determined by me," he said in an off-hand manner. "I am lonely for companionship in this country. I would like a woman to kiss when I am in the mood. In exchange for my help, I will expect a kiss when I want one."

Her pride stung, she said, "So you will not kiss me when I ask you to, but only as part of a bargain?"

Matteo stopped tidying the room. With his back still to her, he hesitated as if unsure what to say or do. "Yes. I will take something from you when there is something in it for me, lest there be any misunderstandings of my motivation. As you have said yourself, and as I have warned you, I am a heartless bastard."

Kieran did not demur, for her pride had been far too injured to worry for his feelings. Before he could add anything more, she sealed the bargain. "Done."

His entire body seemed to stiffen, but when he turned to face her, his expression was smooth and relaxed. "Excellent."

"Will you take your payment now?" Kieran tried to still the tremor of pure anticipation that ran through her body. She would not crave the Venetian's kisses. She would not be left begging for him to come back to her.

But, oh, she did wonder what it would be like to have his mouth move over hers the way it had moved over her neck, lighting that smokeless flame that burned like a thousand tiny fires in her blood.

His expression changed. Those dark eyes moved to her lips, and then her neck. Did he see how fast her pulse throbbed?

"No," he answered casually. He reached into his pocket and withdrew his timepiece, looked at it, and then tucked it back. "Perhaps later. I do not have the time right now. Come."

Matteo turned and led the way out of the ballroom, through the manse and outside once more, back to the out-kitchen. Kieran followed, hating him for making her once again feel artless and humiliated. She'd asked for his kiss, and he'd declined. Again. The bastard.

She thought of the many men who'd come calling, announcing their intentions to Rogan, begging for a stroll in the garden or to hold her gloved hand, so they might press a kiss upon it. She'd spurned them all.

And this man, this romancer, would even not deign to kiss her lips.

Still she followed him, hating herself for not turning her shoulder and leaving. No, she followed, noticing as she did the way he moved, the infuriatingly compelling fluid swagger to his step. And the way his dark hair was curling at his shoulders, his narrow waist tapering into buttocks that looked rounded and firm . . .

Kieran turned her attention to the sky, and forced herself to wonder at the weather, grateful for the coolness of the air and that Matteo's attention was for once, not on her. The hour was growing late, and long, blue shadows stretched across the land as the sun dropped.

Inside the stone kitchen the air was warm and smelled strongly of baking bread and bubbling soup. Kieran looked around, and saw that the stone floor had been swept and scrubbed, the chopping blocks were clean, and the giant hearth showed signs of a recent sweeping. Up in the rafters, though, cobwebs still hung in lacy clumps, and in the corners of the kitchen there were piles of debris that had been swept aside but not yet cleared.

There were three ancient windows along the west wall, a small table and chairs beneath the center window. The last vestiges of sunlight spilled through the wavy, dusty glass.

On the center work table, though, stood crates of root vegetables, beside them, potted herbs. A few slabs of salted meats lay wrapped in paper, and fresh, brown eggs were nestled alongside a rasher of cured bacon. Sacks of flour and oats, and a lump of butter sat beside oils in large, green bottles that bore Italian labels. Wine, spirits, and a few thick, rustic glasses were set in the corner of the table, next to a wheel of cheese.

Matteo went to the simmering caldron and lifted the lid. He took the spoon and tasted the broth, then added salt and a handful of fresh herbs and dried spices. After replacing the lid, he opened the oven and used a huge, wooden paddle to remove a loaf of golden, crusty bread. He set it aside to cool.

"You cook? For yourself?" she asked incredulously.

"Of course." Matteo flashed a grin at her. "I cannot trust the English to cook for me. My English lover adored her native food, going so far as to keep English chefs in her employ, and I thought it disgusting. No soup, no dessert; the meals have no beginning and no end. And when your cooks do make soup, the meat used is disgusting, not fit for a dog." He shrugged. "To each his own, no?"

Kieran could not defend the food in England. After years in Barbados, eating fresh fruits and fish, rich turtle soups and light sauces over vegetables, she, too, found most English fare deplorable.

Nor could she ignore the stab of annoyance she felt at his mention of his former lover.

"My brother has fine chefs. You'll find it much more palatable than the typical boiled mutton," Kieran said, wanting to change the subject.

At the mention of dining with her family, she was reminded of the night she'd revealed everything to Matteo out on the terrace. Apparently, it put him in mind of something else, as well, for Matteo's expression changed again, becoming completely unreadable. And Kieran realized that he did that when he was hiding something; it was his gambler's face. With that knowledge came a feeling of satisfaction, that he was not the only one who could tell when the other was dissembling. What did he hide? she wondered.

A knock sounded on the open door to the kitchen,

and they both turned. The foreman stood there, his hat clutched in his hands. "We're callin' it a day."

Behind the man the sky was darkening. "Of course. I will see you here at dawn. Good work today."

"Right, thank ye," the man said, and after stealing another glance at Kieran, he clapped his hat on his head, turned, and left.

"Soon they will all be gone for the night," Matteo said. "Will you go, too?"

"I have a man here as my guard," she answered him. "And I had hoped to wait for Nilo, if that does not cause you inconvenience."

The truth was, she was not anxious to leave the warmth of the kitchen, where savory soup simmered and the fire crackled, only to ride home in the chilly, damp darkness.

"Your brother will wonder where you are."

"No," she said softly. "He will not."

Matteo hesitated, and then as if to busy himself, he stirred the soup. "Stay, then, and eat with me. There is far too much here for one person."

Kieran plucked at her sleeve and wondered why the mood had suddenly turned awkward. "Very well."

"Sit. I will serve you."

He was gracious as he took her elbow and led her to where a small, rough hewn table and chairs sat beside a window. As if he were attending a lady in a grand manse or aboard his elegant *burchiello*, he pulled out the chair for her as she sat. The stone structure of the kitchen made for a deep windowsill, and on it Matteo placed candles and lit them, their flames reflecting in the wavy windowpanes. He rummaged in the crates by the work area and produced a square of white linen, which he draped over the tabletop. He then lit another stubby candle and placed it in the center, lifting his head to look at her. He watched her for a long moment.

"Candlelight becomes you," he said softly.

"Do you find me too unsightly for sunlight?" she asked, meaning to tease, but she heard the sound of her own voice, full of insecurity.

He only smiled. Reaching out a finger, he touched her face, just above her brow, and then traced down to her jaw and her chin. "Do not be silly."

Matteo turned and fetched earthen bowls and plates, opened wine, cut bread and cheese, and drizzled oil over anchovies. He moved about the kitchen with such comfort, performing tasks that Kieran had only ever known servants to do. Yet, he made them look enjoyable, and somehow turned the musty out-kitchen into a firelit haven that felt more like home than any mansion.

She thought of the ballroom, and how he'd done the same, filling a corner of the vast room with books, music, candles, and warmth. Yes, that was it. Everything he touched, he warmed.

Even her, she realized. Sitting in the kitchen, she felt warm and cozy in a way that had nothing to do with temperature; she'd sat cold and alone in front of many a roaring fire.

He set the table and put out the bread and cheese. He filled wine glasses and ladled soup, carrying them to the table, and taking his seat across from her. He lifted his wine glass and held it up.

Kieran did the same.

"*Tra noi*," he said.

She didn't know what he said, and she didn't ask. She smiled and touched her glass to his. She sipped, and savored the ripe taste of summer grapes with the husky undertones of citrus and lavender. The food smelled so good, and her stomach clenched in expectation. Kieran couldn't recall a time she felt more ravenous.

"Tonight we dine as peasants," he said with a smile. "Someday I will make you a feast."

Kieran smiled in return, and actually hoped that day would come soon.

She tasted the soup, a hearty vegetable beef with thick slices of carrots, onions, potatoes, and turnips, its broth flavored with wine and spices. The bread was dense and crusty, warm enough that the butter melted into sweet, salty rivulets the moment she spread it. The cheese was soft and mild, and she slathered that over the crust of the bread, and ate it with a spoonful of soup.

The fire popped and crackled, and the darkness grew, but did not touch the cozy interior. She felt as if she were wrapped in a safe place, surrounded by light and heat.

Across the table he ate, watching her with the regard of male interest, a sensual look in his eyes that made her wonder once more why he refused to kiss her. He'd said he wanted it too much. That he could lose himself against her lips. Was that the truth? she wondered.

To cover her discomfort, she asked, "Where did you learn to cook?"

Matteo set down his spoon and grinned. "My neighbor, the old woman who lived beside me. The smells that came from her house. *Dio santo!* She made everything, soups, sauces, breads, but she was only one person. She had no family to cook for, but did it for the pleasure. So I made arrangements with her, to pay for meals. So I would come at the same time every night to eat, and, oh, the food was delicious. Ah, so good," he said, leaning in his chair, remembering.

"But I started coming earlier and earlier to dinner, to watch her cook. It was art in motion. She caught onto me, and began asking me for my help. Soon enough, we were cooking side by side. I brought her the produce and the meats daily, and we cooked together." Matteo shrugged and took a bite of bread. He consulted his timepiece and then slid it back into his pocket. "I am curious about everything. Why not cooking, as well? So much to do, so much to enjoy. Why not learn as much as possible in this life?"

"How long did you visit the woman?"

"About three years, nearly every day before she took sick. She died a little more than a year ago." Matteo's eyes turned sad, and he covered his emotion by sipping his wine.

"You cared for her."

"Of course. She was a lovely woman. Kindhearted. There are too few truly kind people. It is always sad to see one go."

"But you must have grown to love her," Kieran said, wondering why he grew philosophical when he spoke about people who he'd lost in some way.

"I cooked with her. I ate with her. I paid for the meals, and I learned a new skill. She found someone to pass her knowledge onto. It was a satisfying arrangement for both of us." He turned his head and looked out the window, even though it was completely dark outside.

"She must have loved you like a son," Kieran said, not caring that Matteo did not seem to want to discuss it. "Imagine how much joy you must have brought her, a lonely old woman who got to pass her art onto someone who enjoyed it as she did. It must have meant everything to her, those afternoons you spent with her in her kitchen."

Matteo turned to Kieran, and for a moment his face was unguarded. He looked young and hopeful. "Do you really think so?"

"Yes," she answered him. Why should that come as such a shock to him, that she might have grown fond of the young, handsome man who came daily for cooking lessons and to share a meal? "I think she must have grown to love you very much."

He hesitated for a moment, and something shadowed his eyes, like the memory of a deep, distant pain.

"She never said so," he replied softly.

Matteo rose and cleared the dishes, puttering around in the kitchen once more, rinsing the plates and bowls in a bucket of water and setting them into a basin to be washed later. He threw a few logs on the fire and consulted his watch once more.

"Are you waiting for something?" Kieran asked.

As if in answer, Nilo appeared in the doorway. He saw Kieran and his face lit in a smile.

"I went to the manor to find you, Miss Keerahn, but you weren't there," Nilo said. He entered into the kitchen, removed his cloak, and hung it on a hook.

"Why were looking for me? Is all well?"

Nilo did not answer her, but instead turned and faced the darkness outside. He beckoned, and in a gentle voice said, "It is good. Safe. Come. Come in."

"Who's there?" Kieran asked, but then froze in place as a girl entered.

She had blonde hair, and an unmistakable birthmark beneath her eye, shaped like a strawberry. Their eyes met, and Kieran felt as though the earth beneath her was made of quicksand, and she was sinking down in it, drowning.

ᔟ15ᔟ

Matteo leaned against the butcher block table and folded his arms, unsure what Kieran would do, or how she would react to being blindsided.

He felt bad about ambushing her with Alva, but knew

that if he'd told her anything about it, she would have run far and long and not looked back. Instead, he'd made plans to have Nilo retrieve Kieran from the manse and bring her, but that had been unnecessary when she'd shown up of her own volition. Nilo and Matteo had discussed the matter, and had come to the conclusion that it was best to simply bring the women together, and let Alva's words offer a semblance of comfort, if possible.

But looking at her now, he wondered if he'd made a huge mistake. Kieran's skin had gone deathly pale, with two red spots flagging her cheeks. Her eyes were wide and unfocused, her lips parted, her breath shallow.

"You," Kieran whispered. Her eyes flicked from Matteo, back to Alva, and then settled on Nilo. They grew wounded and more vulnerable than Matteo had ever seen them. Her voice betrayed her hurt. "How could you?"

Kieran scrambled to her feet and backed away into the shadows of the kitchen. Her hand was pressed to her mouth, which opened like a silent scream as her breasts heaved with each of her shuddering breaths.

"No," she breathed. "Why?"

"This is Alva," Matteo said to Kieran. "She has come to tell you something very important."

Alva hesitated, and looked up to Nilo for reassurance.

Matteo noticed that Nilo had done well with her. He'd instructed him to see to the girl's basic needs, to make sure she bathed, and she had: Her hair gleamed fresh and bright, and her skin was clear and pretty without the layer of grime. Matteo had also given Nilo money to buy Alva a modest dress, and she was appropriately gowned in a simple frock of mauve cotton topped with a brown wool cloak. She did not look like a whore, but like a young farmer's daughter.

And she gazed up to Nilo as if he were Prince Charming himself, her eyes glistening with trust. "Has she gone daft?"

Nilo patted Alva's shoulder protectively. "Miss Kee-rahn needs to know what happened. Then she will be better."

"She's lookin' at me like I'm a ghost."

"You are that. A ghost from her past," Matteo said. Something in his chest hurt as he watched the pain play over Kieran's features, and he wondered if it was his heart. What was it about this girl that she affected him so? "She looks at you, and she relives it. Tell her, Alva, so she can put that night to rest."

Alva took a few steps toward Kieran. Her head cocked to the side and sympathy was written on every line of her face. Kieran took another step back, retreating into the darker corner, and Alva stopped, put her hand on her hip. "Och, are ye that torn up over what I did? You shouldna be fashin' and frettin' over it. My virginity was for sale, and if not that man, it would've been another. They wanted a virgin for a duke or somesuch man who was afraid of disease an didna want a whore. But that man wasna there, and the other decided I'd do just as well for him. It was nothin' ye did, lass. I made my bed when I came to London instead of tryin' to keep body an' soul together at home. I've been lying in that bed ever since, but it was my own makin'."

Alva's fingers plucked at the sleeve of her gown, and she shrugged with the defeated attitude of one who had spent too many years at the mercy of others. "He never would have takin' ye, no matter who ye'd chosen, me or you. You see, when the man tossed ye to the floor, I heard him tell the other one to scare ye good, but not to touch you. He said you were his cousin, an' to leave you alone. Do ye see? The man who swived me wasna allowed to hurt you."

She peered at Kieran in the shadows. "Do ye ken?"

When she received no answer, Alva glanced back at Nilo and crinkled her nose. "I don't think this is workin'. If my comin' here doesna help her, the money is mine anyway, aye? And I can keep the dress?"

A terrible silence fell over the four people in the kitchen.

"What?!" Kieran finally shrieked, as the full meaning of Alva's final sentence sank in. She came out of the shadows like a wildcat, her beautiful face contorted by a fierce snarl.

Matteo involuntarily took a step back.

She was magnificent, he thought at first, and then logic prevailed as he realized the gravity of his mistake.

"Kieran, listen," he began.

"You listen," she hissed, turning on him. "You dare to invade my past by dredging up my deepest disgrace, something that has tortured me every day and every night for years, and you treat it so lightly that you bring her here! Never mind that you did not so much as offer me the option of confronting this, you just bring her here in some high-handed decision that you have no right to make. And then you pay her to lie?"

A sob was on the edge of her voice, threatening a deluge of tears, but she did not give in to them. She rode high on her anger. "Scoundrel! You prodded and poked until I revealed myself, and the very first thing you do is to go digging around until you find the girl who I sacrificed for my own safety, and then you bribe her? You bribe her with money and gowns, and ask her to come and make up some awful lies that are supposed to absolve me of my sins? 'Tis disgusting, because I know that there must be something in it for you, yes? It turns my stomach to imagine what that might be. It sickens me to think how low you can sink."

She turned and faced Nilo, who stood as still as a statue beside Alva. The anger faded from Kieran's face, and an expression of utter betrayal replaced it. "And you," she whispered, "you went along with him."

"Kieran, please," Matteo said softly. "It is not how you see it. Listen."

"Listen. Please," she mocked him. "Words designed to supplicate. To manipulate, more like. Keep your words, for now. I am certain you will find another woman to use them on. Perhaps the Dowager Countess of Perth would listen. Perhaps she would love to hear you play the cello. Maybe she would even want to hear your stories. Tell her the one about your mother; 'twill surely play on her heartstrings. And then, perhaps you can ferret out one of her secrets, and use it against her for your own gain. When you're done with her, you'll just walk away, won't you? It won't matter what you leave behind. You won't be there to see it." She trembled, her lips parted as she looked at him.

Matteo hadn't thought it possible, but he felt ashamed of himself. Not for deceiving Kieran, because he hadn't, but because he had done all those things she'd said to other women.

And why, he asked himself, should she believe the best in him, when he'd gone to such pains to tell her about the worst?

Kieran seemed to withdraw into herself, lost for the moment. And then she glanced around the room, her gaze landing on them each in turn. When she looked again at Nilo, she hesitated as if lost in a sea of emotions she could not fathom.

Before any of them could react, Kieran turned on her heel and ran out of the kitchen, disappearing into the night.

"Wait here," Matteo said to Nilo as he dashed past him.

* * *

Kieran ran into the darkness, not watching where she went. Her breath came in burning cold gasps that stung her throat and lungs. She tripped over a branch and stumbled, but she did not fall. Pressing on, she thought she heard something behind her, and she picked up her pace.

How dare they? The words repeated in her mind again and again. How could they stoop so low, to pay the girl to make up an outrageous lie about that horrible night?

And for what? So she would pull up her skirts and spread her legs in payment to the Venetian rogue? No doubt he thought her a puppet on strings, and he the puppet master.

Memories of that night flared in her mind, of Samuel holding a pistol to the girl's head. He had meant what he said, her virtue or Kieran's. Kieran's choice. She remembered the look on his face, his superior smile, his certainty of what she would do.

He'd meant it. She was certain.

It could not have been a ruse designed simply to show her the depth of the cowardice deep within her own heart.

She hadn't spent three years flogging herself for something that was not preventable.

She felt the wounds on her thigh open up and begin to bleed again, the blood tickling as it ran down her leg. Her corset was a tourniquet around her middle, making her head light with lack of breath as she gasped for air and ran faster. She would soon lose consciousness, but she did not care. The black void would maybe bring peace.

And then she felt a hand clamp down on her shoulder, and another on her arm. Matteo spun her around. As he did, her foot twisted and she lost her balance and fell, hitting the ground hard. Holding onto her, she pulled him off balance. He fell too, hitting with a grunt, taking the brunt of his weight on his side so he would not land on her.

Kieran struggled to get back up, not an easy task when wearing heavy skirts that were pinned beneath a man who outweighed her by at least six stone.

"Are you hurt?" he asked.

"Let me go," she demanded, ignoring the insult of his question. As if he truly worried. Ha! He'd just brought her down like a fox on a rabbit. She tried to pry his fingers from her arms. They encircled her like manacles.

His breath was hot against her neck as he held her down. "Do not be a fool. I will not let you run into the night."

"How dare you! You will let me go or I will cut your heart out and leave it for the wolves." She was breathless and furious, struggling to pull away, to get up. She wanted to run and run, until she collapsed, and then she wanted to disappear. Book passage on a ship, sail away, and be gone from everyone who'd ever known her.

With the tips of her fingers she tried to tug up her skirts, wanting to get to her dagger and show this Venetian bastard once and for all time that she was not some defenseless female who he could manipulate. But she could not reach low enough to gain purchase on the fabric. Frustration seethed in her like molten lava, and she was ready to erupt if he did not release her, soon.

The moonlight bathed them in silver as they struggled on the grass, both breathing heavily, both full of righteous indignation.

And then, pinned by his greater strength, her weapon out of reach, and the memory of Alva's words so fresh and raw, Kieran suffered one of her greatest humiliations. Her rage and frustration and shame melted into a hot stew of emotion and escaping her powers of control, it just happened: She began to cry.

Weeping was something she did in private, but she could not control it, could not hold back the sobs or the tears.

Suddenly his grip changed from confining to comforting. He held her close to his chest, one large hand cupped against the curve of her skull, and she let go.

He stroked her back, shushing her with soothing sounds, murmuring in her ear, "*Per favore non piangere tesoro. No riesco a sopportarlo.*"

Kieran calmed somewhat, but did not pull away. Beneath her cheek his chest felt warm and hard, his greater size a comfort, the beating of his heart slow and steady. The linen of his shirt smelled of him, and she inhaled his scent along with the cool night air.

He pressed a kiss to the top of her head, and he just held her in a way that no one had since she was a child, rocking her slightly, whispering soft, meaningless words, making comforting sounds.

She sighed, sniffed, and used the sleeve of her gown to dry her face. She reclined in his arms, still pinned but no longer struggling. Her hair had fallen down to tumble down her back and into the grass, and her shift clung to the sticky blood on her leg.

The moon was full, ripe and low in the indigo sky, bright enough that Kieran could read Matteo's expression when she looked up at him.

"I am sorry," he whispered. "I meant to help you. I thought that if that girl told what happened, you would find a measure of peace."

Kieran said nothing, but just watched him talk to her. Perhaps it was a trick of the faded light, but his eyes looked sorrowful, sincere, soul deep.

"I swear it to you, I did not pay her for her words. I paid for her time and a new dress because she has become a prostitute. I had hoped to spare you that knowledge." Matteo's fingers moved in her hair, the pressure of his touch making her very aware of just how alone they were, lying in the grass, bathed in the silvery shadows of moonlight.

"I don't know what to believe," Kieran confessed.

Something that looked like hurt flashed in Matteo's eyes, but it faded as fast as it appeared. "Ask Nilo, if you do not believe me. He would never lie to you."

"But how? Why?" She shook her head in frustration. "I just do not understand."

"The story you told me did not make sense. I knew there must be more to what went on, why she was there, why she did not fight, why she brought no charges against him. Those men did not hide their identities, and they just let the girl go. It did not add up.

"And of course, I wanted to know why Samuel left you alone afterward. Why you were untouched. To answer these questions, I needed to find the girl, and thankfully, your Nilo remembered her face, and the address she gave the driver that night. We looked for her, we found her, and she told us what really happened."

Kieran sighed, turned her head away from him, and closed her eyes, needing space from his male nearness, his confidence.

She reached for the anger that had ripped through her, but it was gone. In that wild fury, she'd not thought of anything else. It made her understand why Rogan had climbed in the boxing ring, punching and taking hits until there was no other reality.

Her dagger on her skin had nearly given her escape, but was followed by such shame she did not know if it was worth the price.

Running had felt good, the burn of her lungs, the pain in her gut, the pumping of her legs, becoming lost in the wind. But it was not dignified for a lady to run, and her corset was a vise around her middle that prevented it, anyway.

Samuel, and his absurd marriage proposal. Alva, and her shocking revelation. Matteo, and the confusing feelings he inspired. And then there was the revenge, a thing she wanted and feared in equal measure. Surely it was wrong to desire it, and yet, it seemed worse to be a powerless victim who does nothing in turn.

She was a woman. There was no physical outlet for the feelings that crashed and burned within her.

Or was there?

She turned back to Matteo and shifted her weight so she lay more against his body. He was muscled and warm, so warm. She did not need a cloak when he held her. She did not need a fire when she was near him.

Kieran looked up at him in the semi-darkness. "I do not need to ask Nilo. I believe you."

"I truly am sorry that it shocked you so. I wanted to make you feel better, not worse."

"Make me feel better," she whispered, her cheeks burning with her own audacity. "Make me feel something different, something new. 'Tis your part of the bargain. Take it."

Matteo stiffened against her, tension radiated in every line of his body, the muscles in his arms bulging as if he fought his own instinct.

"Will you reject me again?" she asked softly. "Am I not comely enough? Am I too young? Too . . . inexperienced?"

Matteo looked down on her in the moonlight. She was a painting in motion, fair, creamy skin framed by hair the shade of a dark garnet held to a candle's light. Her eyes were fascinating, narrow in rage, crinkled in laughter, wide with delight when she ate his food and found the taste pleasing on her tongue.

He pictured her head held back, those magnificent eyes closed in ecstasy, her body like it was now, only undressed, supple and willing in his arms, curving against his body in a way that intoxicated his imagination.

Too young, too inexperienced, not comely enough?

More like too beautiful, too compelling, and far too close to his actual heart.

Matteo knew the danger of falling in love. So why was he allowing her such liberties with his emotions?

She would use him as an escape and as an avenger. And when she was done with him, she would move on, likely marry herself an English lord who would clothe her in silks and drape her in jewels. It was what she deserved, he thought, a respectable name to give to her children. It was what she'd told him she had wanted, once.

Respectable. The word burned in his gut like acid. Since when had he concerned himself about such things, he wondered.

The answer came, unbidden, undeniable: Since he'd met Kieran Mullen and realized how much it pained him that he had nothing to tempt her with, nothing to offer her. He could win money to buy her gowns and gifts and jewels. He could woo her with words. Yes, he had so many words at his disposal. Worthless and meaningful words.

He could compose for her, play for her, write sonnets, cook, and paint for her. He was good with his hands; he could build a home for her, paint walls, lay tile, and mortar brick for her. He could die for her if it came to it; he had a life to give. But he still could not give her a name that meant anything more than *bastard*.

He traced the shape of her lips with his eyes, imagined them against his own. If her lips were as soft as they looked, he might never let her go, he might never walk away.

She was his muse, dragged from the water and into his selfish life. She was shadowed light, sweet bitterness, tender toughness.

He wanted to kiss her the way he wanted to breathe.

She was dangerous, so dangerous. Silken destruction and seductive annihilation.

What were the chances he could kiss her and keep his heart safe?

What were the chances he would withstand one more invitation?

Why had he made kissing her part of the ridiculous bargain? He'd told her he was helping her because he wanted something, but he didn't tell her the true reason.

He was helping her because he wanted to see her smile more often. It was the most beautiful thing he'd ever seen, that smile.

Why couldn't he have taken her money? It would have been so much simpler, and then perhaps she would not keep tempting him with her mouth.

If he fell in love with her, he would be that young man again, bringing her little gifts, writing silly poems, hoping for her to love him in return, knowing he wished the impossible.

"Forgive my vulgarity," she whispered. "I sometimes lose my sense of propriety when I am with you."

Kieran made to move away, and suddenly Matteo didn't care if he lost his heart. He began to wonder if he'd ever had it, or if she'd found it at the bottom of the canal and dragged it up with her. He certainly had not been the same since that night.

"Wait," he said, holding her close. "Wait."

Her eyes widened; her lips parted and began to tremble. This would be her first kiss. Matteo had kissed more women than he could recall.

So why did this feel like his first, too?

"You are beyond beautiful," he said to her.

She smiled, and was as radiant as the moon above. "Do you think so?"

"I do." He hesitated, a strange wobbling feeling shook in his body, and he felt as shy as a child. "What do you think of me?"

Kieran reached up and touched his hair, her slim fingers like a butterfly's caress. Her smile changed, grew tender. "I think you are far less jaded than you claim."

"Why do say that?"

"You saved my life. You translated your work. You promised me revenge for my honor. When I told you that I had no honor, you wept for me. And in the dark of night, you went into a strange city and found the truth, just to make me feel better," she whispered in the darkness. "Where is the black heart you keep telling me about?"

Matteo tried to feign his usual carelessness, but she reached beyond his facade and it seemed that in this moment, he couldn't pretend. "Once in a great while, it beats for something else." He cleared his throat. If he was going to be honest, he'd go all in. "Someone else."

"Me?" she asked shyly.

"Yes, Kieran. You." Looking down on her in the silvery light and dark shadows, he wondered if she could ever truly care for a worthless gambler, a needy bastard who could not even inspire his mother's love. "You are unlike any other woman I have ever met, and I find your differences most appealing."

"How so? How am I different?"

Matteo controlled himself. He did not say that she was fiercer than any other woman he'd known, in will, in spirit, and in her heart. Neither did he confess that he thought of her as his muse ever since that day he'd pulled her from the water and found a spitting wildcat sheathed in icy demeanor. He kept to himself that her face made him want clay in his hands, paint on his brush, ink on his quill, and his cello cradled between his thighs. And he left out that the image of that black dagger on her supple white thigh was enough to have him longing for darker, more sensual pursuits of his favorite art form.

"You look for love in every situation, when most others I have met are meeting baser needs."

Kieran turned her head and looked up at the moon, the light of which turned her skin to smooth marble. "I am not looking for love."

"You are, and you find it everywhere: with your brother, Nilo, your horses, the old woman who taught me to cook. You are full of love, but just have not reconciled yourself to its destiny, yet."

"At the risk of sounding maudlin, that gentle emotion is not for a woman like me. I have seen my heart, and it is selfish and self-serving."

"I have seen it, too. I see the way you look at your brother, as if you fear disappointing him. I see the way you look at the duchess; you are awed by her, and you wish you could be more like her. Your Nilo sees it, each time you look upon him. He is more than a guard; he is your friend and you love him. I see the way you stroke your horses, and the tenderness you feel for them. I have seen your face grow soft and full of love when you speak about your mother and father; you love and miss them so much it pains you. I even see it with me, when you point out my smallest kindnesses. I have told you that I do nothing unless it serves me, but you see beyond my bravado.

"I also saw your soul when you told me about the night with Alva. Your heart, Kieran, aches for the torture you did not choose. And so you endure your own form of penance, tormenting yourself because you were afraid." Matteo touched her hair, stroked it back from her face. "Have you not suffered enough? How much punishment do you deserve for a moment of utter horror, and a choice made in complete terror?"

His voice gentled as he watched her expression turn

sad, lost, and lonely. "Does it help to know that you never had the choice?"

Kieran turned to face him again, and she sighed. Her breath was warm on his face, and she smelled of sandalwood and jasmine, that mystifyingly sweet scent that made his chest ache with a longing he could not name.

"I think it does. What's more, it touches me that you would go to such lengths. And for me, when I have done nothing for you," she added, her voice full of wondrous sincerity. "Thank you for that."

There was no more denial left. Matteo was nothing if not self-aware; as a man of letters and a student of the arts, he understood that knowing himself was the first step toward achieving honesty in his art.

His senses were alive, prickling with awareness. The girl beside him in the grass was the only thing that occupied his mind lately, yet he'd made no real effort to seduce her. Compromising her was the last thing he wished for. She deserved only good things.

He could not keep the truth from himself any longer.

The night air was cold, the moon was bright, and the girl in his arms was lonely, complicated, bittersweet and impossibly beautiful.

There, on a tiny piece of English soil near an old, crumbling mansion and beneath stately, winter-stripped trees, Matteo de Gama, the self-proclaimed jaded romancer, abandoned the game, surrendered the stakes, and lost his heart.

He lowered his mouth to hers and breathed her breath into his lungs.

Kieran lost herself in the feel of her first kiss. His mouth was soft and gentle, grazing his lips against hers. He moved so slowly, teasing, sampling, savoring, his breath mingling with hers.

She had expected his kiss to be sensual and practiced, but this tasting felt as if he, too, was experiencing something new. He kissed her almost shyly, and she thought she felt him tremble as if he were chilled by the cold air, at odds with the heat that pumped from him.

Before she could wonder why he shook, he caught her lower lip in his and sucked it lightly before dipping inside her mouth to lick her tongue with his.

As she'd hoped, the rest fell away. There was no more thinking, no more hurting, no more suffering. Here was physical feeling that drowned out anything else.

Heat purled in her blood and made her tingle with warmth.

She slid her arms up and wrapped them around his neck. He bent over her and she felt his hair fall over her cheek in a silky caress. His hand stroked her back, and then pressed flat, pulling her closer against his hard, warm body, deepening the kiss, taking her mouth with a greedy assault that stole her breath.

And she reveled in the feel of him. He was long and sinewy, strong with a tensile strength that was like the man himself, contained and at the ready. Her soft breasts flattened against his hard chest, and the sensation thrilled her. He tasted as he smelled, like spices and citrus bergamot, with the slight tang of wine, smoke, and leather.

He slanted his head and the kiss grew deeper still, his tongue moving in her mouth in ways that made scandalously dark longings curl in her body. No more smokeless flame, this was fire and it burned in her blood.

She heard herself moan, and she felt her body melt against his. She did not bother to pull away; she wanted this more than she cared for reputation or propriety. This was life, raw and untamed, hot with unveiled passions she hadn't known existed inside of her.

No more ice princess. No more lonely heart.

Kieran slid her fingers into his dark hair and curved them around the shape of his skull, felt the bone and the flesh and the heat of him. This was real in a world where little else made sense.

"Kieran," he whispered against her mouth. "Kieran, *angelo mio, anima mio. Voglio accarezzarti aleggiando sulla tua pelle come fossi la luce del sole al mattino. Voglio solo dirti che ti amo. Ti amo, Kieran.*"

"What are you saying?" she asked, her lips still against his, her eyes closed. His tone had made his words sound like a confession and a vow combined. "What does that mean?"

He pulled back and looked at her. She met his gaze. He looked intense, urgent, and somehow fragile, as if a word from her could shatter him.

"You are beautiful," he said.

"It does not take so many words to say that."

"It does when the woman is as beautiful to me as you are," he answered, and then he kissed her again before she could ask anything else.

And she did not pull away to press the question. When his mouth moved over hers and stoked that fire in her blood, she lost all sense of everything else.

She ran her hands through his hair, and then cupped his lean cheeks, delighting in the way his stubble scratched her skin, but his lips were so soft.

He pulled back again, and Kieran held his face. She looked up at him. "What is wrong?"

Matteo pressed a hand to the back of hers, and then took it from his face, pressed a kiss to her palm where his cheek had just been.

"We should go," he said abruptly. "Nilo is waiting with Alva, and he is probably worrying about you."

Kieran didn't argue, for his expression had her wondering about his mood. He seemed suddenly distant, vaguely annoyed.

He stood and helped her to her feet, and they began to walk back to the out-kitchen.

The wind had picked up, moaning in the treetops and rustling the dead leaves in the grass. Clouds drifted in the night sky, casting eerie shadows in the moonlight and beneath the trees.

Matteo walked beside her, his long legs carrying him farther from her as she hastened to keep up. Kieran matched her pace to his and discreetly pressed her fingertips to her lips. They burned and felt swollen, marked by his mouth.

If Rogan saw her, with her hair unbound and full of grass, her skirts stained and damp, her mouth inflamed with kisses and her chin abraded by Matteo's scratchy stubble, her brother would forget his promise to let her manage her own life. How long before he forced Matteo at gunpoint onto the next ship bound for the Americas?

The image raised questions she had been trying to avoid asking herself.

How long before Matteo tired of England's damp cold and sought out more temperate climes? She imagined how England must look to him after Venice. Venice was a warm city painted with a golden brush; England was a damp watercolor, barren beneath winter's clutch.

How long before he sought an experienced lover to warm his bed? Kisses would not keep a man such as Matteo enamored for long, she knew, and her kisses were likely artless and without sensual skill. Perhaps soon he would leave England and seek out a warmer country and an even warmer woman.

Kieran thought of Matteo leaving, pictured him on a ship's deck.

She would not fall to her knees and beg him to stay. But neither could she pretend that it would not hurt her. He might not be actively seducing her with his charm, but his kindness and his kisses were working just as well.

Kieran reached out and grabbed his hand. He glanced over to her, and she saw a question in his eyes. His hand was much larger, harder, and warmer than her own. She tucked her hand in his, and held it in answer. His fingers wrapped around hers, a perfect fit. He slowed his pace and walked beside her. With their hands clasped, they walked together.

And Kieran allowed herself that moment, refusing to think of the future or the past. He would leave one day and not look back, she thought, but he is here now.

~ 16 ~

When they entered the kitchen, the first thing Matteo noticed was that Alva was seated, hunched over a bowl and slurping soup as if she'd never eaten before.

Nilo stopped in mid-step, one hand full of bread and the other bearing a mug of water. He looked guilty, as if he'd been caught in a crime. Setting them down in front of Alva, he turned to Matteo. "She was hungry."

"Of course, Nilo. Thank you for seeing to our guest."

This seemed to put Nilo more at ease, and he approached Kieran cautiously. He looked her over with eyes that glistened like liquid obsidian. "You are doing well, Miss Keerahn?"

"I am." Kieran looked up at him. Her lips trembled, and Matteo wondered if she would weep again. As if undecided herself, she threw her arms around him, burying her face against his broad chest.

At first taken aback, Nilo stood like a statue, obviously

uncomfortable at the physical display from his usually distant mistress. Kieran's shoulders hitched once, then again, and Nilo relaxed a bit in his new role and patted her hair.

Kieran pulled away, brought her gaze to his once more, and simply said, "Thank you."

Alva rose and stood awkwardly by the table. Her expression was that of a girl who felt out of place and no longer needed. Nilo turned and met her gaze, and she smiled tremulously up at him.

"I ought be headin' back." Her cheeks turned red and she shrugged, her hands smoothing her new skirts over and again. "It's growin' late."

It struck Matteo that her speaking of the lateness of the hour did not mean she was fatigued, but that it was time to go to work.

He pictured, in far too graphic detail, the drunk, unwashed men who would be coming to the brothel with their money and their lust, using Alva as if she were meaningless, worthless, and barely human.

Matteo watched Nilo's cheeks grow tense, his brows come down, and his lips flatten into a grim line as he grabbed his cloak from the peg and tossed it over his shoulders.

Matteo had never been the sort of man who concerned himself with the plight of others. So why should he get involved now, in the pathetic life of this young prostitute?

He wouldn't. He opened the door for them. "Thank you for your help, Alva."

Alva nodded and turned to Kieran. "I hope ye can put your heart to rest. I'll pray it is so."

Matteo saw a strange expression take Kieran's face, an odd mix of gratitude and sadness. Alva and Nilo turned to leave.

"Wait," Matteo commanded, perhaps too harshly. But

inside he jeered at himself, trying to save a prostitute was like trying to unsink a ship. But he could not stand the look on Alva's face, her wounded soul. Nor could he tolerate Nilo's expression of frustration and disgust. "Alva, you said you worked as a seamstress?"

She paused in the doorway. "Aye, my stitchin' is second to none."

"I need someone to fashion window hangings, re-upholster furniture, and to sew bed linens. Do you have any experience with these sorts of tasks?"

"Ooh, aye. I've done plenty o' that sort of work, and garments, as well."

Matteo ignored the sound of his internal critic, the sardonic laughter at his futile, ridiculous idea and his absurd meddling.

Alva's eyes had gone hopeful, and Nilo grinned as if he'd just been handed a sack of gold. Matteo didn't risk a glance at Kieran; would she be upset at the idea of seeing Alva again? Would she see it as another manipulation?

He couldn't go back. The words had been spoken and Alva waited expectantly. "Would you be willing to accept this position? It would include weekly wages, and a small sleeping chamber in the servants' quarters." He tried to sound stern, covering his earnestness and his cynicism in equal measure. "I will expect you to work assiduously, and comport yourself decently, as the woman you were before desperation sent you down a different path."

"Oh, yes. Oh. Sire. Yes. I swear it, ye'll not regret me. I'll sew until my fingers bleed."

"Do you have possessions you need to retrieve?" Matteo asked. "I am certain Nilo would . . ."

"No." Alva abruptly interjected. Her hands smoothed her new gown, and then she patted the side of her skirts. "Pardon my rudeness. No. I brought my money wi' me. They can burn the rest, for all I care."

"Your flower?" Nilo asked.

Alva looked up to him, and her face took on such softness that she was nearly beautiful. "Aye, an' it's kind o'
ye to think of it, but I'll just as soon plant a new one."
She turned and looked out the window into the darkness. Her chin came up. "If I do not ha' to go back, I
shallna do so."

Matteo stole a glimpse of Kieran, and was rewarded
with a brief, tender smile before she moved away to
stand closer to the fire. She reached up to fix her hair,
and Matteo itched for paper and quill, wanting to sketch
the feminine curve of her up-stretched arms, her long,
narrow fingers in her tumbled-down hair.

Distracted by Kieran's disheveled beauty and the
memory of their kiss, Matteo said offhandedly, "Nilo, will
you see to Alva's needs? Show her to the servants' quarters. There are blankets and candles in boxes in the
main parlor. Give her what she needs to be comfortable
for the night."

Nilo nodded and as the two made to leave, Alva
stopped in front of Matteo. She bobbed into a little curtsey, which made Matteo feel like an imposter; he was not
a landowner or a noble.

"I thank ye, sire. I canna ken why ye'd do so, but I can
only see ye dinna regret it."

Matteo nodded, uncomfortable in the position of em-
ployer and savior, not certain which felt worse. "Good
night, Alva. Sleep well."

They left, she and Nilo, and Matteo noticed how Nilo
reached for Alva's hand, and placed it on his arm, leading her over the uneven grounds as if she were a high-
born lady. He watched them until they disappeared into
the darkness, and when he turned, Kieran stood by the
fire, studying him. Her face was cast in light and shadow,
burnished by the gold flames.

The mood became awkward, though he knew not why.

"'Twas good of you to help her," Kieran said finally.

"I need a skilled seamstress." He shrugged, trying to seem indifferent. "Be warned: If she does not satisfy my standards, I will dismiss her."

Kieran smiled, and raised a brow. "I told you your heart was not so jaded."

Matteo drew close to her, a mindless moth to a killing flame. He wanted to drop to his knees in front of her, lay his head on her belly, and beg her to stop playing with his heart.

But instead he touched her chin with the tip of his finger, tilted her head back and smiled into her eyes. "But it is. Why do you not believe me when I tell you who I am?"

Kieran's eyes narrowed a bit. "Perhaps I ought to. And while I hear what you say, signore, I also see what you do."

"Remember that a man's most effective way of endearing himself to a woman is through acts of kindness."

The words struck her, hard. He saw the barb sting. And he hated himself.

Matteo wanted her in his arms, in his bed, in his life, and to hell with the ramifications. An idea bloomed in his mind: Compromise her and Rogan will force a marriage.

Matteo did the only thing he could do. He walked away before he descended into the sort of love-crazed madness where such things made perfect sense. He began stacking the dishes Alva had used.

Seeming restless, Kieran began to help him tidy the room. She blew out candles and corked the wine bottle.

Matteo observed her surreptitiously, the swing of her hips, the grace of her movements, the elegance of her profile when limed in the curling gray smoke of an extinguished candle. It was pleasant moving about with her, puttering at mindless domestic tasks while the fire burned cheerfully, chasing the chill of nighttime.

She carried the wine to the center work table and set it down. Flour dusted the surface, and she traced a pattern in the white dust, her mind obviously elsewhere.

She was as remote as the moon and as ungovernable as the wind. Had he only an hour before held her to his body and told her the desire of his heart?

Fool. Beggar. When would he learn?

Nilo returned, the door banging as the wind threw it against the wall. He rubbed his hands briskly. "Alva rests and we should go back, Miss Keerahn. The air blows hard and smells of rain."

Kieran nodded and retrieved her cloak. Matteo banked the fire, blew out the last of the candles, and reached for his own cloak, as well. Closing the kitchen door behind them as they left, he reached out and touched her arm. "When will I see you again?"

Wind whipped her cloak and tore at her hair. And it occurred to Kieran with horrifying clarity that she did not want to leave.

He'd told her his heart beat for her. He'd whispered words in Italian against her lips that had sounded like something far deeper than a compliment.

He'd also told her he could seduce her, make himself the center of her world, and have her licking the floor in front of him if he wanted it.

And she believed him, because she verged on the precipice of becoming obsessed.

"I do not know," she said softly. "But it does not matter. I want to be released from the bargain. Whatever I decide to do, I will do it on my own terms, without your help. Your price is too high to pay, signore."

Matteo's expression was stricken for a moment,

and then it turned blank, once more suavely confident. "As you wish."

Matteo paused, and then he bowed briefly, turned, and walked away.

Kieran watched him go. Better now than later, she thought. She'd had her moment with him, and it only made her want another, and then another. How many moments full of warmth could she withstand, and hope to keep her heart?

Kieran had her pride. Her blasted, never-ending, insufferable pride. It sustained her, shored up her defenses, and she would not sacrifice it to Matteo de Gama's romancing ways.

Glancing at Nilo, she caught him frowning at her. "You do not understand."

"No," he agreed. "I do not."

Nilo took her arm, and without another word, led her through the darkness to the broken-down stables where Nigel waited with the horses. The wind swirled wasted leaves in tiny eddies on the ground and sent the first, fat raindrops of the storm to sizzle in a nearby iron barrel where a bonfire had become nothing more than glowing, orange embers.

The saddle was slick as she grasped the pommel and launched herself up, settled into the familiar seat, and took the reins into her hands.

Why should she worry about that fleeting look of sadness on Matteo's face before he recovered himself? He was nothing more than a player of parts, and she would be a fool to look deeper into his tender kisses and whispered confessions.

What a fool would she be, believing such nonsense when he himself had gone to the trouble to warn her about who and what he truly was.

She thumped the flanks of her mare and launched her into motion. Nilo and Nigel followed her lead.

The rain began to fall in earnest, the fat raindrops turning into stinging, cold barbs as the wind blew cold and fierce. She leaned into the wet and took a circuitous route.

Light slanted from the tall windows in the western wing of the old manse, wavering, golden glimmers that sparkled like a mirage in the cold, damp darkness.

She slowed as she grew closer, the wet earth muffling their approach.

Kieran reined in the beast beneath her, shivering as the rain permeated her woolen cloak and velvet gown. Water trickled down her face, dampened her gloves, and sent shivers down her spine, but she did not rush to depart.

For there, in the ballroom, she watched as Matteo shucked his shoes, pulled off his stockings, and stripped out of his coat.

Behind her she could hear Nilo's uncomfortable shift in his saddle, and Nigel's polite cough.

"Silence," she commanded them.

Someone had lit the fire for Matteo in preparation for the night, bathing him in flickering gold. He'd lit the candles that surrounded his bed, as well, and the pool of light gleamed like a hidden grotto, surrounded by shadows.

He moved around the room, his long shirt untucked, the buttons undone, the open V exposing his chest. He looked every inch the dark, brooding poet, with his ink-stained fingertips brushing back his long, thick hair. He lifted his cello and sat on the stool. Pulling the instrument between his legs, he plucked the strings, his ear cocked as he listened to their sound.

And there, surrounded by the damp scents of fecund earth and pine trees, Kieran shivered, longing for the warmth she had known only with Matteo de Gama.

The mare beneath her quivered and stamped,

snorted, and tossed her head. And in frozen horror, Kieran watched as Matteo stopped tuning his instrument. He held the cello by the neck and moved to the window. Leaning against the glass, he looked out into the dark, raining night. He was outlined by the light, and in the darkness, she could not see his face. It didn't matter. She could feel his eyes on her.

He held his free hand flat against the windowpane.

Her mare whinnied. The rain fell harder. The wind moaned in the treetops.

She'd been right to tell him she could no longer bargain with her kisses for his help. She was not as cold and distant as she'd tried to convince herself. If she kept letting Matteo warm her, she would lose her heart completely.

Rain trickled down her cheeks like icy tears, but in her mind, she was in that cocoon of golden light with him, and it was not the cello he cradled, but her.

Kieran's throat ached, so tight she could scarcely swallow. She thumped her mare's flank once more, and with her guards behind her, rode back to the manse.

She did not look back.

Matteo watched her go, and his desire for music was gone. He turned and glanced around at his surroundings, unsatisfied, unsettled.

Perhaps it was time to go back into London, he mused. But this time, it would serve his own purposes. He called for the carriage and horses that Rogan had loaned him to be brought around, and he returned to his trunks to find something suitable to wear.

Sometime later, Matteo surveyed his appearance in the mirror. The candles illuminated his flamboyant garments: Red silk breeches, frothy purple shirt, vivid green silk brocade jacket, embroidered with yellow threads.

His stockings were also yellow, and his boots were bright red calfskin, heeled and turned up at the tips in a thin curve.

He had pulled his hair back into a tightly clubbed queue, and he settled his hat on his head, a giant, floppy monstrosity made of red felt and embellished with huge plumes of red, purple, and yellow feathers.

He filled his purse with plenty of gold coins and doused himself with a vilely sweet perfume. Every inch of him announced him as a foreigner with money to waste. A final glimpse in the mirror satisfied him. He looked utterly ridiculous.

He went out to the waiting carriage and climbed inside. It rocked into motion after Matteo gave the address of the gaming hall he wished to visit. It was none other than the one frequented by Samuel Ellsworth, according to the whores in the more expensive brothels.

If Matteo would have any satisfaction that night, it would be found in stripping that man of the coin lining his purse.

Days bled into another, until three more weeks had passed, and as before, Matteo kept away from her. This time, however, it was her own doing, for hadn't she severed the bargain herself?

Kieran tried to keep her mind away from the west end of the property. It was not easy, for she found herself daydreaming of moonlit kisses and whispered words against her lips. Words in Italian that she did not understand, and yet, had made a strange visceral impact on her mind.

What had he said, she wondered again and again. She kept hearing his voice, "*Ti amo*, Kieran."

Her pride forbade her from asking Rogan, who spoke a bit of Italian, if he knew what that meant.

Her pride also eschewed her from asking Emeline about Matteo de Gama's progress on the property, though she knew her sister-in-law met with the Venetian once a week.

Now, as she readied herself to take tea with Samuel Ellsworth, she regarded herself in the mirror and wondered if she had the nerve to go through with her plan.

She examined her reflection, saw her blue-gray eyes and her smoothly coiffed hair. Her face was expressionless above her pink, silk gown. She wore a pearl and diamond necklace that had once belonged to her great-grandmother.

She looked every inch a lady, but she was not born to that station. She was the daughter of a common sea-merchant, but the sister of a powerful duke. England's aristocracy had no place for Kieran.

She also looked cool and remote, but only because no one could see the swirling wind that blew inside her, kicking up doubts and disgust in equal measure.

She glanced about her, to the elegant surroundings provided by her brother: peachy silk wall-coverings, Persian rugs of peach, dark copper, and brown wool, and a huge tester bed hung with tapestries.

Samuel Ellsworth was a wealthy aristocrat, as well. He offered titles and entrance to society in a manner that Kieran used to dream of.

He was also a man who'd stripped her naked and humiliated her, before raping a girl in front of her very eyes.

He'd been nothing but a gentleman since he'd begun courting her.

Could it be true that he didn't recall much of what happened that night? she wondered. Could drunkenness completely change a man?

With the flare of silk skirts, Kieran left her rooms, descended the great stairs, and swept into the grand parlor where Samuel waited. She was reminded of a time a few years ago, when she'd come into the same room to meet her cousin Simon, and had been lured to the "house of lords."

Samuel rose to greet her, immaculate and dignified in his dove gray coat and breeches, the white of his shirt crisp and tailored beneath his gray striped cravat.

She envisioned him as he'd been, naked from the waist down, drunk and laughing at her as she tried to cover her own nakedness with her hair. How could the two men be the same man?

"You look wonderful, my dear" he said.

Kieran curtseyed. "Thank you, Your Grace."

"'Tis a lovely day. Would you care to stroll through the gardens before we take our tea?"

"Certainly," Kieran said, and with her distaste well concealed, she placed her gloved fingertips on his proffered arm.

Samuel led her through the manse, chatting affably about his day, the long queue he'd seen extending out of the milliner's shop—isn't that odd? The ducks that waddled across Oxford Street, shutting down the traffic for ten solid minutes—an adorable nuisance.

Kieran listened with half an ear. There was so much going on at the manse these weeks past, planting, the birth of foals, the lengthening of days. Kieran reflected with happiness on Emeline's pregnancy, the growing swell of her belly, and the encouraging news that she was farther along than she'd been with her other failed pregnancies, a hopeful sign.

It made Kieran think of her mother, and she wondered how Camille was and when her parents would finally arrive. Rogan had immediately sent word to them about Emeline's pregnancy, and another to inform them that all seemed well, and urged them to come for the birth of the child.

Strange, but Kieran longed for her mother of late, pining for the sound of her voice, the scent of her skin, her loving presence. She hoped they would come soon.

A thought occurred to Kieran: What would Camille think of her plot to avenge her honor, if she knew?

Kieran wore a dagger that had once been strapped to her mother's thigh, a testament to Camille's determination to be no man's victim.

Perhaps Rogan was correct. Perhaps she was her mother's daughter.

Samuel had asked her something. "I'm sorry?"

"I wondered if you were expecting other guests?" He gestured to the expanse of window that faced the front of the manor, where a livery pulled up the long, curving driveway.

"Not that I am aware of. Perhaps Rogan has a caller."

The butler opened the doors for them as Kieran and Samuel approached, and the driver of the livery jumped down. He tipped his hat respectfully before opening the door and helping the occupant alight. "I'll wait 'ere, miss," he said.

As he moved to retake his perch, Kieran saw who had arrived. She was a dark, exotic beauty with flashing black eyes and ripe, red lips. Her thick hair was the black of a raven's wing, shiny and worn in the Venetian fashion. She wore a gown far too ostentatious for an English afternoon, bright red silk cut low on the bosom and tight on the torso, full and lush in the skirt, and trimmed with black, Spanish lace.

She was the woman from the Doge's courtroom, the woman who had begged for Matteo to come back to her. She was one of his lovers, and she'd obviously come to England for one thing: Matteo de Gama.

Kieran withdrew her hand from Samuel's arm and swept down the stone steps to greet her. Her heart pounded and she was struck with the image of the woman naked with Matteo, his artist's fingers making music in her body.

"Do you speak English?" Kieran asked, her voice sharper than manners dictated.

"Yes. Some." The woman smiled, revealing perfect teeth and charming dimples that flirted at the sharp corners of her mouth. She was devastatingly sensual, everything about her reeked of carnal knowledge. Holding her thumb and forefinger apart, she said, "Not so very much."

Whore, Kieran thought. Tramp. Slattern.

"My name is Carina di Robilante. I come to looking for a man, Matteo de Gama. I am told he is coming here from Venice, yes?"

Her English might not be fluent, but to Kieran, Carina's low, husky voice was made more attractive by her thick accent.

Jealousy had Kieran in a tight grip. She could see Matteo caressing Carina aboard his elegant *burchiello*, amidst warm candlelight with the canal waters lapping softly against the banks.

"Matteo de Gama sailed to England with my family and me," Kieran confirmed stiffly, "but he does not reside here."

"Please, will you direct me to him?"

It was a simple request, really. But it infuriated Kieran beyond all reason. She wanted to scream in the woman's face, *he walked away from you! Humiliated you in front of all those who looked on as you wept and begged for him! Wasn't it enough? Did you need to cross two oceans to give him the opportunity to reject you again?*

Kieran did not reveal her thoughts or her anger. She inclined her head in a gracious manner and turned to call a servant to take Carina to Matteo. But then an idea struck, and it was far more appealing than wandering the gardens whilst wondering about Matteo's reaction to seeing Carina.

She looked at Samuel, and saw him ogling Carina in a way that he clearly thought discreet. Kieran smiled up into his face. "Forgive me, Your Grace, but what say we take our tea on the morrow? I feel 'tis my obligation to take her myself."

Samuel smiled brightly, but his eyes glittered with a different emotion. "Yes, yes. Excellent. Do so. If you'd like, I will accompany you."

"Thank you, but did you not mention you had an appointment later this evening? I should hate to make you late."

Kieran knew the look on his face was a mixture of disappointment and disapproval of her bad manners, but she did not spare a care to that end. Samuel Ellsworth was hardly a person to give lessons in such things. She knew better than most that his manners ran only as deep as his sobriety. "The hour grows late, Your Grace. Farewell."

A tense silence filled the space between them. Samuel openly struggled with his anger at her rude dismissal, and the knowing that if he were to prove himself as different from the drunken brute he'd been, he must do as she asked.

Samuel sighed and gave in to the inevitable. Bowing, he took his leave, slapping his gloves against his thigh as he strode away.

It did not take Kieran long to dispatch the hired livery and call for a carriage to be brought around and for Nilo to escort them to the other property. Kieran climbed into the shady interior and took a seat opposite Carina.

The carriage lurched into motion and Kieran settled back into the soft cushions. Her belly flipped as she imagined Matteo's surprise, his potential reactions.

Would he be delighted to have a former lover bring
herself to him?

And beneath that thought was the ones that had consumed Kieran the three weeks past: did Matteo miss her?
Did he think of their kiss?

Kieran did. Lying awake in the dark of night, she held
her fingertips to her lips and recalled every second of
the warmth and poetry of that kiss.

"Have you been in England long?" Kieran asked
Carina politely.

"No, a few days only."

"How are you finding it thus far?"

Carina shrugged and smiled in a way that made her
look at once vulnerable and cunning. "I am telling you
after I see Matteo, no?"

Hussy. Jezebel. Wanton jade. Kieran smiled back at
Carina sweetly. "'Tis a long way to come for a man. I saw
no shortage of attractive, unmarried men whilst I was in
Venice. I suppose none of them suit you?"

"They are not him," Carina said simply, and she met
Kieran's gaze with bold female knowing in her flashy
black eyes.

"Signore de Gama seems content enough here in
England. And Venice is forbidden to him, for five years."

"Perhaps," Carina said, with the smug attitude of one
who knows something the other does not. "Things are
always changing, no?"

"Things change. People do not," Kieran replied
crisply.

As they pulled up the long driveway to the property
that Matteo was renovating, Carina's demeanor changed.
She leaned forward expectantly, peering out the windows
as if hoping for a glimpse of him.

And Kieran felt content with her decision to keep
Matteo de Gama at a distance. For though she might lie
away nights thinking of him and wishing for another

kiss, at least she was not so smitten that she dispensed of all pride to chase him like a hound on the scent of a fox.

The renovations were progressing beautifully, Kieran noticed as she alighted the carriage. Matteo did have an eye for the beauty inherent in architecture, for he was enhancing the structure with loving details that showed: flagstone walkways connecting terraces and gardens, the shutters painted a warm, rich shade of dark amber that complimented the shades of the stone and the many copper accents. The stone had been scrubbed and repointed, the wood moldings restored and painted, and balconies that once listed were straight and well-supported by new columns the same hue as the shutters.

The activity level was the same as last Kieran had been there, crawling with workers and noisy with banging hammers and the hum of voices. Though the spring air bore the heavy scents of turned earth and smoke, it also smelled strongly of paint and lye.

Nilo called out to one of the men who worked on the stone of the stables. "We're looking for Signore de Gama."

The man jerked his thumb over his shoulder, signaling that Matteo was around the rear of the manor.

Kieran lifted her skirts so they would not be stained with grass as they went to find him. As she walked, she spotted the open field bordered with trees that she'd raced across like a madwoman who wanted escape. And there beneath the trees, she'd lain with Matteo, bathed in moonlight, drenched with heat.

She saw Matteo come from the rear of the house. He walked with the foreman, and used his elegant hands to describe something, sketching the shape in the air as he spoke.

He was so handsome it hurt Kieran to look at him, his lean cheeks burnished and his hair streaked with dark honey from the sun. He wore narrow black leather breeches and knee-high boots that laced up the front, a billowy white cotton shirt, and nothing else. His eyes were animated with excitement, and even from the distance, Kieran could sense his enthusiasm, his passion for the work he was doing.

Beside her, Kieran heard Carina sigh with longing, and she wanted to slap her because the same sigh bloomed in Kieran's own chest, but she did not release it.

Matteo caught sight of them, and stopped talking in mid-sentence. His hands were still in the air, and he lowered them as his face took on myriad expressions, confusion, surprise, delight, before he wiped it clear and smiled.

He said something to the foreman and then jogged over to where the three stood.

His chocolate, amber-lit eyes were on Kieran, and for the briefest moment he smiled at her in an unguarded way that made him look purely happy to see her. In that space of time, Kieran was suddenly very glad she wore such a pretty gown, and that she'd pressed perfume against her skin.

And then he looked at Carina, and he was once more the seducer. He bowed before her and spoke in rapid Italian, before cupping her face in his hands and pressing kisses on her cheeks.

Carina answered him, and the two had a brief discussion that Kieran could not understand, during which Matteo looked stunned and surprised. Hands flew in the air as they talked, and Matteo nodded and said something that caused Carina to lean in and embrace him. Her squeal of delight rang out, followed by her laughter. She was so happy she clapped her small hands together and bounced on her feet, setting her breasts to trembling in her low décolletage.

Matteo turned to Kieran. "My apologies for any rudeness. Allow me to translate. Carina is a friend from home, and she has come to tell me that the Count who charged me falsely has been exposed by his own wife, who, appalled at her husband's indecency, appealed to the Doge on my behalf. She showed proof that the documents were forged, and the gossips say a divorce is pending. Carina brings me my exoneration. My exile has been lifted. I am free to go home to Venice."

∾ 17 ∾

"You are leaving England so soon?" Kieran asked softly, hating the sound of her own voice, full of disappointment. It revealed her feelings, but she was powerless to affect a false mien.

"Of course," Matteo answered casually, but his eyes were on her once again, and they burned. "Venice is my home."

Why was she surprised? There was no answer to that, except the unexpected wave of longing for him to stay. A thousand emotions swirled in her belly, and she could manage only one word: "When?"

Matteo swept his hand to encompass the property. "I will not repay the kindness of your family by leaving the project unfinished. I will see to the final stages, and remain long enough to be assured that I am no longer needed." He studied her with a gambler's knowing eyes.

"You cannot think I could make a home here, after all. I am a fish out of water, remember?"

His reminder of the insult stung, and Kieran felt her cheeks grow hot. "You acclimated quite well. I thought you happy here."

"I am happy here," Matteo said, and he gestured to his mind by tapping on his forehead. "A city or country does not make a man happy, but what fulfillment he seeks, wherever he is. That is the measure of his happiness."

Always the philosopher when talk turns to feelings, she thought to herself. And it satisfied her somewhat, for that told her that he did feel something more than his demeanor suggested.

Carina understood enough of the conversation to have her red lips pursing into a pout. "How long, Matteo?"

"I do not know. A few weeks. Months. I want the stables rebuilt before I go."

"Noo," she whined. "I cannot stay here so long."

"So leave," Matteo said simply. He shrugged. "You could have sent a letter, Carina. You did not have to come so far to inform me."

Carina unleashed a stream of angry words in Italian, and just as in the Doge's palace, Kieran could understand her meaning by her tone and posture. An angry woman, she realized, spoke a certain language that did not require translation.

Matteo was unaffected. He laughed and reached out to tug a loose, shining black curl. "Carina. You are passionate, it is true. I do appreciate your coming all this way to give me the news, but I am not unfettered and cannot leave. I have work here."

"Work!" she spat. "Bah!"

"I agree, it is strange, no?" Matteo laughed again, and he looked to Kieran with eyes that sparkled with amusement. "I would not have believed it, myself."

Kieran could not speak. To cover her upset, she looked about the property and tried to appear at ease. Beside her Nilo leaned down and discreetly asked if he could go check on Alva. Kieran nodded her assent, and watched him lumber away, wondering if her friend was developing feelings for the girl.

"I am waiting with you, Matteo" Carina said, and she surveyed the property with her dark, shining eyes. "I suppose it is not so bad, no?"

"London is rife with comfortable inns," Kieran interjected sharply, swinging around to face the two Venetians. "I do not think my brother should approve of unmarried persons living together under his roof."

Kieran knew that her manners were absolutely atrocious, but she did not care. She also knew that Rogan wouldn't give a second thought to Matteo having a woman stay with him, providing that woman was not Kieran.

She was fueled by jealousy that this woman was so free to do as she pleased. And yes, that Carina would exercise her freedoms with Matteo, mere miles from where Kieran would lie awake at nights, envisioning them together.

A new idea struck, all the better to keep this woman at bay. "Forgive my lack of manners; I was momentarily shaken. You could stay in our home, as our guest. We would be delighted to host you."

Matteo turned his gleaming eyes on her, and looked highly amused. "Thank you for seeing to my honor and assuring my chastity."

"Well, 'twould be most inappropriate to turn a blind eye to such things," Kieran said primly, and she knew she sounded like the ice princess she'd been called, and a prudish spinster, as well.

She most certainly did not sound like the girl who'd lain in the grass with Matteo de Gama, heated with dark, scandalous needs of the most wanton nature. Kieran did not allow either of those thoughts to stop her from her priggish tirade. "Forgive me if I seem overbearing, but propriety must be maintained."

"Of course," Matteo said with laughter in his voice. "The last thing England needs is two unruly Venetians with no regard for society's rules. What will it be, Carina? Will you accept Miss Mullen's generous and most gracious offer of hospitality, or do we need to ensconce you in an inn?"

Carina pouted again, clearly weighing her options. She blew out a little puff of breath, as if she were being taxed beyond her patience. With a roll of her flashing dark eyes she said, "I am already staying in the inn. It is not so far from here. I will be staying there. Thank you."

The woman's impudence would have been fascinating, had Kieran not found it so unspeakable. It was as if the woman had no compunction at all to keep her from openly displaying that she expected to share Matteo's bed.

"As you wish," Kieran said, and she told herself that she had no control over the situation. But it didn't soothe her. She pictured them together, Matteo's hands in all that black, shining hair, his mouth on those red lips, whispering words against it that Carina would understand.

"I must go," Kieran said, and she heard the sadness in her tone. "I need to go home."

"I require a word with you first. I have a message for the duchess," Matteo said to Kieran. "Carina, will you wait here please?"

Carina threw her hands in the air. "In the grass, Matteo? No chair? No shade? No wine?"

"Forgive me, Carina, but this is a private, financial matter, and quite important." Matteo gestured to the front doors of the house. "Go inside, and to your right is a comfortable parlor. There is wine in there, and books. I will not be long."

Carina sucked in a deep breath, causing her voluptuous breasts to strain mightily against the red silk. She pouted and narrowed her eyes, but when Matteo did not relent, she whirled around in a huff and flounced away toward the house.

When she had gone inside, Kieran looked at Matteo. She felt suddenly shy, unaccountably awkward. "What is the message?"

"Come with me, and I will get it. I had written it, and was going to send it by messenger, but you can do me this favor, no?"

Matteo turned and led the way, and Kieran followed him around to the rear of the house, and back to the kitchens that were now immaculate and smelled of roasting meat, dried herbs, and lemon wax. Kieran saw that Matteo had set up the table as a place to view plans; they were spread all over the surface. And there in the center was a sheet of parchment, rolled up and tied with a red ribbon, just like the translated pages of his manuscript that he'd sent her on the ship.

He picked it up, and handed it to Kieran. "I lied," he said simply. "It is not a message for the duchess. It is for you."

Kieran's heart began to pound, and she was suddenly aware that they were alone. "What does it say?"

"It begs to see you. I wrote it weeks ago, and every day wondered if I should send it."

"It begs?" she whispered.

"I beg."

She stared up at him, into those dark eyes that shimmered with amber lights. He looked serious and pained with longing. With his narrow leather breeches riding low on his slim hips, and the billowy white shirt contrasting his dark skin, he looked every inch the artist and poet she knew him to be.

"I am here."

His sensual mouth lifted at the corner, and then shook for a moment, as if he suppressed words he wished to speak. "And I am glad," he said roughly.

Taking her by surprise, he reached out and slid both his hands behind her head, his fingers sliding up behind the thick coils of her hair to cup her scalp. His lips descended down to claim hers in a greedy kiss that took as much as it gave.

Kieran's arms wrapped around his neck and she opened her mouth to accept the erotic touch of his tongue even as she wound her hands in all that dark, soft, sun-streaked hair. She kissed him back, hungry for the taste of him and the feel of his tensile, hard body pressed warmly to hers.

His hands slid down her neck, stroked her jaw, and his thumb pressed on her chin, opening her mouth so he could deepen the kiss. A whimper of pleasure escaped her throat as those clever hands moved to her back, cupped her waist, and pulled her closer still to his heat. The layers of her clothing did not keep her from feeling his strength, his hardness, and against her breast she felt the pounding of his heart, matching the crazy thundering of her own.

His hands moved, his fingers playing up the laces of her gown, over her shoulders, down her arms where they found a bare patch of skin between her sleeve and glove. He stroked that skin as if it were the finest silk, and Kieran's body grew warmer still, even though she shivered. Her wicked heart whispered indecent thoughts, urging her to lie down on the cold stone floor so she could feel his weight on her. As if listening, her knees weakened.

Matteo slid one strong arm around her waist, pulling her up, and kissed her neck as her head tilted back. His lips were soft, his incipient stubble an erotic scrape, and his teeth nipped her lightly. She moaned again, softly, and she knew enough of her body and what passed between a man and a woman to make the shocking realization that she desired him in a way that was hot and wet and visceral.

It was as if her body were an alien thing, ungoverned by moral mores and rational thought. She felt alive and impassioned and yes, she wanted Matteo de Gama to make love to her.

She slid her fingers deep into his hair, cradling the curve of his skull as she inhaled his scent, bergamot and leather and sun-dried cotton. He was the only heat in her cold world, the only laughter in her loveless life, and the only man who made her passions rise like the wind.

He would leave her and go back to Venice.

But Matteo was here now, and Kieran wanted him.

Matteo trembled with his hunger for her. Did she feel it? Did she see the love in his eyes when he looked at her?

He had stayed away from her, hoping that the disturbing emotions would pass. He told himself that it was a temporary thing, understandably arising from the loneliness of a friendless existence in a foreign land.

And then she'd arrived.

Clad in pink silk, she looked like an innocent angel beside Carina's siren scream. Her garnet hair gleamed in the afternoon sunlight, and the oval beauty of her face was nothing less than art come to life. Her eyes were like the canals at twilight, ancient and raw and as he'd seen her then, snapping with female jealousy so potent she fairly vibrated with it.

It was in that singular moment that Matteo de Gama knew that the game was not only lost, but completely over.

She was heaven in his arms, sweet and soft and everything woman, her passionate nature easily unveiled with a single kiss. He knew he could seduce her, in his arms she was pliant and giving and altogether aroused.

But he wouldn't. She deserved much, much more than he could ever give her, and he would not risk her future so he could momentarily enjoy the pleasure of her body.

Kieran pulled back and looked into his eyes, and Matteo saw her desire in the limpid depths, her pupils dilated, her pink lips parted and shining and swollen.

"What are you doing to me?" she whispered.

"Kissing you."

"'Tis dangerous."

"It is," Matteo agreed.

"'Tis wondrous."

"It is that, too."

"Are you seducing me, Matteo?" she asked, and her voice was full of what sounded like fear and hope combined.

"No. I am just enjoying you. Do not worry, Kieran. I will not take advantage of you, I promise. I will not press further."

"Oh," she whispered, and he swore it was disappointment he heard. Her fingers trembled as she touched her lips. "You kissed me with no bargain, nothing at stake."

"To hell with bargains."

Suddenly Matteo felt that he played the part of brute; he'd grabbed her, kissed her, and was prompted by nothing but his own love and desire for her. "Forgive me, Kieran. I should have asked your permission."

She smiled, a tiny, shaking curve of those beguiling lips. "I would have said yes."

Matteo watched the color rise in her cheeks, a blushing innocent with a deliciously wanton nature buried beneath her sense of propriety.

"And if I ask you again?"

"The answer will always be yes," she said softly, and she looked away as if ashamed of her own passion.

So he'd done it, he realized. He'd managed to seduce her without trying, and worse, without wanting to. He would not ruin her because he would leave England, and her life would go on. She deserved the very best. She deserved far more than a man like him.

"I have something to tell you," he said, and he let her go, moving away from her so that he would not reach for her once more. What good could come of it? "I have been busy at night these past few weeks."

Kieran raised a brow in question.

"I have been playing cards in the gaming halls. And as it turns out, one Samuel Ellsworth joined the game some nights ago."

He watched her go stiff, and a look came into her eyes that he could not discern.

"I rescinded the bargain," she said softly. "What are you about? What game is this?"

He forced himself to laugh as if his feelings were not involved. "Do not worry, lonely one, there is something in it for me. The English underestimate anyone foreign." Matteo grinned, this time genuinely, remembering the look on their faces. "I took them for all the coin they had."

She turned away from him, and he gazed with pained longing at the straight line of her shoulder, the curve of her neck, and the small curling tendrils that had escaped when he'd reached his fingers into that shining mass of hair.

He ran his tongue over his lips. He could still taste her.

"Are you upset with me?" Matteo asked.

"No," she replied.

Matteo wanted to reach for her, to turn her shoulders

and pull her against him once more. He wanted to hold her warm and willing in his arms.

"He is a good player," Matteo warned her, hoping she would take care in dealing the man. "He is shrewd and ruthless. He takes large risks and he is an excellent liar."

Kieran let out a little sigh. "He has been coming for tea and openly courts me. Rogan seems glad of it. He says 'tis a good match, if it makes me happy."

"Ellsworth wants something. Make no mistake."

Kieran made a noise that sounded rather like a snort of disdain. "Yes. He wants to marry me."

"Why? He was prepared to do business with your brother before all of this. Surely he does not need to wed in order to pursue such a venture."

His words stung her enough that she whirled around, her eyes snapping with stormy anger. "Is it such a puzzle to you that a man might *want* to marry me?"

Matteo admired her, magnificent in her anger, the passions she hid so assiduously brought to the surface by her insecurity. "You are a beautiful woman, Kieran, there is no doubt of that. Do you think, however, that you are the only beauty in London? Why does this man, a duke, want to marry *you*, when you yourself pointed out that you are not of the aristocracy?"

"He says he wants to atone for what he did to me."

Matteo laughed softly, and watched her anger turn to fury. He had sat across the table from Ellsworth, and knew the measure of the man. "There are many ways to atone, and all can be accomplished without the burden of marriage."

"Perhaps he doesn't see marriage to me as a potential burden."

"It is more likely that he wants something." Matteo shrugged. "You in his bed is a good incentive, I admit, but I think there is more."

"'Tis not as if I want to marry him, signore," she said stiffly.

"You are not softening toward him?"

Matteo watched Kieran's shoulders pull back, and the look in her eyes turn flinty.

"Why would you say such a thing?"

"He offers you very much. A respected name, a title, your society's acceptance. Did you not tell me that you once longed for just those things?"

"I was different then. Naïve."

"So why does it offend you when I suggest he is not some swooning suitor desperate for your hand?"

She did not answer him, and Matteo knew it was because her pride forbade her.

He gave her the way out. "Accept his offer of marriage, if you want to see what he is after. And then, lonely one, you will have the unhappy task of deciding if you care any longer. Most women would choose to become his duchess, accepting that marriage is a business arrangement at best, anyway. Husbands are easily avoided, no? And lovers are easy to find."

"You should know," Kieran said cruelly.

It hurt, the way she said it with such contempt. But despite the pain of her disapproval, he managed to laugh easily. "Yes, I do know. I have comforted many a lonely woman."

"There is one inside the house, as we speak. Your lover sits in the parlor and waits for you."

Jealousy was not what he wanted from Kieran; he could have that from any woman. He wanted more from her than he dared to hope for. Possession. Desire. And, yes, fool that he was, her love.

"Carina is not my lover."

"Does she know that?"

Matteo laughed again, and he knew he courted Keiran's violence. She looked two seconds from slapping his face. "Carina knows what she wishes to know. When

I was her lover, she cared no more for me than any other man. When I left her before her passions had cooled, she fancied herself in love. If I went back to her, she would savor victory for a time, and then she would lose interest. Such are the secrets of a woman's heart."

Kieran's hands were fists at her sides. "You think you know women so well."

"That sounds like a dare," he observed softly. She stood before him full of raw feelings and naked needs, and resentment that he had uncovered them.

"Yes, 'tis a dare. Tell me, signore, all about women."

"Women are not so hard to understand. They are tender-hearted, but tough-minded. I have never met a woman who did not crave the poetry and all-consuming beauty of a passionate affair. But I have also never met the woman who did not also want the power and security that riches and titles bring. I am content to give them a fantasy, for a time, and I never forget that my reality would never be good enough. Women want to be the center of a man's world, but they do not want a man who has nothing more to offer than passion."

"You cannot live on passion," Kieran said defensively. "And you cannot feed your children with it. Women have to place their entire future in a man's hand if they choose to marry. 'Tis not greed to want that he can house you, clothe you, and provide necessities. 'Tis practicality, and would you want a woman so caught up in love and passion that she did not consider the life that such union would offer her?"

"Would I?" he laughed. "Certainly not. Can you imagine a woman wanting to marry a man like me? She would have to be a fool."

Kieran turned her beautiful face away from him. "Are not all those in love fools?"

"Indeed," he answered, and the pain in his chest was the words he did not speak. He did not profess to her that he had become one of them. "But if they can only learn that time will fade those emotions, they can spare themselves much pain."

"Yes, 'tis much easier to not love, than to risk the pain of its loss or its failure," Kieran agreed softly. "And yet, there is love that never fades. I have seen it, with my mother and father. Their love is something magical, so real and strong that you nearly see it with your eyes. I have seen it also with Rogan and his Emeline. My brother is a hard man, but with her he is soft and tender. They are like a dream that has come to reality." Kieran shrugged and sighed, and to Matteo's ears she sounded wistful and full of longing. "So, no, signore, I was wrong. Perhaps those in love are not fools, but rather, they are merely the ones among us who are brave enough to try."

"But why not you? If you have seen it and you believe in it, why do you doubt you could find it?"

Kieran looked up at him, then, and those twilight eyes of hers pierced his soul. "I once hungered for it," she whispered.

"A long time ago?" he finished.

"Yes. I was different then. I never doubted myself at all, really. I knew who I was and what I wanted, and I never thought it possible that I would not get it." She laughed a little, a bittersweet sound. "I valued myself so highly, in fact, I thought I would come to England and that dukes and earls would flock to win my hand. I fancied that I would choose the most handsome and most wealthy, and we would fall madly in love whilst enjoying a beautiful courtship. We would wed in a graceful ceremony, and live the rest of our lives in love and joy."

Kieran sighed again, but this time it was one of regret. "What a child I was. Spoilt and petted so much that I thought all the world would treat me that way. It never occurred to me that I was not special."

Matteo wanted to contradict her, to tell her that if it

mattered at all, a Venetian bastard thought her quite extraordinary. But he held silent.

"And then there was the night with Samuel, where I found out the darker nature of men, and of myself, as well. I vowed I should be alone after that, but men began to seek me out.

"The only suitors who came to call were either men of much lower birth who sought my brother's power and wealth, or men with high titles and impoverished estates, seeking the same. I found I was worth only what I could bring, and not a single man seemed to look much deeper than the gold of my dowry."

He watched as she spoke, and thought her worth more than any riches. "Because everything has a price."

"Yes, even me," Kieran said. She shrugged her shoulders as if to say it did not matter. "I fear I have far too much pride than to sell myself for a title. If there is no love in it, I shall not have it. I have seen great love. I know its value. Sadly, I also know its rarity."

So did Matteo. It was so rare, in fact, that he feared it like a demon that could possess him.

"I know Samuel wants something, and I'm certain 'tis not me," she confessed quietly. "It hurt to realize that you know it, too, and that everyone who finds out he courts me will think it for my brother's wealth. I do not want Samuel; I despise him. But no one knows that. They see only a duke courting the common-born sister of another powerful duke. And then they draw their conclusions, and in them, I am diminished. Marry the girl, join two families, merge the power. It makes perfect sense, really, unless you are that girl. And then suddenly you are a pawn, a means to an end, and if you do as society expects, a belly in which to grow new heirs. Thank you, but no."

"You are no man's fool," Matteo said admiringly, and he meant it. "I told you before that you are unlike any woman I have met."

Kieran turned and walked away, moving to stand near the center work station. Her elegantly winged brows were furrowed as if she contemplated something just beyond her knowing. She lifted a half filled glass of wine that was left over from Matteo's lunch, and she swirled it, inhaled its scent, and set it down. "Perhaps I still think too highly of myself," she said finally. "Always so prideful. Always so stubborn."

"No," Matteo said. He moved to her side, placed his hand on her face, cupping her cheek. He tilted her head up so he could look into those sea-stormy eyes. "You are idealistic, and idealists cannot help but become cynical. They see things as they could be, and despair of the loss of that potential."

"Yes," Kieran said in wonder. "Yes, 'tis exactly as I feel."

He stroked her soft skin with his thumb, brushed it across her lips. They parted in response. *The answer will always be yes,* she'd said. Matteo leaned down to kiss her.

A shriek of rage came from the doorway, and they both turned to see Carina. With her red, black lace trimmed gown, raven hair, and snapping black eyes, she looked every inch the spurned mistress. She pursed her pouting red lips and placed both hands on her tiny waist, before releasing a stream of Italian peppered with such crude and vicious curses that Matteo could only be grateful that Kieran did not understand the language.

And then he saw what Carina had clutched in her hand, and his heart sank.

When her tirade did not cause Matteo to comfort and soothe her, she threw down the papers and whirled on her heel to stalk her way back into the house.

The papers were spread out on the stone floor, crumpled from Carina's hand. There, on wrinkled parchment were sketches of Kieran: on horseback, with her hair streaming out behind her; in profile, deep in thought; at a ship's rail, watching the sunrise.

She brought her gaze to Matteo's in question, and his expression was one of pure embarrassment. He hurried to pick them up, tap them together, and roll them. "It is not what you think," he said.

"What do I think?" she asked softly. Was that a blush darkening his lean face?

"I sketch everything. Birds in the trees, fruit in a bowl."

Kieran gestured to the papers in his hand. "And me."

Matteo sighed in surrender. "Yes."

"May I see them closer?"

He hesitated.

"Please? They are my likeness. Can I not see how you render it?"

Matteo looked pained, and incredibly uncomfortable. So much so that Kieran laughed. She outstretched her hand. "Please, signore?"

"I do not think it a good idea."

"They are me," she pointed out.

Matteo relented and handed them over, before turning to face the fireplace.

Kieran unrolled the papers and saw herself in many poses. The final sheet she viewed had nothing but pieces of her, her eye beneath her brow, closed in one drawing, open in another, widened as if surprised in one more. He'd drawn her hands, holding a horse's reins, cupping a wineglass. There were many line drawings, of shoulder, neck, and collarbone, filled in with the curve of her jaw, the shape of her waist.

And there at the bottom, she saw the distinct curve of a naked woman's hips and legs, and it bore a dagger strapped to the left thigh, shaded in black and gray. Her face flamed as she saw that he'd given attention to the most womanly part of her body, for it was drawn with precision that displayed his familiarity with the female sex. Beneath that particular drawing he'd written two words: *Veiled Passions.*

"Signore," she breathed, her face flaming. "You overstepped your bounds."

"I am sorry, Kieran. I meant you no dishonor."

Thoughts crashed in her mind, and she felt exposed. "How dare you."

"They are meant as an homage to your beauty, nothing more."

"How kind of you to leave them out for the most casual observer. I'm certain your staff of servants and workers have been enjoying this homage."

"They were in a trunk, beneath books. Carina was obviously searching through my things." Matteo cleared his throat and ran a hand through his hair. "Believe me, I draw late at night when no one is awake. No one was ever intended to see them."

Kieran glanced down at the paper and saw her nakedness again, her cheeks burning. She could not quite grasp how he could draw something he had not seen so accurately. And the thought of Matteo de Gama picturing her nude made the fire in her blood grow hotter, the shame of which fueled her anger. "Are there others?"

"Yes," he admitted. "In truth, there are."

"Am I clothed in them?"

"Some of them. In others, no." He spread his hands, his fingertips stained with ink.

Kieran imagined him as she'd seen him from outside his window, half-dressed and bathed in candlelight, only this time, instead of playing his cello, he was drawing her. The heat that burned so hot turned damp and full of desire, and her heart skipped a few beats.

"I am sorry, Kieran."

Her pride, however, had been deeply injured, and for Kieran, it overrode everything.

"Get the pictures. Now," she ordered, and she brought

her eyes up to meet his. "Or I will pull the dagger you so elegantly depicted here."

"I do not think that is a good idea," he said once more, and Kieran lost what little composure she had left.

"Get them," she hissed. "I will not have them lying about for people to see. If a servant finds them, they will pass them around and laugh at my nakedness. That is, until the gossip that I posed for the portraits begins to make its way through the grapevine. Now, signore, I ask that you do me the *honor* of giving me the pictures of my likeness, so I may dispose of them."

Matteo nodded, looking abashed, and he left the kitchen and went into the house. Kieran stood, rooted in place, staring at the drawings. They were beautiful, she admitted to herself, fluid and evocative of various captured emotions.

How could this impropriety make her feel at once enraged, admired, embarrassed, and aroused?

When Matteo returned, he handed her a roll of papers. "I am sorry," he said once again.

"You ought to be," she whispered, and suddenly felt unaccountably shy. He'd imagined her naked, and to stand in front of those dark, amber-flecked, brooding eyes made her feel as if she were.

"I can explain. Please, let me try to make you understand. If I told you how I felt . . ." his voice died off and he swallowed, hard. Kieran could see his throat working, up and down, as if he struggled to form words.

"I'm listening."

"I . . . You are so exquisite," he said lamely.

"We covered that," she said. "But I do not think that finding me attractive gives you such artistic license."

"There is more to it than that," he said.

Kieran held the papers. They smelled strongly of cedar and faintly of ink, and she knew he told the truth, that they'd been in a trunk and not intended for prying eyes.

The thought of her nudity being something private for just Matteo had her blood growing hotter, and she needed to be away from him. It felt as if he wished she were his lover, and a new thought came to her mind, that he might have imagined the act of making love with her as well.

Kieran brushed past him, desperate to get away from his nearness and the eyes that saw beneath her clothes. She left with the drawings tucked beneath her arm, and did not look back.

He called after her, quietly, as if it cost him a great deal to do so. "Please, I know I can explain."

And Kieran kept going, because if she turned around and looked at him, clad in black leather and billowing white cotton, she just might decide that if he wanted her as his lover, he could have her.

∽18∽

Carina strolled into the The Boar, a small, comfortable inn not too far from the estates where Matteo de Gama was staying. The goodwife looked up from the table she was wiping free of crumbs, and her face betrayed her intimidation of the Venetian beauty.

"Can I 'elp ye, miss?"

"No, no. I am to my rooms," Carina said. She picked up her skirts and ascended the stairs with the rhythmic clatter of her heels on bare wood.

Matteo had not said a word to her since she'd thrown the drawings at him and the girl. He'd entered the house, his expression distant, as if she were a stranger. Carina had tried to explain why she'd looked in his trunks; she'd simply been looking for her favorite satire that he'd written.

Matteo had stood stock still, wordless. And then, turning away from her, he'd called for a servant and arranged for her to be driven back.

Why should that be so profoundly disturbing to Matteo, that she'd looked in his trunks? She thought a man such as he would expect it. Would not every woman want to search his things and see if he'd kept the keepsakes she'd given him, the locks of hair, the miniatures, the empty bottle of wine they'd shared in the moonlight? She'd found none of those things, but instead a bundle of drawings of another woman.

It hurt, deeply.

Carina fished her key from inside her bodice and opened the door, entering her suite of rooms with a rustle of silk. It was dark; not even a fire burned in the hearth. As she lit her own candles, she made a silent vow to fire her maid when they returned to Venice.

Carina blew out a breath of annoyance and began to strip off her cap, her jewelry, her gloves. Her gown laced down the side, allowing her to undress herself, and she sighed heavily as she released the binding around her waist.

She slipped into a dressing gown, the silk falling over her skin like a caress, causing visions of Matteo to move through her mind in flashes of memory. He'd been a wonderful lover. The thought of his hands on her made her shiver with longing.

Carina turned and met her reflection in the looking glass. By the light of the single candle, she appeared dewy with youth, as if she looked into the past and saw the girl she once was. She shifted her focus to the woman she had become: fearless, wealthy, and determined. Carina had married well, buried an ancient husband, and spent her remaining youth on pleasure. And when she wanted something, she knew it always had a price.

She thought again of Matteo. A long sigh slipped from her lips. For him, she would pay anything.

And then she thought of those pictures he'd drawn of that girl, and how she had looked upon Matteo with such restrained longing. They were not lovers, that Carina could tell by watching them. The pictures he had drawn must have been inspired by great passion, and a secret one, at that.

Carina had been Matteo's lover, and she had experienced enough men to know how rarely tenderness accompanied skill. He'd treated her well. So well, in fact, that Carina had committed the gravest mistake of all, and fallen in love with the seductive bastard.

Matteo had been kind to her. He'd made her laugh and he'd read her his poetry. He'd played his cello for her, and danced with her beneath the stars.

He'd never, however, drawn a single sketch of her.

Carina looked closer at her reflection. She knew she was beautiful, and she knew the things that Matteo enjoyed.

It mattered not that he thought himself taken with the English girl. Carina knew exactly how to divert his attention.

Kieran had hidden the drawings deep in her armoire, buried beneath winter woolens that would not be aired until the cold weather returned.

He'd said his heart beat for her.

He'd said he was leaving England.

Kieran could not bear to be near him, for it hurt to touch him and kiss him and feel his warmth, knowing he would soon be going home to Venice.

And yes, she admitted to herself, she was a coward. She'd seen Carina's dark beauty, and knew that it was unlikely that Matteo would spend his remaining nights in England alone. Kieran could not endure seeing them together, and so like the fearful spinster she'd become, she stayed away.

Days passed, and became weeks. The winds brought warmth and rain, and the tiny crocuses ushered in the daffodils, the green hills dotted with their sunny, swaying blooms.

Emeline blossomed as well, her belly a large globe beneath the higher waists of her new gowns. The manor hummed with activity as the spring cleaning was completed and the renovations of the nursery were well under way. The midwives and doctors all agreed: The babe was expected in midsummer.

Kieran kept busy, riding, attending dinners and teas with Samuel, spending time with Emeline, and seeing to the fittings of her new spring gowns. She stitched tapestries. She read books. She exercised horses. She wrote letters to her mother, her father, and a few friends from Barbados.

She did not, however, seek out Matteo de Gama.

If Matteo wanted to see Kieran so he could apologize, he knew where to find her. And if he was occupying himself with Carina, Kieran did not care to witness their rediscovered passion.

Kieran returned from her afternoon ride and sought out her rooms to do as she'd been doing these weeks past, killing time before she needed to dress for dinner. She stood out on her balcony, sipping her secret stash of brandy as she stared westward.

Kieran heard her maid approaching. She quickly dumped the brandy over the railing and hid the glass in a drawer. As she breezed back into the sitting area of her rooms, she inwardly grimaced at the taste on her tongue, knowing her maid would smell it and realize she'd become one of "those women."

If her maid took notice, Kieran could not tell. Her toilette continued as always, and left Kieran immaculately groomed in a silver, silk gown. Her hair was coiled atop her head, twined with silver threads, and she wore one piece of jewelry, a stunning necklace of diamonds in white gold.

And with the brandy warm in her blood, she descended the stairs to greet Samuel Ellsworth. His appearance at tea and dinner had become as regular as the timepiece on the mantle.

A servant approached her. "Miss Kieran, His Grace has requested your presence in his office."

Kieran nodded and proceeded to Rogan's office. When she entered, she saw that Samuel was there, as well, seated across from Rogan's desk. Documents were spread out, and quills were stripped and dredged. The room smelled of wealth: wood and leather, smoke and brandy, men's cologne and worsted wool.

Both men stood as she entered. Samuel looked pleased and relaxed; Rogan looked thoughtful and restless.

Rogan, as usual, skipped any preamble. "With our father in Barbados and me as your guardian here in England, Ellsworth has asked me for your hand in marriage."

Kieran was not surprised. She raised a cool brow and swept closer to the massive desk. "What are the terms of this proposal?"

From the corner of her eye, she saw that Rogan stood rigid and tense. Why, she wondered, would he entertain such an offer if he was not comfortable with it?

Samuel bowed before Kieran in a showy display of gentlemanly deference. "Estates in Yorkshire, Westminster, and Kent, along with holdings in Scotland and the Americas. The title of Duchess of Westminster, of course, and all that such status implies. You will dine with kings.

You will dance with princes. You will travel the world, if you choose, or you will command your legions of servants to do your bidding at home, in England. As my wife, you will also be entitled to the ancestral jewels, the value of which cannot be measured. You will, of course, have full access to my stables, and will be free to ride and breed as you see fit."

Kieran was stunned by all he offered. She had known him to be a wealthy man, but did not recognize the extent of his holdings. She also did not underestimate him. Matteo had taught her many things.

"Aside from the husbandly possession of my person, what is in it for you?" she asked. Kieran coolly arched a brow and inclined her head to the papers on the desk. "What is my worth on the matrimonial market?"

Samuel cleared his throat, smoothed his coat, and kept his cool. "Well, there is the matter of your dowry, but I hardly need the coin."

"This many documents for one woman?" Kieran said dismissively, sweeping her hand to encompass the many papers on Rogan's desk. "I might think you were buying livestock."

"Kieran," Rogan said, a warning tone in his voice. "'Tis not necessary to be unpleasant. Simply decline the offer if you are not amenable."

She turned to her brother. "But Rogan, I am merely interested in my worth. What else is hinging on this proposal?"

"Do you insinuate that I would sell you into marriage?"

"Am I to infer that Lord Westminster is besotted with me, such that he is approaching this transaction without his business sense?"

Samuel laughed and leaned his hip against the desk. With his arms folded, he looked down on Kieran with a twinkle in his gray eyes. "You are formidable."

"I am also tenacious. I ask again, what is in it for you, Your Grace?"

Samuel unfolded his arms and clasped his hands together in front of him as he exhaled through his nose.

Samuel struck a lordly pose, and began to speak in a way that suggested absolute reason, as if he lectured a very small child.

"'Tis true that marriage in the peerage is oftentimes a business arrangement. 'Tis also true that your brother and I have similar interests that would be greatly enhanced if we joined together. I came here today to ask for your hand in marriage, and also to discuss a joint merger in a shipyard in Dublin. The two, however, are mutually exclusive. One is business. The other, namely the matter of you and me, is strictly personal."

Kieran cast her attention to her brother. "If I accept the offer of marriage, will you be more inclined to agree to the shipyard merger?"

"Kieran, I am not the sort of man who cares for such things, as you ought to know. Marry him if you wish, or don't. It matters not to me either way, as long as you assure your happiness with your decision. To answer your question, however, 'tis no. I'll make my decision based on numbers and projections, calculations of risk to potential gain." Rogan shrugged and sighed. "That you could think 'twould be otherwise is a real blow."

Kieran faced her brother with a mixture of pride and practicality twisted in her chest. "I fear I cannot muster shame for asking what value is placed upon me. 'Tis, after all, my future and my womb that bears a price."

"I am your brother. Not your keeper, and certainly not your owner."

"Yes," Kieran said softly, and she smiled at Rogan with all the tenderness she felt for him shining in her eyes. "And no girl ever had a better brother. Do not think

I doubt it. But you are a man, and as such, see things differently than I."

"I am your brother first, and a businessman second. Your happiness is worth more to me than any shipyard."

"Very well," she said quietly. "If you say so, I believe you."

Kieran moved to the window and looked out, keeping her back to the two men. A thousand thoughts jumbled in her mind, and from them emerged random, colliding images. What if she abandoned her plan and accepted his offer? She saw herself as a duchess, with all the stature and society acceptance that she'd always craved. And she could also envision herself old and gray, the aging dowager duchess, still alone, still bitter, and forever tortured by the knowledge that she sacrificed her passions for prestige.

She recalled what Matteo had said, when he warned her that she would have to decide if she still cared about Samuel's darker nature when he offered her the moon and all the stars contained in the vastness of the sky.

But what more could she look for, or hope for? Could she ever marry a man and be assured of his love for her, and not his lust for her family's wealth? She saw herself as a spinster, old, childless, and resentful from a lifetime of loneliness.

Kieran recognized that the life she was creating for herself was not bringing her happiness, either. If she wanted something more, something different, she would have to reconcile herself to making real changes.

Kieran turned around to face Rogan and Samuel. "I will need a few days to think about your offer."

And without another word, she swept from the room.

Rogan followed her out into the hallway, grabbed her arm, and pulled her into the library. He closed the doors and scowled down at Kieran.

"Do you know how you've insulted me?" he asked

plainly. "Asking me about business, as if you mean nothing more to me."

"I only wanted the truth of the matter."

"You want the truth? I'll give it to you. Here's the truth, Kieran. I don't like Ellsworth as a person. There's something about him that's not quite right, and I'm forever hesitating to do business with him because of it. I don't like the idea of your marrying him, but I'll not stop you if that's what you want."

Rogan sighed heavily and shrugged his broad shoulders. "All your life you wanted this, aye? Titles and riches and to be part of English aristocracy. I'll not stand in your way of getting what you want, when 'tis being offered to you on a silver platter. So don't you stand before me and question my motives or my love for you."

Through his tirade, Kieran held herself rigidly, shoulders back, spine straight, chin lifted, as her habit dictated. But in the face of her brother's honesty, she let go of a little of her pride. Just as she'd wanted to the night she'd cut herself, she tentatively reached out to him. Immediately, she was rewarded by his grabbing her and holding her in a bear hug that made her feel young and protected.

He spoke into her hair. "I hate the thought of you married to a man like Ellsworth. Find a man you can love, Kieran, if you'll take my advice. Marriage is a blessing when you marry for love, aye? I'd be pleased to see you have something like what I've got with Emeline."

"It seems impossible to find such a thing," she confessed. "I am afraid I never shall."

"It always seems so, until it happens, and then you cannot believe you ever doubted it."

"I hope so," Kieran whispered, not convinced. She held onto Rogan, her arms around his waist, her cheek against his chest. He was warm and solid, and Kieran loved him. "I'm sorry, Rogan. I did not mean to insult your motive."

Rogan held her back so he could look into her eyes. "Listen, aye? Ellsworth is smart. He knows that marrying you will tie him to my wealth. I know what he's after, and frankly, I don't care. If the shipyard is a good merger, I'll do it, regardless of your decision, and 'tis likely that Ellsworth knows that as well."

Shame grew in Kieran's gut. Looking into her brother's vivid green eyes, she couldn't believe she'd ever questioned him, even for a second. "I understand."

"Good. Now off with you, aye? I've got to go check on Emeline."

Kieran bid her brother adieu, and took to the stairs. She stopped briefly to instruct a servant to send word that she would not attend dinner, but would take a tray in her room.

The hour was growing late, and long shadows began to creep in the corners of her rooms. Kieran lit a few candles before she opened her armoire, and dug down into her woolens until she found the sheaf of papers that she'd taken from Matteo de Gama.

She sat at her table and spread them out. Even alone, with no one there to see her looking at the scandalous drawings, her face burned and her hands shook.

Beneath the stroke of his quill, Kieran saw she was beautiful. She was art, sculpture, and poetry in his eyes. He'd drawn her breasts, her waist and belly, her hips and her thighs. He'd drawn her face tilted upward, eyes closed, mouth parted as if on a moan.

And with her entire body on fire, Kieran studied the drawings, running her finger over the lines, imagining his hand on the quill and his thoughts consumed with her form.

She stared at the drawings until a knock at her door startled her, and she realized that it was the dinner tray she'd requested. Kieran stuffed the papers away, took the tray, and ate without tasting.

She rang for her maid, and changed into her night-clothes.

The night was fairly warm. The breeze from her balcony doors wafted into the room, bearing the sweet scent of early roses. But Kieran sipped her tea and shivered.

Kieran pulled the drawings from her armoire once more, and looked at them until the night encroached and the air turned thin and crisp.

She wondered if he had been spending his nights with Carina. The Venetian woman had seemed secure in her place as his lover, despite what Matteo had said.

After all, wouldn't a man such as Matteo take what was being given? Was there a man alive who could resist the lure of a woman like Carina?

Kieran could not deny it any longer: She was becoming obsessed.

He'd said his heart beat for her. He'd said he was leaving England. He'd said Carina was no longer his lover.

He'd told her what kind of man he was, and cautioned her to believe him.

And he'd whispered words against her lips that haunted her without end.

Kieran decided she would discover for herself the truth of the matter.

Kieran rose so quickly that her chair fell over behind her. She rushed to her armoire, pulled out a simple cotton gown with side laces, and quickly dressed herself. A few quick strokes with her brush put her hair in a semblance of order, and despite the belief that it was common to do so, she twined it in a thick braid that hung down her back. She stashed the drawings back into their hiding place, extinguished her candles, and went out to her balcony.

The moon was low and fat in the sky and a few early

stars dotted the sky. Kieran looked down to the ground; it seemed very far away, without a good place to climb.

She bit her lip, wondering at her own madness. Was she truly possessed?

Kieran drew a deep, ragged breath. She should at least wait until the night grew dark enough to hide her. The thought made her giggle a bit hysterically. She really ought not do this at all.

She tucked her gloves into her bodice, straddled the rail, and gripped the balustrade. Lowering herself, she wrapped her legs around the column and carefully shimmied down bit by bit, relying on the strength of her thighs, firm and muscled after years of horseback riding. It occurred to her that it was not unlike when she used to climb up and down palm trees in Barbados when she was a girl.

Kieran paused midway down, gasping for breath, and looked up. How, she wondered, would she get back?

No time to think of that now, she thought. Kieran lowered herself more, the cold, polished marble slick beneath her sweaty palms.

Soon she was lightly skimming the ground, keeping close to the shadows of the manse as she made her way to the stables. Peering inside, she saw that only a lone stable lad was about, yawning as he mucked a stall.

Kieran entered the stable and breezed up to him, tugging on her gloves as if she were completely relaxed. "Saddle two horses for me and my guard, if you will."

She turned and left before she lost her nerve, and waited outside in the shadows. Her belly flipped with nervous turns. What was she doing?

The boy led the saddled horses out, and looked around with eyes that were dimly puzzled. Kieran rushed to speak before he could question Nilo's absence.

"I'll wait with the horses until my guard is finished in the privy. I have no further needs. That will be all."

The lad bowed and entered the stables without a backward glance. When she was alone once more, Kieran quickly tethered the horse bearing the man's saddle to her own, and swung up onto her horse's back. She kicked the mare into motion and rode off into the night, westward bound.

Matteo set down an unfinished glass of port and looked around the huge ballroom with satisfaction. It was nearly finished, the high ceilings had been repainted and the murals were retouched. Everything gleamed gold and cream, except for the punches of crimson red that outlined the handsome moldings and spilled down the sides of the windows in plush velvet.

He should have moved into one of the bedrooms, but that seemed unnecessary now that he knew he would be leaving soon.

Anyway, he liked the way the ballroom was at night, his small corner of it lit with a pool of candle and firelight. With the rest of the enormous room shadowed, he would keep to the light, to draw or paint, compose or play, write or sculpt. Always, though, he hoped that Kieran would once again be outside his window, watching him.

Matteo did not seek her out, except to watch her from a distance. How many times in the weeks past had he lingered in the shadows of a tree and watched her move, smile, speak, and ride?

It was agony, this love. Unrequited, unspoken, unwanted love, bursting in his heart and through his veins like a mutiny within his own vessel.

He wanted to call an end to the work on the property, or at least find a problem that had a long, protracted solution. But the work moved merrily along, nearing completion on the house, and midway through the outbuildings and stables.

Soon he would leave, and all he could hope for was that time would eventually erase the possession she had over his heart.

Matteo sighed and reached for his cello, pulled it between his legs and tuned the strings, his ear low to its neck.

A movement drew his attention to the window. There, out in the darkness, was a glimmer of white. Matteo did not believe in spirits, but then again, he'd thought he did not believe in love.

He rose and moved to the window, and his heart began to pound. Kieran sat on horseback.

Matteo rushed to the door, ran through the long hallway, and burst out onto the terrace, just as she was sliding down from her saddle. She tossed the reins over a post and approached him.

The night air was soft and fragrant, and she was a moonlit fairy, her oval face beautiful and uncertain.

"Kieran," he whispered.

"Can we be honest?" she asked quietly. "Can we set aside all seduction and bargains and silly games, and just be truthful for this night?"

"Of course," he answered her.

"Are you alone?" He could hear the need in her voice.

"I am."

"Carina?"

"No. Not once, I swear it," he answered, to her unspoken question.

A shy, happy smile broke over her face and lifted his heart into his throat.

"'Tis true?"

"It is."

Silence fell between them, the only sound the song of a nightingale.

"Is it a game you have been playing, to make me come

to you?" Kieran lifted her hand to brush back a few wavy tendrils that had escaped her braid. "You stay away from me, and it seems I can bear it for only so long."

"You left angry. I did not think you would want to see me again."

"I am not angry any longer."

"Truly, Kieran, I am sorry about the drawings."

"They are beautiful," she admitted softly.

"You are beautiful," he corrected.

She cast her eyes to the ground. "In your eyes, and beneath your quill."

"Yes. And on horseback, with your hair full of the wind. On my *burchiello*, wet and afraid. In a red silk gown in a lavish mansion. Across a rustic table, eating soup by candlelight. Beside me in the grass, lit with the moon. When I kiss you, it is like kissing beauty, tasting it, feeling it alive and vibrant against my lips."

She laughed, a shaky, nervous sound. "You are a poet, signore."

"Just a man." He shrugged, ashamed of his own mediocrity.

"No. I have never known anyone like you."

"I suppose that is true. A well-bred woman such as yourself would hardly encounter many Venetian bastards."

She brought her jeweled, stormy eyes up to his. "'Tis not what I see when I look at you."

Kieran's eyes roamed over him, and he feared her opinion as much as he craved knowing it. She took a few steps closer to him, and in the golden light cast by the ballroom windows, he could see that her lips were parted and trembling.

"What do you see?" he dared to ask.

"The promise of warmth," she whispered.

~19~

Matteo's knees grew weak; he trembled like a child. To cover, he took two steps back and leaned casually against the column of the grand entryway.

"I am a peasant and a bastard. A gambler and a thief."

She shook her head to the negative. "You are an artist, a poet, a musician, and a man of letters. You are a man of great imagination, passion, and enthusiasm. You see through people better than anyone I know."

Matteo swallowed heavily. He wondered at her mood, and what havoc it would wreak upon his already fragile emotions. "I know who I am, Kieran. Why did you come here?"

She shrugged lightly. "I wondered if you were alone."

"Wondered?"

She smiled, as if in capitulation. "Worried."

"And now that you know the truth, will you leave?"

"Do you wish me to?"

"It is not appropriate for you to be here, alone, at night, unescorted."

"I don't care," she said, the timid softness of her tone belying the boldness of her words. "The night grows colder still. Won't you invite me inside?"

Matteo knew he shouldn't, but he moved to the door, opened it, and held it for her. Kieran ascended the stairs and passed him, and he inhaled her scent as she moved by, sandalwood and jasmine.

Matteo followed her. Her hair hung down her back in a thick, uneven braid, with tendrils of hair escaping in curling wisps, telling him that no maid's brush coiffed her hair; she'd come to him unannounced, without a guard. His eyes swept down to admire the narrow curve of her waist and the gentle swing of her hips. He wondered how padded the skirt was, what was fabric and what was flesh, and then grinned wryly, for that sort of dangerous musing and imagining had caused him to not see her for weeks.

Kieran stopped in at the entrance to the ballroom, and leaned against the open doorway. She studied the interior for a long moment, and then turned to him, her face illuminated in candlelight and shadow. "'Tis as I pictured it. 'Tis what you are to me. You asked me how I saw you, and this is how: A warm pool of light in a vast sea of darkness."

She could not possibly know how difficult she was making things, he thought. He reminded himself: She is a maiden, and does not understand her own feminine power.

"I think you should go. I will escort you back."

"I'm not ready to leave," Kieran said, and she entered the ballroom.

Kieran trembled, her knees nearly knocking together as she walked toward the area Matteo inhabited. It smelled of fire smoke and beeswax candles, pine rosin and old books, leather garments and the ink that perpetually stained his fingertips. In the corner stood a washstand, and on it was a pitcher of fresh water and a dish bearing a soft lump of soap. Kieran moved close enough that she could detect the scent of bergamot and spices.

Turning to face him, a sharp pain filled her chest. He was so beautiful to her, his lean face shadowed and burnished by candlelight, his dark hair streaked by the sun.

His cheeks bore the rakish stubble of a man who had forgone shaving for several days. The white shirt he wore was unfastened, and she glimpsed his chest, dark, tight, and sinewy. As she watched him, she saw his throat work as if he swallowed heavily, and she longed to press her lips to that throat, to smell his skin as his stubble scratched her.

There was no more fighting her passion. When he looked at her with those dark, amber-flecked eyes and told her that he had not resumed his role as Carina's lover, Kieran knew he told the truth.

In Matteo's eyes, she saw the man who'd told her that his heart beat for her. And she realized that she did not want him to ever say such a thing to another woman. She wanted him, yes. But she wanted him all to herself.

Like the other night, she embraced the moment they had in the present. She knew he would leave and return to Venice, but he was here, now.

Kieran walked slowly toward him. He reached out as if he would touch her, but made his hand into a fist and dropped it.

She moved even closer, until she could feel the heat of his body. It reached for her, drew her near him like a magnet's pull. Tilting her head so she could look into his dark, burning eyes, she said, "I have spent weeks remembering every kiss, every touch, and every word you've ever given me, written and spoken."

Matteo took a few steps back. "We should go. Let me take you home."

Kieran advanced on him. "No."

"Kieran," Matteo warned, as he backed away, "stop."

"No." She proceeded to draw closer.

She reached back to her braid and untied the ribbon that bound it. Using her fingers, she raked it free and let it spill and swirl over her shoulders and down her back, as free as she felt in that moment.

"What will you do, signore? Can you call yourself a romancer if you flee from me as if I carry plague?"

Matteo did not stop backing away. "You do not know what you are doing."

"No, I don't."

He tripped over a pile of books but kept moving away from her, his eyes never leaving hers. "You are playing a dangerous game, and it cannot end well for you. You are a maid, and I can only offer you trouble. Let me take you home, Kieran, and tomorrow you will wake and come to your senses."

"I only want to kiss you. Did you, yourself, not once tell me that kisses are a simple thing to be enjoyed? Is this a Venetian problem, signore?"

"There is nothing simple about kissing you," he said, and he backed up until the bed stopped his progress. He muttered searing curses in Italian.

"Matteo de Gama," she whispered, as she stood in front of him. "Will you leave England, and me, behind and return to Venice?"

Something flashed hard and bright in his eyes. Was it pain? she wondered.

"Yes."

"When will you go?"

"When my work is finished here," he replied quietly. "A passenger ship leaves in midsummer. I plan to be on it."

A lump formed in her throat, and it ached like a sickness. "I will not beg you to stay."

"I would not expect you to."

She glanced away from him, stared at the floor where the firelight cast rippling, undulating patterns of gold on the highly polished parquet floor. "Do you have affection for me, Matteo?"

A long silence filled the small gap between them, until he said roughly, "I do."

"Do you remember the girl you pulled from the canal?"

"Yes. She was a tiger in a cage, fierce and afraid, a danger to herself and others."

"I had no one to cry to," she whispered. "I was sad and sick inside, full of a self-loathing for which my pride would allow no cure."

"And now?"

"Now 'tis different. I am different. 'Tis because of you."

"I told you once that your season would come, and that you would bloom. It is not me, Kieran. It is just your time."

"You are wrong," she said, her tone quiet but assertive. "If you had not provoked me into revealing my burden, I would never have let it out. It would still be festering inside me. I also would never have met Alva, and had a new light cast on that night, along with my role in it. You claim you do nothing for anyone unless there is something in it for you, but your actions belie that, and the drawings suggest otherwise, as well. They are not all of my form, but capture my moods, my emotions. I know you are an artist, signore, but I cannot forget that you said your heart beat for me."

"I should not have said that."

"Was it a lie?"

"No. It is a weapon."

"I do not wield it, Matteo. I treasure the words you spoke as nothing else."

He looked at her oddly, his brows drawn down into a frown. "I am ready to return you to the manse."

"I don't want to go."

Kieran reached out a trembling finger and touched his skin, the sinewy valley between the flat, hard muscles that defined his chest. His texture felt warm and surprisingly soft. She boldly ran her finger down to his smooth, muscled belly. His breath hissed between his teeth, and a blush stormed her cheeks at the sound. Kieran pulled her hand away as if she'd touched fire, just as his hand clamped around her wrist.

He held her hard, imprisoning. The gleam in his eyes looked distinctly like anger. "What are you after?"

Kieran's heart beat a rapid tattoo, and her entire body trembled. "I don't know. I can only assure you, I have not found it in my spinster's bed."

The grip on her wrist gentled, and Matteo lifted his hand to cup her face. He held it like a sculpture, and with his ink-stained fingers, he caressed her skin, sending heat and shivers through her body in equal measure.

"There is no shame in hungering for physical release. You are a woman, and your body is made for such pleasures. Attend dinners and balls and go to court, Kieran, and find a man who strikes passion in your heart. Marry him, and go to his bed innocent. The pleasures you find there will be pure then, and not tarnished by an affair with a long-forgotten foreigner."

"I told you I shall never marry, and I told you why." She did not add that she would never forget him; it sounded too much like the needy, begging woman she feared becoming.

His touch was so gentle, and Kieran leaned into it, wanting him to be more insistent, to stop touching her like a maiden.

"I know," Matteo said. "But perhaps if you stop looking for reasons to doubt your suitors, you will find honesty in a few of them. You are a rare woman, and any man would be blessed to make you his wife."

A fire burned in Kieran, ignited months before and now a vast blaze.

He was leaving, and she would never see him again.

She looked at him now, in his unbound shirt. His hair was mussed and hung around his lean, handsome face in dark, streaked waves, and his lips were soft and full. Kieran could recall the precise texture and taste of his mouth, and the memory did nothing to stem the quickening of her pulse.

Kieran's life had not turned out the way she'd thought it would. Everything she'd ever thought she wanted was different now. She was not that young girl pining for a proper English lord to marry her and make her a lady.

Those longings seemed as distant as Barbados and as childish as a fairy tale.

Kieran was now a grown woman, and knew that life was not about how things should be, but how they were. She no longer pined for an English lord. Instead, she burned for a Venetian poet.

"I don't want to be a wife, Matteo," she whispered, and she abandoned her frigid, false demeanor. She was once again that young, petulant girl who took what she wanted and demanded what was denied her. The wild wind inside her body swirled with heat and need, and Kieran nearly laughed with the freedom of it. She was coming back to herself, and it was heady and wonderful. "I want to be fully a woman, and I want you to make me so."

Matteo tried to sidestep her, but she was too quick. Kieran wrapped her arms around him and pressed a kiss against his chest, over his heart. She kissed his skin, her lips warm and moist and greedy, and he weakened. Heat spread through his body, and his arousal became painful as her inexperienced kisses moved to his neck.

"Kieran, you must stop this," he breathed. "I am but a man."

"No, not just a man," she said against his skin, her breath warm and moist. "You are Matteo de Gama, and you are the man I want."

Pain stabbed in his heart. *The man I want.* How he longed for her to say he was the man she loved.

He grabbed her arms and tried to pull them from around his waist. "Enough. You must stop."

Kieran tightened her hold and pressed her breasts

against him. He swore he could feel the erect peaks through her layers of clothing. Matteo groaned and made an effort to wrench away. "I am warning you. Stop this madness."

She laughed, the vixen. With her hair unbound and her simple clothes, she looked like a milkmaid bent on amorous pursuit. Her stormy eyes gleamed wickedly. "Will you subdue me, Matteo?"

She couldn't know what she was doing. Matteo clung to that thought, hoping it would calm the raging desire in his body to take exactly what she was offering.

No. Kieran was a maiden, and he would not ruin her. Matteo took her by the shoulders and held her back from him. He dug his fingers hard into her shoulders, and gave her a little shake, to get her attention.

"You must listen to me. You think this is a game, but it is not. You are a maid, and will remain so. Do you hear me? I am not going to steal your innocence."

"You cannot steal what is given," she said softly, and her lips trembled in a way that made him want to cover them with his own.

"I can refuse it, and I do."

"Do not protect me, Matteo. I know what I want."

"Did you ever wonder what I want?" Matteo asked, and he hoped she did not hear the desperation he felt.

"Tell me."

"I want you to leave me be. I want you to find yourself a man who can fulfill your dreams. I want you to be happy, and I want you to have everything you have always desired."

Kieran's eyes traveled over his face, lingered on his neck, and swept over his chest and belly. Those eyes betrayed her desire and her doubt. She licked her lips as if tasting his skin, and she raised her hands to cup his wrists as he held her from him. Her fingers traced his veins, and lay to rest on his pounding pulse. A smile curved her lips, and she met his eyes once again. She was killing him slowly and he nearly hated her for it.

"Go home," he hissed. "I do not want you."

"Say it again."

"I do not want you."

"Once more."

"Kieran, I do not want you."

Each time, he had less conviction, for her hands were stroking his arms and her perfume filled his senses.

"You are quite beautiful, Matteo," she said softly. "I have never told you that I thought so, but I do."

"Please," he breathed, but he did not know what he begged for.

Her eyelids fluttered down and he noticed that her breath came fast and shallow. A blush rose on her cheeks that spoke of embarrassment. Her lips shook, and she bit at them as if to quell the shaking. A little laugh came from her, but she sounded sad and lost and lonely. "I told you once, I don't quite know what comes over me when I am with you. I lose myself somehow. I don't know how to seduce a man and 'twas madness for me to try."

"You could give lessons."

Kieran brought her eyes back to meet his. "Is that so?"

"I am only a man," he said again, despising the truth of it. He did not know how much longer he could withstand her.

He pushed her further back, let go of her, and walked away. Matteo moved to the fireplace, placed his hand on the mantle, and stared into the flames.

"I am sorry," she said behind him, and she sounded as if she were about to weep. "I will leave. No need to see me back; my brother's property is patrolled on the borders and is quite safe."

His conscience said to let her go, to stay away, and that her tears were better spent now, than later when she would go to her marriage bed with regret.

"Yes, and the moment I dare to behave differently, look how you slap me back into my place. Well done, signore. I was close to seizing my own life, and making a choice of my own. How thoughtful of you to remind me that I do not deserve it by the very virtue of my virtue."

Kieran thumped her mount and wheeled her around, nearly trampling Matteo beneath the beast's hooves. She rode into the wind, leaving him behind. The night was cool and bright, and Kieran urged the horses to a thundering pace.

When she returned to the manse, she left them in the care of the groggy stable lad. She stalked back to her rooms by way of the servants' entrance, and when she was finally alone in her quarters, she slapped her riding gloves down on her table and began to strip off her gown and undergarments.

How dare he? In her mind she could hear him again and again, telling her he would be a fool to love her.

Undressed, she withdrew her nightclothes from her armoire, and yanked the diaphanous silk garment over her head, settling it into place with a few sharp tugs. She raked her comb through her snarled hair and then threw it with a clatter back onto her dressing table.

It was not as if she asked him to profess such before inviting him to bed. Shame heated her cheeks, that she'd stooped so low. How could she have been so close to giving up her virginity for a few well-turned sonnets and well-drawn sketches?

At the thought of the drawings, she retrieved them from deep within her armoire and strode over to the fireplace. She held them above the flames but couldn't bring herself to toss them in. Her anger finally spent, she dropped them to the floor, unharmed.

Kieran crumpled to the floor beside them as tears spilled down her cheeks. She wrapped her arms around herself and rocked back and forth, looking through her tears to the papers where he'd drawn her moods and her body.

Incongruously, she wished for her mother to come and comfort her. An absurd thought, that, because Kieran hardly thought Camille would understand or approve of what she'd been after that night.

Kieran thought about that herself, wondering what she'd been after. Certainly something more than the physical aspect, she'd wanted the touch and taste of him, and to have his complete attention and desire. She'd wanted to feel like the woman he'd drawn: sensual, erotic, and utterly, fearlessly female.

Restlessness curled in her blood and had her tapping her foot. She should have been tired, but instead felt uneasy and unsettled.

The brandy called to her from its hiding place, and Kieran sought out its soothing amber warmth. It glugged from the bottle as she poured a generous draught. She swirled it, sipped, and then sipped again. Lured by the beauty of the clear, cool night, she went out to her balcony to drink.

The fat moon gleamed in the sapphire sky, surrounded by stars. Kieran drank and looked upward, trying to set aside the embarrassment of her failed seduction and her hurt at Matteo's harsh words.

A sound drew her attention, and she searched the darkness on the ground. Soon enough she saw him, illuminated by the moonlight that cast an eerie shine on his black leather garments.

Matteo stepped from the shadows and approached her balcony. He silently looked up at her, and Kieran knew he'd come to make sure she was home safe.

A pang of longing and desire swept through her once again, and a long sigh slipped from her lips. It turned to a gasp as he grabbed hold of the column and began to shimmy up. He reached the balustrade and pulled himself to the railing, hopped over it easily, and wordlessly grabbed her and pulled her against his hard body.

His lips were hot; his kiss was insatiable. No words were needed. Matteo lifted her easily, carried in to the bed, and laid her upon the cool silk coverlet. He lay beside her, and looked into her eyes, his full of questions and declarations he did not speak.

In answer, Kieran slid her hands into his hair and pulled his lips to hers once again.

He deepened the kiss. His tongue plumbed the depths of her mouth until she was breathless. Pulling back, he cupped her face and rained tiny kisses over her closed eyes, across the bridge of her nose, around her cheeks and on her ears. He murmured to her in Italian, softly spoken words that sounded like vows.

But Kieran did not ask him what he said. She did not dare, lest he stop again and leave her alone with the fire in her blood and the rushing in her ears. She arched against him, trembling with needs and passions she barely understood.

His body felt like heated iron, hot and hard. His scent filled senses, leather and bergamot, amber and ink. Through the thin silk of her dressing gown, she could feel his strength and his arousal, a hard, contained bulge pressed to her belly.

He did want her.

Matteo released his hold of her and raised up on the bed. He slipped out of his jacket and stripped off his shirt, and then took her in his arms once again. Kieran touched the skin on his back, so warm and so soft, and felt the movement of his muscles beneath her fingers as he kissed her.

Kieran pulled back, breathless.

Suddenly shy, she realized he would see her flesh, and would know her in the most intimate sense. What if he thought her too thin, or too small of breast?

Kieran did not fear the act of love; Emeline had told her it was wondrous and pleasurable with the right man.

That knowledge, however, hadn't prepared her for having this masculine animal alone in her bed. He exuded strength and sexuality, and it overwhelmed her with the oddest mixture of trepidation and curiosity.

As if sensing her mood, Matteo placed his hand on her thigh, just below her dagger. He traced the shape of it through the silk of her gown, and then slowly, inch by inch, he gathered the fabric beneath his clever fingers, pulling it up until he revealed her weapon.

Her thighs gleamed pale in the candlelight, and the black leather sheath shone like death against her flesh. His breath hissed between his teeth as his fingers moved over the buckles and straps.

And then Matteo froze. Slowly, he touched her other thigh, where two long, thin scars ran in perfectly straight parallel lines, pink and puckered and obviously not accidental. He looked from the dagger to the scars, and then raised his eyes to hers. "Why?"

Kieran did not push his hand away or seek to hide her wounds. No, her days of dishonesty were behind her. She fearlessly told him the truth. "It felt good to feel something."

He seemed to think about that for a moment. Finally he nodded his understanding and bent his head to kiss the scars with excruciating gentleness. A low moan came from her throat when his warm breath touched her in the most intimate of places, and when he lifted his head and looked at her, she realized that Matteo de Gama understood her in ways that no one else ever would.

"Do not do it again," he said simply. "There are better ways."

He leaned forward and kissed her again, and the world melted away. His hands were on her body, touching and stroking her in ways that had her straining against him, her insecurity and worries abandoned.

She lay back, expecting him to lie beside her, but he did not. Instead, he knelt over her and lifted her left hand. He studied it in the golden candlelight, and Kieran saw it as he must, slim, delicate bones and fair, fragile skin.

"If I were your suitor, I would have to wait for months for the privilege of kissing your gloveless hand." He bent his head and pressed a soft kiss on the back of her hand, turned it, and slowly kissed each fingertip, and then the center of her palm. He looked down on her, his eyes obscured by the flickering shadows. "You are a gentle-born woman. Why are you doing this?"

A sigh slipped from her lips. She'd lost so much of her pride, it did not seem as difficult to let go of a bit more. "You will leave England."

"And?" he prompted.

"And I fear that day."

"Why?"

"Because I will miss you. Very much. I picture England without you, and 'tis a lonely, cold place."

Matteo trembled, his hands shaking, like his lips and his body. Strangely moved, wanting to comfort him, Kieran rose up and cupped his face in her hands, kissing his cheeks as if he were a child. A tear escaped his closed eye and she kissed it away, feeling oddly maternal.

"Why do you weep?" she whispered.

"I will miss you, too." He trembled and shook, and looked to the fire, avoiding her gaze.

Pride was a clog in her throat, but Kieran pushed beyond it and said the word that had echoed in her mind since the day Matteo found out that his exile was lifted.

"Stay."

"I cannot."

"Why not? Do you hate it here in England?"

"No."

"Why then?"

He brought his eyes back to look at her and he looked vulnerable and fearful, once again like a little boy trapped in a man's body.

"Why?" she asked insistently.

"Because I love you," he confessed.

∼ 20 ∼

"Fool that I am." Matteo rose from the bed and reached for his shirt and his jacket. "The second weapon I have placed in your hands."

Kieran sat before him, stunned. With his dark hair rumpled, his torso shirtless, and his narrow leather breeches riding low on his hips, he looked like a dangerous romancer, freshly risen from his latest conquest.

It had never once occurred to Kieran that a man like Matteo de Gama could lose his heart to a woman such as herself. She wondered what he possibly saw in her that inspired such a tender emotion, and floundered in his revelation, at a loss for how to respond.

"Do not waste a moment's worry," Matteo said, his voice sounding ragged with emotion. "I have been beset by this problem before. I know that I only need to stay away from you long enough, and I will recover."

He stared at her, his eyes moving from her hair to her eyes to her lips. "It will happen slowly. Excruciatingly. For a time, I will not believe it possible that one day I will not be able to recall the precise sound of your voice, or the exact shade of your eyes, or the way your skin smells and tastes. But it will happen. Time will have its way with me. Eventually, I will struggle to remember the molten garnet of your hair caught in the sunlight, the way you sound when you laugh, and the way you look when you ride, free and caught in the wind."

He slipped into his shirt and shrugged into his jacket, still staring at her as if memorizing her face. "A few details will remain to torture me forever, such as the way you called me the Venetian artist, when you knew me for nothing more than a bastard. I will always treasure the memory of the way you came to me for comfort and warmth when you could have sought out anyone else. These things, and many others, I will cherish the rest of my life, Kieran. Not a single moment with you was wasted."

He moved to the balcony doors, and Kieran realized he was leaving.

"Wait."

Matteo stopped and Kieran rose from the bed to go to him. She wrapped her arms around his lean waist and pressed her cheek against his chest, just above his poet's heart. Tenderness welled in her like a river of warmth, and she held him close.

He kissed the top of her head, and breathed in her scent. His breath was warm as he said, "Do me the favor of granting me your absence. Please, I beg you, stay away from me."

Matteo let her go and went out to the balcony and Kieran rushed after him. She reached out and grabbed his arm. "You have not let me say anything."

"This is not a matter for discussion. It is my problem."

"You trivialize your own emotion, and do not even ask for mine."

In the moonlight she saw his brows come down into a scowl, and she could feel anger brewing in the air, like a lightning storm that blows in from the sea.

"No," he bit out. "I simply do not overvalue it. It is a

feeling, not a need, and it will pass. And as for yours, I am all too aware of the disparity from my own."

But Kieran was still reeling from his admission and the words that followed it. How dare he think he could lay out his heart like that, and then leave her with the admonition to stay away from him?

"'Tis not fair to leave on such terms. Nothing is settled."

Matteo laughed harshly. "Hardly, and it will not be for me for some time."

"We ought discuss the matter."

"I do believe I have said more than I should. Does it please you so much to see me humbled and groveling before you? Have I not satisfied your vanity enough?" His dark eyes smoldered, and he lifted the corner of his sensual lips in a sardonic sneer. "Shall I compose a sonnet for you? You can read it to your children some day, and tell them that once, a long time ago, a poor wretch who did not know his place declared his love to you."

"Matteo," she whispered, hurt to her core. "How could you say such a thing?

He stared at her for a long moment, and then silently grabbed her hand. He looked at it as if it were a foreign object, and then he kissed it fiercely before releasing his hold. Without a word he climbed down from her balcony and disappeared into the darkness.

Kieran ran back into her rooms and pulled the gown she'd worn earlier from her armoire. She tossed it on the chair and withdrew her cloak and riding gloves.

She would be damned if he'd leave her like that. Her blood still burned from his caresses and her heart was full and aching with his words. He'd denied her affections, declared his love, and then acted as though she spurned him.

How dare he think that she would gather tokens of his love, to be shown later in life as some validation of her ability to collect hearts and break them.

A knock sounded at Kieran's door, and she paused in the act of dressing. She glanced at the timepiece on her mantle, and saw the hour was long past midnight. "Who calls?"

"Your mother."

The familiar voice brought a shriek of delight from Kieran and she flew to the door to unlock and open it. Sure enough, there stood Camille, looking fatigued and travel-rumpled and incredibly happy. Her mother, still beautiful in her fifties, smiled at her brightly, her vivid green eyes sparkling with joy.

"We arrived less than an hour ago," Camille said. "But I could not wait until the morning to see you."

Kieran hugged her mother, hard, and then pulled back to look at her. Camille looked much the same as she had a year before: her fine skin lightly aging with the crinkles of contentment around her eyes, her black hair streaked with silver, and her figure petite and slim.

"I cannot believe my eyes. I wrote you a letter only two days ago."

"I did not receive it, my Kieran, and won't for many months," Camille said with a laugh. "What did it say?"

"It asked when you would come, and expressed the hope that it would be soon. I've missed you, Mum."

"And I you."

Camille swept past Kieran, into her chambers. Kieran looked at the rumpled bed where she'd lain with Matteo only moments before, and hoped that the spicy, clean scent of bergamot and leather did not linger in the air.

Her face burned as she realized what Camille could have interrupted, had Matteo not refused her advances.

Camille glanced at the chair where Kieran's clothes were, the side laces designed for a lady to dress without the assistance of a maid, and then to the open balcony doors. She cast her attention to her daughter and with a knowing, perceptive raise of a brow said, "Are you going somewhere?"

"To bed," Kieran said, as if it were obvious.

"Is your maid so lacking that she does not hang your gown after you've worn it?"

"Of course not. She complained of an aching head, and I bid her goodnight before her duties were complete."

Camille lay her hand upon Kieran's cheek and patted it gently before lifting the gown and going to the armoire to hang it.

With her shame for lying compounded by the fact that her mother thought her too high and mighty to hang her own gown, Kieran turned to the fire to show that she was not above taking care of herself in some way. With horror, she saw that the drawings lay on the hearth, untouched by the flames. Kieran rushed over and stooped before the low blaze, surreptitiously stowing the papers in the bottom of her woodbin before adding a few logs to the fire.

A wild look around her rooms revealed no other vestiges of her encounter with Matteo, and she relaxed slightly.

Raking her hair back from her face, she gathered it into a knot, secured it with a comb, and climbed onto her bed, patting the space beside her. "Come, Mum, and leave the tidying. Tell me about home and your voyage. Have you seen Emeline, yet? Her belly is quite large, and growing by the day."

Camille acquiesced and joined her daughter on the bed. "I did see Emeline and Rogan, and yes, 'tis a big belly."

"The doctors say the babe will come in July."

"We shall see," Camille said with a smile. She studied her daughter's face with a mysterious expression, and reached out to smooth a lock of hair that had fallen from Kieran's comb. She tucked it behind Kieran's ear in a familiar gesture from her childhood, and Kieran felt her heart swell with love for her mother.

"So, my Kieran, why don't we put off the chatter. I'm tired from travel and will seek my bed soon. 'Twould be most helpful, darling, if you'd tell me who you've been kissing, and if I'm going to be blessed with a son-in-law any time soon."

Kieran gaped at her mother, who waited patiently. "Kissing?" Kieran managed to strangle out.

Camille sighed and rolled her eyes heavenward, before bringing them back to Kieran, two emerald green orbs that pierced her soul. "Must you drag it out? I see your swollen lips and your abraded chin, raw and red from the rasp of a man's stubble. Will you think me a fool that I don't know what mark a lover's kiss leaves on a woman's face?"

"He is not my lover," Kieran said softly. "I swear, Mum, I have not lain with him."

Camille's gaze swept over her, and Kieran suddenly worried that her mother would see the desire that had pounded through her veins only moments before.

"Who is this man?"

"A Venetian artist in exile from his country. He came home to England with us, and has been working for Rogan these months past."

"Do you love him?" Camille asked.

"He is common-born, a bastard, and a gambler." Kieran heard herself and hated the words as they came out of her mouth, both for their truth and for the fact that it mattered to her. To soften them, she added, "He is leaving England in a few weeks. His exile is lifted, and he is going home."

Camille smiled knowingly. "You did not answer the question."

"I have never loved any man, save Rogan and Da."

Camille's eyes never left her daughter's face, her expression thoughtful. "Does he love you?"

"He says he does." Kieran looked away, ashamed.

"Do you believe him?"

Kieran thought of Alva, and how Matteo had gone to such lengths to find the truth of what happened that night in the "house of lords." She remembered the way he'd looked at her with tenderness, and the words he'd spoken against her lips. She recalled the light in his eyes when he saw her, and the heat in them when he kissed her.

"Yes," Kieran answered. "I believe he does."

"Well then, my child, you must have a care with him. When a man loses his heart to a woman, 'tis usually with great passion and intensity. You must not do anything to add to his hurt and you must honor his heart, the way you would want yours tended."

Matteo's words repeated in Kieran's mind, *Please, I beg you, stay away from me.* And she'd demanded that he discuss his admission, the very thing that he called a weapon. A painful, slow dawning started in Kieran's chest, spreading through her body until her belly ached. She thought of how callous Matteo must think her, naïve and vain.

"Oh, Mum, I fear I have already hurt him."

Camille made a small noise of sympathy, and sighed. "It's likely you have, my Kieran, if you seek only his kisses and not his heart."

"I must talk with him," Kieran began, but Camille quickly cut her off.

"And say what? That you do not love him because he is not good enough for you? It is time you stopped acting like a haughty child. Kieran, you would take care to remember your father, and from where you come. You are well-monied, but not so well-born."

The words were like a slap. Silence fell between them, the crackling of the fire the only sound. Kieran felt an immediate flare of the feelings of her youth, resentment that her mother walked away from the aristocracy with such ease, coupled with the romantic longing for just the kind of love that had driven the decision.

Camille rose from the bed and walked around the rooms. She stopped to lightly touch the carved molding on the fireplace mantle. "This was a cold, loveless house. My mother, Amelia, had it elegantly made, but I do not recall any laughter in these walls. Rogan and Emeline have filled it with warmth and love, and I am grateful for it."

For the first time in her life, Kieran asked the question that had always nagged at her. "I know you love Da passionately, but how did you manage to leave all of this behind, without a glance back? Though you are happily married, did you ever long for the privilege and prestige that was your birthright?"

"My mother was a duchess. It did not make her happy," Camille answered simply. "She had more jewels than she could ever wear, houses she'd never set foot in, and legions of servants to do her tiniest bidding. But none of it was good enough. Nothing satisfied her." Camille shook her head sadly, in memory. "I look back on her now, and I pity her."

"Did you not tell me once that you were betrothed to a man other than Da?"

Camille's brows went up in surprise. "Did I tell you that?"

"Yes. You said 'twas the worst time in your life."

"Well, it certainly was that. If I'd married him, I would have been a duchess in my own right." Camille shuddered a bit, as if she'd tasted something vile. "Lady Misery, the Duchess of Loneliness."

The image of Samuel Ellsworth rose in Kieran's mind, and again, she wondered what her life would be like if she could bring herself to abandon her plan and accept his proposal.

"Do you think I am much like your mother?" Kieran dared to ask.

"Yes, actually, in the best of ways. 'Tis the ways you are like me," Camille replied, sounding surprised. "I am very much my mother's daughter, stubborn and willful and determined. I see that in you, as well, only I'd like to think even more so. Amelia was afraid of my spirit, and she spent my youth trying to break it. I let you have yours."

Kieran thought of how difficult it must have been for Camille to let her come to England with Rogan, and how much she must miss them. A wave of gratitude for her mother's love swept over her, and brought stinging tears to her eyes. She'd been a spoilt child, ungrateful, and demanding. And her mother had never once been anything but loving and accepting, always willing to reason with her, and ready to find a compromise.

"Rogan said I am like you."

Camille laughed. "And did you recoil in horror, to be told you take after your mum?"

"I would have, years ago, because I would have thought that such a thing made me less myself," Kieran admitted. "But now, I find 'tis an honor. I do love you, Mum."

Camille smiled. "I know you do, and that you always have."

With a stifled yawn, Camille consulted the timepiece. "Your da will think I've crawled into bed with you and fallen asleep, as I did when you were small."

"You must be exhausted from your travel. Go to bed, Mum, and we'll talk again on the morrow."

"I am glad I came tonight and risked waking you."

They embraced, and Kieran pressed a kiss to her mother's cheek. "I am, as well. I love you so much, Mum. I'm sorry for every bit of trouble I've given you."

"Don't fret for a moment, Kieran. You've always been

my pleasure. I don't know what good I've done in this world, but it must have been something wonderful for the Lord to bless me with you and your brother."

Camille smiled sweetly, patted her cheek, and moved to the door. She paused, her hand on the doorknob, and turned to speak over her shoulder. "I'm certain 'twill come to no surprise that I'm expecting you'll keep in your rooms at night, and not receive visitors from your balcony. Don't make me post a guard, Kieran. 'Twill just embarrass everyone involved."

Surprised, Kieran could not form a denial. Camille took in the expression on her daughter's face and laughed again. "I was young once, Kieran. And we did agree you're much like me." Camille cast a glance at the balcony doors, sighed wistfully, and left, the door scarcely making a sound as she closed it behind her.

The travel-weary residents of the manse stirred slowly in the morning, as did the others who so happily greeted them in the midnight hour.

As if heralding Patrick and Camille's arrival, the sun shone warmly in the crystal blue skies, a perfect English day in late spring. Emeline's roses held their heavy faces up, their wanton scent drifting on the slight breeze that blew in through the open doors and windows. Out in the paddock the horses tossed their heads and nickered with contentment as the barn cats lolled in warm patches of sunlight.

After a leisurely, late breakfast, Kieran happily went riding with Camille and Patrick, and they enjoyed a long tour of the property.

Upon their return, they discovered Emeline reading in the parlor, her feet propped on a footstool. Kieran regarded her sister-in-law with a sense of awe. She wore a simple gown with a high waist to accommodate her growing belly, and her breasts were high and full and ripe in the square neckline. Her skin gleamed with the luster of crushed pearls, and her sapphire eyes bore the expression of a woman well contented with her life.

Emeline suddenly gasped and rested her hand on the dome of her belly. She smiled, her eyes sparkling. "The babe moves constantly, and at times with such force. He will be as strong as his papa."

Camille took a seat beside Emeline and placed her hands over the swell, before pulling back to wipe away a happy tear from the corner of her eye. "'Tis quite a strong kick he has. Rogan was just the same, always on the go, even in the womb."

Patrick grinned and moved to take a seat across from the women. "'He,' is it? Do you think the babe a boy, Emeline?"

"I do," she replied. Her lips curved in a smile. "I dream of the birth, and 'tis always a son I bear."

Kieran felt suddenly out of place. She considered retiring to her rooms to dress for dinner. As if sensing her mood, Camille turned and held out a hand to her. "And you as well, my Kieran. You kicked as hard as your brother, and so we expected you would be a boy, as well."

"And that's why you called me Kieran," Kieran said softly, remembering the story that Camille had told her many times.

"Aye," Patrick said. He explained to Emeline, "Kieran was the name of my mother, Nuala's, father. We'd named Rogan for my father's father, and so thought it proper to give the name Kieran to my second son. But when, to our surprise, the lad was born a lass, we were so accustomed to calling the babe Kieran, that we kept it. And I think it suits her, for she has the look of my mother's family."

"Truly? I see much of Camille in Kieran," Emeline said.

"Aye, she's as beautiful as her mum, in feature and bone structure. But her eyes and hair are pure Irish."

Kieran smiled for her mother and father's benefit, but

inside she felt the familiar shame at her lack of pride in her heritage. All her life she'd wanted to be all things English and had shunned her common, Irish ancestry.

And yet, looking at her father, she felt an enormous sense of pride that his blood ran in her veins. Patrick was honorable and generous, trustworthy and solid. So Kieran felt very small for her disloyal thoughts, and rose to take a cup of tea from the side cart to cover any emotions that might show on her face.

She wished for someone with whom she could speak about her true feelings, and thought of Matteo. She'd confessed cutting herself and he'd not turned away with revulsion, but had understood. He'd listened to her talk of her greatest shame, and the worst kind of cowardice. Instead of judging her harshly, he had seen fit to find the woman who'd been in the house that night so he could find the truth of the matter and dispel her guilt.

And he loved her.

A warm shiver ran through her body, and her belly flipped. She envisioned his eyes, dark and smoldering with amber lights, and her blood grew warm. What spell had the Venetian cast over her?

From behind her, as if reading her thoughts, Emeline addressed Camille and said, "Signore de Gama accepted your invitation to dinner, Mum. My messenger returned whilst you were riding."

Kieran swung around and gaped at Camille, who met her gaze with a serene smile. "'Twill be wonderful to meet him."

Camille rose and took her seat beside Patrick, leaving Kieran with only the view of the back of her head. Her mother leaned against Patrick's shoulder with the ease of a woman completely in love. Her voice sounded casual as she chatted with Emeline. "What of Samuel Ellsworth? Has he replied to my invitation, as well?"

"Not yet, but I am certain he will want to join us tonight. He will surely want to meet you both."

Matteo and Samuel both coming to dinner? Kieran could have happily throttled her mother. Camille hadn't been in England for twenty-four hours, and had already complicated matters.

"Aye, and we him," Patrick said. He swiveled to face Kieran. "How is that a man asks for your hand in marriage, and we hear of it from Rogan and not you? The entire day I waited for you to speak of it."

An awkward pause fell as Kieran struggled for an answer. How could she explain to her parents that she had not yet decided the course she would take, revenge or marriage.

"You have the look of a blinking owl, not an eager bride," Patrick said with a laugh, clearly at ease and certain of his daughter's intentions. "If that's all the passion the man inspires, I hope your refusal will be worded gently."

"I have not decided to refuse."

Patrick's grin faded and he rose to stand before her, formidable, strong, broad and tall, his stormy blue eyes sparking with Irish indignation. "Oh, aye? And yet you're frozen there, as still and pale as a statue. You're a woman now, Kieran, and as such you ought to be well-equipped to choose a marriage mate. If you do not love this Ellsworth, why would you consider marriage to him?"

Rogan entered the room and answered the question with the smugness of an older brother. "He is an English duke. Isn't that what she used to pine for when she was a girl?"

Kieran faced her entire family: brother, mother, father, and sister-in-law, with as much dignity as she could manage. "Since Rogan is so obviously intent on speaking for me, I leave you all with his devilish interpretation. I find I must retire to my rooms to dress for the dinner that has been so kindly planned without my knowledge. Good day to you all."

Kieran curtsied, and with her shoulders back and her head high, she swept from the room. Let them gossip as they would, she thought with annoyance, knowing that there are no people more willing to meddle in the life of a spinster than those who are happily wed.

With a sigh, she wished for some illness to excuse her from the coming night, but, alas, found herself in perfect health.

As she entered her rooms, she opened her armoire and cast attention to her wardrobe. Gowns of every style, fabric, and color hung there, some studded with jets and lace, others adorned with seed pearls and brilliants. What, she wondered, did a woman wear to dine with her beloved but frustrating family, her wealthy, titled, but despised suitor, and the enigmatic, unsuitable Venetian who claimed he loved her?

Long after the sun had set, the candles had been lit, and the guests had been received, Kieran remained in her rooms. Her mother had come for her, as had Emeline, and her maid as well, all bidding her to descend the stairs and greet those in attendance.

According to Emeline, many other people had also been invited to welcome Patrick and Camille.

Kieran opened her doors and leaned out into the hall. She could hear the sounds of rushing servants, the clinking of glasses, and the very distant strings of music.

She leaned further out, straining to hear more, and nearly toppled over when she heard her brother's voice.

"Are you bent on making an entrance, *sidhe gaoithe*?"

He stopped and his eyes traveled over her, taking in the richness of her navy silk gown. Created in the latest French fashion, with a voluminous skirt and a narrowly nipped waist, it boasted a daringly low, square neckline. It bared the curves of her breasts, and with each step they wobbled in their silken vise. Kieran had never worn something so daring, yet the gown was otherwise so simple and elegant, it did not bear the look of something wanton. Her sleeves were full, gathered above the elbow, and frothed with white lace that fell to her fingertips. She wore jewelry, borrowed from Emeline, finely wrought pieces set with diamonds and sapphires. Her maid had painstakingly coiled and curled her hair, dressing it high, and securing it with brilliant-tipped pins.

"You are stunning," Rogan said, and he grinned at her as only a brother could. "Wearing your best gown to sup with Mum and Da?"

"No," Kieran said defensively. She smoothed her hands over her skirts, the silk like butter beneath her skin, the lace blooming like a flower over her wrists. "'Tis not my best."

"I've never seen you in it."

"I did not say 'twas not new." Kieran stepped from her rooms and tried to reach for some of her battered pride.

"Well, I've never seen so much of you." He glanced pointedly at her breasts and laughed. "Our little girl's grown up, aye?"

Kieran's face flamed red. She placed her hands her décolletage and knitted her brow. "'Tis not too to change. I will ring for Jane."

Rogan took her by the elbow and steered her toward the stairs. "You look grand, Kieran. Hold your head up. Aside from my Emeline, you'll be the most beautiful woman in the room."

Kieran took a deep, shaking breath and nodded. "Thank you, Rogan."

With her hand on his elbow, they walked down the long corridor. Kieran looked up to her brother. He was tall and recklessly handsome. He wore a beautifully tailored dark green jacket with a crisp white shirt, and it made his emerald eyes all the more vivid.

"I'm proud of you, Rogan," she said softly.

He stopped and looked down on her with a quizzical expression. "And I you."

"No, I mean it. You're as comfortable on a ship's deck as in your ducal mansion, and though you bear titles and arms for England, you don't deny your common, Irish heritage." Embarrassment threatened to steal her nerve and her voice. "I often wonder how you manage that."

"'Tis not difficult, Kieran. I am just myself, no matter what. I was not raised to be a duke, or a sea-merchant, or a trader; I was raised to be Rogan Mullen. Honor, loyalty, and truth is what I value, be a man a servant or a king. I require that of myself, and the rest falls into place."

"Yes," she said quietly, and stood on tiptoe to kiss Rogan's cheek. "Thank you for having me here with you. 'Tis beautiful gowns I wear, lovely rooms I sleep in, and magnificent horses I ride. I don't k

Matteo leaned casually against the open frame of the French doors that led out to the terrace. His arms were crossed, and his eyes were on her, a smoldering warmth she could feel from across the room. He wore brown leather garments and a simple cream colored shirt that complimented his tanned skin and chocolate eyes.

He cut a roguish, handsome figure, with his lean, good looks and his tall, narrow frame. Matteo lifted his glass of wine to his lips, and as he did Kieran noticed that his fingers were even more ink-stained than usual. He'd been writing or drawing, she thought, and a dark, delicious thrill ran through her as she imagined his muse.

Matteo met her gaze as if he'd felt it. For a moment she was suspended in time, her only thought, *he loves me.*

And then she remembered that he'd told her to leave him alone, and swore he would forget her.

He did not stare at her like a man who wanted to be forgotten, however. With his dark eyes burning with amber light, he regarded her over the rim of his glass. He lifted erosity for granted."

Rogan lay his hand on Kieran's cheek and frowned lightly. "Don't be daft, Kieran. I've more wealth than any man needs, and 'tis only by birth that most of it's mine. How silly would it be to hoard it, when I have the pleasure of seeing my sister enjoy my good fortune." Rogan's touch grew firmer, and he sighed. "Would that my coins could buy you happiness, Kieran, I would pay any price."

From the bottom of the stairs they heard Emeline. "Please don't make me waddle back up to fetch you, Kieran," she called, a laugh in her voice.

Kieran and Rogan descended the long, curving staircase and joined Emeline. Together they walked the marble halls to the parlor where the guests were chatting and drinking amidst the sounds of laughter and clinking glasses. As they entered Kieran swept the room with her gaze, seeking one person.

it in a little salute, and sipped before turning away.

Matteo cast his attention to Carina, who stood at his elbow.

~21~

Kieran did not have time to react to Carina's presence in her family's home, because Samuel Ellsworth approached with a glass of champagne. He pressed it into her hands and bowed before her. "'Tis beauty's privilege, and worth the wait. You are even more stunning than usual."

an enormous amount of effort to put it together so quickly, we are eager to do so before our child is born and Emeline's attentions are needed at home." He lay a gentle hand on Emeline's shoulders, and she smiled up at him. "'Tis important to us, as well, that we host the ball before Signore de Gama departs for Venice, as without his hard work, I would still be in possession of a rather moldy pile of stones on my western border."

Patrick and Camille went to Matteo's side, and she watched as her father shook his hand and spoke with him. Camille looked from Matteo to Kieran and smiled knowingly, and for a moment, Kieran felt more Camille's friend than daughter, and discovered that it felt quite good.

Samuel took Kieran's hand and placed it on his arm, covering it with his own. He leaned down to speak into her ear. "Have you come to a decision?"

"Not yet," she answered coolly.

Samuel regarded her with a gimlet eye. "I am not a man to wait too long on a woman's fancy."

"I am not a woman to care for a man's impatience. 'Tis marriage we speak of, Your Grace, and as such is a life-long commitment, I feel it bears my careful consideration. If you do not feel the same, perhaps you should withdraw your offer and seek my brother's fortune unfettered."

He spoke quietly, his voice for her ears only. "'Twas an offer made to right a wrong. If making you a duchess and giving you rule over all my holdings does not prove my regret of my actions that night, I cannot think what could. I have apologized and am seeking to do the honorable thing."

"So you say."

"What bars your decision?"

"I'm certain you shall think it a small matter, but I wonder, what of the girl?"

"Who? What girl?"

"The girl you raped."

Samuel smiled tightly for the benefit of anyone who might be watching, and with Kieran's hand still on his arm, he led her across the room and out to the terrace. The air breathed soft and sweet in the treetops and the last vestiges of twilight faded to night.

The moon did not shine down on lovers, but rather cast Samuel's angry face in silver and shadow.

"Let's be clear, name me swine for what I did, and I'll accept your opinion, but do not call me a rapist. I did not rape her. She was a whore."

"She was a virgin."

"Every whore must begin that way."

Kieran pushed, wanting to see if she could get Samuel to reveal some truth that would help her make a decision. Torn between revenge and marriage and spinsterhood she said, "How much did you pay for her virtue?"

"You cannot call a prostitute's virginity her virtue. If she sells her body, she has none."

"What then, Your Grace, did you pay for the privilege of penetrating her hymen?"

His face contorted in disgust. "Such foul speech does not reflect well upon you."

"I am common-born, Your Grace. Do you expect better?"

"You were gently reared, and have been raised to comport yourself with the bearing of a lady."

"Lady or no, being in possession of a hymen of my own, I am curious to ascertain what monetary sum men are willing to pay for it."

Samuel paused, and it became obvious that he realized that Kieran had not been violated that night.

"If 'tis yours we speak of, I do believe the price is entrance to the aristocracy," he sneered. "And as these vulgar words tumble from you mouth, I begin to think the value is set too high."

"Truly, Your Grace? I am a virgin who comes bearing

a fortune in dowry, and the price is too high? Why, you shelled out a few coins to take the other hymen, and now 'tis as if you are being paid to take mine. I should think this turnaround would please you."

"I do not like sharp-tongued women," Ellsworth said in a warning tone.

Kieran knew she played a dangerous game, but she provoked him anyway. "No. As I recall, you prefer them silent and weeping."

Samuel reacted as if he'd been slapped, jerked his head back and let out a barely audible gasp. He straightened to his full height and lifted his head in such a way that he looked down his nose at her. "Why do you consider my offer of marriage if you find me so reprehensible?"

"Wealth and title."

"You want that enough to play the victim?"

"Yes, Your Grace. I want it, and you owe it to me. You stole my innocence; you raped my mind. The wealth you offer doesn't dim my recollection of your actions, but it softens it."

His eyes were lost to her in the shadows; she could not read them. Nervousness gripped her and her belly flipped. She risked everything she'd worked for and planned in the past few months.

To her relief, Samuel laughed. "You're an interesting creature. Most women hide their greed behind pretenses of love and affection."

"I have nothing to hide from you, Your Grace. You've seen me at my worst and showed me my darkest nature."

He fell silent at that comment. When he finally spoke, he looked off into the darkness of the gardens. "I said once that there was something more between us because of what happened. I feel I am beset by you until I make the matter right, and 'tis what I am attempting to do."

"And that is all? You have no other motive?" Kieran asked.

He peered at her in the dim light. "I want to bed you, if that is what you mean. I wanted you the first night I saw you. If that lessens me in your estimation, I am sorry. But you are quite desirable."

"Very well, then. If that is all, I am satisfied." She relaxed her stance and lay her gloved fingers on his arm. "Shall we return to the parlor?"

Samuel exhaled loudly through his nostrils and shook his head as if at a precious child. "Your moods are unpredictable, and you are far more spirited than I prefer a woman be, but I suppose 'tis also beauty's privilege."

"You will find that you are more correct than you know," Kieran said after a moment. His answer had been like the lighting of a candle in a dark room, and suddenly she had her answer.

"Is that an oblique way of accepting my proposal?"

"Yes. I accept. I sought the deeper truth, and I believe I have it now. I ask one thing, however."

"Of course. Anything."

"Do not tell anyone yet. Might we announce it at the ball? I have a liking to see the faces of the women who have spurned me here in England, who have seen me as lesser than they because I am the daughter of a commoner. I want to witness their dismay when they see I will be far wealthier and more titled than they."

Samuel laughed. "Oh, you are a delight. Such venom and wickedness beneath the face of an angel. Oh, Kieran, we will take London by storm, you and I."

They entered the parlor just as a servant announced that dinner would be served. Kieran saw her mother eyeing her, and she smiled brightly to convey her contentment.

"Kieran, come sit by me," Camille said. "It has been far too long since I dined with my daughter."

True to her mother's nature, Camille managed to take a seat that forced Kieran to sit beside Matteo. He quickly took the back of her chair and assisted her as she sat, and she felt the warmth of him as he leaned forward to push in her chair, heard him inhale the scent of her hair.

Kieran closed her eyes for a moment as a sensual river of longing flowed through her. Matteo brushed the back of her arms as he released his hold on the back of the chair, his fingers touching the bare stretch of skin between gown and glove. A frisson of feeling sizzled in her blood.

He took his seat beside her and Kieran gathered her self-control around her like a cloak, for all she wanted to do was bury her face against his neck and breathe in the scents of leather and bergamot.

The chatter around the table was boisterous, many voices mingling with the clatter of servants bearing porcelain platters laden with food and the clinking of many glasses as the wine was poured.

But Kieran was an island in the room, surrounded by a sea of people who did not know the storm of indecision and uncertainty inside her. Less than twenty-four hours before, she'd lain in Matteo's arms and asked him to make love to her. And he'd told her he could not, because he loved her.

Confusing feelings burned in her chest, and she stole a glimpse of him from the corner of her eye. He was smiling as he listened to Carina prattle on, and he laughed easily as she finished her story. The burning turned to acid and felt like a sickness.

Kieran leaned over and her shoulder touched his, drawing his attention.

"Signore, how is it that we are entertaining your former lover as a dinner companion?" she murmured for his ears alone.

He leaned closer to her, and she could smell his clean, spiced, and warm skin. She knew its taste, and wanted more.

"She was present when your brother extended the invitation to me." He moved even closer, and spoke near her ear. "What were you discussing on the terrace?"

"My betrothal."

"Greed or revenge?"

She turned her head to meet his eyes, and nearly melted at the beauty of them, liquid chocolate and amber whiskey. "Can I not have them both?"

Matteo's eyes narrowed and his nostrils flared slightly. His voice was so low she strained to hear him, and then regretted doing so as he said, "The matrimonial equivalent of cutting yourself?"

Kieran feigned a coolness she did not feel. "It has its own rewards, and like the blade, Ellsworth does not deny me."

From across the table, Samuel cleared his throat to draw Kieran's attention. He must have done it several times, because the last one came accompanied with a rattle of silver on porcelain.

Kieran looked to him and saw his growing anger with her quiet conversation with Matteo, as evidenced by the clenching muscle in his jaw and the warning look in his gray eyes.

Pointedly turning her face back to Matteo, she said in a hushed murmur, "Methinks my betrothed grows restless."

"I should have left you in the canal. Your soul would have died, but it would not have been sold."

"Regrets do leave a sour taste."

He grinned rakishly, but his eyes looked sad as they studied her face. "What I really should have done, *cuore solitario*, was go to France. The women there are far less complicated, I hear."

"The one at your side does not seem too complex."

"You are correct, and I know of no better way to forget one woman than to dally with another."

Sick, jealous rage was a fist in her gut. Kieran drew back, ready to scratch his lean cheeks.

"Kieran," Camille said softly. "Regain yourself."

Kieran quickly looked into her lap and twisted her hands around her linen napkin, wringing it the way she wanted to throttle Matteo. She took a few deep breaths and tried to quell the killing urges that pounded like a hurricane against the shore.

A plate was set down before her, an artful arrangement of meat, pastry, and sauce. Kieran wanted to grab it in her fists and smear it in the hair of the Venetian harlot. No, she wanted to draw her dagger, cut that silky black hair from her head in clumps, and rub the food over her shorn scalp.

"Kieran?" Emeline said. "Can you please give me some assistance? I require a woman's help."

Emeline pushed her rounded bulk out of her seat, and when Rogan inquired if all was well, she smiled down at her husband. "I won't be but a minute."

With gritted teeth, Kieran followed Emeline to a room set aside for Emeline's needs, so she did not have to climb the stairs to relieve her bladder.

The small room had once been used as a large cloakroom for guests, but had been cleared of everything save a chair for reclining, a chamber pot behind a screen, and a washstand. Kieran lit a few candles and closed the door behind them.

Emeline stood before her, resplendent in her pale blue silk gown. She pressed her hand on her side, where her waist had once been, and frowned. "What is the matter with you? You look murderous."

"My head aches."

"Liar."

"Truly it does. And my stomach hurts."

Emeline dropped her angry stance and moved closer to Kieran. She studied her face with careful perusal and then smiled. "Flushed cheeks, bright eyes, and a sick belly. I would say fever, but I see 'tis much more serious. You are in love with him."

Kieran felt her cheeks growing warm. "Ellsworth is a worthy suitor, but I do not fancy him overmuch. To call it love is to go quite beyond the pale."

"Don't be deliberately obtuse. 'Tis Signore de Gama who has finally thawed the ice princess." Emeline began pulling up her skirts as she headed behind the screen. "Come hold my hem, Kieran, if you don't mind. 'Tis all I can do to not topple over."

Kieran did as she was asked and as Emeline relived herself, Kieran said, "I should think that you, of all people, would know that I would never cast my affections on a man whose reputation and lineage does not recommend him. My pride would forbid it."

"Love knows nothing of pride."

"He is leaving England and will never return. My life is here."

"Love knows nothing of country."

"He is a bastard."

"Love knows nothing of rank."

"Stop it, Emeline. I do not love him."

Emeline patted herself dry with a scrap of linen and rose to rinse her hands. As she dried them with a flannel, she shrugged and smiled. "'Tis your family's lot."

"What?"

"Your great-grandmother had a love affair with an Irishman, a commoner. Your grandfather was technically, and secretly, a bastard, no? And your mother, the daughter of a duke, married an Irishman. Your brother, in line for the dukedom because of the laws of primogeniture, fell in love and married me, a common-born woman. So, is it really so odd that you would find yourself in love with yet another commoner, and this one a Venetian? I admit, it does break the Irish connection, but then again, you've got enough Irish blood in your veins, don't you?"

Kieran stiffened, at once embarrassed of her ancestry and angered by Emeline's casual discussion of their muddy history. "We have always been friends as well as family, but you are testing that bond."

"Oh, Kieran, when will you drop your fantasy? Love is not something you can arrange, nor can it be willed. It just happens and 'tis not something to fear. Signore de Gama is a good man, and could rival your brother and father with the size of his heart and the goodness of it, as well. Try as you wish to find that sort of heart elsewhere, if you insist, but I can promise you that you will not find its ilk in Samuel Ellsworth."

Emeline held her hands to her belly and sighed. "Thanks to you for your help, Kieran, and now I'm off to feed this baby before it gnaws me raw from the inside out." Turning to go, Emeline paused at the door. "And if you can manage to not look like you're going to slaughter our guests, 'twould be most appreciated. One roasted lamb on the table is plenty; we've no need for a sacrificial one as well."

Emeline sailed from the room as if she had not just lain down the gauntlet and challenged everything Kieran knew and believed about herself.

She most certainly did not love Matteo de Gama. It was, she decided, the most ludicrous thing Emeline had ever said. Kieran could only blame it on the pregnancy, for Emeline was usually a very sensible woman.

Did she desire him? Yes, she could heartily admit she did. The man warmed her, provoked her, and inflamed her.

Kieran would even willingly admit that she had grown fond of Matteo. He was by turns kind and thoughtful, generous and charming. In fact, she laid claim to the fact that she found him irresistible. He occupied much of her thoughts and he heated her dreams. She wanted him with a woman's longing.

But love? Certainly not.

Kieran dismissed the idea as absurd.

She knew love, enough that she knew she would recognize it if it touched her heart. Love was what Patrick and Camille shared. Love was the invisible thread that connected Rogan and Emeline.

And he loves you, her heart whispered. All the things she knew love to comprise, Matteo de Gama claimed for her.

It shook her to the core. Kieran dropped to the chair with a whoosh, her knees suddenly weak and trembling.

A knock sounded at the door, and Camille slipped into the room. Their eyes met and locked. Kieran opened her mouth to speak. Her lips trembled but no words came out.

Camille studied her daughter's face before extending her hand. Very, very gently she said, "Come, Kieran, and bear in mind the carelessness of burdening our guests with displays of unpleasantness."

"I can't go back out there," Kieran said on a breath.

"Why not?"

Answers stormed her brain: _Because he loves me and I can't bear to hurt him; Carina simpers at his side and Matteo all but admitted he had become her lover again; because I said yes to Samuel and am secretly betrothed, the knowledge of which is making me ill._

Kieran took a deep breath and reached for the only answer that did not reveal her true feelings. "I feel poorly, Mum. Will you make my excuses, please?"

"Of course, love." Camille lay a hand on her daughter's forehead. "You do feel warm."

"Yes, I must lie down."

"I'll come up with you."

"No, please," Kieran said quickly. No more conversation, she mentally pleaded. "I only want to sleep."

"As you wish," Camille said, and helped Kieran to her feet. "I'll check on you, though, and will be sure to not wake you."

"Thank you, Mum."

Kieran swept through the corridors, escaped to her rooms, and rang for her maid. She could not seem to breathe, and even after her maid had come and assisted her into her nightclothes she still felt as if she gasped for air.

The madness suffocated her.

Kieran opened her balcony doors and then lay on her bed, willing herself to calm and quiet. She tried to focus on the cool silk of her coverlet and the patterns of shadow that shifted on her ceiling.

The effort proved futile. The relentless ticking of her timepiece seemed to mock her, each snick a countdown to the ball, bringing her closer to the moment when she would have to once again face Matteo de Gama.

This time she wouldn't have the luxury of hiding in her rooms, for in order to deal with Samuel Ellsworth properly, she would need the leverage of his peers gathered in one room.

Kieran did not know how she would make it through the next few weeks, but she knew for certain that neither prospect made for easy breathing.

Early the following morning, Kieran rode with Nilo along a trail deep in the woods behind the manse. Dew sparkled on leafy ferns and trembled from the tips of newly sprouted leaves and in the lacey threads of spider webs. A crisp breeze rustled through the tall treetops and swallows darted like arrows through the copse, skimming the ground and buzzing the treetops.

"You have seen much of Alva of late," Kieran noted.

"I have," Nilo said, and a chuckle rumbled softly in his chest. "She is good company."

"Is this becoming more than a friendship?"

"Maybe." Nilo glanced over to Kieran. "I have been wondering what you would think about that."

"Marriage between the races is not common, but 'tis done, and there is no law against it. But be mindful, Nilo, that prejudice does not mind the law. You and Alva would be shunned by most."

"She is a former prostitute, and I a former slave. People do not respect us, anyway," Nilo answered simply.

Kieran did not argue those facts. "If the union produced children, they would bear your stigma. I only say this to be certain you understand the gravity of such a decision."

"I have already seen my wife and children killed for their color. Think of that, Miss Keerahn, and then ask me if I don't understand what you call a stigma."

Silence fell between them as their horses walked the path, and Kieran felt torn between sympathy and shame. "Yes, Nilo, I am aware of what you say. Remember, I was raised in Barbados where slaves are traded and blacks are born free. I understand well the absurdity of this, and I abhor it. You are a Negro, and you are also my dearest friend. Please, do not mistake my intention. I have always wanted your happiness and nothing more."

"I love her." Nilo spoke so quietly she scarcely heard him. "After my family was killed, I thought: Nilo will never love again. But it happened. My heart healed. And I love again."

Kieran nodded her understanding. "I will do whatever I can to make it possible for you to be together. Rogan will as well, I know it."

"You first," Nilo said.

She glanced over at him sharply, recalling the admonition he'd given her many long months ago at sea. He grinned at her with a wide smile.

"That day may come sooner than you think," Kieran

confessed. Certain that no ears lurked in the cool, verdant light, Kieran spoke to Nilo of her plan.

When she finished, she waited with bated breath.

Nilo reined his mount to a stop and sat in the saddle, wordlessly staring at his mistress with an expression that spoke volumes of his surprise. Kieran waited, and faced him with a mixture of fear and doubt and worry in her gut.

"You could do that?" he asked.

"I *will* do it," Kieran vowed solemnly. "Will you help me?"

～22～

Summer arrived in an assault of vivid green and vibrant flowers. The gentle breezes rustled through the trees, the sibilant sound reminiscent of swirling, silk skirts. The days grew longer, but not calmer, for the manse buzzed with activity.

The invitations were engraved and delivered, the baby's nursery needed final touches, Emeline required a new ball gown sewn to fit her ever-increasing belly. Camille had one made as well, as she hadn't brought a suitable gown from Barbados. Patrick and Rogan spent most of their days at the property where Matteo oversaw the final stages of the renovation. Candles had been ordered by the hundreds, and cases of wine and spirits were delivered. Linens were pressed, flower arrangements ordered, and tables and chairs were carted from Rogan and Emeline's ballroom over to Matteo's.

The day before the ball, the food preparations had escalated to full swing, and the tables would be laden with every manner of meats and cheeses, fruits and breads, salted fish, and pastry. Kieran had surveyed the list some days prior, and swore that the tables would require reinforcement to bear up under the weight of desserts: cakes and pies and tarts and biscuits.

Now, cast in the gloaming as the cloak of night descended, Kieran stood on her balcony, clad in her finest gown. She sipped lightly on a splash of brandy; she would need all her wits about her for the night ahead, but she looked for the calming balm of its burn in her belly. Swirling the amber liquid, Kieran looked into it and saw dark eyes and a slow sensual smile.

Damn him, he even robbed her of the peace of her stolen drink.

Her maid rushed back into her rooms with Kieran's wrap, a waterfall of icy blue silk, draped over her arm. "The stitching is mended, my lady, and is perfect."

Kieran abandoned her drink and entered her rooms to inspect the handiwork. Indeed, the stitches were excellent and the rent in the seam was closed such that it could not be discerned there had been a hole. Kieran took the wrap. "Thank you, Jane. 'Twas a task a bit beyond my skills for mending when the fabric is so fine. What a boon that the seamstress was still here finishing Emeline's hem. Is she ready?"

"Her Grace waits below stairs, and is radiant. The carriages have been brought around, and all is complete. You only need to go and enjoy yourself."

Kieran stood before the large oval looking glass and checked her appearance one last time. Her hair, brushed, oiled, and curled, had been artfully twisted into sleek coils that were wound with thin, sparkling crystal beads and secured with jeweled pins. High and heavy atop her head, it exposed her long neck, showcasing the diamond necklace that had once been her grandmother Amelia's. It circled her neck in a blaze of ice, and seemed to highlight the vast expanse of bare skin between her collarbones and neckline. The curves of her breasts were daringly exposed again in the French fashion, and the crystal encrusted bodice gleamed tightly to her narrow waist and dipped into a V below her belly and at the small of her back. The gown flared out in a swirl of pale blue silk, studded with thousands of tiny crystals that caught the light with flash and fire.

She looked like a fairy, glittering silver and gleaming ice, unearthly pale and ethereally lovely.

"You can do this," Kieran whispered to her reflection.

"Is there something more you require?" her maid asked, confused.

"No. I am ready." Kieran held her reticule, her wrap, and her nerve in a tight grip, and with one final deep breath, left for the ball.

Carriages lined the long, circular driveway in front of the newly renovated manse, and strains of music drifted on the warm, summer breeze. The air seemed to hum with excitement, full of mingled voices and ladies' laughter. The windows spilled light, and lanterns hung from the trees along the paths that led through the gardens and around the manse.

Kieran alighted from the carriage and waited as Rogan handed down Emeline and Patrick assisted Camille. Patrick caught Kieran's eye and grinned. "Are you nervous, lass?"

"Yes, Da," Kieran responded truthfully, and added an explanation that she hoped was plausible. "'Tis been some time since I've attended such a large event."

"Well, 'twas the England you longed for, aye?" Patrick said, sweeping his hand to encompass the aristocrats who entered the manse dressed in their finery.

"Yes, it was," she replied thoughtfully, and silently added: A long time ago.

They ascended the stairs and liveried attendants opened the wide doors for them. Kieran prickled with awareness, noticing the tiniest details. The scents of beeswax candles mingled with the faint smell of fresh paint. What was old had been made new again, from the plastered walls to the coffered ceilings, polished marble, and varnished floors. And her respect for Matteo increased as she saw the admiration of those arrived.

Kieran stood beside her parents in the entranceway, as Emeline took a seat off to Rogan's side. They greeted guests for nearly two hours, and when the waves of gaily dressed people finally seemed to be abating, they were able to make their way to the ballroom.

Flower arrangements marked the way through the long corridors, leading them along to the main event. As they drew closer, the din of music and voices became overwhelming, as did the odors of perfumes and sweat-dampened silks, tables laden with fragrant foods and the sweet reek of wine and gin.

They entered the grand ballroom, and a stab of regret pierced Kieran's heart. Gone was the candlelit nook of warmth and light in the corner of the darkened ballroom, resounding with the sound of one lone cello.

Every chandelier blazed with light, and an entire orchestra poured music into the air. All around the room the French doors were opened wide to the terraces, allowing the summer air to waft in. The alcoves were lit by hanging lamps and bracketed by crimson velvet drapes that could be drawn for those seeking sufficient privacy to hold a conversation or perhaps a liaison of a more amorous sort.

Throngs of London's wealthiest and most powerful people feasted and feted in a colorful, whirling spectacle of unrestrained decadence, their faces flushed with heat, their eyes brightened by the first few glasses of wine.

It reminded Kieran of Carnivale, for though the faces were not masked, not one of them was necessarily who they were perceived to be.

Patrick and Camille greeted old friends and were quickly drawn into the fray, as Rogan and Emeline made their rounds.

Kieran stood alone, searching the room for one face in particular.

There he was, talking in a crowd of young women who flocked around him like brightly colored butterflies. They simpered and giggled as he spoke, curls bouncing and breasts bobbling. One of the bolder girls playfully tapped him with her folded fan as to scold him for saying something naughty.

"Champagne, my lady," a servant murmured discreetly at her side.

Kieran accepted a flute and sipped. The sweet bubbles burst on her tongue as she eyed Matteo. The clothes must be new for the occasion, she noted. Gone were the narrow leather garments. He was dressed in creamy ivory silk breeches and matching jacket, with stockings and shoes of the same hue. His shirt was fitted to his body beneath his ivory waistcoat, a saturated red that accentuated his dark skin and eyes. He'd pulled his sun-streaked hair back into a loose club, tied with a simple piece of ivory ribbon.

The clothes clung to his long, lean body with a Continental panache that Kieran found mesmerizing and distracting. On a plainer man the garments might have looked austere, and if worn by a paler man, he might have appeared washed out and sickly.

But not Matteo. He looked vibrant and coolly elegant, vastly different from the foppish dandies in their vulgar garb and the stuffy aristocrats sweating beneath their padded, stiff clothing.

Kieran started in surprise as someone touched her

elbow. Samuel Ellsworth stood at her side, and he smiled down at her affably. "You look beautiful."

"Thank you."

"I spoke to the orchestral director, and he will call for us to come to the center of the room at 10 o'clock to make our announcement."

"Perfect." She tilted her head back and smiled politely. "I am excited, Your Grace."

"You certainly dressed for the occasion. I will be the envy of every man here."

His words jangled Kieran's nerves further. She made a noise she hoped passed for humble thanks and turned her head to take a deep, trembling breath. She gulped her champagne faster than good sense dictated, and reminded herself to take it easy on the wine. She would need all her faculties.

Matteo emerged from the crowd. His mouth curled in a sardonic grin as he bowed before them. Straightening, he took Kieran's gloved hand and pressed a kiss to the back of it, lingering long enough that she could feel his warm, humid breath on her skin before he pulled away to address Samuel.

"Your Grace, you have the attention of the most beautiful woman in the room. How do you manage it?"

"With better luck than at your gaming tables, de Gama. Did you purchase those garments with the winnings you took from me?"

"Hardly, Your Grace. With those winnings I could buy half of London."

Samuel laughed with Matteo good-naturedly and rocked back on his heels as he swept the room with his gaze. "Good show, de Gama."

Matteo eyed Kieran with a heated look that consumed her bite by bite in greedy gulps. She steeled herself against the desire that swept through her body.

"Signore," she said softly.

His lips curved into a slow, sensual smile. "My lady."

Samuel grew annoyed and took Kieran firmly by the elbow. "Come. We will dance."

He pulled her out into the swirling mass of people and took her in his arm, sweeping her into his arms as the orchestra played a brisk piece by Handel.

"I do not like the way he looks at you, nor you him," Samuel began in a stern tone. "When you are my wife, I will expect you to be dignified, modest, gracious, and appreciative of your place in my family tree. This is England, not some barbaric island, and 'tis most certainly not Venice. There will be no flirtations and intrigues. I will not foster a lover's brat. Are you clear?"

"I understand our relationship perfectly."

"Excellent." He peered down his nose at her and sniffed.

Kieran smiled up at him, directly into his gray eyes. He softened marginally, but said, "I will not be manipulated by your beauty, either."

"I would not expect that of you, Your Grace."

Kieran continued dancing, her left arm around Samuel's thick body, her right hand high in his hand, and gracefully twirled and swirled though the ballroom. Her gown winked and blazed with light, and she knew that a marriage announcement to Samuel would spell envy in the heart of every young, single maiden in attendance.

Kieran was only human; temptation lured her as it would any woman.

The dance concluded and they moved into another, their togetherness and her introductions an effectual sign of their intentions as the formal announcement they would make later.

Before the next song began, Samuel escorted Kieran from the center of the dance floor. "'Tis time we mingled with the other guests."

Time flew as the room grew warmer, smokier, and more redolent of sweaty bodies and perfumed clothing. Demure giggles became shrieks of laughter as the wine flowed and the banter became bawdy. Kieran lost track of the time, and asked Samuel.

"'Tis nearly nine o'clock."

Kieran looked over Samuel's shoulder and saw Matteo watching her. He leaned against the wall, drinking wine. Carina approached him, and Kieran noticed that she leaned her breasts against his arm as she stood on tiptoe to whisper in his ear. Her black curls fell onto his shoulder in stark contrast to his ivory jacket, and when he turned to answer her, she embraced him as she held her ear to his mouth so she could hear his reply.

With sick jealousy that knew no relief, she watched as Carina left the room, and a few moments later, when Matteo left as well.

"I have needs," she murmured to Samuel, and withdrew from the crowd.

Resisting the urge to follow them, she swept out of the ballroom. Leaning against the wall, she pressed her heated cheek to its cool surface.

Somewhat calmer, she walked through the corridor to the library. The doors were opened, and Kieran paused at the sight before her. There in the darkened room, Nilo danced with Alva to the faded sounds of orchestral music.

Feeling like an intruder, she said nothing but watched as they stopped dancing. Alva had her head tilted all the way back so she could stare into Nilo's eyes. Very gently, Nilo cupped Alva's face in his large hands and kissed her forehead, the tip of her nose, and then her mouth.

Kieran turned and quietly left them to their moment. She found an open door to a small terrace and slipped out. The moon beamed in full force, casting silvery light that mingled with the golden lanterns. Leaning against a high wall, she reached for the strength she knew existed inside of her by virtue of the blood of her ancestors.

"You glitter brighter than any star," Matteo said from behind her.

Kieran whirled around. For a moment she could not find his form because he'd dragged a chair out to the terrace and was seated in the shadows. Standing, he moved a bit closer. He loomed like a fallen angel, his ivory clothing reflecting the light, his face still cast in darkness.

"Why do you torment me?" he whispered.

A thrill of fear and a lick of lust went through her, and she could not discern one from the other. His voice was deeper, rougher, and definitely angry. Yet, she longed to touch him, hold him, and taste him. What spell had he cast?

"Where is Carina?" she asked quietly.

"She waits for me in bed."

"Oh." It slipped from her before she could stop it. Toughening her tone, she said, "Will you go to her?"

"Will you marry Ellsworth?"

Kieran took a step forward, drawn to him, yearning for his touch. "Will you leave England?"

Matteo moved closer to her, and she caught a whiff of his scent, bergamot and wine and something more elemental she could not name.

"If I stayed, would it change your mind?" he asked.

Kieran envisioned Matteo staying in England, and a curious heat wound through her chest.

"Where you choose to reside is your decision, signore."

"As is who you choose to wed. Neither observation answers the questions."

"When do you go?"

"A passenger ship leaves for Venice next week, and I have a cabin reserved."

"I do not wish for you to leave," she admitted on a breath.

"It kills me to think of you with him. Please tell me it is part of a scheme."

Kieran opened her mouth to answer, but stopped as she saw Samuel Ellsworth in the doorway. "I suppose we were not clear," he sneered.

Samuel turned his attention to Matteo. "Isn't that bit of fluff imported from Venice enough for you?"

"Is one woman enough for you, Your Grace?" Matteo asked smoothly.

Ellsworth puffed up. "I'll not dignify that with an answer."

Kieran, seeing her opportunity, seized it. "Your Grace, there is a matter that presses."

Samuel swung around to her. In the moonlight his gray eyes shone like hammered silver. "Yes, there is."

Prickles of trepidation ran across Kieran's spine. She swallowed and in a voice full of an authority she did not feel, she stated firmly, "Come with me, Your Grace, if you care to know what your future holds."

"Future? Do you play the soothsayer now?" Samuel scoffed, his annoyance seeming to grow by leaps.

"'Tis not a prediction I will make, but a foretelling. This night will mark the one chance you have to seize control of your fate."

Kieran directed her attention back to Matteo. He was light and shadow, and if not for him she would still be locked in an icy prison. "Signore, you should come as well, if your lover can wait. 'Tis a matter concerning you, too."

"This is preposterous. What you and I need to discuss is no one else's business."

"This is your one opportunity, Your Grace. My advice for you is to dispense with your pride. You will not be needing it this evening."

Kieran brushed past him, counting on curiosity to bring the men to the library.

The candles had been lit, and as she entered her nerves

churned like nausea. The room had been beautifully restored just like the rest of the manse. It boasted floor to ceiling bookcases, huge trestle tables for reading and ledgers. Along the back wall, flanking the cavernous fireplace, two alcoves held cushy chairs and had been draped with gold, velvet curtains, so one could curl up and read the day away, if she chose. And for Kieran's purposes, she'd chosen the room because it did not have an exit to the outside. Samuel would be a captive audience, just as she planned.

Samuel and Matteo came in behind her as she politely stood in the doorway, and when they passed Kieran closed and locked the doors. Gesturing to a chair in the corner she said to Matteo, "Please."

With an expression of bemused interest, Matteo took the proffered seat.

A tremulous smile curved her lips and she said to Matteo, "If you don't mind, signore, I would value your silence. 'Tis time for reckoning, and 'tis only fitting you witness what you set into motion the night you pulled me from the canal."

"'Twas you?" Samuel blurted. "At Carnivale, 'twas you on the waters?"

Matteo did not reply, holding his silence as Kieran had asked him to do. But with a mocking smile, he bowed his head to Samuel.

"Bastard," Samuel whispered. "You came to my gaming tables knowing full well who I was to her, didn't you?"

"He did," Kieran stated, her voice ringing out. "He knows everything of that night."

And as she faced Samuel, she saw he simmered with anger.

"You are a vain bitch," he bit out.

"Bitch I may be, but 'tis vengeful as well as vain. I spent three years tormented by a night that you scarcely recall. But I recall it, every moment of it. I remember your laughter as you stripped me in front of your friends. I remember the cruel jests you made about my virginity, and the way you spoke about my body, as if it contained no soul. I wept and you laughed. I fought and you degraded my efforts. I begged for mercy, and you took delight when I was forced to deny it to another."

Kieran found that her nervousness lessened as she warmed to the task, and the words she'd needed to say flowed freely.

"You stole my innocence, and vain bitch that I am, I valued it. No man had ever seen my skin, until you made me stand naked before a group of leering, laughing men. I never knew what a man's body looked like, until I saw yours. My first knowledge of intercourse is still you, thrusting your way into an unwilling woman, and as the virgin I am today, I have that image burned in my brain. How dare you think that marriage to me is some sort of balm that eases that pain? How dare you have the audacity to scold me on my behavior and consul me about decorum? You, *Your Grace*, are about as decorous as a shithouse."

"I do not need to stand here and listen to your vulgar diatribe," Samuel said haughtily. He made to leave, tossing a final comment over his shoulder. "The offer of marriage is retracted. I leave you to your bitterness."

"You're not leaving until I grant you the privilege." Kieran lifted the key to the doors and displayed it in her palm. "We're not finished."

"You overstep your bounds."

"No. I'm taking them back."

"You will open this door, madam, or we will have trouble."

"Yes, I thought it might come to that."

Nilo and Alva emerged from a dark alcove and stepped into the light. Nilo had his African luguru ax slung causally over his right shoulder, his huge hand riding lightly on the handle.

"Consider this a court," Kieran's voice rang out. "I am the judge and Alva will be your jury. My man, Nilo, will be our guard, to make certain the accused comports himself, and Signore de Gama will bear witness."

"I am not taking part in this ruse."

"Part? No. You are center stage, Your Grace. Take your seat. We will begin."

"No."

Nilo stepped closer, his hand tightening on his ax. He looked to Kieran, waiting on her word.

"Sit."

Ellsworth visibly swallowed, but did not back down. "I will not be cowed by your slave. He'll hang before dawn if he does not retreat."

"You'd need out of this room to make that happen. It could be that you're dead in a ditch before midnight, with my *free* man sailing away on one of my brother's ships before you're even noted as missing." Kieran gestured to the chair at the head of the table. "Sit."

Ellsworth sat. But he held his hand up and seemed to strive for reason. "I told you before, I was very drunk."

Kieran met his eyes and distinctly said, "Being drunk is not an excuse for cruelty. Are we clear? Each time you blame your actions on your drunken state, I grow angrier. Am I any less damaged from that night because you'd imbibed too much gin? Did your insults hurt less? Was I less humiliated? Less degraded?"

"No, of course not," Ellsworth said. "I am not excusing what I did, but pointing out the reason for which the unfortunate events occurred."

"Are you sorry?"

Ellsworth's eyes narrowed; he clearly did not like her tone. But to his credit, he answered her. "I am. I am sorry."

"Tell me, Your Grace, how sorry are you?"

"Sorry enough to offer marriage."

"But as I come with dowry and a family of great influence, how am I to believe that is your true motivation?"

Ellsworth's eyes flicked to Nilo and the wicked, double-bladed ax. He seemed to resign himself to settling the matter. "I told you before, your dowry is meaningless to me; I do not need the coin. As for your brother, he admitted that he would not be less or more inclined to do business with me."

"Let's get down to the crux of the matter. We don't have all night." She rapped on the table with her fist. "The court is in session. Justice will be served."

Kieran's skirts swirled and flashed with prismatic light as she walked toward Alva. She took the girl by the hand and led her to stand in front of Ellsworth.

"How much did you pay for her virginity?" Kieran asked, her voice firm and clear.

"I don't recall. I was drunk."

Kieran asked Alva. "How much for your services that night?"

"A pound," Alva stammered. Her cheeks flushed with color, and Nilo moved a step closer.

"One pound," Kieran said to Ellsworth, "and you have forgotten her value. Used and discarded and dismissed. Look at her," Kieran commanded.

Ellsworth turned his head, but he did not meet Alva's gaze.

Kieran's voice grew harder. "Look in her eyes. You were the first man she ever knew, and you took her while she wept. Tell her you're sorry you held a gun to her head and made her fear for her life. Look at her, and tell her you are sorry that you took her in front of other drunk, laughing men. Tell her you're sorry that you couldn't just give her that meaningless, forgotten pound without raping her in exchange for it."

A long silence fell over them all; only the faint music

from the orchestra could be heard, along with the muted conversations and the tinkling of laughter from those who enjoyed the festivities.

Samuel slowly raised his eyes and looked into Alva's. She shook with the effort of holding her composure, her face deathly white but for the vivid red splotch of her birthmark. Her blue eyes filled with unshed tears as she pressed her lips in a thin, tight line above her pointy, trembling chin. With her hands twisted in the skirt of her simple, cotton gown, she seemed as young and vulnerable as she truly was, a girl of only nineteen.

"I am sorry," Samuel told her. For once, he seemed to understand the words, and mean them.

Alva bobbed her head in a nod. One of the tears she held back escaped, tracing a shiny track down her cheek.

"Well, then. Thank you for the humbling." Samuel rose from his chair and bowed to Alva and then Kieran. "Good evening."

"This is a court of justice," Kieran said distinctly. "We do not leave here until 'tis served."

Samuel heaved a sigh and flopped back into his seat. "I am growing tired of this charade."

Kieran spoke over him. "I asked my brother about my dowry. You can imagine my shock to find that my worth is set at 100,000 pounds. 'Tis a staggering sum. And it has occurred to me that there is a great, vast divide between the value placed on me, as compared to the single pound you paid for Alva's virtue."

Kieran squared her shoulders and raised her chin. "Justice, Your Grace, demands equality and fairness. 'Tis only fair that Alva's virginity be given the same value as mine."

The dawning of her meaning showed on Ellsworth's face. "You've lost your mind."

"No. I've reclaimed my heart," Kieran said in a voice that was menacing for all its quiet softness. "Fool that you are, you do not recognize such things when they are right in front of you. Do you not see? I spent years chained to the shame and the guilt for my part in another woman's rape. I went cold inside, deadened by disgust with myself. Alva became a prostitute, and spent every day in a hell that began with you. Yes, she suffered the most, and no one cared for her plight. But you did not suffer, Your Grace. You carried on as normal, and paid no price save one pound for a virgin's blood and an aching head when morning came."

Kieran gestured to Alva, Nilo, and herself. "But we paid, Your Grace. We paid with our souls, and now 'tis your turn to balance the scales of justice. The cost of my virtue has been named, and 'tis out of joint with Alva's. 'Tis time to settle accounts."

"I am not giving this common whore 100,000 pounds."

"I am more than willing to negotiate the terms of resolving this dispute," Kieran said reasonably. "After all, that weighty sum is not simply for my virginity, but also to allay expenses you would most certainly sustain for the support of my person. Now, mind, all of that must be balanced by my services as your wife, my position as a potential mother to your children, and of course, my wifely due. You did make it clear you wanted me in your bed, no?

"However, let us not undervalue the actual virginity. A man does not, as you so eloquently put it earlier, want to foster a lover's brat. If she comes to his bed intact, he at least knows there have been none before him who may have planted a seed.

"'Tis common practice that when a man kidnaps or rapes a woman, his penalty is to pay her dowry. You held a gun to Alva's head and threatened rape, did you not? Me or her, you said. And you made me choose. If 'twas not rape, why did you call it such? And if 'twas not rape, why was it done for the amusement of other men and my horror?"

Kieran laid her hands on the table and leaned forward. "This court finds Samuel Ellsworth in Alva's debt.

You will pay her 30,000 pounds, minus the one already paid, and we shall consider the matter settled."

Alva gasped and opened her mouth to speak. Nilo took her by the arm before a sound came out, and led her to the alcove. With a softly spoken word, he bade her to wait before he took up his guard once more. He stood by Kieran once again, bearing his ax without expression.

"There is a place for you in Bedlam," Samuel stated flatly, and he again stood. "This matter was settled three years ago. I paid what the girl charged for our encounter."

"She did not consent to having the act done in front of all those other men. You raped her sensibilities as much as her body. You owe her this debt, and you will pay it."

Samuel moved closer to Kieran and leaned down so he could speak softly for her ears alone. "I don't understand what you're after."

"Justice," Kieran replied quietly. She brought her eyes up to meet Samuel's, and to her relief, realized she no longer felt revulsion of him, nor fear, nor anger. She had truly exorcised herself of that night, and as the weight of it melted away, she felt like the phoenix, risen from its own ashes to fly again.

She cast a glance to Matteo, who watched silently. He nodded, once, as if urging her on, and the intense look in his eyes filled her with all she needed.

Kieran continued. "Listen well, Your Grace. I plotted my revenge on you. I planned to accept your offer of marriage and had every intention of walking down the aisle. And there, in front of all your peers and everyone who you held dear, I was going to tell them all in explicit detail what you did and why I would never, ever consent to be your wife."

Samuel grew pale. "'Tis disgusting, and 'twould have brought shame on you and your family as well as mine."

"Do you think Rogan would have cared more for the

disgrace or for your actions? I know my brother well, and he cares nothing for the nattering opinions of the peers at court." Kieran cocked her head to the side, and a slow smile curved her lips. "What do you think, come to that, my father and my brother would do to you if I were to go out and tell them now? Do you think that Rogan would still want to do the shipyard deal, or do you think 'tis more likely that my father would have his Irish, common way with you before dawn touched the sky?"

With his skin turning paler still, Samuel drew back his shoulders and stood his full height. Peering down his nose he regarded her with derision. "So 'tis blackmail, then? I pay the girl or you will tell your father and brother."

"The terms are elegantly simple, aren't they? Pay her what she is worth, and I will keep the secret forever. Go and have your shipyard deal; I care not if you've made good with Alva. But think to not pay her, and I will reveal you and your actions. I swear I will."

Samuel seemed to mentally weigh his options. Kieran knew he realized that business with Rogan would surely yield him much greater wealth than he would spend on Alva. She also knew that it offended his pride to be pushed into a corner.

Kieran held her breath, hoping she appeared careless either way. The truth was, she did not want to reveal herself, but she would if it came to it. The time of lies and secrets and hiding had come to its end; she would see the matter to a resolution, one way or the other, and she would sacrifice her pride if need be. Lord knew, it had not served her well these years past.

"The money is nothing to you," Kieran appealed to him quietly. "To that end, 'tis nothing to me, as well. I don't work for my keep, and I have my virtue and a dowry, should I decide to seek marriage or spinsterhood. But to her, the money spells choices. It means she will not toil over stitches by candlelight until her eyes weaken and even that honest work is denied her. It means she will not ever have to lie beneath a man for money ever again. And most of all, it means that she can wed the man of her choosing, and can enter that union with enough coin to see to the comfort of her family."

Samuel tapped his lips with his forefinger. "How do I know you would truly hold silent if I did as you said? This could all be a plot to take my money before exposing me, anyway."

"The thought occurred to me to do just that, if you want the truth. However, I want the secret kept as much as you do. If you make good with the girl, I swear I will consider justice served and the matter put to rest. I give you my word."

"As an extortionist?" he asked sarcastically.

"As a woman who does not profit either way," Kieran replied on a breath. She closed her eyes and whispered, "You are not the only one who needs to do the right thing."

Samuel blew out a breath as if deflating. "Very well. I'll pay the girl."

The relief that swept through Kieran nearly brought her to her knees. But she showed no sign of it. Pointing with one long, slim finger to the writing desk against the wall, she said, "I've written down our agreement. Fill in the agreed amount, sign it, and press your signet ring into the wax."

"I think 'tis best we don't put things into writing."

"'Tis best we do. We did it your way for three years. 'Tis time for mine. Sign it."

He folded his arms in front of his chest. "No. I'll pay the money, but I'll not sign anything."

"You will sign it, or by God I swear that I will march out into the center of yonder ballroom and our ten o'clock announcement will be quite different from the one you had planned."

Time passed in what seemed like excruciatingly long

intervals, each second drawn out like a torture device that had Kieran inwardly screaming. But she held her ground and met Samuel's gaze, seeing to it that her lips and chin did not betray her fear.

Samuel glanced around the room, from Matteo and Nilo to the shadowed alcove where Alva watched and finally to Kieran. He strode to the writing table and snatched up the paper to read what Kieran had written.

She'd tried to be fair. It stated in clear, simple language what had transpired that night, and that a balance was owed to Alva. He could write the amount, 30,000 pounds, minus one.

Kieran held her breath, not releasing it until he dipped the quill and scratched out his name. He heated the wax and poured a small pool onto the bottom. As it cooled from liquid to solid, he pressed his ring into the soft wax, leaving the indelible mark of the Duke of Westminster.

Standing, he handed it to Kieran. In the flickering candlelight he stared down at her. "They say your grandmother was a self-righteous harridan."

"Bring the money here, tomorrow at three o'clock."

"You're well on your way to taking her place, aren't you?"

"Do not be late. My offer expires at one minute past."

"I would have married you," he sneered. "You could have had the world laid at your feet."

"The nature of my choice ought speak volumes, Your Grace. Both of you, and of me."

Her insult hit its mark, and he stiffened. His cheeks turned ruddy as he exhaled through his nose. "I'll count the coin well-spent, as it rids me of you."

"As you wish." Kieran dipped into a low curtsey. She straightened, moved to the door, and after unlocking it, held it open. "Now get out."

~ 23 ~

Alva crept from the dark alcove and emerged into the light. With her wide eyes and hunched posture, she looked like a criminal awaiting a flogging.

"What'd ye do?" she whispered to Kieran accusingly. "What possessed ye to go an' do such a thing?"

"'Twill be fine, do not worry. Don't you see? You'll have choices that only money can buy." Did the girl have no gratitude? Kieran had just secured her a fortune.

"Aye, an' I'll have the likes o' him huntin' me down to get his money back."

Kieran waved the paper. "This bears his seal and his signature. It says the money is yours."

Alva grabbed at her own hair, twisted it into her fists. She whirled around to Nilo. "Do ye hear this? Do ye ken? What am I going to do? Paper canna protect me from the likes of that man. Where will I go? What will happen to me?"

Nilo reached out and took her hands, gently dislodging them. "It will work out. Miss Keerahn is doing right by you."

"Nooo. I dinna want this. I dinna need this. I've a sewin' job an' a place to lay my head. That's all I want and all I need and I'm grateful for it."

"I did not mean to upset you, Alva. I wanted to help. To right a wrong done to you," Kieran insisted, her tone growing desperate. "After everything that happened, 'twas the only thing that seemed right."

Tears began to burn behind Kieran's eyes; her throat

grew tight. All the emotions of the day conspired to break through her tightly held composure. "Alva, money brings choices, and I wanted you to have them. I wanted to do the right thing."

Kieran's chest hitched and she nearly lost what remained of her resolve. Her lust for revenge had turned to a thirst for justice, and she thought she'd achieved it for the girl who deserved it most. She'd thought she would find a sense of relief and redemption, but in the face of Alva's upset, she felt lost and adrift once more. Could she do nothing right?

From the corner of the room where he'd sat as an observer, Matteo moved into the light. He approached Kieran. She looked up into his dark eyes and enough of her pride slipped that she dared to ask, "Did I do it wrong, signore?"

Matteo lay a finger on her lips to quiet her. Leaning down so he could speak into her ear, he whispered, "You were wonderful."

Matteo left Kieran's side and approached Alva. He laid a comforting hand on her shoulder. She turned her wide, blue eyes up to him with reverence for the man who'd taken a chance on her when she'd been nothing more than an unwashed prostitute.

"Sire," she whispered. "Will you have no need of me anymore?"

"There is little more here for you to do, and I leave in a week's time. What will become of you when I return to Venice?"

She twisted her hands in her skirt the way she'd had them in her hair, knotting the fabric tightly. "I dinna ken, but that money? It's not mine. I didna earn it."

Matteo lowered his voice, the soft tenor soothing. "It is frightening, no? You know how to be poor, you know how to be hungry, and you even know the price for which to sell your body. But you do not know how to have more than you need, do you, Alva?"

The slim, Scottish girl shook her head furiously, causing a few of the tears she held back to fall.

"I understand," Matteo continued. "You see, I was quite poor once, running the streets and stealing every coin I could just to keep going, each day like the next, hungry, desperate, and afraid. It was comfortable, though, in its own way, because I knew how to be hungry, desperate, and afraid."

Matteo put his arm around Alva's narrow shoulders and turned her so she faced Kieran. "This is not over. You will need to trust that you will be cared for. I am certain that Miss Kieran will help you set up your accounts and will even aid you in managing the funds until you are comfortable. I am also certain that she will assist you in making these new choices, and will rise to your defense if Samuel Ellsworth makes any effort to take back the money due you."

"I will do those things, Alva," Kieran promised, not caring that her earnestness could be easily heard. She wanted desperately to put her demons from that night to rest, and knew that could not happen until the accounts with Alva were balanced and settled. "I will do whatever I must."

Alva took a deep, tremulous breath. Her eyes, full of trust in Matteo, turned questioningly to Kieran. "If I take this, will ye sleep easy?"

"I believe I will."

The two women regarded each other in a moment filled with memories of violence and humiliation. A frown troubled Alva's brow and she let out a little sigh.

"Fine, then," Alva said. "But this marks the end of it. I want to bury the past, an' if I'm to do so, I need ye to do the same. I dinna want ye lookin at me an' seein' that night. The prostitute is dead and gone. I'm just Alva, now. If I take it, that'll be the last I ever hear of the past. Do we have a deal?"

"Deal," Kieran said, her voice shaking. "'Tis a deal."

Alva reached out to Nilo, and he enfolded her tiny, white hand in his large mitt. She smiled up at him. "We didna finish our dance."

Nilo returned her smile, and his happiness was so evident that Kieran could feel it herself. He led the way from the library, leaving Matteo and Kieran alone as they went in search of a darkened room where the strains of music could be heard.

Matteo remained, watching Kieran with eyes that burned in shades of amber. He seemed remote and yet he was so close to her that a few steps would close the gap between them.

Feelings stormed Kieran's body, released by her actions that evening and set to tremble in her blood. And there was Matteo de Gama, the man who'd first spoken words of revenge and inspired Kieran to reach for her own justice.

"Many months ago, wet from the canal and cold in my heart, I stood on the deck of your beautiful *burchiello* beneath the moon in Venice, and you urged me to find the peace in my soul. Without your provocation, I might still be *cuore solitario*, the lonely heart."

"It is impossible to see that frightened girl in the woman standing before me."

He'd promised he would not leave England until all was well with her; she supposed he had kept his promise. Still, she ached to think of his leaving. She hoped he knew how much he had changed her for the better, and she realized that everything Matteo de Gama touched was made warmer, more beautiful. Especially her.

"Thank you," Kieran said softly. "For all you have done for me, a thousand times, thank you."

"I did nothing. It was all you, and I am very proud. You did well for yourself, Kieran."

Heat gathered in her belly, her heart, and pinked her cheeks with pleasure at his praise. He stood before her, so handsome that looking at him and yearning for him became a physical pain. He'd said he loved her, yet another woman warmed his bed.

"Will you keep Carina waiting?" Kieran whispered.

"I do not want Carina."

"She is in your . . ." Kieran began.

Matteo cut her off. "Because she tries to seduce me. She wants me as she wants a favored pet, something to decorate herself with, a distraction, an amusement. I am not interested in being that anymore. Not for her, or any woman."

"But you said otherwise. You said dallying with her would make you forget me."

"I said it is the best way," he corrected her.

"I stayed away because I didn't want to see you with her. Every day I envisioned you and her together, and yes, I admit it, I was jealous."

"I considered becoming her lover again. I even longed for it, for I wanted to stop this sick madness." He looked down at the floor. His hair slipped from his loose ribbon and fell over his lean cheeks. He brought his smoldering gaze back to hers. "But in truth, I have not availed myself of such a remedy."

"No?"

"No."

A thrill ran through her, increased desire for him and palpable relief that he hadn't shared Carina's bed.

"So you are still ailing, signore?"

"I am. So sick, in fact, that I do not want the cure."

"Do I truly hurt you?" she asked him shyly, thinking of her mother's admonition to have a care with his heart.

"'Tis not my desire. You have been nothing but wonderful to me, and I am so grateful for all you've given me.

Every word, every drawing, every kiss. I cannot bear to think I wound you in return."

"You do hurt me. You cut me with every glance, stab me with every smile, and flay me with every touch. Therein lies the rub, however, for you kill me with your absence."

"If my presence cuts and my absence kills, perhaps 'tis a kindness for me to remain? Where should I go, signore, and what should I do?" Kieran took a few steps, moving close enough that she could catch his scent, craving it as she desired breath. "'Tis not my wish to further poison you."

Matteo's lips quirked up at the corners but sadness was in his eyes as they moved over her face. "I am already a dead man."

Matteo reached out and grabbed her hand. He pulled her to him, crushing her to his warm, hard body as his lips took hers in a heated assault.

Kieran buried her hands in his hair, curling her fingers against his skull, pulling him deeper and deeper into her mouth, wanting to be one with him. She could feel the urgency of his body against hers, exciting her with his strength and heat and size until she felt she would die if he stopped touching her.

And then he pulled away and let go, his breathing shallow and ragged. "No more of this," he said roughly. Looking away, he muttered low in Italian to himself.

"Matteo," she breathed. Her lips were swollen and throbbing; her body thrummed with desire.

He brought his gaze back to her. "Give me the key."

Kieran fumbled for it, handed it to him with a hand that shook. He went to the doors, closed and locked them, and came back to her. Candlelight illuminated his lean cheeks in burnished light and roaming shadows, his eyes lit with flecks of glowing amber and gleaming chocolate.

"There is no going back once the deed is done," he warned her.

"You're right," Kieran whispered, reaching for him. "There isn't."

And with those words, he was kissing her again.

Matteo could not keep his hands from roaming over her, touching the silk of her neck, the softness of her cheeks, the delicate shape of her ears. She was heaven in his arms, magic against his lips, and a raging fire in his blood.

Nothing put out the flames, not the drain of his art or the exhaustion of manual labor. She consumed his every thought and had galvanized his heart.

And now, in the face of her passion, he could deny her no longer.

He kissed the long, elegant column of her neck and shook as he heard her sigh with pleasure. He gripped her waist, wanting the feel of her beneath the thick crust of her sparkling, jeweled gown and the rigid stays beneath it. But there was not time to undress her and feast upon the bounty of her body. They'd already been gone from the ball for so long, people were no doubt already wondering where they were.

Matteo lifted her so she sat on the table, and as he stared into the limpid depths of her stormy blue eyes, he began slowly pulling up the length of her skirts. The library was silent, so quiet that he could hear the sizzle of flames against wicks, and the steady dripping of melted wax against the brass candleholder. Every sound seemed amplified, her ragged breathing, the rustling of her rich, jewel-crusted silk as he pulled up her skirts, the ticking of the timepiece on the mantle.

His breath hissed through his teeth as he looked down and saw the dagger against her white, trembling flesh. He touched her silk-clad legs, calves, knees, thighs, every inch of her supple and sleek and perfect. Even her scars inflamed him, two long, parallel lines of pain that only he knew about, an intimate knowledge that he alone shared with her.

She clung to him, her head tilted back, lips parted as she sighed, just as he'd drawn her. And he wanted those sighs to become moans, her warm flesh to sweat with the dew of her passion, her slim, narrow hands clenched against him as she experienced the ultimate gratification.

He dropped to his knees before her and parted her thighs, kissing their sweet softness above the silk garters. Her trust in him inflamed him further; he'd expected some virginal shyness, but found none. Matteo caressed her flower, so soft and small and delicately made, her nub swollen and tight and round.

She moaned as he touched her, and he trembled as her hands found his hair, her touch gentle and light. Her scent was like heady perfume, filling his senses, drawing him closer. He licked her lightly, not wanting to frighten her, and was rewarded as he felt her body tighten and heard her exhale in a long, soft sigh that ended on a moan. Only when he was sure she was ready did he dip his finger inside her, stretching her a bit as he licked and nibbled. Her noise was his melody, and he licked and laved her tender bud until she sang the song of building pleasure.

Matteo stood then, touching her with one hand as he released himself from his breeches with the other, and moved between her thighs.

"You're certain?" he whispered against her ear.

Kieran answered by grabbing his arms as if to prevent him from leaving.

Matteo let go of her long enough to withdraw a hand-kerchief from his pocket, and he placed it beneath her to catch her virgin's blood. Her body wept with desire, humid against his hands as he touched her again, and when her sighs became moans once more, he gripped her hips, delighting in the feel of them. He pressed inside of her, gritting his teeth with the effort of moving so slowly.

She was hot and wet and soft, gripping him in a silken vise that threatened his control. Her hands were in his hair again, and her body went rigid. He held still to allow her to adjust to his size and the intrusion in her body.

"Do I hurt you?" he whispered raggedly.

She met his eyes and he saw her expression, wonder, uncertainty, and amazement. "*Magnifico*," she breathed, and a small smile curved her lips.

He grinned and pressed a bit deeper, and then deeper still, feeling the tug of her virginity give way as he slid all the way inside, watching her eyes go wide.

She clenched around him, her legs instinctively wrapped around his thighs, and her breath hitched and then exhaled. He held perfectly still, letting her grow accustomed to the sensation.

It was killing him, her clenching muscles a sensual massage that wrecked havoc on his control. He tried to think about something else, anything else, desperate to stem the tide of pleasure that rolled through him with each rippling contraction of her body.

He couldn't help it; he moved, just a bit, pulled back a fraction and thrust back in.

"Oh," she whispered, and she closed her eyes. Her back arched and her fingers dug into his arms. "That is something."

He moved again, and Kieran's head fell back. Again, and her fingers gripped him harder. Again, deeper, and the silken vise that gripped him grew wetter and hotter still. A little faster, and her moans came in time with each thrust until her body stiffened in his arms and he felt the undulating of her climax.

And because he loved her, he withdrew and gripped

himself. She was limp against his chest, his cheek was pressed to hers as his hand moved, her breath stirring his hair. It didn't take but a second and he was spilling his essence into the handkerchief, breathing in her scent as he did, lost in his love for her.

"*Ti amo*," he said softly against her hair, and hearing his words, Kieran held him tighter. He tried to ignore that she did not say it back. He tried to forget that he would leave and never see her again. And he knew he would spend the rest of his life longing to hold her again.

He gently cupped her face and kissed her cheek, tasted the salt of his own tears on her skin, and reveled in the moment that was just like Kieran herself, bittersweet and incredibly beautiful.

Kieran held to Matteo, suddenly unsure and insecure. His tears confounded her, touched her heart and pierced her soul.

He pulled back to look at her. "How are you?"

"A little embarrassed," she confessed.

"Why?"

Kieran glanced down and grimaced. Matteo laughed lightly, and reached for his handkerchief. Wrapping it into a ball, he shrugged easily. "Such is passion."

"You didn't . . ." she began, and then dispensed with modesty. "Finish . . . in the normal way."

"The world doesn't need more bastards," he said, and his face grew darker. Matteo fastened his breeches and turned his attention back to Kieran. He brushed her cheek with the backs of his lean fingers, the gesture so gentle it made a pain bloom in her chest.

She felt her cheeks turn red as she said, "I see now why Carina waits."

He lifted her hand to his mouth, pressed a tender kiss on the backs of her gloved fingers. "It gets even better."

"Truly?"

"Indeed."

The thought staggered her imagination, and she reached for him as he evaded her grasp. "Your absence at the ball will surely be noticed," he said, and he sounded strange. Distant.

"Oh. Yes. I should return." She hesitated. "Did I do something to upset you?"

He looked pained. "I hope you will not regret this. I never intended to let it go that far."

Unsure of what to say, Kieran shrugged and glanced away. She felt immature, foolish, once again like an artless child.

Kieran reluctantly slid from the table and stood. Her skirts dropped around her shaking legs, and between her thighs she ached and burned. The fresh memory of their coupling pierced her with new desire. So this was why Emeline gave that secret smile to Rogan in the early mornings, and why her parents still reached for each other after all their years together.

Kieran stood back as Matteo unlocked the door. Feeling awkward, she reached for his hand. "Will you not join me?"

"Go alone," he answered softly. "There will be gossip if we appear together, and I know you do not wish others to think you are courted by me."

She couldn't read his expression, for he once again seemed distant though he stood right before her. It was as if their lovemaking had caused a great divide instead of bridging a gap.

"I care not what they think."

"No, my love, you do. You care." The candlelight was behind him, throwing strange shadows over his face. "Go, dance, and celebrate your victory over Ellsworth. The night is still young."

Confused, Kieran said, "What about you?"

"Kieran," he whispered. "Go."

"I don't understand." She heard her own voice, full of confusion and yes, she admitted it, hurt. Why was he behaving so strangely after they'd shared such intimacy?

His dark eyes betrayed his emotions; for once it seemed he could not hide his feelings behind his gamblers facade. He looked vulnerable and sad. "I once said there was nothing simple about kissing you. I take it back. Kissing you was the least of it."

"Signore, I fear I have done something to wound you, and that was not my intention." Her face grew hot, but she did not let embarrassment stop her from speaking her mind. "If you are feeling guilt for the loss of my virginity, please don't. I absolve you."

Matteo looked away. "I should have done better by your brother and your father. But most of all, Kieran, I should have done better by you, and dare I admit it, by myself."

"So you say it was a mistake?" Tears nipped at her eyes, and all she could manage further was a whisper. "You regret it?"

He brought his eyes back to meet hers, and she saw that he, too, held back tears. "Making love to you was the best thing I have ever experienced," he answered her. "And I will never recover from it."

Kieran stood before him, trying to understand what had just happened and why his demeanor had changed. She did not have long to contemplate it, however, because Nilo came running down the long hallway.

"Miss Keerahn, your mum sent me to find you." Even in the dim corridor, Kieran could see Nilo's embarrassment as he looked at the wall rather than meet her eyes. So he knew what she had been doing in the library, Kieran realized with a hot flush of shame.

As Nilo spoke, Kieran knew her newest secret was safe with him, as were all her others. "I told her you had an aching head and had taken yourself to lie down. She bade me come tell you that Her Grace labors with the child. The waters came with her pain, and she's been rushed back to the manse. Your mum and da rode with them, and Mister Rogan said to tell you to get yourself home. There's a baby coming."

"The baby comes early?" Kieran said in a rush, all her worries for herself forgotten as tension and anticipation filled her. A new life, a niece or nephew, and Rogan and Emeline's greatest joy. "Wait just a minute, Nilo."

Kieran threw her arms around Matteo's neck, pressing a kiss to his cheek. "The baby comes, Matteo. Oh, signore, this is everything they've wanted. I'm sorry to abandon this conversation, but I must go. I will return tomorrow."

She whirled around and smiled brightly. Her eyes sparked with happy tears and her heart pounded. "Come, Nilo, and let's rush home. A baby is coming!"

The manse vibrated with tension and anticipation. Kieran paced downstairs with Patrick, as Camille and Rogan were in the birthing chamber with Emeline, the doctors, and the midwives.

"How long does it usually take?" Kieran asked Patrick, glancing at the clock for the millionth time that night. Hours had passed and dawn had begun to break. "It seems so long. Too long."

"It can take many hours and sometimes days, *sidhe gaoithe*. Why don't you go to bed? I'll rouse you when there's news."

"No. I will wait. 'Tis not possible I could find sleep."

Kieran wrung her hands and glanced at the clock again. Only a few seconds had passed. A servant entered bearing a tray of steaming tea and warm biscuits that smelled freshly baked. Kieran smiled at this, for even the cooks did not rest, but relieved their stress by baking Emeline's favorite treats.

"Any word?" the servant asked.

"Not yet," Patrick replied.

Kieran poured herself a cup and added a spoonful of sugar, cupped the hot porcelain and moved to the window to watch the sunrise. Patrick joined her with his own cup.

"We didn't see much of you at the ball," he observed casually.

"I took a little lie down," she answered, and sipped her tea, wincing as she found it too hot to drink.

"You seem well enough."

"I am fine, Da. Much better, actually."

"I couldn't help but notice that Signore de Gama was also missing from the festivities."

"Was he?"

"Aye."

"Oh." Kieran's cheeks burned and her ears felt as if they were on fire. She opened her mouth to mention Carina but was interrupted by Camille as she swept into the room, her face wreathed in a beaming smile.

"Twins!" she announced.

"What? Two?" Kieran swung around, spilling her tea.

"Two boys, both beautiful, and Emeline rests as Rogan weeps. Come, come!"

Camille, Patrick, and Kieran took to the birthing chamber that had been set up on the first floor. They slowed their pace as they approached so as to not disturb the new family's peace, and entered quietly.

Emeline reclined on pillows, looking exhausted but incredibly happy with a swaddled babe in her arms. Rogan sat beside her holding another, and both looked stunned at their embarrassment of riches, two healthy babes when they'd dared to hope for one.

Patrick and Camille leaned over the bed, admiring the

babies, but Kieran could not approach. Gratitude and awe had filled her to bursting, and she stood and wept with happiness for her brother and sister-in-law.

Rogan stood and approached Kieran, gently laying his bundle in her arms.

"Congratulations, Auntie Kieran," he said, and Kieran could not reply because her throat had closed. She nodded, smiling tremulously, and looked down on the child, who slept in peaceful perfection, wrapped in a blue blanket that Emeline had knitted herself.

As she admired his features, so tiny and new, he opened his eyes, still watery and somehow otherworldly, and met her gaze.

"Nice to meet you," she whispered to the baby, and leaned down to press a kiss on his forehead.

Emeline laughed tiredly, looking from her arms to Kieran's, obviously still amazed at her bounty. "Two babes. It explains all the kicking."

"Have you chosen names?" Camille asked.

"Aye, well, we'd decided on one for a boy and one for a girl, but 'tis a good thing we'd discussed what we would name another son, if we were so blessed in a few years," Rogan said. Gesturing to the baby in Emeline's arms, he said, "This is Padraig Charles Wolfe, and in Kieran's arms is Aidan Patrick Wolfe."

Patrick grinned at his son, his face beaming with pride. "I'm honored, lad."

Rogan returned the smile with one of his own, and simply said, "I love you, Da."

The two men clasped each other in a hard hug, and then Rogan returned to his wife's side to take Padraig from her arms. "Charles is for Emeline's father, and Wolfe is Emeline's maiden name. The boys are as English as they are Irish, and so we thought it fitting they bear both our names."

Kieran could not take her eyes from Aidan's face. His

features were so little and perfectly made, his lips pouting and pursed, his brows nothing more than a winged wisp over his eyes. He had a bit of dark hair on his crown, swirled against his scalp, still damp from his first washing. He smelled elemental and sweet, his little body so trusting and vulnerable in her arms, and yet solid and warm and weighty. She touched his fist, and fresh tears fell from her eyes as he wrapped his hand around her finger, his grip surprisingly strong.

Irish and English, she thought, blended blood making for tough, hardy people, and looking at the babe, beautiful ones, as well. Why, she asked herself, had she never thought of herself that way?

A strange, new, and curious pride welled in her heart for her family and her heritage. Irish and English. Common stock and noble blood. This was her family. These were her people. And she vowed to herself that she would never, ever again forget exactly what that meant to her.

"Aidan Patrick," she whispered to the baby in her arms, "a fine name for a strong, strapping little laddie."

❧ 24 ❧

Kieran slowly woke, noticing the bright lines of sunlight that peeked through her closed drapes. Her room was dim and cool, her sheets sliding silkily over her body. She stretched like a cat, cozy and comfortable and filled with a sense of deep peace that she hadn't felt in years.

Memories of Matteo made her lips curve, and she

wrapped her arms around herself, remembering every touch, every breath, every caress. And most of all, the pleasure. The thick fullness of his manhood deep inside her. It left her yearning for him, wanting to see him, hoping to hold him close and join with him again.

Rolling lazily over in her soft bed, she glanced at the clock and sat straight up, her languid bliss forgotten. The hour had long passed noon, and she had an appointment with Samuel Ellsworth at three.

Rushing through her toilette and her breakfast, Kieran called for a mount and Nilo's escort, and left word to fetch her from the nursery when it was ready. She hurried down the long corridor to seek out her new nephews, eager to see the babies before she left. Emeline and Camille were there, Camille holding Padraig as Emeline nursed Aidan.

"I still cannot believe you had twins," Kieran said, leaning over Padraig, who slept contentedly in Camille's arms.

"I know. The midwife had mentioned she thought she felt two babies, but I didn't believe it. I dared not hope for it, and told myself 'twas just the constant movement of one vigorous babe." Emeline gently patted Aidan's bottom, watching him as he ate. "I should know better by now, that 'tis safe to dream as big as I dare."

Kieran glanced up and met Emeline's eyes. "You deserve every bit of happiness."

Emeline smiled at her and said nothing, but the look in her eyes was plain enough, a silent admonition that Kieran did, too.

"They look different, I think," Kieran said of the babies.

"Yes, they do. Fraternal twins, the midwife said."

"Perhaps one will be light and one dark, like salt and pepper," Kieran laughed. "Two sons, one as fair as his mother, and one dark like his papa. You ought to dispatch a notice to all parents of new daughters in England, warning them of the Mullen twins."

The women chatted for a while, and Kieran took Padraig from Camille's arms to cradle him closely. Emeline spoke of the birth, and Kieran was glad to hear that it did not go too hard for her. She smiled as she heard how Rogan had held Emeline as she pushed, whispering encouragement in her ear. He was a good husband, and would make an excellent father, Kieran thought of her brother.

"What of you, Kieran?" Emeline asked casually. "I saw you dancing with Samuel Ellsworth quite a bit last night. Have you made a decision concerning his proposal?"

"I have told him I am not disposed to marriage."

"What a relief," Camille said on a breath. "I did not fancy the thought of you married to him, and frankly, did not care for the man at all."

"'Twould be odd to have a son-in-law your age, wouldn't it, Mum?" Emeline said on a laugh. "Let's hope Kieran finds herself a man young enough to lift his babies."

"Let's not hope," Kieran replied dryly, addressing them both. "Marriage is not the answer to the questions that burn in my heart, such as: Why am I cursed with such a meddlesome family?"

Both women giggled at her glib retort, unaffected. A servant appeared in the doorway and informed Kieran that her horse had been saddled, and Nilo waited. Grateful for the reprieve, Kieran breathed a sigh of relief.

"Where are you going?" Camille asked.

"Riding." Kieran's face grew warm. To cover, she pressed a kiss on the baby's forehead before handing him back to Camille. "I will be back in time for dinner."

"Would you like company?"

"No, no, I will be fine. Nilo will accompany me." Kieran kissed her mother quickly on the cheek and bade Emeline farewell, making her escape before anyone could question her further.

As she left the room, she heard Emeline call out, "Bid good day to Signore de Gama for us."

Their laughter spilled from the room and followed Kieran down the corridor.

As Kieran rode up the long drive to the property, her heart began to thump. Anticipation brewed in her belly and her hands shook.

It was not worry over the transaction with Samuel that set her nerves on edge. No, she only had one thought in her mind as she slid from her horse's saddle and handed the reins to Nilo. What, she wondered, would Matteo say when she abandoned her pride and asked him to stay in England?

As she entered the house she was greeted by the smells of lemon wax and soap as servants toiled to clean up the mess left by the ball. Kieran inquired of Matteo's whereabouts, and smiled to herself when told he was in the library.

Moments later she stood in the doorway, watching him as he sat at the writing desk, penning a letter.

"Good day, signore," she said softly.

He looked up and her breath caught in her throat as he met her gaze, his dark eyes warm and lit with pleasure. "And to you, my lady. How is the duchess?"

"Very, very well, and in possession of two new sons, both healthy, both beautiful, young Master Padraig and his brother, Master Aidan."

"What a happy day, and I am glad I was here long enough for the event. I will come by tonight to see the *bambinos*." He smiled broadly and then laughed. "Two, you say. How wonderful!"

Kieran laughed, too, pure happiness effervescent in her blood.

"And you. How are you?" Matteo asked her. It seemed

he had recovered from his strange mood. His eyes were warm, his lips inviting. She glanced at the table and then back to Matteo.

A light blush touched her cheeks. "I am very well."

His eyes moved over her in a way that had her body growing warm. "You look it."

Kieran smoothed her riding gown, a simple, sturdy garment of pale blue cotton. "'Tis plain."

"I did not speak of the gown, but I do like how the color suits your eyes."

"I like how you notice," she said with a smile. He drew closer to her, showed a fine leg in a courtly bow as he lifted her hand and pressed a kiss to her glove.

"I have a little gift for Her Grace. Would you like to see it?"

"Of course."

Matteo moved to a shelf and took down a scroll. He untied it and unraveled it on the trestle table.

Kieran gasped with delight. He'd drawn Emeline, standing by an open door, as if poised to step through into a new life. In the picture her face was downcast, contemplative, her hands and her attention on the round dome of her belly, and the expression he'd captured was one of maternal wonder.

"Oh, Matteo," Kieran whispered. "'Tis beautiful. She will treasure it always, I am certain."

"I hope so. I thought she might like a sketch of how she looked when ripe with her child. Well, children," he corrected, and grinned.

"She will love it."

"Good. It will give her something to remember me by, as well."

"You speak of leaving, and that is something I wanted to discuss with you, signore."

A servant appeared, discreetly knocked on the open door, and leaned in to announce Samuel Ellsworth's appearance. Matteo bid entrance, and Ellsworth strolled into the room.

Dropping a packet of papers on the table, Ellsworth dusted his hands as if they were something distasteful. "There you go. I had the funds set aside in an account for the girl, and as you seemed to take a proprietary interest in her, I named you as the fiduciary. If that doesn't suit you, go see Nigel Lowry at the bank and he will make whatever changes you decide," Samuel said to Kieran. He looked her up and down briefly, his patrician features communicating dismissal in a way that only an English lord could manage. "Good day."

He turned to leave but Kieran stopped him with two quietly spoken words. "Thank you."

Samuel inclined his head and his expression changed. "'Tis over, then?"

"Yes."

"And you're at peace?"

"I am."

"Good," he said gruffly, and seemed to mean it.

"Your Grace?" Kieran ventured tentatively.

"Yes?"

"If you need to hear me say it, here 'tis: You have proven me wrong. You are not evil. And for what it might be worth to you, I forgive you your weakness that night as I forgive myself of my own."

A strange expression came over his face, and he swept into a grand, formal bow before her. When he straightened he met her eyes and said, "Farewell."

She watched his back as he walked away. And as Kieran lifted the papers and looked them over, she knew that the matter was finally settled. No pain seared her heart when she thought of Ellsworth, and no more regrets plagued her conscience.

Most of all, Kieran knew the peace of letting go of guilt. She'd done her best to rectify her actions, and recognized

that she could do no more than that. And in the tranquil-
ity of that knowledge, Kieran finally reclaimed her soul.

Emeline had been correct; forgiveness was not weakness, but was the heart's truest strength.

Full of fresh discovery, she faced Matteo. "Signore, i
is truly finished," she breathed. "I am free of it."

He studied her, and the amber lights in his eye
gleamed. "I knew the night I pulled you from the cana
that you were formidable. I did not anticipate just hov
much so."

Emboldened, Kieran cleared her throat and dared to
say, "Speaking of Venice, I wondered what is your rush
in returning? Perhaps you might consider staying in
England a bit longer, and we could pursue this nev
phase of our acquaintance."

She studied his expression as she spoke, and saw the
veil come down behind his eyes.

"You want me as your lover?" he said bluntly.

"I do believe you have already become that, no?" she
answered. "Did we not become lovers last night?"

"We did." Matteo moved to put Emeline's scroll back
on the shelf and then faced her, his face devoid of any
emotion. "I fear that staying here is not possible. The
ship leaves Friday on the evening tide. I will be on it."

"But I had hoped," Kieran began.

"I am sorry for any disappointment you might feel,
he said, cutting her off. "But you see, I have a life in
Venice. A *casino*, a gondola, a *burchiello*, and many
friends. I am a writer there, and I miss the untrammeled
idioms and nuances of my native language. My days and
nights are full there. I cook, I paint, I play cards, and yes
I take lovers. That is my life. And I am going to return to
it, despite the considerable intrigue of your offer."

He had told her he could, and would, walk away from
her, no matter what. Why had she not believed him?

Embarrassment threatened Kieran's composure, fo

she'd already abandoned her pride in asking him to stay, and his rejection stung her exposed emotions. She lifted her chin and affected a cool mien she did not feel at all. "Very well, signore. I asked and you answered. Consider the affair ended."

She strode away from him with as much dignity as she could muster, hating herself for asking the question to which she should have known the answer.

And yes, she hated him for letting her go.

He'd said he loved her, and fool that she was, she thought that alone might keep him in England.

Riding up to the stables, Kieran saw a hired livery in the driveway, the garish lettering on the side boldly announcing the name of the company, drawn by four horses wearing brightly braided tack. Prompted by curiosity, she approached on horseback. The door hung open, and in the shady interior she saw Carina had come calling.

"Have you lost your way?" Kieran asked sweetly. "Signore de Gama is located about seven miles westward."

"It is you I am coming to see."

"Oh? For what?" Kieran's mare, excited by the presence of the livery's stallions, began to prance. With a firm hand she reined her in, peering at the Venetian woman through narrowed eyes.

"Matteo comes home to Venice."

"I am aware. He has made that abundantly clear."

"He is needed there, and I want you to stop all this . . . how do you say . . . interfering."

Kieran lifted a brow. Mimicking Carina's hesitant speech, she said, "How do you say in Italian . . . does it translate . . . Mind your own business."

"He comes home with me," Carina added smugly.

"He told me himself that he is not your lover any longer."

Carina laughed easily, setting her black curls bouncing and her breasts bobbling. "He says that? Ah, Matteo, Matteo, he is a seductive bastard, no? Never one woman for Matteo."

"I must be on my way. If there's something you want to say, come out with it," Kieran demanded, her tone acid.

"Let me do the guessing. He had you begging for him to take your flower, no? Begging, oh, Matteo, I am wanting you, I am needing you." Carina laughed again, and clapped her hands as her dark eyes flashed with amusement. "Oh, he is good, is he not? So good."

"I understand, Carina. He left you waiting in his bed to come to me, and the jealousy sickens you," Kieran said with mock sympathy, trying to forget when Matteo warned her that he could do just that, have her licking the floor in front of his feet if he asked her.

"Waiting? No, no. Satisfied and wanting more. I am so sorry to hear you got the second helping, but I am not so sorry that I got the first. If you cannot be a woman of the world, knowing how a man such as Matteo is, you do not deserve to be his lover. And if you believe the things he is telling you when he wants to be making love, you deserve your heart being broken."

Visions of Carina and Matteo at the ball haunted Kieran: their laughter; Carina's hair falling over his ivory silk; their mutual absence.

Carina leaned out the door and smiled brightly as she bent forward, her luscious curves encased in yellow silk. "I was coming to tell you that Matteo is very needed in Venice for important business, so you would not be keeping after him. I see now I was not needing to come here. Matteo de Gama will be coming home with me. There are only foolish virgins here in England." Those sharp, black eyes swept up and down Kieran's form. "Well, maybe not any more a virgin, but still foolish, no?"

Carina thumped the roof of the livery and it lurched

into motion, leaving Kieran to manage her frisky mare. She whirled her around and headed toward the stables, and in her mind she heard Matteo's voice, repeating over and over until she thought she would scream. *Why do you not believe me when I tell you who I am?*

She rushed through the house by way of the servant's entrance to avoid seeing her family. Alone in her rooms, Kieran let the tears come. She wept long and hard into her pillow, and when they were finally spent, Kieran lay in her bed, harrowed and hollow.

She must have slept, for when she opened her eyes, twilight had come. Ringing for a bath, she sat numbly waiting, and when it arrived, Kieran slid into the warm, scented water without any sense of pleasure.

Dressing for dinner, she reached for the red gown, hoping to recapture some of the icy fire she'd felt the night she'd worn it. If she could only reclaim that cold indifference and the white hot anger that burned beneath it, perhaps she could find relief.

But none came. She was laced and perfumed and coiffed, gowned and bejeweled and gloved. Looking into the mirror, Kieran only saw a naïve fool, a rube taken for her virtue in a game she never understood how to play.

Matteo knocked on the door of Rogan's home with real nervousness in his gut. And as the butler admitted him, his tension increased.

It took every bit of Matteo's considerable nerve to face Rogan and Patrick after his night with Kieran. Though it had been many months since Rogan's warning to him regarding his sister's virtue, Matteo was convinced his opinion had not changed. And to that end, he was just as confident that her father would feel the same.

He was escorted to the parlor, where Rogan and Patrick each held an infant as they stood by the cold fireplace.

The room smelled heavily of the numerous floral arrangements that had been delivered as news of the twins spread, and the French doors were all opened wide to the soft evening air that swirled in, scented with summer. Two glasses of whiskey were on the mantle, and they chatted comfortably as they cradled the sleeping babies.

For a man who'd never known a father, the scene struck Matteo in the heart. Patrick and Rogan, father and son, but also friends, and now, their offspring: Two boys who would be raised with loving guidance from a man who claimed them, loved them, and wanted them.

Jealous of two babies, Matteo chided himself, inwardly laughing at his own melancholy thoughts. He pushed them aside, philosophizing that if he'd grown up any other way, he would be a different man in the present.

Matteo bowed as he entered, relieved to see that both men greeted him affably, and accepted a glass of whiskey from the attending servant.

"Congratulations, Your Grace. I hear you are doubly blessed."

"My thanks, signore." Rogan shrugged his broad shoulders. "I could not have imagined such a blessing, but words can't express my gratitude."

"So it is only us men in the parlor this evening?" Matteo asked with a laugh, gesturing to the babies even as he wondered where Kieran was, and if she would join them.

"Aye, Emeline and my mum are both resting," Rogan replied.

But Kieran, Matteo wondered. Where is she? He longed to see her again, wanted to drink her in as many times as possible before he left.

Instead of asking, however, he lifted the scroll in his hand and then set it on the table. "A gift for your wife."

"You'll see her before you go, won't you? I know she'd be disappointed to not say goodbye."

"I will leave it, in case." Matteo moved close enough to

inspect the child in Rogan's arms. He saw the beauty of his mother in the shape of his mouth and the lines of his father's brow. "He has the face of an angel, Your Grace."

"Aye, and he squalls like a sailor when it's feeding time. He's content now, though. You're welcome to hold him."

"I will decline, but please take no offense. I have never held a baby before, and though you have one to spare, it seems you are attached to both."

Rogan laughed easily, shifted the baby in his arms and sipped his whiskey. "Ah, 'tis good, Da. This is the stuff you brought?"

"Aye," Patrick answered. "I bought a few bottles from an Irish trader years ago, and I've been saving the last one for a special occasion."

"This certainly counts as one," Rogan said, and he sighed with contentment. He cast his attention back to Matteo. "Signore, there is a matter we need to discuss before you go."

Before Matteo could respond, Kieran swept into the room, and he noticed she looked pale and wan, her eyes sad. He watched her face react with surprise and then anger as she saw him there, her clenched hands buried in her swirling skirts. With a cool nod of greeting, she turned her back to Matteo by bending over the sleeping baby in Patrick's arms.

"Is all well with you, *sidhe gaoithe*?" Patrick murmured.

"Yes," Kieran replied. She gestured to the baby. "May I?"

Taking little Aidan into her arms, Kieran moved over to the open French doors where the breeze stirred the curls that lay on her white shoulders. With the baby in her arms and the sunset on her face, Matteo had never seen her look so lovely. Nor as uncomfortable. Did his leaving really trouble her so much, he wondered.

No, he answered himself, jeering at his foolishness for even considering such a thing. She must sting from the rejection.

Rogan recaptured his attention, saying, "Signore, as I was telling my father, several men made offers on the refurbished property at up to five times what I paid for it. Emeline wants to keep that particular house and so I declined the bids, but I see a real opportunity here. It occurs to me that there are many such estates in England and also many houses in London that have fallen into disrepair. I'd like to buy them as they are, renovate them as you did to the western property, and resell at profit."

Matteo grinned broadly, full of enthusiasm and pride for the house he'd lovingly restored. "I think you will find your new endeavor vastly rewarding. I am the first to admit I was surprised at how much I took pleasure in it. Honest work had never held much appeal, for winning money is so much easier than working for it. But in truth, I loved what I did here, and I will miss the challenge."

He gestured to the scroll he'd set on the table, and with sincerity he said, "I wrote your wife a letter telling her of my gratitude for giving me the opportunity. Please, if I don't see her before I go, do tell her I mean every word."

"I had hoped you felt that way," Rogan said. He walked over to where a purse lay on a writing desk, and gave it to Matteo. "This is for you, a payment for a job well done. And I have an offer for you, as well. I want to hire you to oversee my future renovations, if you'd be willing to stay. My wife was correct; 'tis a job for a man with vision. You are just such a man. So, please, signore, consider my offer before you leave. I would see to it you were very well compensated, and would give you a percentage of the profits. So if you decide that working is more satisfying than winning, stay on here and work with me."

Matteo held the purse, heavy with coin, and for a moment he had no words. No one in his entire life had ever handed him money for a job well done, and no one had ever treated him as someone who could be trusted.

It sent a shockwave to his core, for Rogan Mullen was a man whose respect was not given easily. Knowing he'd earned it made Matteo feel incredibly pleased. "I am honored, Your Grace," he managed to say.

"Rogan. I don't work with people who don't call me by name." With his child cradled in the crook of his left arm, Rogan extended his right hand to Matteo. As he took the firm grip, Matteo was reminded of the day of his exile, when Rogan had offered passage to England. And suddenly Venice felt like a distant life, far away and unappealing for its decadence, and Matteo did not long to make the journey back.

"Tell him you will not stay," Kieran said from across the room, her tone so quiet it belied the sharpness sheathed within it. She turned to face the men. "And then, signore, why don't you tell him why?"

The atmosphere in the room turned uncomfortable, and Matteo wondered why Kieran's eyes glittered with the unmistakable shine of female jealousy. "I have made it clear. Venice is my home."

"A *home* is a place for family. What you have there, signore, is an *existence*, and 'tis a bleak one, if you ask me."

"Kieran, regain yourself," Patrick instructed, and though his tone was mild, it brooked no argument. He went to his daughter's side, gently took the baby from her arms, and frowned down at her. "Where are your manners?"

"I left them with Signore de Gama's mistress. Perhaps he should go speak with her and see what she's done with them." There was an obvious sob in her voice, and hearing it herself, she put her hand to her throat. Kieran met Matteo's eyes for one moment, and in them he saw betrayal before she whirled around and went out the French doors to the terrace.

Matteo made to follow her, but found his arms being filled with an infant as Rogan handed Padraig over to him. "Support his head in the crook of your elbow. Aye, like that."

"Your Grace, Rogan, this is not a good idea," Matteo protested.

"You're doing fine. I've a need to speak with my sister."

Rogan strode from the room, leaving Matteo to stand frozen and stiff, holding the baby who stirred, a bit bothered at being disturbed.

Patrick eyed him and laughed. "You hold him as if he were about to explode."

"He is so small."

"They're stronger than they look."

Matteo shifted the baby awkwardly in his arms, wary of this new fragile life that was for the moment, entrusted to his care. The baby settled back to sleep, his tiny fists up by his ears.

And then Matteo looked up to the Irishman whose daughter was no longer a virgin, and wished he had done better by this man. "About Kieran," he began.

"She is, as well." Patrick grinned and glanced to the door where both his children had exited. "Stronger than she looks, and always ready to explode. I've seen her grow cold these years past, and I've seen her come back to herself of late. She's a headstrong girl, sweet in her heart but stubborn as any mule. She's always so set on seeing things as she wishes they were, instead of how they are. But don't worry, son. She'll get a handle on herself, and when she does, you'd best be prepared."

Son. Matteo swallowed heavily. No man had ever called him that. How could it feel so good, and yet hurt at the same time? "Prepared?"

"Aye," Patrick said slowly. His dark blue eyes, so much like Kieran's, assessed him critically. "There's a storm brewing."

* * *

"Stupid fool," Rogan said as he came out onto the terrace. "What's wrong with you?"

Kieran kept her back to Rogan so he would not see the tears that had returned to torture her. "Leave me be."

"No. You'll explain to me why you're acting like a jealous tart."

"Go away, Rogan. I don't answer to you."

"Are you weeping?" He put his hand on her shoulder and turned her to face him, and as he saw her tears, his brows came down in a fierce scowl. "Oh, this is not good."

Kieran couldn't help it; the tears were there and they would not be denied. Her pride forgotten, she threw her arms around her brother's waist and buried her face in his chest. "Rogan, he lied to me."

"Lied?"

The truth poured out as Rogan patted her back. "He said she was not his lover, but she came and she said she is."

"The Venetian woman? Carina?"

"You know about them?" she wailed.

"What? Know what?"

"They are lovers? 'Tis true?"

"Did she say as much?"

"She did! I just told you she did!"

"Well, why would she lie?"

"To keep me from him," Kieran snapped, wondering how her brother could be so intelligent and yet so dense.

Rogan fell silent and his patting stopped. He thought for a long while and then put his hands on her shoulders and held her back so he could look into her eyes. "Have you fallen in love with him?"

"No, of course not."

"If not, then why the tears? How did Signore de Gama lie to you, and why does Carina want to keep you from him?"

"I don't know," she said with real exasperation. And

again she spoke the truth, for she had no idea why it should bother her so, when she'd known from the very beginning exactly how it would end.

Rogan narrowed his eyes. "Do better than that."

"I don't love him," she said stubbornly.

"Why not?"

"What?" Kieran said, surprised at the question.

"Tell me why you don't love him."

"He is common, a gambler, a liar, and he is Venetian." But her heart spoke as well, from the warm recesses where only Matteo de Gama had reached: An artist, a poet, and a man of letters. She silenced that inner voice, and spoke her truest worry. "People will say I could not do better."

"Kieran," Rogan said, his voice hard, "grow up."

"I am serious, Rogan."

"I know you are. That is why you need to grow up."

"You don't wish better for me?"

"What is better? An English lord? Ellsworth? Is he a better man than Matteo de Gama by virtue of his birth?"

"No, of course not."

"What of Da? He is common, the grandson of a pirate, nothing more than a sea-merchant, and he won Mum's heart with the goodness of his own. Is he not good enough for you?"

"Of course he is," Kieran said quietly.

"And my Emeline, common and with a past that many would judge her by. Or your Nilo, a former slave, with black skin that many despise. Or Orianna, a gypsy," he said, speaking of his first wife. "Or me. A half Irish sea-trader turned boxer turned duke, the latter simply because too many of our relatives had the misfortune of dying young. There is hardly an Englishman in the House of Lords who thinks I deserve a seat there, but there I sit, Kieran, because until the day that I think I am not worthy, I know I am worthy."

"You humble me," she whispered, as fresh tears spilled down her cheeks.

"Yes, I do, and rightly so. If you do not love him, say 'tis so, and nothing more needs be said. But do not stand before me and claim he is not worthy of you, even as you weep because another woman lays claim to him." Rogan shook his head as if deeply ashamed of her, and his disapproval reached Kieran's heart as nothing else could. "Pine for your knight on his shining steed if you choose, but don't abuse another man because he is not what you want."

"'Tis not my desire to hurt anyone."

"Then don't," Rogan said simply. "Do not put down Signore de Gama's life because it doesn't suit your high standards. And do not stare at him with moony eyes that beg for his attentions, only to reject him because he is not all the things you decided you wanted when you were a little girl."

Kieran hung her head, deeply ashamed of herself. She'd been acting like the spoilt child she knew she used to be, petulant, demanding, and selfish. It seemed that healing the pain of the past three years had returned her to her former self, and Kieran realized that her brother was correct: it was time for that bratty girl to grow up. "You are right in everything you said, Rogan. I will take your words to heart, and I am very sorry for my unpleasantness."

Her humility seemed to soften Rogan's anger, for he hugged her close and kissed the top of her head. "Good."

"Rogan?" she began, looking up to him. "Would you mind if I had a word alone with Signore de Gama? I believe I owe him an apology."

Matteo stepped out on the terrace, wiping the sleeve of his leather coat with a damp cloth. "The baby vomited," he said, clearly disgusted.

"Spit up," Kieran corrected with a smile. "'Tis not sickness. They all do it."

The sun had set and in the twilight he looked at her. "You have been crying."

"Because I am sorry for how I've treated you."

"Carina came to see you?" he ventured.

"She did. And like a fool, I believed her."

Matteo shrugged. "She is a vain woman. It is hard for her to accept that our affair is over."

"Will it resume in Venice?"

He stared at her for a long moment. "What difference will it make to you?"

Kieran sighed and gave up her jealousy. "None, I suppose. In truth, 'tis not what I wanted to say. I just cannot seem to help myself, and for that, also, I am sorry. You do not owe me an accounting of your actions. I have no claim on you."

Matteo turned away from her, casting his attention to the gardens. "Is that all?"

"May I ask you something?" she managed to say, her throat tight with embarrassment at her former actions and the carelessness with which she'd treated his heart.

"Of course."

"Why?"

Matteo flinched slightly. He knew exactly what she meant. He did not look at her but kept his gaze fixed on the flowers that swayed in the gentle breeze. "Do you need more weapons in your arsenal, Kieran?"

"No, not at all. More like, I cannot see in me what you find admirable. I have courted your passion but not sought your heart. I have been selfish and self-serving and in truth, signore, I do not deserve your tender affection."

Matteo laughed softly, but it was not a happy sound. He turned to her, his face drawn as if with pain. "Do I deserve to see, when others are blind? Do I deserve to walk, when other men who are much better than I, are crippled? Do I deserve to live, when other men who are fathers and husbands die young? Sometimes, Kieran, we receive gifts we do not deserve. Perhaps you do not deserve my love, and perhaps you do not look at it as a gift, but I give it to you anyway. Such is the nature of that ungovernable beast, the heart."

"Signore, I am sorry. Of course your love is a gift, and I am not worthy of it."

"Use my name when you apologize."

"Matteo," she whispered. "Matteo. Matteo, I am sorry."

"Kieran," he replied, his tone still full of pain. "I forgive you."

"The failing is all mine. I am shallow and proud."

"You are," he agreed softly, and his lips quirked up on the sides in a ghost of a smile.

"You said you will forget me."

"I will do my damndest."

It struck a pain in her chest to imagine him in Venice, romancing another woman, all vestiges of his love for her gone. But Rogan had reached her heart; she would not abuse this man any longer.

"Before you do, please write to me and let me know you made it home safely."

"I will."

But she didn't believe him.

She stared up into his eyes, melted chocolate and amber whiskey. "I will never see you again, will I." It wasn't a question.

"No, my love. You will not."

Kieran stood on tiptoe and cupped his lean cheeks, her fingers brushing over his stiff stubble and warm skin. She breathed in his scent, leather and bergamot and clean spice. With lips that trembled she kissed him, tasting her own tears in his mouth.

His arms went around her, at first as if he were reluctant, but then he pulled her to his body, hard and hot, and kissed her with all the passion he had.

Just as abruptly, he let her go. Standing before her in shades of twilight, he again seemed distant and remote. "It is time for me to go."

"I will miss you," she said, and a sob threatened her thinly held composure. "I will never forget you."

He lifted her hand, pressed a kiss to her glove, and then just as he swore he would, he turned and walked away.

Kieran did not leave her bed for three days, but lay there, convinced some illness had befallen her. What else would explain her extreme lethargy and her utter lack of appetite? By the time Friday came, she had a troubled belly and an aching head.

She glanced at the timepiece for the millionth time. It was after two; Matteo was probably already at the docks.

The thought had her wanting to vomit.

Her arms were empty without him, her bed cold and lonely. No warmth lay at the west end of the property; she could ride to the house but knew she would find it echoingly hollow, devoid of music.

A knock sounded on her door and at her call, Patrick entered. When he saw she was still abed and in her nightclothes, his face betrayed his worry.

"Not feeling any better?"

"Just tired, Da."

Patrick sat on the side of her bed and pressed a hand to her forehead. "You're not warm."

"I don't know what's wrong with me," Kieran said, and she realized she'd probably never spoken truer words.

"Ah, well, I'm sure 'tis nothing that time won't resolve." He took her hand and held it in his own. "Mind if I sit with you awhile?"

Kieran shook her head and shifted in bed so she lay on her side. She caught sight again of the clock. Only a few short hours until the evening tide. Her chest ached and her belly hurt.

She brought her gaze up to her father. Still handsome, he wore his age with craggy ease, his auburn hair pulled back from his face in a loose club. His hands were big and warm, and made Kieran feel like a little girl again. He was her port in any storm, a father who listened, who accepted, and who always understood her.

"I love you, Da."

"I know you do, lass." He spoke slowly, imbuing his words with inflection and meaning as only he could. "You know, recently I've been reminded of a story. 'Tis actually a tale I told you mum, the very first day we met. Would you like to hear it?"

"Please." Kieran snuggled into her pillow, ready to listen.

"Well, you see, it's about a warrior who lost his love, both his lady and his ability, in one battle. It wasn't a battle for land or honor or even glory, but was a fight within himself, you see. And those battles, they're the hardest to fight, aren't they? Our warrior had much in the way of what a man wants, strength, vigor, valor. But he was vain. He was prideful. He was haughty of his worth."

Patrick took his time in the telling, his deep, smooth voice as mellow as the man himself. "After a battle in a faraway village, he came upon a beautiful peasant girl, who was wise beyond her years and capable of tremendous understanding. She saw into him, past his fleshly scars, and to the ones on his soul. And she loved him. She loved him for exactly who he was inside, and didn't judge him. She just loved, purely. She held her warrior and when she saw his pain, she wept for him, tears for the wounds he couldn't weep for himself.

"And for a while, he let himself get caught up in her beauty and her understanding. He took her love and let it heal him.

"But our warrior was so prideful. After a time, his arrogance grew. Her love had healed his heart, but sadly, had not rid him of that pride, and after a while, he found he could not accept the love of a peasant girl. For he was a great warrior, aye? And his heart, healed of its hurts, longed for something greater than such a simple abundance. And so he left her there, off to search for an elusive greatness that he just knew he deserved, and his peasant girl was left to cry for him for all eternity. The legend has it that the silver river that flows through that ancient village is made of her tears, pure as her heart, and crystal clear."

Patrick fell silent as he finished his story. The only sound in the room the ticking of the clock on the mantle.

Kieran waded through a welter of emotions even as memories stormed her thoughts. Of Matteo's confession that his mother had never loved him. And of his former lover, the one who'd taught him everything he knew, and her casual rejection. It must have wounded him so deeply.

Even the old woman who'd taught him to cook. Kieran remembered her words to Matteo. *She must have loved you like a son.*

And his expression, for a moment unguarded, young and hopeful. *Do you really think so?*

Kieran's response, mystified as to why he would doubt it. *I think she must have grown to love you very much.*

His hesitation, the shadow in his eyes, like the memory of a deep, distant pain. *She never said so.*

She saw Matteo in a thousand ways, memories crystal clear: sardonic on his *burchiello*, mocking her stiff pride; on the ship, the cello between his knees; in front of Lyman, awed by the horse's beauty; talking as he walked, his hands gesturing in the air; smoldering across the room, his eyes burning with emotion as he looked at her. And on and on the memories went until she finally understood with her mind what her heart had known for months: She loved him.

Pure, unadulterated love and longing sang in her heart for him, now unfettered by the prideful immaturity of her girlishness.

Her heart was full of love for a gambling bastard who played the cello, painted, wrote poetry, and cooked in the kitchen. She wanted to bask in his warmth. She wanted the taste of his skin on her tongue. She wanted to dine with him, sleep with him, live with him, and laugh with him.

What she'd dismissed as lust ran so much deeper, for no other man spoke to her heart the way he did, and she lay sick with his loss for days on end. England was a cold, desolate place without him, and the days loomed, lonely and cold, stacked end on end, each like the day before it, worthless in his absence.

Kieran had been like the warrior, smug and haughty, full of her own worth. And Matteo had given and understood and loved, pure and simple, and she'd taken it, let him help and heal her, and when she no longer needed him, turned it away as if it meant nothing.

Shame for her actions mingled with sadness for the hurt she must have caused him. As Rogan had told her, it was high time Kieran grew up and put aside her childish nonsense. There was no more denying the truth.

Kieran sat up in her bed and met her father's eyes. "Da. I love him."

"Aye, I know you do, lass," he said with a slow grin. "We all know you do."

"But he doesn't know."

"No. Don't you think you might want to tell him?"

Kieran bounced from the bed and glanced to the clock. "Have a carriage brought around, please, and send up my maid so I can dress. Ask Rogan to give the driver directions, and tell Nilo we are going to the docks."

Patrick went to the door as Kieran raced to her armoire to pull out a gown. She stopped in mid-motion.

"What if he leaves anyway?" she whispered, her old pride still warring with her new love. It would hurt deeply to tell him how she felt and then watch him walk away. She hesitated, afraid that she would be left on the docks, looking every inch the fool as his ship sailed.

"What if he doesn't?" Patrick asked her.

In a flash of clarity, Kieran knew that it didn't matter. She would tell him how she felt, and she could not control the outcome. There was peace in that knowledge. But even more, she knew the risk of playing the fool was the price she would pay. If she didn't, she would forever regret letting him go without his knowing that for what it was worth, she loved him.

And as she yanked out garments and rushed to pull a brush through her unbound hair, she realized that she was praying. A silent prayer that promised and begged, beseeched and hoped. The night in the "house of lords" had destroyed her faith. How many times in that one night had she asked God to spare her? How many times since had she asked him to help her?

She remembered a verse from her childhood schooling, a promise that His will cannot be rushed, but will be done.

Well, perhaps this was His answer.

She stopped in her motions and bowed her head. Clasping her hands together, Kieran prayed to God for the first time in three years, thanking him for the gift of Matteo de Gama's love, thanking him for her healing, and thanking him for giving her back her heart.

And then, she dared to ask one simple word, again and again.

Please.

The crowded docks bustled with activity, the excitement thick in the air. The tall ship crawled with people as the crew loaded the last of the goods onto the decks. Men hung up high in the rigging, dangling ropes and calling out to each other, securing sails and tightening lines. The summer winds were fierce, blowing scents in swirling eddies that reeked of rotted fish and coal smoke, hot bridies offered by vendors and the smells of crated produce and cured meats that would carry the passengers and crew through the long voyage.

Matteo leaned against a wooden pillar, keeping a close eye on his belongings as pickpockets and thieves preyed on the unwary. He kept his leather-encased cello cradled safely against his side so he could bear it safely aboard, watching as Carina ordered a crewman about in shrill, broken English, bidding him to see to it that her steamer trunks had been placed in the proper cabin. She made a comical sight in her flashy silks and Italian laces, her giant hat bearing plumes that kept whipping around to hit her in the face as the winds raced across the Thames.

He bore a heaviness in his chest.

His arms were empty, his heart desolate.

And he swore to himself that never, ever again would he succumb to the force of love. The pain of having it unrequited was too great to justify letting go of his guard. He envisioned his life as it had been before Kieran Mullen had fallen into the canal and incited his response. From that moment on, it seemed, he'd always been saving her from something.

No more. He would slay that man and his fragile principles and unwanted nobility.

The gambler and thief he once was knew no pain. Selfish, independent, and alone, he would resume his life without the complications of vulnerable girls with bruised honor and hidden passions.

His life in Venice had been full. It would be full again. He would see to it.

A crewman shouted for all to board. He hefted his cello and began walking up the long gangplank.

Carina rushed up to walk beside him.

"I cannot wait to be home," she cooed, and she held onto his elbow, leaning against his arm.

He didn't answer.

"You will not be this sullen on the entire trip, will you?" she demanded, her annoyance evident. "You have scarcely said three words in as many days."

Matteo glanced down to her, silent, and wondered if he would ever again see beauty in dark, flashing eyes and red, ripe lips. He wanted to gaze into eyes as blue and stormy as the sea, set in a face as delicate as a porcelain sculpture, framed by hair the color of a molten garnet.

A rumble of a carriage drawn by six prancing horses came from behind him, accompanied by a few startled cries of pedestrians who scurried out of the way. As if bidden by his deep wanting, he heard, "Matteo de Gama, wait!"

The voice made his heart stop.

Slowly he turned around and saw Kieran jumping out of the carriage, followed by Nilo. She wore a rumpled traveling gown and her hair was unbound, streaming over her shoulders and down her back as she fought her way through the throngs of people. The winds whipped her hair from her face and lifted the auburn tresses as she lifted her skirts and broke into a run. *Sidhe gaoithe*, his mind whispered.

She rushed up onto the gangplank, panting, her face flushed, her skin glowing, disheveled as if freshly risen from bed.

"Matteo," Kieran breathed, and she reached out to him, her hands empty and supplicating. "Please don't go."

Carina gripped his arm, her long nails biting through his jacket. She hissed in his ear in Italian, "She just cannot bear to lose you to me."

Matteo shook off Carina's hands and faced Kieran. How much pain could this one girl heap on him? He leaned his cello against his chest and looked into the face that had captured his imagination and his heart. "What are you doing, Kieran? We said our goodbyes."

The crew milled around them and the gangplank beneath their feet swayed and creaked.

"The tide doesn't wait, mate. Get up on deck," a crewman called as he ushered other passengers up the gangplanks.

"I have to go, Kieran."

"No, please, no. Listen." The wind tore at her hair and she brushed it out of her eyes. Desperation etched her face and sharpened her features. "I have been a fool. Always so prideful, so haughty, so stupid and childish. I didn't see what was so plain that all my family knew it and I did not. But my da came, and in his way, made me understand how I treated you, and oh, Matteo, I am so sorry for it."

"I told you the other night: I forgive you," he said, hearing his own ragged voice.

"But that is not all." Kieran glanced around at the crowds, passengers who boarded, jostling past them and casting curious glances at the girl with the tousled hair, and then to Carina. "Can we please find a place to speak privately?"

"No. I am leaving. The ship will not wait."

"But, Matteo, please. There is something you should know before you go."

Carina let go a stream of vicious insults about Kieran and her parentage. Matteo turned to the dark beauty and snapped, "Go, then. I do not hold you here."

"Come with me," Carina demanded, and she tossed her head in the direction of the ship.

"Matteo," Kieran beseeched softly, her lips trembling and her eyes full of desperation. "Please."

The ship's captain himself came to the rail, annoyed that Matteo, Carina, and Kieran stood on the planks. "We need to unfasten the hawsers and untie! You're holding up the entire ship, mate. Get on or get off."

He blew out a sigh. There had to come a time when he denied her; if he did not, he would never reclaim himself. "Goodbye, Kieran. Farewell," he said, and he turned and began walking up the gangplank.

"*Ti amo*, Matteo de Gama," Kieran called after him. "*Ti amo.*"

Afraid he did not hear her correctly, he slowly turned. And there, all vestiges of her stiff pride completely gone, was Kieran Mullen on her knees, begging. Nilo stood behind her, always at her back, a fragile girl and her hulking guard. Tears fell heedlessly down her cheeks, and she held her hands out to him.

"I love you, Matteo. I love you. 'Tis true, and 'tis what I came to tell you. For three days I have lain sick in my bed thinking some illness laid me low, but now understand what I have been feeling. I am lovesick. Absolutely sick with love for a Venetian artist who warms me as nothing else ever has. Will you stay, and heal me?"

Carina grabbed Matteo's arm once again, pulling him toward the ship's deck, speaking quickly in Italian for Matteo's ears only. "Everyone waits, Matteo. Do not fall for her stupid words. She is manipulating you, and nothing more. I came all the way to England for you. If she loves you, let her follow you to Venice and prove it."

"Whatever Carina is saying, I don't care," Kieran told him. "Maybe she does not believe that I love you, but I do. I swear I do, and if you'll stay with me, I'll spend the rest of my life proving it to you."

Her words washed over Matteo like a tidal wave, crushing him as much as they lifted and carried him to another place. His breath left him, his heart pounded in his throat.

Doubt and hope ran in tandem through his blood. Could it be true, he wondered, even as he was certain she did not speak the truth.

God, he wanted to believe her. He wanted her love as he wanted air and food and water. He craved it as life itself.

But he'd wanted it before, and never found it. How could it be that this English girl who thought herself too good for any other suitor would want him, a man who lived on luxuries that were all but stolen at gaming tables? How soon before she tired of his bastard name and his lack of stature? How long before she grew bitter toward him?

"You only think it now, because I am leaving. You would soon feel differently," he told her quietly, his voice lost in the winds and the noise on the docks.

But she heard him. "I lost my heart to you the night on the ship, when you saw beneath my cold exterior and reached for the lonely girl within. You are the only one, Matteo. The only one who understands me. The only one who healed me. The only one who warms me. But above all, you are the only one I love. Leave if you must. I cannot stop you. But don't you think it might be worth it to stay a little while, and test my love? Test it, Matteo. I invite you, I dare you: Test it. You will find it true."

He hesitated, his need nearly overwhelming his fear. The captain shouted for his men to physically remove the passengers from the gangplank. The tides were high, and they waited for no one.

"I know you are afraid, Matteo," Kieran said. "I know, because your mother and your English lover and the old woman who taught you to cook, none of them said the words. You spent your whole life living without love, and so you don't believe me. You are afraid I will wake one day and my love will have faded like a summer's bloom that wilts on a vine. But the truth is, I am afraid, too. I am afraid you might wake one day and look at me and wonder what you ever found worthy. I am afraid of all of it, but I love you enough to take the risk."

"Look at me," she said. "My pride is gone, my worth forgotten, and yes, I beg." She reached her hand farther out. "Take the leap, love. Take it with me."

The crewmen came down the planks and Matteo held up his hand. "No need. I am not boarding."

He lifted his cello and walked toward Kieran. Her face showed her happiness and she rose to her feet.

"You're staying?" she whispered, and her smile dazzled him.

"Now we leap, my love," he answered.

Carina shrieked in Italian at Matteo, gesturing wildly as she stamped her feet.

Matteo hesitated, knowing that she would descend into a screaming, passionate display intended to bend him to her will. In years past, he never would have given her another thought; he would have allowed her to continue her tirade as he walked away, leaving her to her own emotions.

This time, however, he let his compassion move him enough that he turned to face Carina. In Italian, he said, "Go home, Carina. Godspeed you safely there, and may you find love like I have."

"I did, Matteo," Carina insisted. "With you, my love. With you."

"No," he said quietly, and despite the noise of the docks he knew she heard him. "No, I know you did not. Because when you do, Carina, nothing will keep you from saying so."

"What is this delay?" the captain shouted behind them, furious that his crewmen hadn't removed the passengers from the planks. "Get on or off!"

Matteo raised his hand in a wave, and then walked to Kieran. He heard Carina weeping, but did not turn to see her being escorted onto the ship. He didn't wish to be cruel, but he walked toward love and left his old life behind.

The winds grew stronger, blowing debris in swirling eddies. Hustling, the sailors untied the ship and unfastened the hawsers. The final gangplank was pulled up onto the ship, slammed down on the deck with a resounding boom. Chains groaned and the tall masts creaked as the sails were raised. A giant clapping sound resounded as the wind caught the sails and filled them.

Kieran stood on tiptoe and kissed him.

He held her close, nuzzled her ear and whispered, "*Ti amo.*"

Leaning back, she met his gaze again in a seeking, serious gaze. "I love you, too. I swear you shall never doubt it."

He smiled like a fool. He would never grow tired of hearing it.

The winds that had been whipping over London finally blew in rain, and as it began to pelt them, they climbed into the carriage. Kieran nestled close to Matteo and lay her head against his shoulder as it rolled into motion.

Suddenly she gasped and looked up at him with wide eyes. "All your belongings are on the ship!"

Matteo grinned and shrugged. "My Venetian clothes off to Venice. Ah, love, it does not matter. I will have new clothes made, and will send for the rest of my things to be returned. In the meantime, I have you. I have my cello. Life is complete."

Kieran nestled back into his arms. "'Tis for me, as well."

His heart grew in his chest until he thought it would burst with happiness. She was in his arms, his love, his muse, his wind fairy.

"You have to marry me," she whispered.

"Have to?"

"Yes." She tilted her face up and smiled sweetly. "If you decline, I shall tell my father and brother of the night at the ball, and they will force the issue."

"I could tell them you seduced me," he said against her ear. "They know how obstinate you are. They might believe me."

"Then I would be forced to show them the drawings."

"You are playing a dangerous game. Did I not warn you of men like me?"

"You did. But did I not warn you, signore, that I am spoilt? When I want something, I stop at nothing to get it."

Could something so wonderful be true? If he was dreaming, he prayed he would never wake. He heaved a mock sigh of capitulation. "Well, Kieran, if you insist on depriving me the pleasure of asking for your hand, I suppose I will allow you to force me into marriage."

Kieran pursed her lips. "You make a good point, signore. Go ahead. Ask. I should very much like to hear you say the words."

In the rocking carriage, Matteo hunkered down on the narrow floor on one knee. When life handed him such a moment, he knew to savor it. He lifted her hand, peeled away the glove with slow deliberation, until her creamy, soft, slender hand was revealed.

He lifted it to his lips and pressed a gentle kiss on her skin, feeling the pulse of her heartbeat in the veins. His love, his life. "Will you marry this Venetian pauper, take him for all that he is, and love him despite all that he is not? If the word is yes, I promise I will spend every day seeing to it that you are rich in the ways of love and passion."

Kieran held her breath as she looked at her hand cradled in his warm, ink-stained fingers. It amazed her the way the simplest touch from him could mean the world. She placed her finger beneath his chin and tilted his head up so she could look into his eyes, those beautiful, soul-deep eyes.

He was warmth and art and music and passion. How could it have taken her so long to realize that her life had never been richer since the day he stepped into it? Well, she answered herself, she would play the fool no more.

Pauper or prince, she cared not. He was not a man to be defined by a title, nor the lack of one.

But he'd defined himself, hadn't he? The Venetian. And a slight worry nagged at her. "Will you miss your home too much? Now that the babies are born and my parents are here, I would hate to leave England."

"You have not answered my proposal."

"Matteo, I love you. I want to marry you. Of course the answer is yes, but I want us both to be happy."

"Then never fear. Be your answer yes, I am home. I am home, my love, and I am so very happy."

And so, finally, was Kieran.

✍ EPILOGUE ✍

1778

As a girl, Kieran had dreamed of her wedding day. In those dreams, she'd fancied a gown to rival that of her favored monarch, Queen Elizabeth. With the help of Camille, Emeline, and the finest atelier in England, she got it: a sublime creation of incredible richness.

The gown itself took nearly as long to be created as the wedding itself took to be planned, nearly a year to the day that Kieran came to the docks, confessed her love, and begged Matteo to stay. It took three embroidery houses, many, many spools of silver thread, crystal beads and chenille work, to produce the snowy gown that shimmered in contrasts: satin sheen and matte organza, sparkling crystals and luminescent pearls. It displayed her figure to the fullest, low on the breast, framing her face with a stiff collar that fanned around her slim neck, and showcasing her narrow waist in an unforgiving corset.

Her hair gleamed in dark red contrast, worn high and dressed with brilliants, a long veil of silk lace so fine it was like the breath of an angel spilling behind her in a gossamer drape.

And now, many hours after the morning ceremony that joined her to Matteo, when the champagne had been drunk and the celebratory meal eaten, the congratulations and well-wishes received and the dancing done, Kieran could not wait to remove the garment.

But instead, she stood in the cool green grass beneath tall stately trees, bathed in the pinkish gold of the setting sun. And there before her was her love, Matteo, resplendent in his ivory satin garments, furiously sketching her on a huge canvas that he'd set up outside on an easel.

It was, he had told her, the very spot where he had lost his heart, and so it was there that he wanted to draw her on the day that he claimed her as his own.

He worked until the light was gone. As the stars made their appearance in the darkening sky, he abandoned the easel, lifted the canvas in one hand, and took Kieran's in the other. Both content and chatting about their magical day, they walked across the fields and past the gardens and the restored copper fountain, over the repaved cobblestones, and up the steps to the grand home that flourished beneath Matteo's vision.

Her family waited inside for them to finish, and by the sounds of laughter, the party continued. As Matteo went to put the canvas away where it would not be disturbed, Kieran followed the laughter into the main parlor.

The twins, always underfoot now that they were both walking, had busied themselves by investigating a cabinet, climbing inside, closing the doors, and back out again to repeat the process.

Camille and Patrick were seated by the far window, and Camille had her bare feet, sore from dancing, propped on an ottoman as she sipped tea.

Kieran accepted another glass of champagne from Rogan and Matteo came into the parlor. He poured a glass of wine before coming to Kieran's side. His hand went around her waist, but he came in contact with nothing but crusted crystals and pearls. He tried instead to touch her shoulders, but found the same.

Seeing his expression, Kieran laughed. "I will have to change so you can touch me again."

He grinned and pressed a kiss to her cheek, and nuzzling her neck, spoke for her ears alone. "Please do. This man is in desperate need to touch his bride."

Kieran blushed lightly, and shared his excitement. Since they had decided to wed, Matteo had insisted on treating her with all propriety. They would make a fresh start, and have a proper courtship, he'd said. His days as a woman's lover were over. He would be a husband, faithful and true.

Eager to end their abstinence, Kieran said to Emeline, "We should go home so I can change out of this gown."

"No need," Emeline replied easily. "You don't live there anymore."

A slight wrinkle formed between Kieran's eyebrows. The past year it had been decided that Matteo and Kieran would primarily keep their belongings in Kieran's rooms at the manse, and would rent townhomes near to whatever property Matteo renovated for Rogan.

"Pardon?"

Emeline's golden beauty was such that at times she could look angelic, and it was thus when she turned her most innocent expression to Kieran. "I had everything moved here."

"Here?"

"Yes," Emeline said. "This is your new home. 'Tis my wedding gift to you and Matteo, and a warning to your brother to not wager against my intuition."

Rogan laughed as he scooped Aidan and Padraig up into his arms and out of mischief. Talking to the babies he said, "Tell your mummy that your da knew what she was up to."

Emeline smiled and rose from her seat to embrace Kieran, who stood, stunned. "'Tis selfishness on my part, Kieran. I would hate to have you too far."

"Thank you," Kieran breathed, and looking to Matteo, saw her incredulously happy expression mirrored on his. "Such riches."

Matteo stammered, his accent thickened with his emotion, "It is too much."

"No, it isn't," Emeline said calmly. "'Tis part of Kieran's dowry, is all."

"'Tis the least you can do for us, signore," Rogan said with an evil grin. "To take the girl off our hands, 'tis a bargain, really."

Kieran lifted a pillow from the sofa and threw it at Rogan, sticking out her tongue at him as it hit him squarely in the chest.

"And when you're ready, son, your services will be needed again," Patrick said to Matteo from across the room.

Turning to Patrick, Matteo bowed slightly. Their relationship over the last year had made Kieran's entire being tighten with joy as she watched Patrick teach Matteo what having a father could mean. "Sire? What do you need?"

"A house," Patrick answered simply. "Rogan says he has found one that needs renovating, not too far from here. We won't be going back to Barbados. I've a need to see my grandsons grow up, and Camille does as well."

"Mum! Da!" Kieran gasped. "'Tis the best wedding gift of all."

"I hoped you would think so," Camille said with a smile.

Kieran turned to Matteo, saw the emotions playing over his face, and knew he was struggling with the enormity of it all. A year hadn't been long enough for him to fully accept his place in their family, to grow accustomed to generosity, to feel at ease with accepting love.

She reached out and took his hand, and as he met her eyes she smiled softly up at him, leaning in close to his warm body. For his ears alone she whispered, "This house is yours, Matteo. Without you, it would not be a thing of such beauty. I will be so proud and so grateful to live here, surrounded each day by the artistry of your vision."

He hesitated, caught between his emotions and her words.

"My love," he whispered in reply, "there is so very little I can give you."

Kieran's heart was full, so full it felt it would burst.

"Today I am Kieran de Gama, wife, lover, and muse to a Venetian artist who warms me as nothing else. Please, my love, please tell me that it is enough for you to have me as I am."

He laughed a little. "Enough to have you? You are everything I have ever dared to hope for."

"There are things you can give me, Matteo," Kieran said on a breath. "Things I truly want from you, and no one else."

"Anything," he said, leaning down to her. "Anything."

"I want you to draw my nude form, but this time from true knowledge rather than your imagination. I want you to compose sonnets for me. And someday, I want you to put a baby in me, and always, always, always, I want you to know the joy of being loved."

His eyes glistened, so dark and beautiful and soul-deep. "All of that and more."

"Yes, Matteo, I do want more." Kieran smiled and said, "Signore, as this be our home, I will want a bed in the ballroom and the library."